SECRETS
OF
TAMARIND

SECRETS OF TAMARIND

NADIA AGUIAR

FEIWEL AND FRIENDS
NEW YORK

A FEIWEL AND FRIENDS BOOK
An Imprint of Macmillan

SECRETS OF TAMARIND. Copyright © 2011 by Nadia Aguiar LLC. All rights reserved. Printed in May 2011 in the United States of America by R. R. Donnelley & Sons Company, Harrisonburg, Virginia. For information, address Feiwel and Friends, 175 Fifth Avenue, New York, N.Y. 10010.

Library of Congress Cataloging-in-Publication Data

Aguiar, Nadia.
  Secrets of Tamarind / Nadia Aguiar. — 1st ed.
      p. cm.
  Summary: Four years after leaving the lost island of Tamarind, Maya, Simon, and Penny Nelson return to stop the Red Coral Project, a sinister group mining the magical mineral ophalla there and, in the process, ruining the magnificent island.
  ISBN: 978-0-312-38030-4
  [1. Adventure and adventurers—Fiction. 2. Islands—Fiction. 3. Magic—Fiction. 4. Brothers and sisters—Fiction. 5. Mines and mineral resources—Fiction. 6. Environmental degradation—Fiction.]
  I. Title.
  PZ7.A26876Sec 2011
  [Fic]—dc22

                                                              2010050898

Map illustration copyright © 2010 by Jeffery L. Ward

Book design by Barbara Grzeslo

Feiwel and Friends logo designed by Filomena Tuosto

First Edition: 2011

10 9 8 7 6 5 4 3 2 1

mackids.com

For Tim

I must go down to the seas again . . .
—John Masefield

Prince's Town

Cabarro

Grandfather Mountains

Moraine of Lost Loved Ones

WESTERN TAMARIND

Nallansha River

Hetty's Pass

City of Children

Maracairol

Printing House

Jai River

Overview of Greater Tamarind

EASTERN LANDS

NEGLECTED PROVINCES

WESTERN TAMARIND

Red Coral Ship

Flori

Floriano Ha

GREATER TAMARIND

Mumbagua Falls

Red Coral Camp

Little Blue Door

Ruins

Emerald Oasis

NEGLECTED PROVINCES

...LANDS

Reappearing Village

Ror River

Entrance to Caves

Green Vale

Pamela Jane

©2010 Jeffrey L. Ward

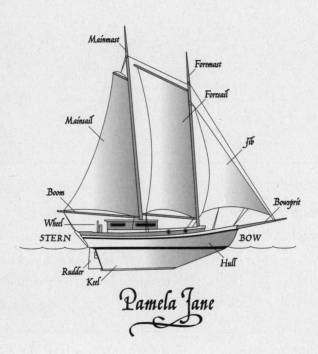

Mainmast

Foremast

Foresail

Mainsail

Jib

Boom

Wheel

Bowsprit

STERN

BOW

Rudder

Hull

Keel

Pamela Jane

❧ CHAPTER ONE ❧

*The Watchers ❋ Granny Pearl's House ❋
The PAMELA JANE ❋ A Gloomy Illumination ❋
"It was unmistakable"*

Simon's school bag bounced on his back as he ran. When he reached the bend in the road he stopped and looked back. His sisters had gotten off the bus with him but they were lagging behind. With a running leap he vaulted onto the mossy boulder that sat on the verge of the road and climbed quickly to its top. From there he could see out to the choppy winter sea around Bermuda and hear the whistle of the wind. The slate gray sky was heavy with clouds and the day was already growing dark. He wished that Maya and Penny would hurry up. Recently their parents had forbidden them to walk home alone, so Simon had no choice but to wait, even though he was impatient to get to the boatyard. He and his friends had spent the past month rebuilding an old speedboat and it was almost ready to put in the water. It was all he had thought about all day as he endured the slow crawl of the hands around the big round clock at the front of the classroom.

Through the treetops Simon could see the crisp white limestone roof of Granny Pearl's house. Even though they had lived there for nearly four years now—and it was the only real house any of them had ever lived in—they all still called it Granny Pearl's house. If he stood on his tiptoes he could just see the kitchen garden with parsley, thyme and the frothy green tops of carrots, and lettuce that grew crisp and cool deep inside the ice green heads. Around the side of the house was a milkweed patch where flocks of monarch butterflies massed in the summer. The house overlooked a small green cove, sheltered from the open ocean, with a narrow slip of sandy beach and a mat of rubbery sea daisies. The family's boat, the fifty-two-foot schooner, the *Pamela Jane*, rocked on her mooring, her yellow hull the brightest thing on this gloomy afternoon.

Something stirred in a nearby tree and Simon instantly thought of Helix, happier in trees than with his bare feet on the ground. But it was just a branch bobbing after a bird took flight. Their friend had disappeared so suddenly and had been gone for so many weeks now that Simon wondered if he was ever coming back.

Maya and Penny finally appeared—Penny hopping ponderously on one foot—and Simon slid down from the boulder and went to meet them.

"You should have waited for us," Maya said crossly when they reached him. "What'd you need to go rushing off for?" Maya was sixteen, which meant she thought that she was in charge of Simon and Penny. Simon had just turned thirteen and he hated anyone telling him what to do, most of all Maya. Since nothing irritated her as much as being ignored, he didn't answer and instead swung five-year-old Penny up onto his shoulders so fast that she squealed. He made up a silly song that made her giggle and began walking.

"Frog!" Penny shouted, catching sight of a muddy-backed bullfrog on the side of the road, and she wriggled until Simon put her back on the ground.

Maya dawdled with Penny, who was prodding the reluctant frog to hop in front of them, and Simon turned onto the shortcut, a narrow packed-sand path between the trees to Granny Pearl's house. Old Man's Beard hung like fog from gnarled branches. The light that managed to make it through the thick clusters of stubby palm trees and the heavy climbing creepers was dim and eerie. High in the spice trees, the wind creaked ominously, a sound that reminded Simon of the wind moaning in a ship's rigging, but the air on the path was strangely still, as if it were sealed off from the rest of the day. He stopped to wait for his sisters and peered uneasily through the trees, trying to see if he could make out one of the watchers. The strange men were here all the time now.

He looked back. "Hurry up!" he shouted.

When he saw them, Maya's scowl had fallen away and her face was lost in the hazy drift of a daydream—Maya was *always* daydreaming. The frog leaped into a clump of ferns and Simon, not liking the dark stretch of the path, took Penny's hand and pulled her firmly along.

The house was cool when Simon came in, and the tiny television on the kitchen counter was spouting yet another news report about the mysterious glowing sea creatures that were being found dead in the waters all around the Caribbean and South America. Simon's mother wasn't home from the laboratory yet, but Granny Pearl was listening to the report as she chopped vegetables at the sink. Simon swooped down to give her a kiss—he had grown three inches in the past few months and he was doing a lot of swooping to low places, as well as stretching to high ones, reaching up nonchalantly to rap his knuckles on every door frame he went under.

"How was your day?" his grandmother asked

"Boring," he said. "But yesterday I figured out what was wrong with the boat engine. The old fuel had thickened to varnish and the jets were clogged. I'm going to take the carbs apart and clean them—I think we can have it in the water by this weekend." He glanced out of the window. "Are they still out there?"

His grandmother nodded. "They've been lurking around all afternoon."

"They can't just invade our yard," he muttered. "Why doesn't Papi get rid of them?"

"Sometimes things are more complicated than they seem," said Granny Pearl.

Simon's gaze fell on the television, where an old fisherman was holding up a dead octopus, its faint glow ebbing even as Simon watched. "*Found it in my nets,*" he said. "*Second this month—I been fishing here since I was ten years old with my father, in fifty-five years I've never seen a thing like this before . . .*"

The television still babbling tinnily, Simon went to change into his old grease-stained clothes for the boatyard, hearing the screen door bang shut as Maya came in behind him. Usually these days he breezed right by his father's study, but today he stopped and looked in.

Dr. Nelson's ear was pressed to the CB radio. With one hand he was turning the knob, listening to the series of pops and whines and static that sputtered from the speakers. With the other hand he was making notes. His beard, white since his time in the Ravaged Straits, had grown long and his skin, no longer exposed to the sun as they sailed from port to port, had faded. Frown lines deepened into grooves as he concentrated.

A year ago, the first thing Simon would have done when he got home from school would have been to head straight to Peter Nelson's study. All of them would have, Helix, too, but Simon always stayed the longest, telling his father about his day and sitting at the desk opposite his father's to do his homework. He'd browse through Papi's books, poring over the scientific illustrations. He loved the treasures on the shelves: marlin bills; exotic shells; starfish and octopus and coiled water snakes that floated in a solution in rows of big glass jars. Simon had a steady hand, and his father often asked him to sketch things he saw under microscope slides. But these days his father was preoccupied, and he rarely talked to the children except to yell at them when they were too noisy.

"Papi," said Simon. His father didn't hear him.

Messy piles of coffee-stained papers teetered precariously under sea stones and open books were stacked on top of each other on almost every inch of the floor. Behind his father's desk was a large map studded with colored drawing pins that plotted the locations of the reported sightings of dead, glowing sea life. Simon felt a sudden rush of annoyance at the shambles of his father's office.

"Papi!" he said, loudly this time.

His father looked up, startled. "Simon," he said. "Home already? What can I do for you?"

"I just saw that someone found another glowing sea creature," said Simon. "Did you hear about it?"

"I did," said his father, looking back down at his papers. "Very troubling business."

"What do you think is making them glow like that?" Simon asked. He had been hovering in the doorway but now he stepped inside, dropping his school bag to the ground.

"Anything I could say now would only be speculation," said his father. "And I'd rather not speculate."

Simon frowned. He wished his father would stop being

so infuriatingly vague. He looked out of the window. "You know those men are still out there," he said.

"Yes, I'm aware," said his father, sifting through the jumble on his desk in search of something.

"I could help, you know," said Simon. "We could go outside right now and tell them to get lost!"

His father looked at him. "That would be very foolish," he said seriously. "Those men are dangerous—it isn't a game. Steer clear of them, Simon. I mean it."

"What do they want?" Simon pressed.

When his father didn't answer Simon changed the subject. "What about Helix?" he asked. "It's been weeks—can't you at least tell us where he's gone, or when he'll be coming back?"

Dr. Nelson sat back, rubbing a bony knuckle over his bushy eyebrow. "I wish I did know where Helix was," he said. "I'm worried about him. He took it upon himself to—Oh, never mind. He thinks he's helping us."

"I want to help, too," said Simon.

"You're too young," said his father.

"Helix isn't that much older," argued Simon.

"Helix is different," said his father.

"That isn't a good enough reason," Simon objected in frustration. "I don't understand why no one will tell me anything!"

"Please, Simon," said Papi. "I'm very busy. Was there something specific you wanted?"

"No," mumbled Simon. He picked up his backpack and

went the rest of the way noisily to his room. He could get there now in just three long strides and—*whack*—one especially hard knock on the door frame.

✖ ✖ ✖

When Simon got back to the kitchen his mother had returned home from the laboratory. Her lab coat hung over the back of a chair and she was helping Granny Pearl make dinner. "I'm going to the boatyard," he told them, bending down to tie his shoelace. Maya had gone to her room and just Penny was there.

"Can I come?" she asked.

"Nope," said Simon breezily.

"I won't say anything," said Penny. "You won't even know I'm there."

Simon shook his head.

"Please."

"Hang on a minute, Simon," said his mother as he headed out of the door. Simon knew from the tone of her voice that she was going to say something he wouldn't like. He had almost made it. He stopped and turned around, but kept his hand on the door.

"Those men are outside again," she said. "I'd be happier if you stuck close to home, okay?"

Simon's heart plunged. He *couldn't* stay at home. He hated being there these days. The only thing he really looked forward to was the boatyard. Maybe Maya was happy to sit in her room and read a book, but he had to be out. He had to be *doing* things.

"But I have to go," he said. "If I'm not there Dennis will be the one to put the last bits of the engine back together and then he's going to act like it's *his*." It was true. That was exactly what would happen.

Mami hesitated, frowning as she wiped her hands on a tea towel. "I've had a funny feeling all afternoon," she said. "Something's in the air. I'd like you to stick nearby—just for today."

When Simon opened his mouth to argue she looked at him so seriously over her glasses that he stopped. Outside the screen door, he could see his bicycle leaning against the poinciana tree in the yard. He felt the afternoon sliding away from him, like a wave being sucked back out to sea.

"A feeling," he grumbled. "That isn't very scientific."

"Not everything is," said his mother.

⚔ ⚔ ⚔

Simon shuffled outside and flopped down on the porch steps. A perfectly good afternoon, ruined. Now what was he going to do? At this very moment he should have grease all over his hands and engine parts spread out on the ground around him. He scanned the garden but the men who had caused all the trouble were nowhere to be seen. It was all so stupid. The light was fading fast and the fact of the short winter days only sharpened the injustice.

The dreary day reflected Simon's thoughts.

A cool wind rustled through the trees and rattled the *Pamela Jane*'s halyards, and his gaze wandered down to her. Until four years ago, Simon, Maya, and Penny had lived on her, sailing the open seas with their parents, who were marine biologists. Back then the *Pamela Jane* had been kept in tip-top shape: Simon and his father used to dive beneath the water and scrape the barnacles from her hull, her yellow paint was fresh, her name was proud and bold, and the waters she sailed over were sometimes four thousand fathoms deep. Each day her brilliant white sails were filled by the salty Atlantic wind.

But now she sat there as if abandoned, chained on her mooring. Scummy sea moss waved around her in the current, making her appear to drift in and out of focus. Her paint was cracked and faded, her sails furled and her masts stark and lonely. Rust bloomed around her fittings, and underwater, chains of olive green barnacles plated her hull like armor. The wind drove seaweed in through the mouth of the cove and it floated over to become tangled in her anchor line. She looked like a neglected, sea-worn old hulk— bewitched and unlucky—destined for nowhere but the sea floor.

And now Simon and his family were what the old salts who hung around at every port called "landlubbers." Landlubbers—*blecch!* Simon missed the days when the family had sailed from port to port, never waking in the same place. But the best place they had ever been—the most exciting and the scariest—had been Tamarind, a mysterious island not on any map, where they had lost their parents in a storm, met Helix, and gone on a wild adventure to rescue their parents.

For a long time after they returned home and moved in

with Granny Pearl, Tamarind had been all the children could think or talk about. Simon, Maya, and Helix had formed the Tamarind Society. Sometimes, when she proved useful, Penny was brought along, too. They had played on the *Pamela Jane* or in a tree house in the garden, pretending it was in the Cloud Forest Village. Maya pretended to be Evondra or Mathilde, Simon played Rodrigo the barge captain or the pirate Captain Ademovar, Helix was always himself, and a night heron pecking for hermit crabs in the rocks of the cove would be Seagrape, Helix's green parrot that they had left behind. No other kids ever joined in these games. Simon and Maya's parents had made them solemnly swear never to breathe a word about Tamarind to another soul—*It may be the most important secret you ever keep*, Simon's father had said—and none of them ever did.

But time passed and Tamarind began to seem very far away. Simon could still remember the day when Maya had finally sighed and said to him, *Tamarind was just something that happened to us a long time ago.* She began hanging out with school friends and had little interest in Simon as he sat alone at the edge of the cove, stirring the water into a tiny maelstrom with a stick, like the giant Desmond had done, watching bits of twigs get sucked down into the whirlpool as the pirate fleet had on one of their last days in Tamarind. His parents told him that there was no way ever to go back to Tamarind, but sometimes, on days like this, Simon wished he were there again.

Though they lived in the same house and shared the same family, they didn't seem to be really *together* anymore.

Simon's parents acted weirder and weirder. They would never talk about Tamarind or the Red Coral Project or their old friend and colleague, Dr. Fitzsimmons, who was the reason they had ended up in Tamarind in the first place. Simon's parents felt Dr. Fitzsimmons had betrayed them, leading them to believe the Red Coral Project was a simple scientific study, when in fact he knew it was a dangerous investigation to find the secret island. Simon's parents had resigned from the project as soon as they had returned home, but the Red Coral had never left them alone.

In all that time, Simon had kept the secret of Tamarind faithfully, but now his parents were keeping secrets from him . . . it wasn't fair! Helix, too, had grown cagey. Before Helix disappeared a few weeks ago, Simon had several times interrupted hushed conversations between him and Simon's father, which had ceased when Simon was noticed in the doorway.

Though the Nelsons considered Helix part of their family—Simon considered him practically a brother—Helix in many ways remained a mystery. He perched on furniture, never getting too comfortable. Simon had never seen him really sink easily into an armchair or couch. He took school seriously and was a diligent student, though he had little obvious delight in learning, unlike Simon, who actually secretly liked many of his schoolbooks. Helix had been orphaned as a small child and brought up by an island tribe. The Nelson children met him on their first day in Tamarind, and from the moment Simon had seen him—when Helix had freed him from the carnivorous vines of the Lesser Islands—Simon had liked him. Helix had tattoos made of jungle pigments all over his skin, his hair was knotted and dirty, and he had carried a spear. In Tamarind he could disappear into the jungle and survive on his own for months at a stretch. Sometimes Simon thought the only surprising thing was that Helix had stayed with them as long as he had.

As he sat there on the porch steps, Simon longed for a moment to be back in Tamarind when, in spite of all the trials they'd faced, life had seemed simpler somehow, his purpose important and clear. The place he had worked so hard to escape from was now the place he desperately longed to return to.

It had already grown darker in the short time Simon had been sitting there, and the next time he looked up, to his surprise, he noticed a pale light glowing from one of the *Pamela Jane*'s portholes. At first he thought it was an illusion caused by the reflection of gray water and sky, but then he felt his heart quicken. Why was there a light in the boat and was someone on board? Everyone else was still in the house. Simon glanced around him. One of the watchers was walking around the other side of the house; the other was nowhere in sight. Simon ran quickly down the stairs, across the grass, and down to the cove, where he ducked behind the mangroves. The little rowboat was there but he wanted to get to the *Pamela Jane* unnoticed, so he stripped off his shirt and waded into the water, which lapped cold over his bare ankles. Another quick glance behind him told him no one was looking, so he began to swim out toward the schooner.

Whoever was responsible for the light could still be inside the boat, so Simon swam hidden underwater as far as he could. He popped up on the starboard side and swam along in the cool gray shadow the boat cast on the water, passing the black-stenciled letters of the *Pamela Jane*'s name, where a chiton had made its home over the N. He crouched for a moment at the top of the ladder up to the deck, making sure that no one on land was watching him, before he crept quietly to the hatch. He pressed his ear to it, but heard no one in the cabin below. He opened it and, taking a deep breath, dropped into the companionway.

To Simon's relief the main cabin was empty. He closed the hatch softly behind him. The portholes were frosted with salt and the light was dim. He waited for his eyes to adjust, listening to the familiar creaking of the boat. It felt as if an old friend were talking to him, but through a dream, the words distorted. Though he stood still, straining his ears, Simon had no sense of whether he was alone or not. He wished he had brought something more than the flimsy pocketknife he always carried, but it was too late to do anything about it.

The light had come from the captain's quarters at the bow of the boat, where his parents had slept, so Simon tiptoed cautiously forward. He went past the upper and lower bunks that had been his and Maya's (how had they ever fitted into the tiny beds?); past the sling that Penny had slept in that had never been taken down and still hung from a center beam; past the galley, the cupboards bare, no smell of meals cooked thousands of miles out at sea lingering on the stove. He inched up to the doorway of the tiny laboratory, where once their parents had studied the mysterious, ethereal sea creatures that had led them to Tamarind in the first place, but it was silent and empty.

Simon's next step squeaked on the deck and he stopped for a moment to steady his nerves. Sweat trickled down his back and he felt clammy and light-headed. He had only a few paces left to the door to the captain's quarters. What if one of the men who had been lurking around the house was waiting for him? There could be more than one, even. What would they do if they caught him? He realized his hands were trembling. But he was more afraid of turning back than going forward. Bracing himself, he turned the corner.

The captain's quarters were empty.

But his sigh of relief was cut short when his eye fell on the source of the light he had seen coming from the porthole.

A glowing foot-long gouge, half an inch deep, ran horizontally across the inside of the hull.

It was the last thing he would ever have expected to see.

He came and crouched next to it, his heart beating quickly. In the dim cabin, the cut glowed with a blue-green light, a color like phosphorescence stirred up in the sea on a summer night. It looked hard and polished, like deep ice under the sun, but its radiance was neither cold nor hot.

It was unmistakable.

"Ophalla," he whispered.

Simon leaned in to peer at it more closely. A thin veneer of wood had been cut through to reveal ribs of ophalla that lay beneath it. Fine shining dust, like the talc from moths' wings, spilled from the cut and lay in a small motionless heap, glowing softly in the dark. He reached forward and rubbed some of the ophalla powder between his fingers. There was no breeze inside the boat, but the *Pamela Jane* rocked in the waves stirred up by the wind and groaned on her lines.

What was ophalla doing here? The precious ice blue mineral was from Tamarind, where it had long wielded a mysterious power over the people. Wars had been fought over it, children had been enslaved to work in mines deep underground (Simon and his sisters had been taken prisoner at one—a memory that still made him shiver), and it had created more havoc and chaos in Tamarind than any other single thing ever had or should. Yet it also possessed rare healing powers—Simon had seen it cure his father after he had been trapped in the inhospitable salt islands of the Ravaged Straits. And it had been here, beneath their noses—beneath their very hands and feet—for years and they had never known. Simon's skin prickled with excitement.

He kneeled, deep in thought, and stared at the whitish dust. He was oblivious to everything else around him for a few minutes so he was startled when he heard the footsteps on the deck. Someone else had come aboard the *Pamela Jane*! He looked around frantically for something more threatening than his pocketknife to use as a weapon, but the captain's quarters were bare. Whoever it was had opened the hatch and descended the companionway and was now walking softly down the short corridor. Simon ducked behind the door and held his breath. To his dismay he remembered that he had swum to the boat and his shorts had been soaked—his wet footprints led from the companionway through the main cabin and down the corridor, directly to where he stood right now. Whoever was coming knew he was here and knew exactly where he was. Simon clutched the pocketknife and his knees began to quake as the footsteps stopped outside the door.

"Hey!" said an indignant voice. "Where are you? What are you doing in here?"

Simon almost leaped out of his skin.

"Maya!" he said, furious. "Why did you sneak up on me like that?"

"You're the one sneaking around," said his sister. "I saw you swim out here. What's going on?" Simon could tell that she had been scared, too. He was surprised she had come out here on her own and he felt a bit embarrassed by how afraid he had been. They both looked at each other angrily, Maya shivering in her wet clothes. Then she caught sight of the glowing cut. She sucked in her breath and hurried past Simon to see it.

"I saw light coming from the porthole, that's why I came out here," whispered Simon. "I think it's fresh." He came closer to peer at the cut with Maya. "You don't know anything about it?"

"No more than you," she said. They spoke in whispers. "Ophalla," she murmured, incredulous. "Do you think those men who've been hanging around the house did this?"

"I haven't seen any of them coming out to the *Pamela Jane*," said Simon. "But . . ." he whispered, "I don't know who else would have."

He looked closer at the glowing scar. It wasn't a gash, he noted; the cut was neat and precise and shallow. The culprit had been gentle.

"Whoever it was knew what they were looking for," he said thoughtfully. "It's not random. And they didn't want to damage the boat—it's not vandalism." He paused. "I think they suspected there was ophalla here, and they wanted to know for sure."

"But how would they know?" Maya asked.

Simon shook his head, mystified.

Maya turned to look all around the cabin. "Do you think it runs through the whole hull?"

Simon had been wondering the same thing. He took out his pocketknife and went to the hull on the opposite side of the cabin. He began to score a line through the wood.

"What are you doing?" hissed Maya.

Simon ignored her, and a few moments later the scratch in the wood began to glow and a fine powder of blue-green ophalla trickled to the floor. Simon stopped. He tried a few other spots around the cabin. In some there was nothing; in others fresh ophalla was exposed.

"It's in the main beams," he said excitedly. "This is incredible! It's almost as if there's a skeleton of ophalla inside the boat and just a thin layer of wood covering it. It would have been really hard to build. Whoever did it would have had to know how much ophalla the frame could bear before it became too heavy to float, and all sorts of other things. But there must be a reason why she was built this way—I wish I knew what it was!"

Maya looked all around them in wonder. "How did we never know?" she whispered. "We *lived* here for years!"

Though she had belonged to their family for years now, the children knew little of the *Pamela Jane*'s past before the day she had drifted into the little cove at Granny Pearl's, her sails in shreds and her hull encrusted in barnacles, back when Maya had been just a baby and Simon had not yet been born. It wasn't until after the great storm that took them to Tamarind that they even learned that she was *from* the mysterious island. Whatever secrets were locked within her timbers were hers alone. The day had changed irrevocably, and the boatyard and Simon's friends suddenly seemed very far away.

"We have to tell Papi," said Maya.

"I guess . . ." said Simon grudgingly. Part of him wanted to keep the secret until he had time to investigate further.

When Maya shivered again they decided to go back to shore. They drew a chest in front of the glowing scratch to conceal its light, then climbed back up to the deck. The water was chillier the second time, and as the wind picked up from beyond the mouth of the cove, the *Pamela Jane* rocked from bow to stern. Impulsively Simon swam along the lee and took his knife out of his pocket. He pried off the chiton from the *Pamela Jane*'s name and, feeling a moment of small triumph, watched it wobble down through the water and come to rest in the turtle grass beds below. Then he swam back toward the little beach. The clouds were thickening in the sky and the first raindrops were splashing down, dimpling the surface of the water.

❧ CHAPTER TWO ❧

Note in the Conch ❋ *The Red Coral Project* ❋
Faustina's Gate ❋ *The Compass and Strange Stromatolites* ❋
"Hello?" ❋ *One Extra*

There were two chairs empty at dinner that night. Helix's, of course, had been empty for weeks, and tonight Simon's father was too busy working to come out of his study. Through the closed door everyone could hear the wheezing and crackling of static on the CB radio. Simon wondered who he was trying to talk to. Simon and Maya had told their parents about the ophalla as soon as they returned from the boat. Marisol and Peter Nelson had not seemed as surprised as Simon would have expected, but when the children left they had talked privately behind the closed study door.

Now Granny Pearl and the children's mother met eyes and Mami nodded.

"Come on, Penelope," said Granny Pearl. "Time for your bath."

Penny scrambled down from the table and she and Granny Pearl left the room. The children's mother waited until they were gone and then she looked at Simon and Maya.

"You both know things have been a little strange lately," she said delicately. "And now this thing with the

Pamela Jane . . . We don't want you to worry, but until we know more we want you to stay close to home after school. Just to be on the safe side for a little while. And I'd like you to help Granny Pearl keep an eye on Penny."

Simon dropped his fork and looked angrily at his mother.

"We know those men are from the Red Coral," he said. "Why don't you just tell us what they want!"

His mother didn't answer.

"They can't do this to us!" said Simon. "They're trespassing—it's illegal! Why don't you and Papi just call the police?"

"Your father and I have our reasons," said his mother. She leaned her elbows on the table, chin in her hands. Simon noticed dark circles under her eyes.

"I'm thirteen," he said resentfully. "I shouldn't have to be stuck at home. I'm not scared of those men. I can take care of myself, you know."

Maya looked concerned. "Don't worry, Mami," she said. "We'll be okay. And we'll watch Penny. It doesn't matter if we have to stay home for a little while." She looked pointedly at Simon.

Simon glared at her. Just because she was older didn't mean she could act like she was his mother. He picked up his fork and pushed it through the cold potatoes left on his plate. He wasn't hungry anymore.

"I haven't done anything wrong," he said, "so I don't see why I'm being punished." He pushed his plate away. "May I be excused?"

His mother sighed. "Go ahead," she said.

Simon brushed his teeth and put on his pajamas and threw himself on his bed.

He couldn't believe this was happening. One afternoon missed at the boatyard was bad enough, but now his parents were being unreasonable. It was like torture.

He hated the Red Coral Project.

Simon was fed up with his parents. Why didn't they take charge of the situation? He wouldn't have let anyone push him around—why were they? It didn't make any sense.

Through the window, Simon heard footsteps on the darkened grass and saw a shadow slip into the trees at the eastern end of the garden. The watchers were still out there. The rain had stopped and a sallow moon was out and bats were in the throes of a mad, erratic ballet in the purple sky. A fine rain began, rustling on the grass.

Simon wished Helix were there. His bed, empty all these weeks, sat on the opposite side of the room. It was crisply made, but lately Simon had begun to throw stuff on it. When they were younger they used to stay up late talking, and they'd whisper loudly to Maya across the hallway, too, until Mami or Papi or Granny Pearl would come and tell them to be quiet. If Helix were here they could figure out what to do about the Red Coral! Why had he left without telling Simon he was leaving or where he was going? He was supposed to be Simon's friend.

Simon imagined weeks and possibly months ahead

sprawling out before him—a barren wasteland, heaps upon heaps of hours, living like prisoners. Their lives would contract to a monotonous routine of school and home. Friends would fall away. There would be no afternoons at the boatyard, no exploring in the boat he and his friends had built, no riding around on his bike—no freedom. The same slithery thought he had so often these days crept back in: Something very big was happening right under his nose and he didn't know what it was.

He turned his shoulder into the mattress and pulled the sheet up over his eyes. It had been a long day; he just wanted to escape into sleep.

"Simon . . . Simon, wake up."

He opened his eyes.

It was Maya, standing in her nightgown in his doorway. Outside the moon was high in the black sky.

"*Simon*," she whispered. "*Helix is back.*"

✸ ✸ ✸

Maya came quietly into the room, shutting the door behind her. Eyes shining, she handed Simon a folded slip of paper. "Before Helix left he told me to look in the conch shell on the porch every night," she whispered excitedly. "There was never anything there until now."

Leaning sleepily on one elbow, Simon opened the paper. On it was scrawled: *Meet me by the mangroves tonight. Don't tell anyone*. It was definitely Helix's handwriting—he had only learned to write after he had come to the Outside and his writing didn't look like anyone else's, or much like writing at all, for that matter. Suddenly Simon felt wide awake. He looked quickly out of the window. The mangroves were down by the cove. If Helix had left a note in the conch maybe he hadn't wanted the watchers to know he was back. He had been a hunter—he could perch in the crook of a tree unseen for hours if he had to. How long had he been there?

Simon scrambled out of bed and grabbed his dressing gown. A moment later he and Maya were climbing out of his bedroom window. Checking to make sure the watchers weren't in sight, they ran across the damp grass down to the mangroves.

Clouds shrouded the moon and the *Pamela Jane* was silhouetted starkly against the midnight sky. The sand on the tiny crescent of beach between the dark mangroves and the water was cold beneath Simon's feet. The spot was hidden from the view of anyone looking out from Granny Pearl's house or from anywhere in the garden, which is why Helix must have chosen it. Maya saw him first.

"*Helix!*" she whispered joyfully.

"*Shhh . . .*" said the boy, putting a finger to his lips.

Simon could only just make out Helix in the darkness, but there was enough light to see the familiar angles of his face and mop of dark hair. The shark's tooth necklace he had worn since the first day they'd met him was there, knotted on a string around his neck.

"Leave the flashlight off," said Helix in a low voice as Maya went to turn it on.

"But I want to *see* you!" she said. Even in the darkness,

Simon could feel her beaming with happiness. She hugged Helix. "Why did you just disappear? Where have you been?" She and Simon sat down on the sand beside Helix.

Simon was relieved that their friend was okay, but angry that Helix hadn't taken him with him—or even trusted Simon enough to tell him where he was going. Simon was tired of being left out of everything.

"You didn't even tell us you were leaving," he said.

Helix sighed. Simon thought he looked older somehow. Suddenly those three inches Simon had grown didn't amount to much. He felt like a kid.

"I'm sorry I left like that," said Helix. "I thought it was safer if none of you knew where I was."

"What's going on?" Simon asked suspiciously.

Helix exhaled slowly. "Tamarind is in trouble," he said.

"What do you mean?" asked Simon. Suddenly the chill in the air felt colder, creeping through his clothes. He and Maya edged closer to Helix.

"It started with those unusual sea creatures washing up dead," whispered Helix. "Your parents think they're from Tamarind, and that something bad is happening there that's killing them, and somehow they're washing in across the Blue Line."

"But how is that possible?" asked Simon. "The Blue Line is a barrier."

"Your parents don't know how it's happening," said Helix. "But . . . what we do know is that the Red Coral finally found a way into Tamarind."

"What!" exclaimed Maya. "How do you know?"

"I knew a little about what was happening—the dead marine creatures and the fact that the Red Coral were still hassling your family," said Helix. "And I kept asking your parents to let me help. But they wouldn't. They didn't want me to get into trouble. Finally I snooped around in your dad's office until I found some leads that helped me track down the Red Coral headquarters in St. Alban's. I hitched a ride on a cargo ship there and back. But I was too late—when I got there the headquarters were abandoned. I found out that they had a hundred-and-fifty-foot steel ship, but that's gone, too. About a year ago they bought a supply of diesel, batteries, canned and dried food, medicine, engine spares . . . and ammunition. After that there's no record of them anywhere. It's as if they walked into thin air. Except they haven't."

"They're in Tamarind," said Maya, looking worried.

"But I don't understand," said Simon. "If the Red Coral are already in Tamarind, what do they still want with our parents? Why don't they leave us alone?"

"Because of Faustina's Gate," said Helix. "They think your parents know where it is."

Faustina's Gate. Simon wracked his brain but he was sure he had never heard of it before.

"The Red Coral believe it's the secret to getting across the Blue Line," said Helix. "They managed to cross the line once, but I don't think it was easy—you remember the storms. They need an easier way back and forth. And they think that Faustina's Gate is it."

"Is it a real gate?" Maya asked curiously.

"No one knows," said Helix.

"Why don't we go in the house to talk?" said Maya, shivering and pulling her sweater down over her hands. "It's silly to be out here like this."

"I'm not going to the house," said Helix. "I don't want to risk having your parents see me. I wanted you to meet me here so that we could leave right away." He paused and took a deep breath and looked at both of them. "I need the *Pamela Jane*. And I need you to help me get through the reefs. I'm going back to Tamarind."

Simon and Maya were stunned for a few seconds.

"Back to Tamarind?" Maya asked incredulously. "How?"

"The ophalla in the *Pamela Jane*'s hull!" cried Simon suddenly. "It has something to do with getting back to Tamarind—you were the one who made that scratch!" He scrambled up so he was kneeling. Suddenly he felt jittery with excitement. The water lapped softly on the sand.

"*Shhh,*" said Helix. "Yes, it was me. While I was gone I came across another Tamarinder who had come to the Outside like me, but a long time ago. Don't look so surprised! I knew as soon as I saw him he was from Tamarind. Anyway, he must be nearly a hundred now—he's a fisherman in St. Sylvan. He told me a lot of old stories. One of them was that a long time ago in Tamarind there were boats made from ophalla, built to cross the Blue Line. As soon as I heard that I knew the *Pamela Jane* must be one of them. That's why after that storm, when none of your navigation equipment would work and you couldn't stay on course, the ophalla in the *Pamela Jane* was naturally pulled toward the Blue Line and across to Tamarind. I don't know how it works, just that it does. All I have to do is sail back to the place you were in when the storm struck that took you to Tamarind—the *Pamela Jane* will do the rest." He paused. "So you see," he said, "we *can* go back."

Back to Tamarind. Simon had never thought it was possible. He felt a shiver scuttle down his spine. "And you want to leave tonight," he said.

"Tonight!" exclaimed Maya. "Tonight?" she repeated softly. "This is happening way too fast. I think we should go and wake up Mami and Papi and talk to them—"

"Do you really think they'd let me go?" asked Helix.

"Well . . ." said Maya, then stopped.

"Of course they wouldn't," said Helix. "But now that I know Tamarind is in trouble I have to go. I can't wait another day. I've already drained the fuel tank on the Red Coral men's boat. They won't be able to catch us. I want to leave before the tide goes out. I'm not asking you to come to Tamarind with me—I don't know what's happening there; it might be dangerous. But, please, I need your help to get the *Pamela Jane* past the reefs outside the cove. I'm not a good enough sailor—I can't make it through them, especially on a night like this. If you can help me get through them, you can row back to shore in the rowboat. Once I'm in open water I'll be fine. I can go alone from there."

"So you wouldn't even be telling us you were leaving unless you needed our help right now!" said Maya. "We'd just wake up and you and our boat would be gone!"

"*Shhh,*" said Helix, looking back toward the house.

Simon stopped listening as Maya and Helix bickered softly. He looked out at the cove. Helix was right; the tide was going out and if they didn't leave soon they would miss their chance. Clouds hid the moon. Conditions were perfect. Suddenly he remembered the first day in Tamarind—the heat, the butterflies as big as bats that had drifted around them, the twinkling chimes of the flying fish. He remembered the tree houses high in the Cloud Forest Village where they had lived for a time, running across rope bridges far above the ground, the air thick each night with jungle fireflies and the scent of orchids. In Tamarind he and Maya and Penny had been brave and independent and free—they had rescued their mother from a pirate ship and their father from the ghostly salt islands of the Ravaged Straits. They had helped to start the Great Peace March that had finally brought generations of a bitter war to an end.

Suddenly the boatyard didn't matter anymore. Simon could do something much bigger and more important! He would stop the Red Coral himself! He'd show his parents he wasn't just a kid. The breeze blew and Simon smelled the sea. His face felt hot. His fingers and toes began to tingle, as if they had been asleep and now the feeling was returning. He turned to Helix.

"I'll go, too," he said boldly. "Not just to get past the reefs. I'll go to Tamarind with you."

Suddenly the breeze became a gust, whipping up small waves on the surface of the cove. "This is crazy," said Maya authoritatively. She stood up, her hands on her hips, and glared at Simon and Helix.

"It isn't crazy," whispered Simon. "I think it's very rational. We know that something hasn't been right for a long time with our parents, and that whatever it is has to do with the Red Coral Project. Helix has just told us that the Red Coral are in Tamarind now and whatever's happening there is bad—so bad that things from there are dying and washing up on the Outside. Who knows what's actually happening *on* the island? Once I heard Papi tell Mami that the Red Coral would tear Tamarind apart to get their hands on ophalla. We can't do anything here—even Mami and Papi haven't been able to. But over there we can do whatever we want! We'll be free! We can actually *do* something to help our family—and Tamarind. We'll go and we'll be back before we know it."

"Please, Maya, all I'm asking is that you help me through the reefs," said Helix. "Then you can go home."

"And let you two go off without me!" said Maya. "Especially after you just came back, Helix!"

She looked at them, conflicted, but she sat back down again.

Simon knew that all Maya had ever wanted was to live a normal life on land. He also knew she would never tell their parents that Helix was back if he didn't want her to. And Simon was pretty sure that she wasn't about to be left behind while he and Helix went off on an adventure without her.

She turned and looked out at the *Pamela Jane*, tugging on her mooring. The wind blew her hair and she pushed it behind her ear. She was wavering. She loved Tamarind, too. They heard the urgent whistle of the wind across the surface of the sea, the swish and churn of the waves. Simon and Helix waited. Then Simon saw a familiar determined look come into her eyes. She took a deep breath.

"I'll come, too," she said. "To Tamarind."

The air seemed filled with electricity. The three of them looked at each other. Simon felt the hairs on the back of his neck go up. It was all beginning again.

Simon and Maya had to run back to the house to get supplies. In his room Simon dumped his schoolbooks out of his backpack, and threw in spare clothes, his pocketknife, and his binoculars. He rummaged through drawers—where was his compass? They couldn't go without one. When he couldn't find it anywhere he remembered that his father had one in his office. He slung his bag over his shoulder and crept down the hall.

To his relief, his father's study was empty. No light came from under his parents' bedroom door—they must be asleep. The study door was open and Simon slipped inside. Moonlight glowed on the glass jars in which sea creatures were trapped forever in their lifeless drift. The last time Simon remembered seeing his father's compass it had been on one of the bookshelves. He scanned the rows of titles:

Coral Spawning: A Mysterious Season; Life Cycles of Coral Reefs; Blue-Green Algae . . . Ah, there it was, sitting in front of *Strange Stromatolites* and behind the jar with the water snake. When he moved the jar, the formalin sloshed gently from side to side and the snake appeared to wriggle as if alive.

Simon pocketed the compass, but before he left he paused to look once more around the room. He let his eyes rove over the storm of papers on Papi's cluttered desk. He felt a pang as he remembered their exchange earlier. Was he really leaving like this? He wished he could say good-bye or even just see his father for a moment. Simon was lingering by the desk when the radio hissed beside him. He nearly leaped out of his skin. For a minute he could only hear the pounding of his heart. Then a staccato code was tapped out. Then a voice: *Are you there?*

"Hello?" said Simon softly.

Peter? said the voice. *Who is this?* But then the static rose and the reception was lost.

Simon fled the room and found Maya in the kitchen, packing food into her backpack. "Got everything?" she asked.

"Yup, ready to go," he said.

Before Simon could tell Maya about the voice from the radio, they heard something rustle in the doorway. They looked up to see a small figure illuminated in the moonlight.

"Penny," Maya whispered. "Go back to bed, baby. Come on, I'll take you."

Penny was rubbing her eyes, looking past Maya curiously at the things spread out on the table.

"Where are you going?" she asked.

"Going?" Maya asked lightly. "We aren't going anywhere."

But Penny, no stranger to her older siblings' duplicity, glared at them.

"You're going somewhere and I want to come," she said. She got a stubborn gleam in her eye.

"What are you talking about?" asked Maya. "The only place we're all going is back off to bed." Penny didn't budge. Maya decided to switch tactics. "Let's play a game," she said cheerfully.

Penny pressed her lips together tightly and shook her head.

"Penny," said Simon, "this is serious. We aren't playing anymore. You have to go back to bed, *now*."

"How about I come with you," said Maya. But when Maya smiled and reached out to take her arm, Penny took a deep breath and opened her mouth wide, ready to holler.

"Stop," Simon said to Maya. "She'll do it."

Penny began to hum warningly under her breath.

"What are we going to do?" asked Maya.

"Take her with us?" asked Simon.

"Be serious," said Maya.

"If we wait now, we'll miss the tide," said Simon. "You'll just have to come back with her in the rowboat. It's lumpy out there tonight—I need your help to get through the reefs."

34

"Me!" whispered Maya, glaring at Simon. "Why me? I'm the oldest—I'll go with Helix. *You* take Penny back."

When Simon didn't answer and began stuffing more food from a cupboard into his backpack, Maya turned to her sister. "Oh, Penny!" she whispered fiercely. "Can't you just go back to bed?"

The tide was going out and the smell of the sea moss exposed on the rocks came through the window. If the tide got too low they would be in danger of hitting the *Pamela Jane*'s keel on the rocks, and if they waited for the tide to come back in it would be daylight and they would have lost the chance. "Come on," said Simon. "Helix is waiting for us. It's now or never."

"We're going to play a game," he said to Penny. "And you have to be absolutely silent—absolutely. You understand?"

Penny bit her lip to stop smiling. She nodded.

Maya wrote a note.

> Dear Mami, Papi and Granny Pearl,
> Simon and Helix are taking the Pamela Jane back to Tamarind. I'm going to help them through the reefs. Penny woke up so I have her with me. I'll explain when I get back. Sorry.
> Love,
> Maya

PS, added Simon. *Don't be mad. We'll be home soon.*

Maya put a vase on the note and left it in the middle of

the table. Simon got the backpacks they had packed with clothes and food—bread, peanut butter, apples, bottled water—and they slipped quietly back to Simon's bedroom and climbed through his window. Then taking Penny's hands, the three of them crouched and dashed across the open grass down to the cove.

❧ CHAPTER THREE ❧

Underwater Maze ❋ *Decision Time* ❋
On a Winter Sea

The breeze was dead inside the cove, but outside it Simon could see whitecaps whipped up by the wind until the moon slid behind a cloud. The *Pamela Jane* creaked on her moorings.

Helix was waiting for them in the mangroves. When Penny saw him she flung herself into his arms.

"Hey," he said, catching hold of her. "Starfish!" He frowned at the others. "What's she doing here?" he whispered over her head.

"She woke up," said Maya in a low voice. "We couldn't get her to go back to bed."

"We can't take a five-year-old with us!" said Helix. "What are we supposed to do now?"

"There wasn't anything else we could do," whispered Maya. "Don't worry, I'm going to take her back in the rowboat once we get past the reefs."

"I'm going to be good," Penny whispered loudly.

"*Shhh,*" said Simon. "Our voices will carry across the water."

Simon and Helix flipped the overturned rowboat and palmetto bugs scurried out. They carried it down to the water and all of them stepped in. Simon rowed as silently as he could, and when they reached the *Pamela Jane* he tied the rowboat to the stern and they climbed on board. Maya slid a life jacket on Penny and sent her to the cabin. Simon and Helix released the mooring bridle as carefully as they could so it wouldn't jangle. It was fine until the last moment, when the last links of the chain slid over the *Pamela Jane*'s gunnel with a brutal zipping sound. Simon cringed and looked quickly back to shore but there was no sign that anyone had heard. He and Maya worked quickly to rig the sails. They raised the jib first, since it was easiest and would attract the least notice from shore. In a moment it caught the breeze and the boat began gliding cautiously out toward the mouth of the cove. Simon glanced over his shoulder, holding his breath, but the shore was dark except for the light on Granny Pearl's porch.

Just when Simon started to think that perhaps they would be out of the cove and on their way before the men even noticed the boat was missing, they saw the first of the flashlight beams swinging along the shoreline. The drumming of footsteps carried across the water, and moments later, to their delight, the children heard an outraged cry as the empty fuel tank was discovered.

"Okay, hurry," said Helix. "That's not going to stop them for long. They'll go to the boatyard and get hold of another boat."

Pale moonlight filtered through the heavy clouds, and as they rounded the rocky head the wind rose. The ghostly white bloom of the jib led them out of the cove and into the channel between the reefs.

"We have to be careful, the next bit is tricky," said Simon. He stayed at the wheel and Maya went to look out from the bow. Helix alternated looking out from starboard and port.

A perilous maze of jagged reefs spread before them in the darkness. There was a single, narrow, winding channel running for about a mile through them and out to the open sea. One false move, even by a few degrees, and the hull would crunch into the rocks and the boat would sink right out from under them. Without the GPS plotter, which the Red Coral had stolen long ago, Simon had to navigate from memory. Only someone who knew the reefs like the back of his hand as he did would be able to make it. He decided to continue with only the jib until they reached open water. For now, precision seemed wiser than speed. As it was, they were missing reefs by mere inches sometimes—Maya or Helix would spot one, looming craggy and treacherous, and Simon would have just seconds to spin the wheel in time to avoid a collision.

Behind them they heard an engine choke and splutter, then with a tortured wheeze it roared to life. The Red Coral men had found a new boat. Soon it was whizzing around the coast, the raw buzz of the engine reverberating off the shore. Simon's knuckles were white on the wheel, but he tried to steady his nerves and stay focused: steer to port, right the wheel, call to Maya to shorten the jib, now turn a little to port. Behind them the rowboat sloshed in the swells.

"There they are!" Helix shouted suddenly.

Simon glanced back at the motorboat, bumping over the waves at high speed toward them. It gave no indication of slowing.

"They're coming up fast!" Maya called. "Simon, we've got to hoist the mainsail!"

Simon spun the wheel just in time for the *Pamela Jane* to narrowly miss grazing the toothy ledge of another boiler reef. He broke out in a sweat.

"I need more control!" he called. "We can't handle more sail yet! We have to get into open water first!"

Stay calm, he told himself. The Red Coral boat would hit the reefs if it kept going at that speed. Open water was still a quarter of a mile away, but the motorboat was drawing closer and closer. Simon could now see the silhouettes of the two figures in it. He looked back at the floundering rowboat, half-filled with water from the mounting seas. It was slowing them down and making it difficult to steer. The Red Coral boat would reach them within a minute or two. Simon agonized, then he took a deep breath.

"Cut the rowboat free!" he shouted.

"But—" yelled Maya, taking her eyes off the water to look back at her brother, "that means . . ."

"There's no time!" Simon shouted. "We have to!"

Maya ran in a crouch to the stern cleat and unknotted the rowboat and cast it loose. Free of its drag, the *Pamela Jane* surged forward in the water. They were so close to the end of the reefs. They only had to make it a little farther.

But their pursuers showed no sign of slowing. For a

terrifying moment Simon thought that they would be caught after all. But the motorboat dropped suddenly into idle and began nosing slowly through the water. Simon heaved a sigh of relief.

"They've reached the high reefs!" he called. "They don't know the way!"

Simon looked behind him and saw Granny Pearl's cottage. In terms of distance it was still close, but from the other side of the torturous path through the reefs it felt immeasurably far away.

At that moment the *Pamela Jane* passed between the last of the reefs and the seafloor dropped off suddenly as the boat entered open water.

"More speed!" shouted Simon. "Hoist the mainsail!" Pulling with all their strength, Maya and Helix hoisted the sail. The mainsail gave a mighty shudder and bellowed in the wind. When it reached its full height it fell suddenly silent, shining like a great white wing, majestic in flight over the dark sea.

A thrill went through each of them.

"We're free!" cried Maya gleefully.

"Barely," said Helix. "That was close." But he was smiling.

Euphoric, they turned to look behind them. The motorboat had become hopelessly lost in the maze of reefs. The lights from the shore danced between the swells, already getting farther away. The wind was in their favor and the *Pamela Jane* was making good speed. She had shaken the mustiness out of her sails—spiders and long streamers of cobwebs had blown away wildly into the night—and the salt spray struck her sides and washed her clean.

"The rowboat!" cried Maya suddenly. "Penny! What are we going to do with her?"

They looked behind them but the rowboat had disappeared quickly in the darkness.

Simon knew that to head back to shore against the wind would be tricky. The waves were rising and the lights from the shore were lost each time the boat dipped down into a trough. It was dark, the winds were blowing twenty knots, and every now and then waves broke on the tops of the swells. It would be easy to run aground on a night like this. It would also give the Red Coral men time to find their way through the reefs or to turn back and find a safer channel out to sea. The *Pamela Jane*'s motor no longer worked, and even if they had a good head start, once out in the open water a faster boat would catch them easily.

But it was more than that. Now that they were out there on the open sea with the wind at their backs it seemed harder and harder to imagine returning. The pull of the ocean was strong. Simon already felt closer to Tamarind than to home.

Penny had crept back onto the deck without the others seeing her.

"I want to go with you," she said. She stood there stoutly, still in her pajamas. Her orange life jacket dwarfed her. "I want to go to Tamarind."

They looked down at her.

"No way," said Helix. "Your parents are already going

to kill me. We're going to head back to shore farther down and you're going back to Granny Pearl's."

"Helix is right," said Maya reluctantly. "I have to take you home."

Penny looked crestfallen for a moment, but then the familiar obstinate thrust returned to her chin. "I've been to Tamarind before, you know," she said indignantly.

The truth was that none of them wanted to go home.

"If we try to head back in to drop Penny and me off we'll give them time to catch us," said Maya. "And then all this will be for nothing—we'll have lost our chance."

"Then there's only one thing to do," said Simon. He pulled his gaze away from land and kneeled down and took Penny's hands firmly.

"We're in charge," he said. "You have to do everything we say, the second we say it. It's very, very important. And you can't change your mind and decide you want to go home in a little while. We don't know how long we'll be gone. Do you understand?"

Penny nodded fervently, her cheeks flushed. "I understand," she said.

"You have to wear a life jacket all the time," said Simon. "And if anyone ever yells, 'Come about!' it means the boat is going to tack or jibe and you have to duck immediately because the boom will come cracking around. It's very dangerous. Got that?"

Penny nodded.

"Now go down to the cabin and stay there," said Maya. "The ocean's too rough for you to be on deck tonight!"

Beaming, Penny hurried below. A moment later she was kneeling on a bunk with her face pressed to a porthole, looking out in wonder as the foaming black sea slid past and the tiny boat headed into ever greater darkness.

"We all need to be on the lookout," called Simon. "Maya at the helm. Helix, take starboard, and I'll take port and the wheel for now."

It was astonishing how swiftly Bermuda dwindled to a tiny pinprick of light in the distance and then was lost to sight. After that they weren't so afraid of being caught. Even if the Red Coral men made it past the reefs they wouldn't be able to find the children out in the middle of the immense night ocean.

❧ CHAPTER FOUR ❧

The Storm

Though it had been a long time since Simon and Maya had worked as a team on the boat, the memory of how came back to them and they worked in harmony, adjusting the sails to marshal the power of the wind, waiting for a glimpse of the North Star through the clouds, and righting the boat's course to sail directly south. They ran the sails full—it was almost dangerous to have that much canvas up on such a night—but the *Pamela Jane* plowed gallantly through the darkness. *It's lucky Helix isn't on his own out here*, thought Simon, *the seas are too rough for one person to handle.*

They were out in deep water now. In the inky fathoms below them were whales so large they dwarfed the little ship; nighttime hunters like tiger sharks; and deeper yet, where the ocean floor was cold and still, eerie creatures that were little more than filaments of light blinking on and off. But here, on the surface, the winter night was wild. After a while, Maya and Helix joined Penny in the cabin to warm up, but Simon put a safety harness on and stayed on deck, keeping a watchful eye for other boats' lights. He was wet and cold but he didn't care. The past months and years seemed to fall away, and he felt somehow *alive* again, as if

45

he had woken from a long sleep. This morning he had dragged his heels to school, yawned, and doodled through classes, and now here he was out on the open ocean, salt spray dousing him, rinsing off the tedium of life on land. Nervously, he wondered if they really would find the Blue Line.

The wind dropped out after a few hours and Maya joined him in the cockpit.

"I just remembered that my note said Penny and I would be back," she said unhappily. "Mami and Papi and Granny Pearl will wake up and find us gone . . ."

Simon felt a twinge of guilt but he quashed it.

"Don't worry," he said. "They're smart. They'll figure out what happened. And when we come home and tell them we stopped the Red Coral Project, think how happy they'll be."

Helix appeared and sat down with them. He seemed more relaxed now and he looked at them both properly for the first time.

"Hey," he said to Simon. "You grew."

Simon was just about to say he'd grown three inches when Helix grinned and said, "Had to happen some time, shrimp."

Simon was alone at the wheel on the second night when he first heard the storm in the distance. He stood still, listening. Excitement made his hands prickle. Oily black waves slithered over the hull. At first it was just a light show on the horizon, miles away, illuminating only a tiny fraction of the great darkness that surrounded them. Clouds sat heavy on the fields of black water. Then in seconds, the storm began moving toward them. A great flash lit the sea all around and Simon saw something that made his heart skip a beat.

For a moment he was rooted to the spot, staring at it in awe, then he ran to the hatch to call Maya and Helix.

Shaking off sleep, they appeared on deck and joined him at the stern. They had to wait until the next flash of lightning to see the strange, deep turquoise band.

"The Blue Line!" said Maya in amazement. "I don't believe it—we found it!"

The lightning illuminated the sea and sky as bright as false day, and lit the line an unearthly, mesmerizing aqua, distinct from the rest of the sea. It looked like a second horizon tracking toward them. Rain began to stab the deck and blur the seas rising around the *Pamela Jane*.

"Furl the sails," said Simon. "We don't have long!" The wind snatched his words and ferried them into the night.

An instant later rain was drumming deafeningly on the deck. The world around them shrank to the boat herself— Simon could barely see past her railings. Thunder boomed overhead and immense banks of clouds massed and multiplied, hurling javelins of lightning. When he had tied the wheel securely, he rushed to help Maya and Helix, who were struggling with the mainsail. Great sheets of salt spray and foam drove through the air, knocking their feet out from under them.

"This is it!" Simon bellowed when everything was finally battened down. "Get belowdecks!"

Maya slid down the hatch first, followed by Helix, and with a last look at the Blue Line—they were nearly upon it now—Simon ducked and pulled the hatch down over his head and slid the lock across it. Within moments the storm had swallowed them whole. The boat lurched as if she had run aground and the three of them pitched forward, tumbling into one another. Penny woke sobbing and Maya crawled over to her. The four of them huddled where they could, bracing themselves against the bunks to keep from being tossed around.

Waves struck the *Pamela Jane* broadside and spun her around. At first the children tried to shout to one another, but they couldn't hear over the wind and waves. The ophalla in the captain's quarters had started to glow furiously, casting a weird light that turned their faces ghostly blue. Waves crashed on the deck and Simon watched water creeping in through the hatch. Through the porthole he glimpsed cliffs of black water. The boat's timbers groaned and sometimes it sounded as if she was splitting into pieces. The children couldn't have said how many times the boat rose dizzyingly on crests of waves and plunged into cold dark troughs, but it began to seem as if they had been in the storm their whole lives and there was nothing in the world beyond the howling void.

Gradually Simon realized that the winds had started to subside and the boat was no longer at the mercy of the mountains of waves. A current caught the *Pamela Jane* and bore her swiftly away from the foul weather. Through the portholes the children watched the dark water rushing past. Simon climbed the companionway and opened the hatch to look out at the black cluster of clouds, buzzing with lightning, receding farther and farther into the distance.

"The *Pamela Jane* made it through," he said. "Brave ship," he whispered, patting her deck.

Maya put Penny back to bed, and exhausted by her ordeal, the little girl fell asleep at once. Maya and Simon and Helix left the cabin. They stood on the deck, bending their knees in the gentle swells, and looked around them in wonder. It was as if they had passed some invisible shield and sailed on into warm, calm seas beneath a sky that had suddenly cleared to reveal a brilliant husk of moon and thousands of stars. Around them the sea spread silver with moonlight. The air itself smelled different—the pungent odor of strange seaweeds reached their noses and the faint rustle of it could be heard somewhere in the distance. A shiver passed through Simon. They had crossed the line once again. Tamarind lay ahead.

They examined their bruises, coming up black in the moonlight, but were relieved to see that the *Pamela Jane* was undamaged. They checked and retightened the stays, then they hoisted the sails and were soon sailing along quickly.

"I'll stay on watch," Simon said to Maya and Helix. Helix still looked a bit green-faced.

"Are you sure?" asked Maya.

Simon nodded. "I don't think I could sleep now anyway," he said.

The others headed for bed. Simon wasn't alone for long before he heard Maya's footsteps in the cabin and a moment later she emerged on the deck. She had a blanket wrapped around her shoulders and had brought another for him.

"Penny's asleep," she whispered. "Helix, too. I'd rather sleep out here, anyway." She sat down next to Simon, pulling her blanket tightly around her. Above them thousands of stars glittered in the clear crystal sky. "Remember last time we did this?" she asked.

Simon nodded. They had been younger then, and shocked and afraid after their parents had been lost overboard. Maya had had first watch but Simon had come up and slept on deck near her so she wouldn't be alone. "Thank you," he said.

"No problem," she murmured, lying down and drawing the blanket up to her shoulders. "Good night."

She didn't sleep, though, because a moment later she said, "I've been thinking about what we're going to do when we get there. I think we should find Isabella. I bet she'd help—I'm sure she doesn't want the Red Coral in Tamarind, either. She'd probably be exactly the kind of person who could do something. Look what she managed last time."

Isabella Obrado, the young girl at the head of the Sisters for the Peaceful Revolution, had planned the Great Peace March that ended many long decades of war. Maya was right—if anyone could help them, Isabella could.

"That's a really good idea," said Simon hopefully.

Maya's breathing grew deep and even, and Simon knew

she had fallen asleep. He was alone with his thoughts. The warm breeze blew over the deck. Strong currents propelled them forward and miles of sea passed beneath them. Hearing a soft splashing, he looked to starboard, where dozens of turtles heading to shore lifted their heads, their ancient carapaces catching the moonlight. Their quiet gasps sounded like the wind through trees that they were still many miles from. Simon was tired and his thoughts wandered and ran into each other.

A memory returned to him: He was eight or nine and the family had still lived on the boat. They were out at sea and he was standing at the helm with Papi, who had one hand around Simon's shoulder and with the other was pointing at a giant blue marlin leaping through the air like a missile, the wind strong in the sails, the day hot and the sea a deep, brilliant purple-blue so beautiful that Papi said it could knock you over. Simon had been purely happy in that moment. Then he remembered the day before, standing in the doorway to his father's office. All he had wanted was to talk to him. He didn't know why everything was so different now.

The sea murmured softly on the *Pamela Jane*'s hull. It felt good to have made it through the storm. Bioluminescent creatures glowed in the waters around the boat and Simon could see their lights off the port and starboard, mysterious and strange. Every now and then something glided through the water, leaving a fizz of blue-green bubbles.

He wondered what they would find when they got to Tamarind.

Helix said the Red Coral were desperate to find Faustina's Gate.

Faustina's Gate.

What was it?

Why did the Red Coral Project want to know?

And if Simon and the children found it first, could it help stop the Red Coral?

❧ CHAPTER FIVE ❧

Trouble in Tamarind ❂ An Overburdened City ❂
"Madam President!" ❂ The Red Man ❂
Bird of Milagros ❂ A Bolt of Green

The following morning dawned blue and clear. The children ate breakfast on the deck—apples and bread that Maya had packed—and enjoyed the sun on their shoulders. There was a brisk but gentle breeze and miles of ocean sparkling all around them with not another ship in sight. To everyone's relief, Penny had not cried since the storm or asked for their parents, and seemed pleased simply to be included on an adventure with the older children. Since they hadn't brought spare clothes for her, she was still wearing her pink pajamas, which Maya had rolled over her knees and elbows.

Simon chewed on a hunk of bread. Even stale bread tasted delicious out on the water. He tossed his apple core overboard, where electric green fish lifted their gleaming scales into the sun as they nibbled it to its seeds. His skin was salty, his hair was stiff with salt, his feet were bare, and after years of waking up in the same place each morning, in a home rooted solidly to the ground, he had woken in the cabin of their beloved boat as she rushed through the dawn waters. Except for the occasional twinge of guilt about his parents, he was happy. Tamarind lay up ahead and there

53

they would be able to confront the Red Coral Project—
Simon would finally be able to *do* something.

"Land!" Maya shouted suddenly.

Simon leaped to his feet and for a brief second he
caught sight of a brilliant green speck on the horizon before the boat dipped back down and he lost sight of it.

"Is this it?" Maya asked excitedly. "Are we there?"

Helix ran to the bow to look out, hand shading his
eyes. A moment later he turned back to them, smiling from
ear to ear. His shark's tooth necklace gleamed on his dark
chest. "We made it!" he shouted. "Tamarind!"

A turquoise swell lifted the *Pamela Jane* and Simon felt
as if he were flying. Maya shouted joyfully and Penny began
hopping up and down with excitement. Simon ran to
the wheel and turned the *Pamela Jane* to head toward the
green mote, already growing bigger. The wind was in their
favor and the ivory sails billowed. Brilliant schools of fish,
bright as parrots, swished past the sunny yellow hull. As
they drew closer, the island seemed to expand like a sponge,
growing before their eyes into soaring hills and valleys,
green as jade against the airy white mists breaking upon the
shores.

In another half hour they were close enough that through
his binoculars Simon could see gannets diving from sheer
cliffs and turtles basking on sand twinkling with ophalla
dust. Schools of flying fish emerged from the darkness of the
jungle, sparkled in the sunlight for a moment, then dissolved
back into the canopy. Birds perched along swaybacked palms
and a family of long-tailed monkeys swung from branch to

branch along the jungle's edge. It was as he had dreamed of it each night for so long after they had returned to the Outside. He felt his heart catch in his throat.

"Home," Helix said softly.

Maya lifted Penny up so she could get a better view. The last time she had seen Tamarind, she had been a baby, strapped to a sling around Maya's shoulder. Now her nose quivered, smelling the cinnamon and nutmeg, the fruit trees and the hot jungle air that came to them across the water, and very old memories stirred in her.

The wind was changing direction and Simon called to Maya to help him as they approached a green head of land jutting out from the island. This time they did not arrive in the Lesser Islands, with the secluded green coves and the vines that swam in the air like tentacles. Instead, to Simon's surprise, what now came into view as they rounded the head was a great, glittering city built upon a sweeping hillside. A monumental stone fortress loomed on its highest point. From a distance its flags seemed frozen stiffly in the air, but through the binoculars Simon could see that they waved furiously in the wind. A long coastal road led in and out of the city.

"Hey . . ." said Maya. "Can I have the binoculars?" Simon tossed them to her and a moment later she looked back up, excited. "I remember that road—I'm sure I do! I walked it on my way to find you and Penny!" She passed the binoculars to Helix. "It's the capital," she said. "It's Maracairol! Isabella lives here—this is perfect!"

But Helix didn't share her enthusiasm. "It *is* Maracairol," he said, squinting at the shore. "But I don't think we should land here. Let's go somewhere more out of the way until we figure out what's going on."

"But why?" asked Maya. "We couldn't have landed in a better spot."

"We don't know what's happened here since we left," said Helix soberly. "We don't know what the Red Coral are doing or where they are on the island. Maracairol may not be safe." He touched the knife on his belt and looked darkly at the city as it grew closer.

Simon's initial joy began to fade as reluctantly he remembered why they had come. Helix was right. They had no idea what was happening in Tamarind.

"I agree," he said. "Better to be on the safe side." He steered to starboard to find a quiet place to come ashore. The winds drove them around the head, and as they sailed into its cool shadow Penny was the first to notice the bloated carcass of a dimly glowing fish drifting by. As they watched, the creature bumped gently into the lifeless form of an octopus. Its arms, so tangled and busy in life, were now stretched out flat like a starfish's. When Simon looked up he saw shadows of countless other creatures nodding limply in the dark green water.

"Why are they all dead?" asked Penny.

Simon remembered the reports of glowing marine life washing up at home. Helix had said their parents believed they were coming from Tamarind.

"Can they really be getting to the Outside somehow?" murmured Maya.

"I don't understand how," said Simon, frowning. "The Blue Line should stop them." But it seemed too much of a coincidence. Simon wished that his father had talked to him about his concerns and that he knew more. The dead creatures felt like a bad omen.

The children were so absorbed by the lifeless army floating past that the violent explosion from shore startled even Helix. Penny cowered behind Maya. Simon's first thought was that they were being fired on.

"Take Penny belowdecks!" he said quickly.

"Wait," said Helix. "The explosion was too big—it's not a cannon. I don't think it had anything to do with us."

They listened as the sound echoed in the hills and slowly faded. A dark cloud of smoke rose deep in the jungle, casting a shadow over treetops that moments before had been gleaming in the sun. Then Simon noticed that there were other, similar clouds here and there, going deeper into the island, previous explosions whose clouds were now turning white and thinning. The birds roosting in the palms took flight and a lone yellow jaguar prowling the shore turned and vanished into the jungle, leaving not a soul on the beaches. The bitter scent of smoke wafted across the water.

"What do you think it is?" asked Maya.

"I don't know," said Helix. "But we have a bigger problem—look."

The next time the *Pamela Jane* reached the crest of a swell Simon saw a pair of clipper ships under full canvas, making their way at speed toward the *Pamela Jane* from the direction of Maracairol.

"Is it pirates?" Maya asked anxiously.

Simon fumbled with his binoculars. "I don't think they're pirates," he said in relief. "It looks like soldiers on board— I'm guessing they're military ships."

"I have a bad feeling about this," said Helix. "Can we make a run for it?"

Simon shook his head. "They're much bigger than us. They'd overtake us in no time."

In minutes the clipper ships had drawn a hundred yards on starboard and port of the *Pamela Jane*. The soldiers' shouts—too far away to hear distinctly—were clearly intended to direct them in to shore. Simon took a last glance at the soup of dead creatures sloshing in the current before he turned his attention back to sailing between the two ships.

The winds led them in easily and soon they entered Maracairol's harbor. Coral glinted in the seawalls. Fishermen, skin copper from the sun, were hauling in nets of silver fish that slapped wetly against the stone docks. Blots of shadow wagged beneath palms bent permanently in the wind. The air had again cleared of smoke. They were instructed to tie the *Pamela Jane* to a mooring a few hundred feet from shore, and a large rowboat with two armed guards met them.

"Get in," barked one of the soldiers.

"We're friends of Isabella Obrado," called Maya.

"Outsiders have no friends here!" snapped the guard.

Maya's smile faded, and Simon felt the first twinges of doubt. He looked to Helix.

"Don't talk for now," whispered Helix. "Where are you taking us?" he called to the guard.

"Ashore," said the soldier. "To the president."

The president? There had been no president when they had last been in Tamarind. There had been only war and chaos.

"Why would someone as important as a president want to see us?" Simon whispered.

"No more talking," snapped the other soldier. "Get in the boat."

Simon felt uneasy leaving the *Pamela Jane* like that, but there was nothing they could do. They would be back to her soon. Taking their backpacks with them, they stepped into the rowboat. Penny climbed dutifully into Maya's lap, where she sat quiet as a mouse while they were rowed to shore, where more soldiers awaited them on the beach.

"What should we do?" Simon asked Helix in a low voice.

"Just do what they say for now until we find out what's going on," said Helix under his breath.

Flanked by soldiers, the children were led up steep, mossy steps to the city. The steps were huge for Penny's short legs, so Helix and Simon took her hands to help her. Soon the strenuous climb was all Simon could think about. When at last they reached the top, the soldiers stopped to mop the sweat from their faces and the children stood there breathing heavily, looking around them in surprise.

Maracairol had undergone a transformation in the years since they had left, and now they looked upon smooth streets, windows flung open, and walls freshened with new coats of paint. The war over, the rubble of destroyed buildings had been carted off, and tidy green parks created where they had stood. People moved busily along the streets. Children slurped on watermelon in doorways and workers balanced bamboo baskets of cassava and dragonfruit and great spiky durians from farms outside the city. A fisherman's wife went past, hawking strings of pungent sardines rolled in shimmering crusts of salt.

But as Simon followed the soldiers through the narrow, winding streets, it quickly became clear to him that something was awry. The parks were crowded with people living in makeshift tents. Women cooked over open fires in the gardens. The city gates were clogged with caravans of people, their belongings bundled precariously high on wobbly carts. Why were they coming here? What had happened? The new arrivals wandered up and down, faces eerily blank, searching for a spare few feet of earth where they could settle. Many of them struck camp in already crowded dead-end alleys. Simon caught a whiff of fetid air each time they passed one.

He realized they were being taken up to the imposing fortress that sat above the city. A single high watchtower loomed over one corner, casting a thin, cold river of shadow down the hillside. There were no windows except for a row spaced along the top of the high, thick walls. As they reached the hilltop, the powerful wind that flapped the flags overhead dried the sweat from their skin. Maya shivered suddenly. Simon looked down to the town far below, where even now more tents were going up, blooming like mushrooms in the crowded squares. Then the fortress's massive

60

wooden gate swung open a few feet and the newcomers were ushered unceremoniously inside and the gate was swiftly closed behind them. Penny jumped as a heavy bolt slid loudly—*chunk*—into place.

"I don't like this," she whispered. Simon squeezed her hand.

Inside, the wind dropped away at once and they found themselves standing in an eerily deserted courtyard. The guard led them beneath a portico and through a series of rooms and stone corridors. It seemed increasingly clear that this president they were going to see had purposefully secreted himself away deep within the fortress.

They mounted a winding staircase that seemed to twist around forever, growing narrower and narrower and more and more claustrophobic. Finally they reached a small wooden door and were led into the circular room at the top of the tower. The floor was made of polished ophalla that looked like ice that never melted. On all sides of the room, open windows overlooked the city and surrounding jungle and the broad sweep of the sea. A figure stood at the window, her back to them.

"Madam President," said one of the soldiers, "your visitors are here."

The person who turned to face the children was tall, with long, jet-black hair caught in a clip made out of a tough seashell. Her face was young and unlined, and she had a sharp jaw and piercing eyes that looked down the bridge of a nose grown too long to be pretty. In her crimson, flowing pants and shirt, she looked like she belonged to a different world from them. Beside her a gold telescope pointed out to sea.

Simon heard Maya gasp softly. "Isabella . . . ?" she asked in amazement. "It's you! *You're* the president?"

A brief glimmer passed over the young woman's face—pain or worry—but she answered briskly. "I am," she said.

Unlike Maya and Helix, Simon had only seen Isabella fleetingly the last time he had been in Tamarind. Back then, she and Maya had borne a striking resemblance to each other, but any similarity they shared had been left behind in youth. But even though Isabella looked both sharper and harder than his sister, she was still only Maya's age. How could she be in charge of Tamarind?

Though Isabella remained impeccably composed, the color rose to her cheeks when her gaze paused on Helix. An expression flickered across her eyes, fast as a shadow, too quick to be readable, and then her gaze roved on to the others.

"We were hoping to find you, and here you are!" said Maya. "I was scared when the ships came to get us—I wish we'd known you had sent them!"

But Isabella looked at them coldly. "When the spotters saw your boat coming in I thought it was another Red Coral vessel," she said. "Then you got closer and I saw the name of your ship and all of you on it. Why are you here?"

The children had expected a warm reception from their old friend, but now Simon saw that it wasn't going to be that easy. Maya stood there, looking awkward and increasingly bewildered. Simon met Helix's eye and Helix gave him a look that meant he didn't know any more than they did.

"We've come to help," said Maya, more timidly. "We heard that the Red Coral Project had found a way to get to Tamarind, and that the island was in trouble. We're here to help stop them."

"Yes, the Red Coral are here," said Isabella. "But you're late—they arrived here nearly a year ago, in a huge metal ship . . . Only I'm not concerned with them for the moment—how have *you* managed it? So few Outsiders ever make it to Tamarind, but to *return?*" She paused. "How do I know you're not Red Coral yourselves?"

"Of course we aren't Red Coral!" said Maya indignantly.

"Maybe you are, maybe you aren't," said Isabella. "Outsiders are Outsiders—how am I supposed to tell you apart?"

"But don't you remember?" asked Maya. "We helped you before."

Isabella shrugged. Her thin, narrow shoulders were so tense they seemed brittle. "That was a long time ago."

Simon could see that this wasn't going well. Maya was already frazzled and Helix was looking quietly furious. There was nothing Helix hated as much as feeling trapped, and Isabella had already held him prisoner once before. Afraid that things would quickly go from bad to worse, Simon tried to sound as friendly and reasonable as he could. "Well," he said, "you know that we're not with the Red Coral because Helix is a Tamarinder."

"Yes," said Isabella bitterly. "A Tamarinder who has been to the Outside, and lived among Outsiders." She turned to Helix who glared back at her.

"I think this is a misunderstanding," Simon began to say when a violent explosion in the distance made them all jump and turn to face the windows.

The initial boom was followed by a sound like thunder, rumbling toward them. A few seconds later a hot wind blew from a few miles away and rolled out across the city. It rushed through the windows of the tower with a *whoosh*. In the town below flags beat against themselves, the boats in the harbor pitched and their masts clacked together and their ropes groaned, and palm trees bowed and thrashed their fronds against the hot, bright sky. The burning odor that Simon had smelled earlier was stronger now, and he and Maya put their hands up to cover their noses. Penny coughed.

"What was that?" asked Maya.

"That was the Red Coral," said Isabella. "They're blasting for ophalla. They're right outside the city now."

Simon could see that she was angry and frightened. "Please," he said. "I promise you, we came here to help."

Isabella looked at him dully. "At first we had an agreement with the Red Man, but he broke it months ago," she said. "Most of the old villages were built on ophalla deposits, and now the Red Coral men are evicting people and tearing down homes and burning jungle to reopen the mines. Just a few months ago there was only a trickle of people arriving in Maracairol—now they're pouring in. We can't protect them. Soon we're not going to be able to feed them, either."

Suddenly all the people they'd seen coming into the city made sense.

"They're taking over more and more of Tamarind," said Isabella. "They've hired the Maroong—a people from the East who have always been mercenaries. They're ferocious warriors—they shave their heads and paint them, and people are terrified of them. Four days ago they kidnapped my mother and brother. I'm the acting president only—taking over for my mother, who was made president during Reconstruction after the war. We don't know where she is." She paused, then said softly, "I know they're coming for me next."

For a moment Isabella looked as young as she really was. Simon thought how strange it was to see someone their own age with such responsibility.

"I'm sorry," said Maya, looking genuinely upset. "We want to help. We'll do whatever we can—"

"You can't help," said Isabella in frustration. "Milagros is the only one who can." She turned to Helix.

There was a tap at the door then.

"Come in!" Isabella called briskly.

A guard came in, holding what appeared to be a large cage, draped in a lemon yellow silk cloth, which hung on the end of a pole. From inside the cage came muffled scratching and murmuring sounds. Whatever was in it wanted freedom desperately. In two strides Helix was across the room. He threw back the cloth and in a flash he had unlatched the door of the cage and an angry green blur burst out. The parrot flew violently around the room twice, diving viciously at Isabella, before coming to land on Helix's shoulder. Helix swiftly untied the string that bound the parrot's beak shut.

Rrrraaaaaaack! squawked the bird, sounding like an unoiled hinge, but lifting her satiny jade cape of wings so they rose over her, majestic and intimidating. *Rrraaaaack!*

"Seagrape!" cried Simon and Maya.

"Seagrape," whispered Penny, gazing in fascination at the bird she only remembered from stories.

Helix ran his fingers over the parrot's wings, her head and neck, her talons, but she was unharmed. She made soft grumbling sounds and gnawed his knuckles gently.

"So she *is* yours," said Isabella, unable to hide her excitement. "I remember you, when you were tossed off the pirate ship four years ago and I had you put in jail. I knew then she was a bird of Milagros—I saw the tattoo beneath her wing!"

"What are you talking about, she's a bird of Milagros?" Helix asked angrily. "Why do you have her?" Seagrape nuzzled his neck and he stroked her feathers gently.

"I haven't been able to find Milagros," said Isabella. "Finally I issued an order for people to catch her birds and bring them to the capital, in hopes that the birds would lead me to her. But this is the only one that was captured, and she's refused to budge. I knew she looked familiar, but it wasn't until I saw you sailing here that I remembered where I had seen her before. Anyway, that's not important.

What's important is now that you're here, you can help me." She took a step closer to Helix but withdrew when Seagrape squawked warningly. "I *need* to find Milagros," she said. "Where is she? How can I reach her?"

"Helix, what's she talking about?" Maya whispered.

Helix looked blankly at Isabella. "I have no idea who Milagros is," he said. "I've never heard of her, so how could I know where she is?" He turned to Simon and Maya and shrugged. Simon knew he was telling the truth.

"Don't you see?" asked Isabella impatiently. "There isn't time to waste! Milagros is the only one who can help save Tamarind from the Red Coral—she can tell us what we need to do to stop the destruction! It's critical that I find her. She wouldn't have given that bird to just anyone. You must know her!"

"I already told you I don't," said Helix.

"Then how did you get this bird?" Isabella demanded.

"I don't know," said Helix. "I've had her as long as I can remember."

"Who are you?" Isabella asked.

"I was raised by the Coboranti tribe, in the jungle," said Helix, glowering.

"You aren't Coboranti," said Isabella.

"I didn't say I was," said Helix sourly. "The Coboranti found me. I was lost in the jungle when I was a child. They raised me and I lived with them until I was old enough to leave to hunt on my own."

"But who were you before that?" Isabella pressed. "Before the Coboranti found you?" She held her breath.

67

Helix scowled but was quiet. "I don't know," he said finally. "I wish I did."

Isabella stared at him intensely, then her shoulders drooped. "You really don't know who you are," she murmured. "Then you can't help."

Simon wished he knew what was going on. He could see that Isabella was desperate. Why did she care so much who Helix was? He'd already told her he didn't know where Milagros was. And why did she think that Milagros— whoever she was—could help Tamarind?

"Who *is* Milagros?" he asked.

But before Isabella could answer, Seagrape suddenly flapped her wings and squawked. Bits of downy green feathers flew out in the air. Isabella sneezed and shot the bird a dirty look. Halfway through lifting her handkerchief to her nose, she paused as if she had just thought of something. Then she turned to the children.

"I'm afraid we have to take your boat into custody," she said.

"You can't do that!" replied Maya at once.

"I'm going to have to insist," said Isabella in a falsely rueful tone. "You'll stay here until we know more."

"But we aren't Red Coral," said Simon urgently. "We hate the Red Coral—they've been hurting our family, too!"

Isabella cut him off. "Outsiders are Outsiders," she said, unmoved. "I don't know anything for certain. And I can't take the chance. I'm very sorry, but I have to think about what's best for Tamarind."

Simon could hardly believe it—they had barely arrived

and already they were prisoners and their boat was being seized! He hated the thought of anyone else sailing the *Pamela Jane*. Everything was happening too fast and he didn't know what to do.

"One of you can go back to your boat to retrieve any belongings you need," said Isabella. "You," she said, nodding to Helix. "The others stay here."

Before the children could protest, two guards escorted Helix from the room. He was stone-faced. He stole a last look over his shoulder at Simon and Maya, but if he was trying to tell them something they had no idea what it was. In dismay they watched him go, Seagrape on his shoulder. Behind him the door was shut firmly and a bolt slid across it, echoing in the stone chamber.

Maya turned furiously to Isabella. "We were planning to find you when we got here," she fumed. "We were going to *help* stop the Red Coral!"

Ignoring her, Isabella went calmly to the window at the far end of the room and looked out at the harbor below.

"I can't believe this is happening," said Maya through gritted teeth. "I could kick myself—what was I thinking of, trusting her! She betrayed us last time, too!"

"Let's not panic," whispered Simon. He was distressed, too, but he knew they should stay calm and think logically. "We just need some time to win her over. We'll wait until Helix is back and we're alone, then we'll figure out what to do."

Maya growled something inaudible under her breath. "Come on," she said at last. "Maybe we'll be able to see him." Simon gave her the binoculars and he and Penny followed her to the window farthest away from Isabella.

As Maya waited until she could see Helix, Simon took a deep breath and looked slowly over Maracairol. The wind changed direction and the late-morning air was once again sweet and warm. A breeze billowed through, running over the coral walls of the ramparts and teasing the hanging vines. Laundry fluttered like sails from the windows of red-roofed houses. Silhouettes of boxy fishing boats hovered in the diamond-bright twinkle of the sea. From here the day seemed slow and peaceful, and trouble far away. Simon took a deep breath. Maybe things weren't so bad. Isabella had a right to be mistrustful—they just needed time to win her over. He sneaked a quick look at her. Her body was inclined forward, tensed and catlike, as if she were watching and waiting—but for what?

"Hey," said Maya suddenly. "They're taking the *Pamela Jane*!"

Simon took the binoculars and scanned the harbor, but their boat was no longer at the mooring. His eye ran over an empty sweep of blue water until, to his great surprise, he saw her already five hundred yards out to sea, surging through the water, ropes coiled neatly on her sun-bleached deck, full sails catching the brisk breeze! A solitary figure stood at her helm. Simon focused the lenses.

"It's Helix!" he whispered.

He saw Seagrape flying back and forth, a bolt of green across the pure white sail.

"Where's he going?" Maya whispered, taking the binoculars from Simon.

"What's happening?" clamored Penny.

"He's alone on the boat," said Simon. "He's escaping!"

At first a thrill went through Simon, but in the next moment he realized that Helix was leaving them behind. Maya glanced triumphantly at Isabella, but then her excitement gave way to confusion, too. Penny jumped and craned her neck, trying to see.

Only Isabella didn't seem perturbed. She watched calmly as the *Pamela Jane* moved farther away. None of the other ships in port left to give chase and the rowboat was heading slowly back to shore. A sick feeling began to grow in the pit of Simon's stomach. Helix was getting away and Isabella wasn't doing anything about it.

The door opened and a guard entered. "Your orders have been followed, Madam President," he said, bowing.

"Good," said Isabella. "Wait until he's past Holloua's Rock and then follow him at two leagues, unless the weather closes in. Don't let him know he's being followed. Mobilize the watches along the coast and alert the fleet at Balla."

Isabella turned to the children. "I knew he would take it if he had the chance," she said. "I simply gave him that chance. I suspect he knows more than he shared with me. Maybe more than he shared with you, too. And even if he doesn't, that's a bird of Milagros—it's going to lead me exactly where I want to go."

Simon felt as if the wind had been knocked out of him. Without Helix, he suddenly felt like a stranger in Tamarind. He watched as the *Pamela Jane* rounded the head and disappeared and the sea was again a blank blue slate.

Isabella headed for the door. "The guards will bring you down to the jeeps," she said. "We're leaving right away."

Simon and Maya stood there, stunned. It was all happening so fast.

"Where are we going?" Simon managed to ask.

Isabella disappeared in a swirl of crimson down the stairs, but she shouted back up to them.

"To the City of Children!"

✦ CHAPTER SIX ✦

A Figure from the Past ✵ Back in the Jungle ✵
Simon and Maya Disagree ✵ Wasteland

Two guards shuttled the children back down the winding steps.

"Stay close," Simon whispered to Penny, squeezing her hand. His mind was racing. He had no idea where they were going, but if the opportunity to escape presented itself he wanted to be ready to take it.

Outside the fortress, two ramshackle trucks with cobbled parts and ancient engines awaited them. Moonshine fuel, smelling of palm oil, dripped onto the ground beneath them. Isabella was there already, winding a sheer veil around her face to disguise herself.

"You may know things about your friend that will help the director locate his file," she said. "That's why you're coming. We'll ride separately. The Red Coral are all around the city, so hang on—we'll be going quickly."

With that she turned and headed for the first truck. Three guards accompanied her. The children were left with their driver, a brawny figure who pushed them into the backseat and knotted a rope around Simon's and Maya's ankles, tying them together and to a bolt in the floor of the vehicle. Penny was allowed to remain free. He shut the door and locked the outside with a bamboo stick. The children would have to climb through the windows if they wanted to escape. *Not that there was much hope of that at the moment*, thought Simon as the engine rattled to life and the truck began to pick up speed down the hill away from the fortress.

"Are we going to meet Helix?" Penny asked.

Simon was grateful that she seemed more curious than afraid and he was eager to keep it that way. "Well, yeah," he said. "But first we're going into the jungle. If you look out of the window, pretty soon I bet you'll see monkeys and parrots and other animals!"

"Monkeys!" breathed Penny, then she scrambled over Maya and kneeled at the window to look out eagerly.

"How are we going to get out of this?" Maya whispered. She bent down and tried to unknot the rope around her ankle, but only succeeded in making it tighter.

"We'll keep our eyes and ears open and as soon as there's an opportunity we'll act fast," said Simon. He looked at Penny. Acting fast with a five-year-old wasn't going to be easy.

"I can't believe he just left us like that," whispered Maya.

"Here, look, use my pocketknife," said Simon, sliding it out of his backpack and surreptitiously passing it to Maya. "I'm sure he saw a chance to escape and he took it," he whispered, trying to sound more confident than he felt. "What would be the point of coming back and getting locked up in the tower? That wouldn't help anything. He probably thought we'd be safe here until he found out more about the Red Coral and could figure out a way to free us."

"I guess," said Maya. "Anyway, at least Isabella doesn't have our boat."

Though Simon believed what he had told Maya—that it made sense for Helix to have taken his chance to escape—it was hard not to feel abandoned.

As they drove through Maracairol, the powdery burning odor of the explosions lingered faintly, but was overpowered by the strong smell of cooking fish. The market was open, the late-morning light falling blue through the tarpaulins onto heaps of apricots and dates and guavas. Massive green pumpkins sat on the earth beneath the tables. Strings of cowry shells rattled in doorways. Dusty children waited in line at a well and women sat outside their tents, scraping shellfish to cook on the stones of smoky fires. Their eyes met Simon's dully as the truck bumped past. Even though he wasn't one of the Outsiders who had caused them to lose their homes, Simon felt strangely guilty and frustrated. The Red Coral were ruining everything.

Soon they left the city and headed up into the hills of the jungle. The car picked up speed, the driver keeping a wary eye on the trees around them and the road behind them. Met with stony silence, the children finally gave up trying to get him to answer their questions. The canopy closed over the road and suddenly, to Penny's delight, a dozen squabbling monkeys appeared, leaping from branch to branch to keep up with the truck. One jumped down and rode along on the roof for a while. Its tail hung tantalizingly in the window, but Maya wouldn't let her touch it.

Simon took over with the pocketknife, which unfortunately was too dull to cut the thick rope quickly. A fine dust of fibers trickled down, making his ankle itch. He struggled to put himself in Helix's position. If he were Helix, where would he have gone? If they could just get out of this mess and find him, they could start over and do what they had come to Tamarind to do.

They had traveled quite far from Maracairol, the deep green jungle passing in a blur, when it came to Simon. He sat up and turned to Maya, his eyes shining.

"*Faustina's Gate,*" he whispered. "That's where he'll go."

Maya frowned. "But we don't even know it's a place," she whispered. "We don't know what it is."

"We'll find out," said Simon. Checking to make sure the driver wasn't paying attention, he resumed sawing through the rope with renewed vigor when he heard an ominous whine coming from somewhere in the jungle, a sound so high-pitched he could almost feel it in his teeth. Penny looked all around. Both drivers had heard it, too, and they slowed for a moment to shout back and forth to each other.

"They think it's the Red Coral!" said Maya in alarm.

An instant later the driver accelerated and the children were flung against the backseat. They slid from one side to the other as they bounced wildly over potholes and the jungle flashed past the windows. Clouds of red dust spun up from the tires, thickening the air and coating big banana leaves on the roadside. The drone of the Red Coral was growing louder. Then without warning Isabella's truck braked. The children's driver slammed on his brakes and their truck fishtailed to a stop behind it. The driver leaped out. Simon leaned out of the window to see what had happened.

He sat back in a hurry, his heart pounding. "There's a big tree that's fallen across the road," he said. "There isn't room to pass it—they're going to push it out of the way before we can keep going. Now's our chance!"

The Red Coral hadn't appeared yet but they were getting closer. Their wheels made a snapping and crackling sound over the undergrowth—it sounded as if a fire were eating its way towards the children.

Maya hesitated, but the Red Coral was only getting louder. "All right," she said, seizing Penny's hand. "Let's go!"

Simon snatched his backpack off the floor and, with a final swipe of the pocketknife, the last fibers snapped and the rope slid loosely down his and Maya's ankles. Up ahead they heard the great tree being dragged out of the way.

"We're going to run into the jungle and hide," he told Penny. "You have to go as fast as you can!"

He climbed out of the window and reached in to haul Penny out. An instant later Maya was free, too. Her feet had barely hit the ground before the driver saw them and began shouting.

"Run!" hissed Simon. "Don't look back!"

The children ran as fast as they could off the road into the jungle. The foliage was almost impenetrable. Simon kept a firm grip of Penny's hand and held her close so branches wouldn't fly back and swat her. Roots tripped them. Vines got tangled around their arms. Their crashing feet sent lizards streaking up tree trunks and spiders bouncing across trampoline webs. Behind them they could hear Isabella shouting. Penny fell and Simon covered her and grabbed Maya. They dropped into a huddle and lay there trembling, trying to slow their ragged breathing. They had not come very far at all and could still see the road.

The driver and another guard had dashed into the jungle after them, but had quickly lost them in the opaque undergrowth, and were now running back to the road. Another guard rushed Isabella back to safety in the first truck. The drone of the approaching vehicles rose to an almost intolerable pitch. Penny covered her ears. The men finished dragging the tree out of the way so the trucks could pass. Then they pulled it back into the road before they hopped into the trucks and peeled off down a side road that headed back in the direction of Maracairol.

Seconds later the Red Coral jeeps burst onto the road, but the tree brought them to a screeching stop. A haze of dust from the road hung heavy in the air.

Hiding beneath billowy leaves, the children watched as men got out of the jeeps and pulled the tree out of the way once again. The jeeps were shiny and new and looked like they had come from the Outside. The men had shaved heads dyed with bloody-looking jungle pigments and they appeared to be incredibly strong. Simon thought they must be the Maroong people that Isabella had told them about. Penny wriggled close to Maya. There was one Outsider among them, a man in faded gray trousers and a tan shirt, who was clearly the one in charge. When he turned, Simon saw his face. His heart quickened.

Simon hadn't seen him in four years and the man he was looking at had changed. He was thin and his face was half hidden beneath a broad hat. But when he took it off and wiped his forehead with it, Simon saw his bright red hair, and he was certain.

It was Dr. Fitzsimmons.

Simon's first impulse was to run out of the jungle to their old friend. Perhaps he could help! Once he saw who they were he wouldn't hurt them. He could sit them down and offer some rational explanation for everything that had happened. But as he started to get up, Maya squeezed his arm, hard enough that it hurt.

"We can't trust him, Simon," she whispered. "He's the Red Man."

The Red Man? Dr. Fitzsimmons? Simon frowned, confused, but sank back down into the leaves. There had to be some mistake—their old friend couldn't be the man who had broken an agreement with Isabella, the person responsible for the upheaval in Tamarind. Simon wanted to argue with Maya, but some instinct made him stay silent and watch.

As the men heaved the tree out of the way, Dr. Fitzsimmons turned and scanned the jungle slowly. In spite of himself, Simon felt a chill creep over him. But Dr. Fitzsimmons's eye passed over the children and he turned to the men and shouted for them to hurry up. When the jeeps were ready to go again, he climbed back into one of them, which snarled and shook as the driver gunned the engine, and the fleet sped after Isabella.

Too scared to move, the children waited until the whine of the engines faded. Activity in the jungle that had stopped during the commotion resumed. Long-winged dragonflies zizzled through the air. A large, neon ladybug sauntered down a swooping vine. Monkeys swung hooting from branches. Frogs croaked from thick pink lotuses on a softly gurgling stream. Beyond the vivid world immediately around the children, the jungle darkened into murkiness. The stench of mushrooms in a rotting log rose to their noses.

"I think we're safe," said Simon. "They're gone . . . at least for now."

The children crawled cautiously back to the road. The monkeys had capered off. Thorns had snatched holes in the children's clothes and Penny's pajamas were grimy.

"Are those bad men going to come back?" she asked, looking fearfully down the road.

"No, Pennymouse," said Maya. "It's just us now." She kneeled down to brush the dirt off Penny's skinned knee.

The three of them were alone in Tamarind again, and though he knew he should be worried, Simon couldn't help smiling for a moment.

What now? he wondered. As Maya tended to Penny, he chewed his lip, thinking. Green light dappled the road. "It looks like Isabella headed back toward Maracairol," he said. "So . . . I think we should keep going to the City of

Children to find out what we can about Milagros. Isabella was convinced Milagros could help. Maybe she'll know about Faustina's Gate, too."

Maya stood up. "I think we should try to find a town farther down the coast, where Helix was sailing," she said. "Someone will have seen him."

"But in the city we can find out about Milagros," said Simon.

"We don't even know who Milagros is," said Maya. "All I want to do is find Helix. Mami and Papi aren't here, that means I'm in charge."

Simon gave her a surly scowl. "Fine," he said at last. "If you're in charge, you can tell us which way to go to get back to the coast so that we don't end up right back in Maracairol with Isabella."

Maya gazed around the endless dark green jungle. "I don't know," she admitted finally.

"The City of Children is probably up ahead," said Simon. "I think we should keep going on this road."

"Oh, all right," said Maya a bit huffily. "If nothing else, someone there can tell us how to get back to the coast somewhere safe outside Maracairol. For now, anywhere that Isabella isn't sounds good to me." She picked loquats and bananas for them and peeled a banana for Penny. Hoisting their backpacks on, they set off on foot, following the same road they had been on before. Penny kept her eyes open for monkeys, but Simon could only think of one thing.

"Do you really think Dr. Fitzsimmons is the Red Man?" he asked Maya.

"It looks like it," said Maya. "I was hoping that he wouldn't even be here, but he is."

"But we know him," said Simon. "We know he couldn't be someone that bad. There must be some explanation. Maybe we should have talked to him when we had the chance."

"Don't be naive," said Maya dismissively. "Mami and Papi were his best friends, and look how he tricked them."

"I'm not being naive," argued Simon, frowning. "I just don't want to jump to conclusions before we have all the facts."

"What more do you need?" asked Maya. "I think it's pretty obvious."

"Who is Dr. Fitzsimmons?" asked Penny, chewing on her banana and watching a blue velvet moth fluttering nearby, drawn to the sweet scent.

"He used to be Mami and Papi's friend," said Maya. "But not anymore. I don't know what happened, but he changed." She looked pointedly at Simon. "He's not the person we used to know anymore."

Simon ignored her. Maya didn't really know anything. Simon had spent more time with Dr. Fitzsimmons than Maya had—*he* was the one who used to hang out in Dr. Fitzsimmons's lab whenever they stopped in port in St. Alban's. He marched a little ahead to show her that he wasn't going to be bossed around.

But what *was* Dr. Fitzsimmons doing in Tamarind? The scientist Simon had known almost his whole life was a great fuzzy bear of a man with a startlingly red beard and eyes that twinkled. His hands, surprisingly large, could handle the most delicate of specimens with gentleness and agility, and he had a big, deep laugh that made everyone with him smile before they knew what they were smiling about. He had a hearty appetite at mealtimes and though he towered over Simon and Maya when they were young, Simon had always felt safe with him. Dr. Fitzsimmons had always made it seem as if he and Simon were friends. Like Simon's father, he would talk about science with him—everything from the distant dance of planets and asteroids to the tiny emerald ripples of flatworms visible only beneath the powerful microscopes in his spotless white laboratory. He had loved the creatures of both land and sea—how could such a man be part of anything bad? Simon's parents had never proved that Dr. Fitzsimmons had betrayed them. They just refused to talk about him. He didn't care what Maya said—there had to be more to the story.

But after they had been walking for a while Simon forgot to be annoyed with Maya. The heat was steamy and enveloping. Their clothes were damp with sweat and dust from the road clung to their skin. A stream came out of the jungle and murmured along beside the road. Lilies grew thickly on its banks. Plants with leaves as big as sails soared over the travelers, and in the humid green gloom they walked past shaggy palms and clots of vines, and scented orchids that spilled—ivory, mysterious, opulent—from the mossy forks of branches. Jewel-colored birds swooped and dived on the fringes of the jungle, their cries pealing through the black caves of air between the trees. They were back in Tamarind, walking through the jungle together, and for a while Simon's mind was emptied of anything but a fierce love and wonder of this place.

But then he noticed that the lush, emerald trees were beginning to peter out and the jungle had fallen curiously silent.

"Where did all the animals go?" asked Penny.

The shadowy jungle grew brighter as the trees dwindled. Then abruptly the jungle ended altogether and Simon had to squint and shield his eyes from the blinding glare. The scene they came across took his breath away.

The jungle had been slashed and scorched, and the earth stretched barren and blasted to a horizon distorted by bitter rafts of smoke. The burned ruins of a village lay slumped beneath a chalky film of ash. Charred corpses of animals had been picked clean by scavenger birds that had now moved on. The chirping, hissing, clicking, warbling, and swooshing of wings that formed the incessant backdrop of noise in the jungle had been erased and the air was eerily silent. Nothing grew—no fleece of green had arisen to suggest the soil would be renewed; no hardy stalk left standing had turned its face to the sun. Even the trees and plants along the border that had not been cut down or burned were gray and lifeless, as if the destruction was somehow contagious and a cold death was spreading across the land. Deep pits yawned open, and here and there brittle shards of ophalla stuck out of the ground. Simon's stomach lurched as he realized what he was looking at.

"They're ophalla mines," he whispered.

84

"This is what the Red Coral have been doing," said Maya in a low rage.

This was the smoke they had seen as they sailed into Tamarind; the explosions they had heard in Maracairol. This was what Isabella had told them was happening.

Simon felt as if he had been punched in the stomach—Dr. Fitzsimmons was part of this. He may even have ordered it himself.

Simon remembered the army of glowing creatures they had seen, swishing lifeless in the current—were they somehow connected to this destruction? With a sinking feeling, he realized that the problem was much bigger than he had imagined.

For the first time since they had arrived in Tamarind, Simon felt truly afraid.

This was wrong. It was very, very wrong.

Then anger began to bubble in him. He realized he was clenching his fists. "We have to stop them," he said.

❧ CHAPTER SEVEN ❧

City of Children

A few hours later the children had left the desolation behind and were making good time along the wide dirt road through the jungle. Finally, through a break in the trees, they saw a town sitting snugly in the valley below. When they reached the bottom of the hill, the city gates came into view, and over them a stone arch that read CITY OF CHILDREN.

They passed beneath it and walked slowly on, peering curiously around. The town was neat and orderly. The streets were swept and there wasn't a scrap of litter for the lazy breeze to catch. The buildings, made of stone walls and tin roofs, were new and gleaming. Lush vegetable gardens grew around a long, open kitchen and communal dining room. A ball game was going on in a field on the outskirts and they could hear the thump of bare feet kicking a coconut husk wrapped with lizard skins. Small children were sitting in a circle under a tree, learning a lesson from their teacher. Through the windows of classrooms the familiar litany of times tables was being memorized. Signs pointed the children in the direction of RECEPTION, THE HALL OF RECORDS, THE INFIRMARY.

The recess gong rang and children poured out of their classrooms. The sight of so many children all together made Simon think of the child prisoners in Evondra's mining camp the first time he had been to Tamarind, and he felt a pang at the memory of the starving slaves. But these children were well cared for. Girls and boys in brilliant yellow and green uniforms were hurrying to a table for sliced cantaloupe and mangoes when they suddenly spotted the newcomers. They galloped toward them on bare, nimble feet. Alarmed, Penny took a firm hold of Maya's hand and stuck close as the children swarmed around them.

"Hello!" shouted dozens of voices. "Hello, hello!"

"Are you coming to live here?" piped one.

"Do you need a place to stay? There's space under my tree!"

"Have you lost your parents, too?"

"Hello," Simon finally managed to say. "We're trying to find our friend."

Immediately the city children began babbling all at once again.

"Who is he?"

"What happened to him?"

"Is he lost?"

"Sort of," said Simon. "We're trying to find his family."

"His family?"

"Did he lose his family like us?"

"His family will be in the Records! Take him to Sorella! She'll know!"

Immediately a contingent ran off calling for Sorella,

whoever she was, and Simon, Maya, and an uneasy-looking Penny were carried amidst an eager tide of children toward a building marked HALL OF RECORDS. As they got closer Simon heard a funny rustling, fluttering sound, like hundreds of dry leaves scraping along a pavement in a breeze.

A woman appeared on the wooden porch and came out to greet them. She was a plump, comfortable-looking woman, with olive skin and soft arms. Her skin glowed from the humidity.

"All right, all right," she said. "Calm down and give our visitors some room to breathe!" She held out a moist hand for the visitors to shake. "I'm Sorella Banza," she said. "Secretary in charge of Records of the Disappeared in the City of Children. How may I help you today?"

"We're looking for our friend," said Simon, after he had introduced them and explained how they had come to be in the city. Upon hearing that the Red Coral had been chasing Isabella, Sorella grew deeply concerned. A few more women poked their heads through the door of the building and listened somberly.

"Isabella is very dear to us," said Sorella. "She was the one who created the city, to reunite children and their families who had been separated during the war."

Simon remembered that Isabella had helped in a war orphanage the last time they had been in Tamarind, too.

"Now," said Sorella. "You said you wanted to find your friend's family?"

"Yes," said Maya. "Isabella hoped you would have a record of him here."

"What is his name?"

"He goes by Helix," said Simon. "But we don't know his real name—he doesn't, either."

Sorella looked doubtful. "I'm afraid I need more to go on than that," she said. "What else can you tell me about him? How old is he?"

"Um, about seventeen," said Maya. "Maybe. He doesn't really know for sure."

Sorella sighed. "Come with me," she said.

They entered the cavernous building and the children saw where the fluttering sound had come from. Tables stretched across the room and on them, weighted under stones, were pictures and paper documents, their edges flapping in the breeze that sailed in one set of open windows and out of the other. Women were hunched over, sorting through them.

"Since the City of Children was founded, we've opened files for hundreds of children," said Sorella. "These are the ones who have been successfully reunited"—she paused to point at a tiny cabinet—"and these are the ones still searching." She indicated rows of files, stacked on top of the other, spilling in a dizzying maze around the room. "Unfortunately your friend's story is all too common since the war. Without a real name, or the names of family members, or anything at all to go on, I wouldn't know where to start. There must be something else you can tell me?"

Simon looked around him in amazement. Had Isabella really thought she could find information about Helix buried in these files? It would take years to go through all of them! He felt discouraged. But he had a feeling that Isabella wouldn't have been deterred. If there was something in here about Helix, there must be a way to find it.

"Helix had a green parrot that Isabella believes someone named Milagros gave him to protect him," said Simon. "Isabella thought that if she could find out who Helix's family was, they could lead her to Milagros. She said that Milagros is the only one who knows how to save Tamarind from the Red Coral."

"Milagros—Milagros the Dark Woman?" exclaimed Sorella, her eyes widening. "But they were all hunted in the war—no one has seen a Dark Woman in so many years! Who knows if any are even still alive . . ."

Milagros was a Dark Woman. Simon swallowed. The last time they were in Tamarind an evil Dark Woman, Evondra, had held them prisoner.

"It was believed that a few escaped and went into hiding," said Sorella. "Milagros may have been among them." She paused, thinking. Shooing away giggling children who were peeking in the window, she motioned to Simon, Maya, and Penny to sit down at a wobbly table in the corner.

"If Milagros sent the bird to protect your friend there's a good chance that his family knows her and knows where she is," said Sorella. "I'm sure that's what Isabella was thinking. They say that Dark Women were the ones who saved Tamarind the last time the island was under threat."

"What are Dark Women, really?" Simon asked.

Sorella got up and closed the window, then drew the green curtain so that the children, their tiny faces still peering in, sticky with mango, couldn't hear. The daylight through the curtain cast a murky green light in the corner. She came and sat back down, dabbing sweat off her brow.

"Dark Women are closely tied to the earth," she explained in a voice barely above a whisper. "They're attuned to its vibrations, they sense its moods and shifts, from the tiniest trembling fern to the herds of wild animals that live in the Borderlands to the very rock we stand on, to even— and especially—ophalla itself. You see . . . Tamarind *is* ophalla. It lies deep beneath our soil, the roots of our trees are tangled in it, we've fought countless wars over it, and our most precious things are made from it. Every step we take, somewhere deep below us is ophalla. And the Dark Women know more about its secrets than anyone."

Penny looked troubled. "Are Dark Women bad?" she whispered.

"No," said Sorella, smiling gently at her. "They're strange, but most of them are good. You don't have to be afraid. I bet you like animals, don't you?"

Penny nodded.

"Well, Dark Women can communicate with animals," said Sorella. "Milagros's gift is with birds."

She turned back to Simon and Maya.

"But now that the Red Man is here bad things are starting to happen," she said quietly. "People say there are storms happening all the time on the coast. Fish have been washing up dead for months. And now trees are starting to die— even ones far away from the mine sites. Look around, you'll see them. Yesterday I was walking outside and I saw flying fish drop dead in midair. Something is wrong, and people say it's because too much ophalla is being taken out of the ground."

The children listened soberly.

"How can Milagros help?" asked Simon.

"I don't know *how* myself," said Sorella, sitting back in her chair. "But if Isabella believes she can, then we'll do whatever we can to help you find her," she said. "Give us some time. There are a lot of papers to go through, as you see. But if Helix's family has been here looking for him, there will be a record of their request somewhere. We'll do our best with the clues we have. You can stay here with us tonight. Why don't you go outside now—the children will show you around."

Several children hovering in the doorway waved eagerly to Simon, Maya, and Penny.

Sorella returned to the records, and Simon, Maya, and Penny joined the children on the dusty porch. After a while, Simon joined some of the boys playing football, while Penny played happily with some of the other children. When it grew dark they were called to a long outdoor table, lit by candles, where the city children sat to eat. Penny was chattering with her new friends at another table. Everyone lined up and had cassava stew ladled on top of soft brown rice in their wooden bowls. Simon was famished, and he dug in hungrily. A dessert of sweetened yucca wrapped in banana leaves was passed around.

"I've been talking to some of the girls," said Maya,

looking serious. "All the kids here are like Helix. They all lost their families in the war."

But she was interrupted by Sorella, who was walking quickly across the yard. She sat down with them, her cheeks bright, the hem of her skirt dusty, and leaned in so she could talk without anyone else hearing.

"I think we've found what you're looking for," she said eagerly. "It could be that your friend Helix has an aunt—Señora Conchita Rojo Valdez—from the old Valdez family. Her nephew was lost when he was a small child, at the height of the war, somewhere in Robiando Province. He had a green parrot given to him by Milagros. He would be about seventeen now. This could be Helix. Señora Rojo has come here in search of news about him many times. She's one of the benefactors of the city, in fact. Her address is here." She handed a slip of paper to Simon and Maya.

Señora Conchita Rojo Valdez, 24 Rua Santa Flora, Floriano

"Helix has an aunt?" murmured Maya. Until then she had not really believed that Helix would have a family other than them. She looked up at Sorella. "What about his parents?"

Sorella hesitated. "His aunt is the only one who has been here," she said.

"Is Floriano far?" Simon asked.

"Not far at all," said Sorella. "Several hours on the road straight from here. There's a cart leaving here early tomorrow morning, taking produce to the North. A couple of our boys are leaving us, sadly, and are going with it. You can ride with them as far as Floriano. You can stay here tonight. I've arranged for a few extra hammocks to be hung for you beneath the eba tree."

Simon turned to Maya. "If it really is Helix's aunt, she'll help us," he said. "I think we should go."

"It seems like the only thing we *can* do," agreed Maya. "If she really is his aunt," she added.

"Thank you, Sorella," said Simon.

"Yes, thank you," said Maya. "You've been very kind to us."

"Oh, you don't have to thank me," said Sorella, blushing in the candlelight. "I very much hope that you'll be able to reunite your friend with his family. And that you'll be able to find Milagros, too."

✳ ✳ ✳

After dinner the city children hung their colorful cloth hammocks from the broad branches of eba trees and settled in beneath insect nets for the night. The nets were woven out of spidersilk threads that glistened in the light from the yellow tree-oil lamps that the teachers left burning here and there on the ground. Simon, Maya, and Penny climbed into their hammocks. There was a peculiar light in the sky to the south that Sorella had told them was the glow from the Red Coral mines.

Maya rocked Penny in the hammock between hers and Simon's and Penny fell asleep almost instantly.

"It's hard to imagine that Helix has a family," said Simon, looking at his little sister.

"I know what you mean," said Maya. She was quiet for a moment, then added softly, "But—we're his family now, really."

Deep down Simon felt a tiny grain of doubt about this. He remembered again watching the *Pamela Jane* sail from view, Helix and Seagrape on it, and a tiny part of him wondered if Helix had always secretly planned to leave them when they returned to Tamarind. He hated to think it might be true, but perhaps Helix had other reasons for returning, reasons he had kept from them.

"It was smart, what you did today," whispered Maya, "realizing we should escape when we did. I probably would have waited too long and it would have been too late."

"Hey, thanks," said Simon. "But I'm sure you would have," he added generously. He smiled as he looked up into the dark branches. Maya never usually bothered to praise him anymore. Suddenly he felt happy they were there together.

Simon lay awake for a while after the murmur of children's voices died down as the city children faded off to sleep. Maya and Penny slept peacefully nearby. Occasionally he heard the swish of leaves in the jungle as animals made their way on their night travels.

He fell asleep, but woke a few hours later in a cold sweat. He sat bolt upright and got tangled in the silken threads of the insect net. The tree-oil lamps had burned out and it was pitch-black. It took him a few seconds to remember where he was. In his dream Dr. Fitzsimmons had been chasing him—his hands had been only inches from Simon's neck. Heart thundering, Simon sat there listening carefully, but the only sounds were insects buzzing outside his net and a child coughing in his sleep. The Red Coral weren't here, at least not yet. Penny stirred, mumbling something in her dream. Simon wished she were home safely.

He lay back down, but it took a long time before the fear of the dream left him. He had to admit that nothing had happened the way he'd expected since they had arrived in Tamarind. They had assumed they would be with Helix and they had counted on him to lead the way once they were there. But now Helix was gone, their boat was gone, the children were on the run from Isabella, and the Red Coral were wreaking havoc across the countryside. Simon didn't have any real idea how to find Helix or go about stopping the Red Coral, and the woman who was ultimately supposed to be able to help them was a creepy Dark Woman, who, if she was even still alive, was deep in hiding somewhere. He tossed and turned, trying to get comfortable.

All they had were three clues.

Faustina's Gate.

Milagros.

Señora Conchita Rojo Valdez, 24 Rua Santa Flora, Floriano.

Three clues to stop the Red Coral and save Tamarind.

❧ CHAPTER EIGHT ❧

24 Rua Santa Flora ✦ The Señora, the Doctor,
and the Colonels ✦ An Uncanny Likeness ✦
Glinting from Above ✦ Between Bird and Beast ✦
A Mysterious Glow

In the morning, Simon felt brighter. The hammocks were taken down and folded up. There was a lot of chattering and teasing as the city children gathered around to bid farewell to Jolo and his little brother, Small Tee, who were leaving the city to join their cousin in the North and become fishermen. An old, patient brown horse with big, dusty hooves the size of dinner plates was hitched to a wooden cart, ready to take them. The cart was laden with star fruit, cassava roots, and the biggest pumpkins Simon had ever seen.

Sorella spoke quietly to Simon and Maya as they got in the cart. "Be very careful if you see the Red Coral," she said. "Don't let them see you. They're very bad men."

"We will," said Simon. Thanking Sorella profusely for her kindness, he, Maya, and Penny hopped in after Jolo and a tearful Small Tee.

Simon felt the cart lurch forward and begin to wobble down the road out of the City of Children. Children ran and waved behind them.

"Good luck, Jolo and Small Tee!"

"Catch lots of fish!"

As the cart got farther away the merriment fell away. Then the cart rounded a corner and left the city behind and headed out on a dirt road that Simon, Maya, and Penny had not traveled on before. It ran through farm fields, silver with morning dew, which ended in jungle on either side. Simon realized that from here on they were going to have to be vigilant. The Red Coral could be anywhere and they no longer had the adults in the City of Children to protect them.

Though he claimed he was older, Jolo looked to be around the same age as Simon. He was wiry and had dirty knees. He picked through the cart till he found some ripe mangoes and dragonfruit and tamarinds and passed them gallantly around to everyone. Maya split open one of the brown, leathery tamarind pods and gave the sweet pulp to Penny. Small Tee gave a shuddery breath but sat up and ate the mango that his brother gave him, the juice dribbling down his chin. He couldn't have been much older than Penny, Simon thought.

"Why are you leaving?" asked Maya. "Couldn't you stay there longer?"

"We're on our way to meet our cousin on the north coast," said Jolo. "He left the city last year. I'm going to be a fisherman with him there. I wasn't going to leave my little brother behind."

"What about your family?" asked Maya. "How will they find you if you leave?"

Jolo snorted. "No one's coming," he said. "Everyone who's left in the city now just waits until they're fifteen and old enough to leave. I turned fifteen last week. I don't need school to be a fisherman!"

"Aren't they nice to you there?" Maya asked gently.

"Sure," said Jolo agreeably. "But the city is for babies."

Small Tee sniffled. He started to suck his thumb but his brother knocked it gently out of his mouth. He curled up with his back to a pumpkin and watched the big bright birds hopping between branches on the trees they passed. The dew was drying on the fields and Simon breathed the fresh morning air deeply. They spent the next hours talking to Jolo, hearing about his life and telling him about Helix and Dr. Fitzsimmons and Isabella. Jolo whistled when he heard that the children used to know the Red Man, as he called him, and he was impressed that they had been in Maracairol with Isabella.

"Isabella comes and reads to us every week and helps us with school," he said. Maya looked surprised. "Tee loves her, don't you, Tee?"

Hearing Isabella's name, Small Tee looked up hopefully. Lulled by the rising heat and the rocking motion of the cart, he and Penny dozed off. Dappled light slid over them as the cart rattled along the road.

"We're almost in Floriano," said Jolo.

Soon Simon saw the shining rooftops of a town nestled a few miles down in a shallow valley that led down to a milky sea. The driver pulled on the reins and the horse came to a stop.

"Thanks for your help," said Simon, hoisting his pack onto his back. "And good luck in the North!"

"Good luck to you, too," said Jolo. "You'll have to jump down. You go first and I'll pass the baby down to you."

"I'm *not* a baby," said Penny, and after Simon had hopped nimbly down she insisted on jumping into his arms herself.

"Good-bye!" Simon, Maya, and Penny called as the cart rolled slowly off. Then they turned and set off on foot down to Floriano.

"I think that little kid Tee wanted his mom," said Penny, taking Maya's hand.

Maya glanced at Simon. "Do you miss Mami?" she asked Penny.

Penny didn't answer but her eyes filled with tears. "I'm sure Mami misses you," said Maya. "But we'll be home soon."

⚘ ⚘ ⚘

Floriano was a very big, old town with buckling streets and dusty olive trees and clusters of palms growing from behind high, cracked walls. They passed a few old ladies returning from the market and a pack of stray dogs trotted by, but otherwise the streets were sleepy. Apparently the Red Coral Project hadn't reached there yet. They asked someone the way to Rua Santa Flora.

It was early afternoon when they approached the house. Number 24 sat behind a heavy wooden door that opened directly onto the deserted street. The windows were barred and the curtains drawn, so the children couldn't see inside. Simon had expected something grander for a family that was supposed to be so important. They hesitated. Now that they were there, they were afraid to knock. Who knew what the people inside would be like?

Maya combed the knots out of her hair with her fingers and dusted off her and Penny's clothes. "Remember," she said, "she might not even be his aunt after all."

Simon glanced behind them. The street was cool and dusky from the shadows of trees overhanging the high wall that ran along the opposite side. Beyond the wall was a steep, tree-covered hill. Something flashed from the hilltop, blinding him momentarily. He blinked and squinted. But when he shaded his eyes and looked up, there was nothing but a large old mansion peeking through the leaves high on the hill. Perhaps the light had caught a window. Still, it made him nervous—who knew where the Red Coral would show up next? He turned back to the door and rapped the knocker solidly three times. The children stepped back and waited.

The knock interrupted a low murmur of voices inside the house, then a pair of footsteps approached and a bolt slid back and the door opened. A woman stood there. She was old—close to seventy, Simon guessed—but her back was straight as a mast and her hair was jet-black and combed into a bun so tight that not a single strand had a whisper of hope for escape. Age spots drifted on her face like shadows on water. Her deep-set eyes regarded the children coolly. An ophalla cameo on a moss-colored choker nestled in the hollow of her throat.

"Yes?" she said in a low, gravelly voice.

"Good afternoon," said Simon politely. "We're looking for Señora Conchita Rojo Valdez."

"I'm Señora Rojo," said the woman. There was no welcome on her face.

The children stared at her. Could this truly be Helix's aunt? It seemed impossible to believe, first that Helix even had an aunt, and second that they should be standing on her doorstep.

Simon swallowed. "My name is Simon Nelson," he said. "These are my sisters, Maya and Penny."

Just then the light flashed again. Señora Rojo squinted and shaded her eyes as she scowled up at the hill.

"Come in," she said. "Quickly."

She stepped back and the children followed her inside. They were in a small, high-ceilinged room with black-and-white-checked tiles. Potted ferns hung from ropes attached to the ceiling timbers. The air smelled of a cooked lunch, which must have been finished not long before. Simon's stomach grumbled. The furniture was made of dark carob wood and upholstered with the silken threads of seapods, and framed maps and oil paintings of old battles adorned the walls. A topaz-colored cloth hung peculiarly in the middle of one wall. Doors opened onto a tiny central courtyard with a fountain. In the far corner a circle of settees and chairs were positioned around a low table, and in them sat a group of very old men in the middle of a card game. The men had stopped playing and turned to face the newcomers. There was something creepy and unsettling about their collective stare and Simon felt the hairs rise on the back of his neck. Penny stood behind Maya and peered out cautiously.

Then Simon realized: The eyes gazing at him were not all real. Some of the men had one real eye and one made of glass: one was amber, one was aquamarine, another black as an inkwell, but each was fixed in an unnatural and brilliant stare beside its living partner. At the same moment that he realized this, Simon saw that some of the men were also missing limbs. A few of them had empty shirt or trouser legs, ironed smooth and pinned up neatly. A collection of ornate canes lay beneath the chairs. Polished medals pinned to the men's lapels twinkled like dim stars. *Old soldiers*, Simon thought. They had been ravaged, first by injury and then by time, for they were all ancient, with drooping whiskers and sagging jowls, and whatever battles they had seen had been long before Simon or Maya or Penny had been born. Simon noticed then a faded old flag hung in a corner.

"Play on, please, gentlemen," said Señora Rojo. "I'll sit out the rest of this hand. Now," she said, turning back and looking at the children imperiously. "What may I do for you?" The cameo shone darkly on her neck.

"We've come from the City of Children," said Simon. "They gave us your address." He fumbled in his pocket for the crumpled piece of paper and handed it to her.

"We think our friend is your nephew," said Maya. "We came from the Outside together, but we lost him . . ."

Two spots of color rose in Señora Rojo's cheeks, but

she spoke with regal composure. Only a slight tremor in the corner of her lip betrayed any apprehension. She turned to the men playing cards.

"Gentlemen," she said, "I'm sorry, but I'm afraid I have to ask that we adjourn the game early. Colonel Lorca, I believe that makes you the winner today."

With some difficulty, the men got to their feet. In a moment canes were tapping on the floor and they were shuffling toward the door. Señora Rojo turned to a distinguished-looking, silver-haired gentleman who had risen to leave with the other men. "Dr. Bellagio," she said. "Perhaps you'll stay?"

"Of course," the man replied. Unlike the others, he did not appear to have been wounded. His back was proud, and the starched corners of his elegant collar touched a tanned face that was shaved smooth but for a plump, perfectly curled silver moustache. His thick hair was combed smoothly back with the hard gloss of pomade.

"We were having our weekly baccarat game that Señora Rojo hosts," he said amiably. "Colonel Lorca will be happy you arrived when you did—another few minutes and Colonel de Silva might have gone home with Mrs. Lorca's necklace."

The card players left and the tapping of their canes faded down the street. Señora Rojo motioned the children to sit down. She perched on the edge of a settee, her hands clasped tightly. "Now, tell me why you believe you know my nephew. And I warn you," she said, lowering her voice, "I'm not patient with tricks."

Fumbling at first, Simon and Maya began to tell them

about Helix, Isabella, Milagros, Dr. Fitzsimmons, and the City of Children. Señora Rojo and Dr. Bellagio listened in silence. When they finished there was a long, heavy moment of quiet. Simon felt the backs of his knees beginning to sweat. He desperately wanted to be back outside, not trapped in a room with such old and strange people. A breeze brought in dust from the street and stirred the hanging plants. Simon heard the squeak of decrepit ropes on the wooden beams and was aware of the faint smell of rot in the fibers.

Abruptly Señora Rojo stood up and, with her back to them, walked to the wall near the courtyard doors, stopping in front of the square of topaz-colored silk curtain that Simon had noticed earlier. With one hand she slowly drew back the panel, revealing not a window, but a painting concealed behind it. It was a portrait, done in thick daubs of sumptuous green and brown oils, and when the children saw the face gazing at them from within the gold frame they all drew in their breaths.

"That looks like Helix!" exclaimed Penny.

"So," said Señora Rojo, without even turning around to see the children's expressions. "He looks like her."

The children studied the woman's strong jaw, her deep olive skin, her dark hair, her bright and intelligent eyes— she was the spitting image of Helix. On her shoulder sat an unmistakable green parrot.

"His mother, Lejandra," Señora Rojo said, gazing at the painting. "My younger sister, with the bird you call Seagrape, which was sent to protect my nephew when he was born."

"Is she . . ." Maya began.

"Dead?" asked Señora Rojo. "Yes, for many years now."

She released the curtain and it fell lightly back over the painting, and the woman's face—at once so familiar and so mysterious—was hidden again.

"You *are* his aunt," said Maya. Simon could see that her sympathy was greater than her fear of losing Helix to this other family. "I'm sorry," she said gently. "It must be a shock, after all this time . . ."

"He's my only nephew," Señora Rojo said at last. "Lejandra's only child. Against our father's wishes, she eloped with a commoner from Robiando. He was a guerrilla fighter in the war and was engaged in the most dangerous operations—all those men lived like outlaws. My sister—she was twenty years younger than me—moved several days northeast of here to be closer to him. We begged her not to go, but she didn't listen. He settled her in a small jungle village—I doubt it even exists anymore. It was barely a few huts at the time—many of those villages melted back into the jungle as the war went on. She thought she would be safe there, in the middle of nowhere, and he was able to sneak away sometimes to see her. That's where my nephew was born—Inigo, or 'Helix,' as you call him."

"Inigo," Maya whispered.

The next part of what Señora Rojo told them matched the story that Helix had confided to Maya—in the fragments that he remembered—years ago on a mountaintop on their way to the North. The señora's story filled in the missing gaps. Helix and his mother, with a driver, had left

their village by car and were driving through the jungle—
Señora Rojo believed she had most likely been going to
deliver a war message, as women often did then. Helix's
mother and the driver were discovered the next day, shot in
an ambush. Helix, only three years old, was never found.

"After my sister's death, we—I—did everything in my
power to find my nephew," said Señora Rojo. "I scoured the
island, searching high and low. I left clues everywhere I
could, so that he could try to find his way to me. But there
was never a trace of him after that day in the car. It was as if
he had never existed. People said that even if he had somehow escaped the robbers, he would have been devoured by
wild animals in the jungle. When the war ended a few years
ago, after the Peace March, the City of Children was estab-
lished and I thought there was reason to hope again. But
still—nothing. He was such a small child when he was taken
that, even if he were still alive, who knows what he remembered? How would we recognize him, grown up more with
each passing week and month and year? Today is the first
day that I've been given any reason at all to hope."

She closed her eyes and stopped talking, but when Dr.
Bellagio rose to check on her she waved him away. Simon
looked at her fearfully. She was old and frail—what if the
shock was too much for her? He felt shocked himself.
Helix had a family, a whole past that he had never known
about. His father had been a guerrilla fighter! Maya looked
shocked, too.

When Señora Rojo opened her eyes again she had composed herself.

"What about Helix's dad?" Simon asked as tactfully as he could.

"He was never the same," said Señora Rojo. "He blamed himself. I saw him a few times after my sister's death, but not again. He had never been close with our family. I don't know what became of him."

She sighed and ran her hand over the arm of the chair.

"So," she said gruffly. "You returned to Tamarind with my nephew to stop the Red Man. That's a tall order."

"We know," said Simon, glancing at Maya. "We told you that Isabella is looking for a Dark Woman named Milagros. She thought that Milagros was the only one who could stop the Red Coral, and she thought that you would know where she was."

"Milagros is a crazy old woman," said Señora Rojo firmly. "She's best left out of this. We'll find my nephew without her. He's all I care about right now." She got up and went to a bureau and opened a drawer and began rummaging around.

Bored with all the talking, Penny tugged on Maya's shirt and asked if she could go and look at the fish in the fountain.

"Go ahead," said the señora, waving her on. "She'll be all right," she said. "All the doors from the courtyard just lead into other rooms in the house. The only way back to the street is through the door you came in from."

Penny scampered outside.

"What about Faustina's Gate?" Maya whispered to Simon. "Do you think it's okay to ask them?"

"I think so," whispered Simon. "Do you know about something called Faustina's Gate?" he asked. "We know that the Red Coral is looking for it, and we think it's where Helix might go."

Señora Rojo stopped rooting around in the drawer and looked up at him blankly. "Never heard of it," she said. Dr. Bellagio shook his head, too.

"We hoped you'd know . . ." said Simon. They had come to Helix's aunt—a member of one of the great old families of Tamarind—expecting answers, but instead all they had found was a salon of old people!

"Here we go," said Señora Rojo, withdrawing a map. She brought it to the table and the children and Dr. Bellagio gathered around. "This is one of General Alvaro's old battle maps," she said.

"Who is General Alvaro?" Maya asked.

"He was the greatest general of the war," said Señora Rojo, sighing. "It's the best map of Tamarind there is. Let's have a look and see if we can figure out where my nephew would go."

The map was detailed and precise, drawn by someone with a meticulous hand. Simon saw Maracairol and Floriano on the southwest coast. In the middle of the island was a large barren expanse called the Neglected Provinces. Just east of this was a strip marked *Borderlands*. In the north hunched a misty blue chain of mountains, and above them a string of coastal towns. Three silver rivers carved the map in half. The island was dotted with Xs and arrows signifying military maneuvers. The oilpaper was yellowed and in script in the bottom right-hand corner was written *Map of Western and Middle Tamarind*.

"Now," said Señora Rojo. "We are down here, and there's Maracairol. When you saw—Helix—leaving Maracairol, he was heading northwest?"

The children nodded. Señora Rojo traced her finger through the blue waters along the western shore of Tamarind, heading north. "If he left Maracairol, sailing west, the winds at this time of the year will carry him up the coast without too much trouble, and would also keep him quite close to shore. How fast is your boat?"

"If the winds are optimum, she can go about ten knots," said Simon. "But that's pushing it. But sailing alone, Helix probably won't be able to go quite that fast. Say he was doing seven knots, that's reasonable. He's been gone now for, what is it? Twenty-four hours. Twenty-four hours at seven knots would put him—if the scale on the map is right—about here." He pointed at a light blue stretch of coastline in the north.

"That's if he hadn't stopped at all," said Maya.

"Right," said Simon. "So that means this is as far as he could have gone, and he's likely to be somewhere in this range now. But he could have stopped to hide in a cove. Helix is good at hiding—if he didn't want them to find him they wouldn't have a chance. Or he could have turned around and gone back the other way, or even abandoned the boat and gone on foot. He could be anywhere by now."

Just then a faint drumming sound came from the hill.

Señora Rojo hurried to the window to peek through the curtain, then she spun around. "You have to hide, children!" she hissed. "Hide in a room in the back, don't make a sound. Now, go, quickly." She began drawing the curtains.

"Where's Penny?" Maya asked suddenly. The courtyard was empty and the little girl was nowhere in sight. "Penny!"

"Hurry," Señora Rojo urged. "You mustn't be seen!"

The thundering sound grew louder and Simon felt a chill, remembering how the Red Coral had chased them in the jungle. Were they the people coming now? Had they found out that he and Maya and Penny were here? Through the window he could see that whatever was coming was making its way to them at a great speed. He could track its progress from the cloud of pollen kicked up through the trees.

Señora Rojo was still struggling to close the curtains when a tall narrow gate across the street flew open and a violet blur charged out. It was some sort of great feathered creature, which carried a passenger aboard its back who ducked her head to peer in Señora Rojo's window as she passed. A second later there was a furious knocking at the front door.

"Blast that woman!" roared Señora Rojo. "How dare she spy on me! Oh, don't bother hiding now," she said to Simon and Maya. "It's too late."

She stamped heavy heeled to the door and flung it open. Simon and Maya gasped and took a step back.

The door was almost entirely filled by a creature some-where between bird and beast, something that looked like a giant purple ostrich. Simon and Maya looked at it in amazement. It was terribly tall; even Simon couldn't see over its back. Beady black eyes, like those of a sea snail, sat on the end of two tentacles in the middle of its dark violet face. Its neck shone like the shimmer on a greenfly and hung down in great saggy wattles. Its head was hairless except for a cap of purple feathers, and it had a heavy train of tail feathers like a peacock's, the tips dirty where they had trailed on the earth. It had two long, strong legs—clearly it was a runner. Its large talons had riven deep scratches into the dirt road. Stunted wings, mere ornament, drifted out at the sides—the creature was flightless.

Astride the creature, framed by its enormous lavender tail feathers, was a tall, regal, surprisingly old woman with graphite gray hair, whose face, though longer and thinner, bore an unmistakable likeness to Señora Rojo's. The rider swung down from the giant bird, deftly tied its bridle to a nearby post, and stepped up to the door, breathing heavily.

"Conchita."

"Estella."

The two women regarded each other icily.

"Good afternoon, Dr. Bellagio," said the newcomer, nodding at him.

"Señora Medrano," said the doctor, bowing his head. "A pleasure."

Señora Rojo turned to the children. "This," she said through gritted teeth, "is my eldest sister, Señora Estrella Medrano."

Simon's and Maya's mouths dropped open. Helix had another aunt!

The new aunt slammed the door shut on the giant bird and, pushing past Señora Rojo, strode boldly into the room.

"Well, who are these?" she asked, scrutinizing the startled Nelsons. "My sister never has young people around her—I know something's up. I've been watching you from the hilltop."

"Spying on me!" bellowed Señora Rojo. "Spying on me from my own family home!"

"It's not my fault you moved out!" said Señora Medrano.

"I'm Maya and this is my brother, Simon," said Maya quickly. "We're looking for our friend—we came to Señora Rojo for help."

Señora Medrano looked suspiciously at her sister. "What is this about?" she asked.

Señora Rojo stared sullenly at the ground. Dr. Bellagio clasped his hands behind his back and kept his eyes averted.

"Well?" asked Señora Medrano. "Conchita," she said, her voice rising like a kettle rattling softly on the stove. "I'm warning you . . ."

"Simon," whispered Maya. "Where's Penny?"

But Penny was nowhere to be seen. Simon suddenly felt nervous. "Penny!" he called. "Penny!"

Maya was running to look in the courtyard when the children heard a rustling sound. In a dark doorway there appeared a peculiar ghostly light, hovering about two feet off the ground as it approached. It grew brighter—blazing brilliantly for a moment—then suddenly it was extinguished and Penny stood there. She held something in both hands. "Look what I found," she said.

"Penny—no touching things that aren't yours," said Maya. Penny was holding an old newspaper, but Maya quickly took it from her, intending to hand it to Señora Rojo. But as she did so it fell open and the same strange phosphorescent light spilled out and illuminated the room, swallowing the shadows and casting an icy blue-green glow on the faded furniture and paintings. Simon, Maya, Dr. Bellagio, and the two señoras all stared at it, spellbound.

"See?" said Penny, reaching out to touch it.

The newspaper was very old, almost crumbling at the edges, its pages darkened by time to rich sepia. Columns in an ornate, old-fashioned typeface with lavish flourishes and curlicues were inset with small, grainy photographs. But what Simon and Maya could not take their eyes off was the largest image in the middle. It looked like a photograph, but it was from this that the weird light spilled forth. In it boats sailed together in a harbor under a brisk wind, and three thin waterfalls dripped down stately mountains in the background.

The image appeared lit from within somehow, as if the light emanating from it was coming from the day the picture had been taken. It seemed to tremble with life. Simon took a step closer and peered into it. The crispness of detail was remarkable. A feather falling from a gull's wing as it flew. The stitches around a patch in one of the mainsails.

Individual bubbles in the lacy surf breaking around the bows of the boats in the foreground. And then, most astonishing of all . . . Simon had to squint to make sure his eyes weren't deceiving him . . . but, yes, it was unmistakable. There, stenciled in black letters on the hull of one of the boats, a familiar name:

"The *Pamela Jane*!" he cried.

❧ CHAPTER NINE ❧

A Very Old Feud ❀ *"This, dear child . . ."* ❀ *The GAZETTE EXTRAORDINARIO* ❀ *Further Study of the Ophallagraph* ❀ *The Dark Women* ❀ *"Tamarind is ophalla . . ."* ❀ *A Gift for a Rainy Day*

"That's our boat!" said Simon excitedly. "We sailed here in her!"

"I'll be deviled," said Señora Medrano, her bright eyes flickering over the image. The light poured from it, glowing on her face and illumining each crease and hollow. "Wicked woman!" she cried. "You kept one. Sneaky, wicked woman!"

"I was tasked to keep it," Señora Rojo shot back, her eyes smoldering with rage.

"That's a lie!" shouted Señora Medrano. "None of us were! What are you up to, Conchita? Who are these children?" She took a step threateningly towards her sister.

"They're friends of our *nephew*," she spat.

Señora Medrano was stunned into silence. For the second time that day, the children watched a person absorb the news that Helix was alive.

"It's true," said Señora Rojo, relaxing now, confident that she had gained the upper hand. She took the paper from Maya and closed it and the room dimmed.

"You weren't going to tell me," said Señora Medrano in disbelief. She turned to the children. "Where is he?" she asked.

Once more the children told their story.

Señora Medrano listened, astounded. Then she looked at the newspaper again, a bit of light still leaking from its pages. "You know what this means," she said slowly. "It's beginning. It's time. Milagros has to be told before it's too late."

"You've lost your mind!" snapped Señora Rojo. "The woman is a lunatic. She may even be dead. All I want to do is find our nephew—he's all I care about."

The sisters' eyes crackled as they looked at each other. Penny retreated behind Maya.

"You can't bury your head in the sand!" said Señora Medrano. "It isn't a coincidence! The Outsiders have been tearing up Tamarind—mining more than has ever been mined before—and now these children have come from the Outside with our nephew in a boat that they say is in this ophallagraph . . . an ophallagraph that has begun to glow! Do you have any better ideas than going to Milagros? Because I don't."

Suddenly the fight seemed to go out of each of the old women.

"You should have come to me right away when it started to glow," said Señora Medrano reproachfully.

"I should," said Señora Rojo. "But I didn't want to believe it." She sank heavily onto a faded seapod-silk chair. "Everything we planted all those years ago, coming alive again. Who ever thought it would be in our lifetimes?"

Señora Medrano sat down opposite her.

Señora Rojo's hands quivered in her lap. "All right,

we'll go to Milagros," she said resignedly. "We'll ask for her help."

"Us?" Her sister laughed. "We can't make it all the way there—look at us! We aren't the age we were when we did these things. It's not up to us this time."

"But he's our nephew," objected Señora Rojo sorrowfully. "We can't trust anyone but ourselves to do this."

"It's too far for either of you," said Dr. Bellagio. "It would be extremely reckless."

"If you tell us where Milagros is, we'll go," said Simon. "We've made it this far."

Señora Medrano looked at the children, her eyes traveling over each of their faces. "For thirteen long years, since the day he disappeared, we've searched, Conchita," she said. "We've never found even a hair from his head or a thread from his clothes, not the tiniest clue. This is the closest we've ever come—they've brought him back into our lives. Let them go now. If anyone can bring him home to us, they can. He's their friend. They'll find him."

Señora Rojo dabbed the corners of her eyes. "All right," she whispered finally. "All right."

Simon cleared his throat. "We don't really understand what's going on," he said politely. "What is that glowing picture, and why is our boat in it? And how is Milagros supposed to help?"

"And what does Helix have to do with any of it?" asked Maya.

Penny tugged on Simon's elbow. "Why were they fighting?" she whispered.

"*Shhh,*" said Simon. "They're Helix's aunts. We'll tell you more later."

"All right," said Señora Rojo, sniffling as she collected herself. "Please, sit down. Let's start with what we have in front of us. This," she said, regarding the children with a smile that was both proud and scornful, "is the *Gazette Extraordinario.*" She opened the newspaper to the illuminated image once again, and in its glow for a brief moment she seemed youthful. The children, Dr. Bellagio, and Señora Medrano all gathered around. "It used to be the most important newspaper in Greater Tamarind in the Extraordinary Days."

"The Extraordinary Days?" asked Simon.

"It's the name people gave to a time in Tamarind when we were young," said Señora Medrano. "More ophalla was being mined than ever before. The island was prosperous and there were miraculous plants and animals everywhere you looked. The war over ophalla was still only a minor skirmish in the hills and crazy things that had started to happen in nature were still isolated incidents, little more than side stories in the *Gazette Extraordinario*. The paper was owned by our family and came out three times a week and it reached every corner of Western Tamarind, from Maracairol to the north shore."

"The photograph looks *alive!*" said Maya.

"It's like you could walk right into it," said Penny, who had climbed onto Maya's lap to see.

"It's not really a photograph—it's an ophallagraph," said Señora Rojo.

"An ophallagraph," said Simon, looking curiously at the image. "What is it? How does it work?" He reached out to touch its edge—it was cool and dry.

"Oh, some trick with ophalla," said Señora Rojo dismissively. "One of Davies Maroner's inventions."

"Why is the *Pamela Jane* in it?" Maya asked.

"I don't know," said Señora Rojo. Señora Medrano and Dr. Bellagio shook their heads, too. "But ophallagraphs contain clues, and I suspect that your boat is a clue somehow. Though what it means, I can't tell you."

"There's more than one ophallagraph?" asked Simon.

"Yes," said Señora Medrano. "I don't know how many, but there are others like it, and together they reveal a secret that was hidden long ago—a secret that might save Tamarind now."

A shiver passed through Simon. Penny stopped fidgeting and they all listened carefully.

"You see," said Señora Rojo, "sixty years ago the skirmish in the hills escalated into a terrible war—the same war that only truly ended with the Peace March four years ago. The North and South began fighting each other over ophalla. Soon after that, something very strange began to change in Tamarind. First of all, people started to see fish dying. Once a thousand octopuses were stranded on a single beach in the Southwest overnight. Then the weather started to change. There were floods in provinces that had never before seen rain, drought in lands that had been lush jungle; if it was sunny and hot at breakfast, by lunch a frost could have withered the fruit off the trees. Everyone had a story to tell about some strange phenomena they'd seen.

"The Dark Woman Milagros had been a friend to our family for generations," Señora Rojo continued. "When she started to notice the first perturbations in the natural world, she came to our father. She claimed that we were in danger of a catastrophe greater even than the war itself, greater than any we could imagine. She said that the natural disasters were being *caused* by the mining, and would only get worse if something wasn't done. The natural balance was being disrupted too quickly, and she predicted that if ophalla continued to be taken from the earth, Tamarind itself *would not survive*."

"But our father didn't believe her," said Señora Medrano. "He was a businessman and had little patience with what he saw as witch doctoring from an older age."

"But after he was killed, there was no end to the war and the mining for ophalla, and the chaos in the environment just grew worse," said Señora Rojo. "Storms ripped across the island from north to south and east to west. Coastal towns were swallowed up by huge waves, the people who lived there never seen again. No one knew what was happening.

"At that time, we—Señora Medrano and I, and Dr. Bellagio and General Alvaro, and a handful of others—went to Milagros to ask for her help. By then people believed that the Dark Women were to blame for all the natural disasters happening across Tamarind, and the Dark Women were being hunted and slaughtered."

"We asked Milagros for help, but as it turned out, chance alone saved Tamarind that time," said Señora Medrano. "The mining stopped abruptly, you see. Most of the ophalla deposits that people could reach had already been mined. Most of these had been in the Neglected Provinces, where the ophalla deposits were very shallow. There seemed to be nothing left to take. It was too late to save the Neglected Provinces, but the damage stopped just in time to spare the rest of Tamarind.

"Milagros told us that if people ever started mining too much ophalla again, there was something that must be done to restore the balance in nature," said Señora Rojo. "She told us there was a place deep in Tamarind that could save it. A sacred place that ancient people in Tamarind had known about."

"What place?" asked Simon, almost in a whisper.

"She was forbidden by the Dark Women's code to come right out and tell us," Señora Medrano answered. "The secret was too dangerous and too important for any one person to know. In the wrong hands, you see, misusing the secret could lead to Tamarind's destruction as surely as not using it at all.

"Milagros came up with a way to hide the secret. She decided to share it between many individuals, most of whom were unknown to one another. Each of these individuals then took their part of the secret to one man—the scientist-inventor Davies Maroner. Davies had invented a new process using ophalla in pictures—ophallagraphs, he called them—and he concealed the parts of the secret in these images."

"The trick," interrupted Señora Rojo, growing excited, "is that the ophallagraphs would just look like ordinary photos unless ophalla in Tamarind once again became out of balance. The ophallagraphs were sensitive to changes in ophalla in the earth. If it were disrupted, the ophallagraphs would begin to *glow*.

"The ophallagraphs were published in the *Gazette Extraordinario*—only Davies Maroner knew who received the special copies for safekeeping. Sometimes the people they were given to had no idea what they were for; they only knew that they were important and must be kept safe."

Simon frowned. "What marked the papers as special back when they were printed?" he asked. "How could you tell?"

"You couldn't," said Señora Rojo, smiling. "That was the point. The clues in the ophallagraphs would only be revealed in time, when they were needed again. That way no one would ever know the Dark Women's secret unless it became absolutely necessary for Tamarind. The papers were entrusted secretly to members of the Extraordinary Generation. One of the colonels gave me this one before he died."

"The guy who made the ophallagraphs, Davies Maroner, maybe he can help!" said Simon. Simon put a lot of faith in scientists—good ones, like his parents.

"Rest his soul," said Señora Rojo. "He was mixing chemicals in his laboratory—working on some new invention, when the whole thing went up in flames. He didn't have a chance . . ." she trailed off.

"Oh," said Simon. There went that idea. "But Milagros might be able to help."

"Where *is* Milagros?" asked Maya.

"In a place north of here," said Señora Rojo. "In a village on a lake." She turned to General Alvaro's map and waved her finger vaguely over a barren stretch of it, where a tangle of blue rivers and soupy green lakes and estuaries met and diverged and met again.

"There isn't a village marked there," said Simon.

"There wouldn't be," said Señora Rojo. "It's a hidden village."

"How do we get there?" asked Maya.

"I'll take you as far as I can," said Dr. Bellagio.

"Of course," said Señora Rojo excitedly. "Dr. Bellagio has a car—the only one in Floriano. You can take it as far as one of the last towns, before the road runs out. You'll have to get a boat from there, and travel upriver, through the wetlands to the Reappearing Village." She looked at Penny and frowned. "Can the littlest one keep up?" she asked doubtfully. "Maybe she should stay here?"

Penny looked at her siblings in alarm, but Simon quickly put his arm around her. "We all stay together," he said firmly.

"Well," said Señora Rojo reluctantly, "I suppose there's no time to waste."

Maya looked troubled. "But what about Helix?" she asked. "I don't understand how this will help us find him."

The señoras were quiet for a moment. Dust drifted in a slow dance in the afternoon light.

"Tamarind is on the verge of great trouble," said Señora Medrano finally. "It needs your help. And so does our nephew. All of you came here together to help Tamarind—your path will surely cross with his. But even if it doesn't, Tamarind must still be saved, and there may not be much time left."

Dr. Bellagio left to get his car, and Señora Rojo went to the kitchen to pack food for them—leather canteens of water, rice wrapped in banana leaves, white sapotes, guanabanas, and raw sugarcane for Penny. Señora Medrano gently tore the newspaper away until only the stiff square of the ophallagraph was left. Looking at the curiously luminous image one last time, she handed it reverently to Simon. When they heard Dr. Bellagio return, his car popping and jangling down the street and then his brisk knock on the door, the señoras walked the children out.

Penny jumped, startled to see the giant purple bird tied to a post outside the house.

"It's an ostrillo," Dr Bellagio whispered to the children. "Preposterous looking, but harmless, and very handy most of the time."

The creature looked up from nibbling moss and made a squeaking noise. Señora Rojo gave Simon General Alvaro's map, and the señoras hugged each of the children tightly in turn. Before she let them go, Señora Medrano squeezed Simon's and Maya's hands, tears welling in her eyes.

"Find our boy," she said.

"Bring him home to us," said Señora Rojo.

Simon noticed a funny look cross Maya's face but she said nothing.

✳ ✳ ✳

Dr. Bellagio's car—an open-top, beat-up old jalopy that, like most things in Tamarind, ran on some kind of homemade fuel—rattled along down the streets and out of Floriano. A sickly yellow haze filled the sky and the air was muggy.

"Why do the señoras hate each other?" Maya asked. "What happened?"

"Old feud," said Dr. Bellagio. "They were both in love with General Alvaro—the man whose map Señora Rojo gave you."

Maya gasped and leaned forward, intrigued.

"Oh, brother," muttered Simon.

"The señoras haven't spoken in nearly twenty years," Dr. Bellagio went on. "Their old family house is at the top of the hill here. After their falling out, Señora Rojo moved out and Señora Medrano has become a recluse—today was the first day she's left her hillside in years. They're the last two, really, as the rest of the family has died out. Your friend is the last of the line."

"What happened to the general?" Simon asked. The general at least was someone he could be curious about.

Dr. Bellagio hesitated. "He, well, he's not with us anymore."

"Oh," said Simon.

"But when he was, he was something!" said Dr. Bellagio.

"He routed the Northerners at Hetty's Pass and then his men escaped into the nearby tunnels they had mapped and overtook the northern towns—it was the most heroic campaign of the war. The general was daring—sometimes *too* daring. That's what got him into trouble with the señoras."

The car rattled on and through the window they saw people carrying baskets of produce on their heads, walking toward Floriano. Black clouds mounted in the sky and the day was darkening. Simon could smell rain coming. He noticed stray flying fish that lay rotting on the roadside, and observed that every so often a tree had shed its leaves and stood dead and ghostly.

"Did you know Helix's mother?" Maya asked.

"I did," said Dr. Bellagio, veering to avoid a pothole. "She was a great beauty in her day—all those Valdez sisters were admirable-looking women, but neither of the older sisters could hold a candle to the youngest one. She was a remarkable creature. And a gentle soul.

"Anyway," Dr. Bellagio continued, sighing, "she was lost in the war, like so many others. Now all of us who are left are just relics from another time. From the Extraordinary Days. The men you saw at Señora Rojo's today— the card players. They were all army men—Colonel Francisco led the Tambenno Assault, Colonel Luisio was in command of the forces at Gallolo. Yes—it's all the greats who come to Señora's salon. They *were* the greats, anyway. Now they're made of wood and sand and glass! I stitched them all together myself at one time or another. I cut off

Colonel Luisio's leg and sewed his arm back on. Yes, those days were something. And now . . . now I sense that another Great Time is upon us. Yes, it's happening, and you children and the señoras' nephew are part of it."

They were passing through a tiny village when they noticed that people were coming out and clustering in the streets and whispering to one another, their eyes wide and fearful.

"What's going on here?" murmured Dr. Bellagio.

He slowed down, the engine sputtering noisily, and waved down a woman walking quickly down the road, carrying a small child on her hip.

"Isabella Obrado's been kidnapped!" the woman said. "It happened yesterday but word just reached us. She was heading to the City of Children when the Red Coral captured her! There's no government anymore—the Red Coral have taken over!"

"Oh dear," said Dr. Bellagio and drove quickly on. "This is terrible," he muttered. "Terrible. That brave young lady was a beacon of hope to many people."

Simon felt sick at the news but he said nothing. They drove on in silence. Finally Dr. Bellagio eased on the brakes. Up ahead the road was impassable. An ancient tree lay felled across the road.

"Storms!" said Dr Bellagio. "They've stalked us these last months—the weather's changing all over again. This is as far as I can take you. You have to be very careful from here on." He hesitated. "I didn't want to say this in front of the señoras and alarm them more, but if the Red Man doesn't know you're here already, it's only a matter of time before he does. He wanted your parents—he'll be after you, too. Don't for a moment think you're not in danger. Keep your wits about you. That goes for the Reappearing Village, too. For centuries it's where convicts, thieves, and hunted men have fled to hide—the place is a snakepit of them."

Dr. Bellagio did not leave them empty-handed. Bowing gallantly, he gave Maya a first-aid kit that he assembled quickly from his doctor's bag. "And," he said, handing a furled umbrella to Simon, "since we never know what the weather will do next anymore—a gift for a rainy day."

"Thank you," said Simon. The umbrella was made of sturdy, chocolate brown fabric and had an ornamental handle made of ophalla that looked very old.

"It was given to me by Colonel Arturo Silva on his deathbed," said Dr. Bellagio. "Doctors receive all sorts of gifts from dying patients. But I'll tell you this, I knew the colonel for years and he kept nothing ordinary. Everything had a secret purpose. I kept it all this time, as I promised him I would, but I've decided that it may be more valuable to you now than it ever will to me."

Simon wasn't exactly sure how helpful an umbrella was going to be, but studied the exquisitely carved handle with interest. Its surface shone ice white, but when the light caught it just so, deep inside he thought he could glimpse a faint blue-green hue. A natural swirling pattern in the stone looked like a twist of candle smoke.

"I hope you'll find it useful," said the doctor, looking at Simon with his clear blue eyes.

The children had not been walking for long when the rain—with a sudden rush of ozone and a shiver of leaves—began. Simon snapped the umbrella open above them. It was surprisingly capacious, and once up, not a drop of water touched them. The drumming rain created a din, but beneath it was cozy and dry. Only their feet, slopping through puddles up to their ankles, got wet as they walked. Each step took them farther from the señoras and Dr. Bellagio, and closer to Milagros and the elusive Reappearing Village.

Dr. Bellagio's words had alarmed Simon. The doctor was right. Look how the Red Coral had tormented Mami and Papi—surely once Dr. Fitzsimmons discovered that the children were in Tamarind he would want to find them. Simon, Maya, and Penny would be valuable pawns to use against their parents. The Red Coral would hunt them down. Simon began to wonder what they had gotten themselves into. Or what *he* had gotten his sisters into. Maya would never have agreed to go if he hadn't encouraged her, and if he hadn't been so impatient to leave right away, Penny would be safely at home where she belonged.

"Isabella might have told the Red Coral that we're here," said Maya quietly.

"I know," said Simon. "We're going to have to be really careful and keep our eyes open."

In an hour the rain tapered off and the sun emerged on the dirt road the señoras had described, flanked by trees and farm fields. It was muddy from the rain but it was there, where it was supposed to be, and they knew they were going the right way. Occasionally a cart with a farmer taking his produce to market in Floriano passed them, but after a while they saw no one else and the road was empty. Simon shook out the umbrella, closed it, and strapped it to his backpack.

They heard the busy blue river before they saw it. The river had more traffic than usual, Simon realized, because of the dozens of boatloads of displaced villagers on the move. The Maroong had invaded villages overnight and driven everyone out. Everything people had taken with them was bundled in pale silkworm cloth and tied with fishing line onto their rafts, which floated like dirty white cumulous clouds down the river. Villagers sat perched on top, huddled with their knees under their chins and the same blank expressions on their faces. The children easily caught a ride on a produce skiff on its route between towns. For the next few hours they listened as their fellow passengers told wild tales—herds that showed up in a town one day, so thin their bones almost pierced their hides; another village that had been buried in mud from freak rainstorms. On the shores the children saw birds that had fallen dead out of the trees and fish that had washed up lifeless. Sometimes they had to cover their noses against the reek of death. Once they had to crouch, hiding behind wooden boxes, as they passed a handful of Maroong on the riverbank, loading giant, shining blocks of ophalla onto a boat to carry upriver.

Later, when the other passengers had disembarked and

the captain was out of sight at the stern, Simon took out the ophallagraph to study it more closely. He felt it was more important than ever that he figured it out.

"I can't put my finger on it, but something in this is just off somehow," he said to Maya. He scratched his knee, his brow furrowed in thought. "I'd almost say it's not made from a real photograph. All the bits in it were added separately—the boats, the hills in the background—even those skinny waterfalls look weird. I don't think this is a real place, it's all just bits and pieces of things and places, doctored together."

"Well, how does that help us?" asked Maya, "if everything in it is just wrong?"

"It isn't wrong," said Simon slowly. "It's deliberate. There's a big difference. It would mean that everything in here is a symbol or some type of clue." He chewed his lip and studied the image. "The señoras said you need to have all the ophallagraphs together in order to make sense of them. I wonder how many of them there are?"

After a while, Penny fell asleep. Maya sat with her chin on her knee, lost in her own thoughts. Now that he had a quiet moment, Simon missed his parents and Granny Pearl. The hastiness of their departure weighed on him. It had been four days since they left—their family must be very worried about them by now. He wondered what they were doing at home. As Simon sat there, clouds moved in and covered the sun. The river turned dark beneath them.

Trying to put his family out of his mind, he glanced down at the ophallagraph once more. Now that the day had dimmed and it was the main source of light, he noticed that the three thin waterfalls in the background had begun to glow more brightly, purposefully calling attention to themselves. Why? Simon's eye roved over the harbor in front of them, where the ghostly, glowing *Pamela Jane* sailed on.

❧ CHAPTER TEN ❧

The Children Are Shadowed ❁ *The Reappearing Village* ❁
Bird Woman ❁ *Faustina's Gate* ❁ *In the Golden Birdcage*

It wasn't until late that afternoon that the telltale walla-walla birds appeared and the fields turned to marshes. As the señoras had instructed, at the sharp bend in the river beneath the great landowega trees, the children left the skiff. They found the tiny tributary the señoras had told them about and walked along its bank. The ground grew muckier and muckier and with each step it became harder to walk. Maya was hot and irritated by a fly buzzing around her head, and Penny's pajamas were covered in mud. When Simon saw a half-sunk abandoned rowboat he waded into the water up to his waist and, with considerable effort, dragged it up to the shore.

The planks had swollen apart, leaving big gaps. Simon thought for a moment, then he took out his pocketknife and cut a few reeds. He flipped the rowboat over, and using a stout branch as a chisel and a rock as a hammer, he packed the reeds tightly into the loose joints.

They climbed in and Simon broke off two paddle-shaped tree branches and he and Maya began to steer. Penny bailed water out of the leaking hull with a coconut shell as they drifted along on the current. They had left the traffic of the river behind when they had turned onto the tributary, but soon Simon became aware of another small boat behind them. Each time they turned a bend the tip of the other boat's bow was just appearing around the last, so he could never get a good look at it.

"I see it, too," Maya muttered to Simon under her breath so that Penny wouldn't hear and be frightened, and they picked up the pace paddling.

It was probably just someone from a nearby village, but Simon couldn't shake the sense of foreboding that hung heavier on him with each stroke of the paddle. What if Isabella had given them away and the Red Coral had tracked them down? Eventually, to his relief, he could no longer hear the lap of oars behind them. The other boat was gone and they were alone in the wild, watery place. Evening was almost upon them and the light was beginning to fade. The reeds grew thicker and thicker but the current kept pushing them through.

"We're supposed to come out in a big lake inside the marsh," he whispered, saying it aloud in hopes that it was true.

"If this was the right way," said Maya. "And if this place really exists at all . . ."

Just as Simon was wondering if the señoras had unwittingly sent them on a wild-goose chase, with a final crackling and shuffling, the tall stems parted and before them was a large, pale lake. Simon quickly grabbed the reeds to hold them steady before the current could pull them out into open water. Golden light suffused the surface but the shadows near the shorelines were black and glossy. There was no village in sight, however. The lake was empty. The bad feeling that had been nagging Simon grew worse.

"What do we do now?" Maya asked. There was the gentle *shhh* of water leaking into the boat.

Simon was at a loss. All the señoras had said was that the village was near a lake. But what if it didn't even exist anymore? The señoras were old. Things could have changed since they had last left Floriano. The sky over the lake was already darkening. Except for a flock of birds flying silently high overhead, there was no sign of life. What were they going to do if night fell and they were stranded there in the leaky rowboat?

"If it's such a big secret, it can't be that easy to find," said Simon, feigning cheer for his sisters' sake.

As he was speaking he heard a hissing sound in the reeds nearby. Something was coming toward them. Simon remembered the boat he had seen following them earlier and his stomach lurched. Instinctively the children remained silent, hardly daring to breathe. Simon didn't know if he should keep paddling to get farther away, risking that the splashing of the paddle would betray them to whoever was coming, or wait and hope that they weren't noticed. The *wssssss*ing sound was getting louder as whatever it was came closer. Then he realized that there were more sounds coming from deep in the reeds all around the lake.

The rowboat had been taking on water and Maya resumed bailing again as quietly as she could. An unseen bird began to shrill, loud as an alarm. The hissing rushes grew louder and louder and began to shake and rattle. Whatever was there was very close now and in a moment would be upon them—they had to move! With a mighty drag of the paddle through the water, Simon drove them out of the reeds into the open lake.

They were exposed now; anyone could see them. Sweat poured down Simon's face. They had moved out of the way just in time. The singing reeds behind them were reaching a fever pitch when all of a sudden something burst out into the open lake. The children turned and gazed at it in surprise for just a few seconds, because that's how long it took before a current whipped it back into the reeds a short distance away. But they had seen it: a raft, upon which was built a dilapidated wooden house with a green roof and a rusted railing around its porch. If anyone was on it they were hidden safely inside the house. Thoroughly spooked, Simon was eager to hide again. But when he tried to paddle back toward the reeds he found that the current was too strong. With growing horror he felt the rowboat pick up speed.

"Give Penny the bailer—I need you to help paddle!" he cried to Maya.

But it was no use. They were powerless to resist the powerful current, which was bearing them swiftly toward the middle of the lake.

Then, from the rushes all around them, birds began to rise—hundreds then thousands of them. They scattered over the lake, hiding the last of the setting sun and casting dizzying maps of shadow on the water. The children found themselves suddenly disorientated in a vertiginous world of shadow and reflection and mirage. Across the vast lake other currents became visible, lightly foaming streams that ran this way and that with no apparent rhyme or reason.

"Stay down low, Penny," Maya whispered.

The sky lightened as the flock seemed to melt, then instantly re-formed as a dark, bristly V in the sky. The leader dived recklessly toward the lake and the others followed as if they were being poured out of the sky. Simon looked up and saw they were headed directly for the rowboat. He panicked and with a shout he lifted the flimsy paddle to shield them. But a split second before the birds would have struck, as if the creatures had suddenly changed their minds, they dropped their chests and lifted their wings and rose again to swirl in a darkening circle above the rowboat. More birds exploded from the rushes and a shrill cacophony rang out. Then all the birds together fell silent and began to ascend in the sky until they were too far away for the children even to hear their wings. Simon looked up, the paddle trembling in his hands. The last of the sun had disappeared while the birds had blocked the light. Now they were in the witching hour, the water and sky a deep purple. The black silhouette of rushes bristled around the lake.

A giant red albatross appeared, flying low toward them across the water. Simon paddled with all his strength, but couldn't fight the current. The boat was taking on water fast and Maya dropped her paddle and began to bail furiously. The albatross was above them, hovering just off the stern. A strong wind blew from its great wings. Simon felt the rowboat being blown from the current they were in and into another and then another again. It was almost as if the bird was driving them across the lake. Then it occurred to him: Sorella had said Milagros's gift was with birds.

"It could be one of Milagros's!" he said, looking up desperately. "Maybe it's trying to help us!"

The great bird navigated them from one current to another until they ended up in one that was running swift and straight toward the center of the lake.

Then Simon saw movement on the lake's fringes. He watched as a quivering light emerged from the reeds. Gradually, through the gloom, he saw that the light belonged to a lamp that hung from the porch of what appeared to be another small hut floating on a raft. One and then two and then three appeared after it—a collection of strange beacons all approaching the center of the lake. Maya's jaw dropped and she stopped bailing. The raft-boats pulled alongside one another, then locked together. Others were coming out of the reeds and across the lake to join them. To the children's amazement, a village began to assemble like a great jigsaw puzzle before their eyes. Wooden streets formed from the edges of connected rafts and shadowy figures moved along them. Canals ran through the village and bridges arched over them. Torches blazed on poles and candlelight shone from the windows. Already people were busy, crossing the bridges, gliding down the canals in sleek gondolas, stringing laundry out to dry in the warm night, lighting cooking fires and casting fishing lines. In moments a whole miraculous world had materialized out of thin air and been brought to life.

Night was fully upon them now, the lake and sky black but for the stars. The albatross dipped back down toward them and flapped his magnificent wings once more before taking off across the dark sky, and the little rowboat was given a final push toward the village. The boat had taken on too much water, though, and the children could no longer bail fast enough. They reached the edge of the village and just as they scrambled up a wooden ladder onto a raft, the rowboat sank beneath them, disappearing down into inky black water zipped with phosphorescent streaks. The children crouched there for a moment, waiting for their hearts to slow. Simon expected to be stopped and questioned, but the village was busy and nobody paid attention to them. Late-coming raft-boats were sailing in on the currents and joining the edge of the raft they were on and soon, without having moved, Simon, Maya, and Penny were deep inside the maze of interlocking streets and canals.

A gondola slid past them and the passengers looked wordlessly at the children—a man with great, beefy arms and an oily slick of black hair and pocked face; a hard-eyed woman swaddled in bright flowing garments who carried a basket of dried eels on her lap; an old man with a greasy beard down to his knees, who slept with his eyes open and only the whites showing, who seemed to be in the grip of a terrible dream. With a shiver that was not from the night air on his wet skin, Simon remembered what Dr. Bellagio had said: For centuries the village had been a place where convicts, thieves, and hunted men had fled to live in hiding.

It was up to him to protect his sisters. He and Maya each took one of Penny's hands.

"How will we find—" Maya began.

But she didn't need to finish her sentence.

It was obvious where Milagros lived. A soft storm of birds circled above one house like smoke from a chimney.

The children made their way cautiously toward it, water squelching in their soggy shoes, a rickety bridge creaking beneath their steps. Nighthawks darkened the air around them, their sharp wings like knives in the air. The moon came out and the limbs of the water-trees were pale silver and their bark shimmered as if covered in fish scales. When the children reached the house they saw that it was a single wooden room on a raft that was latched onto the far corner of the village. Its roof sagged, its paint was peeling, and scraggly nests burdened its eaves. No light came from its boarded windows. Waterweeds clotted the railings that ran around it.

The door was ajar, hanging half off its hinges.

They paused in front of it. Simon could feel the water moving beneath the planks under his feet. He thought he had better go in alone. "Wait here," he said.

"No," whispered Maya quickly. "We'll go with you."

Simon swallowed. *There's nothing to be afraid of*, he told himself. The señoras wouldn't have sent them here if Milagros were likely to harm them. Gathering his courage, he called softly into the dark room.

"Milagros?"

When there was no answer he pushed the door open warily—the wood was swollen and it creaked as it swung slowly in. The room was dark and smelled of rotting wood and bird droppings. Simon heard the flutter and rustle of feathers as soon as he stepped inside. Through the gloom dozens of tiny, shiny eyes peered at him.

"Milagros?" he repeated.

The houseboat swayed gently on the current into the moonlight that streamed suddenly through broad, open windows that ran along two walls of the room. In the middle of the room sat a woman—a great heap of a woman—who was looking with interest at the visitors.

Simon knew at once it was Milagros. She was a vast, heavy figure, with a large head and droopy eyes. A ruff of grizzled hair hung over her forehead. A few long, matted braids, tied with feathers, hung over her broad shoulders, where birds were perched staring at the children—theirs were the glowing eyes that Simon had seen. She wore a brown burlap dress, tied with twine around her waist. Her skin and eyes and hair and teeth were all the same color. The great, immovable mass of her sat planted in the middle of the room. She could not have been less birdlike, less likely to take flight. She looked instead, it occurred to Simon, like a nest. Downy feathers gathered in the folds of her dress, bird droppings frosted the tops of her shoes.

"I am she," she said. Her voice had a gravelly warble to it. "I am Milagros."

Only Penny didn't seem shocked by the filth in the

room. She stared in fascination at Milagros and the birds on her shoulders.

Simon's throat was dry and when he went to speak no sound came out. Milagros spoke instead.

"I presume that your visit has something to do with the other Outsiders who have followed you here," she said. They trailed her eyes to the window, through which they could see several lights bobbing on the other side of the lake, at the point where Simon and Maya and Penny had entered. Simon's heart skipped a beat—the Red Coral knew they were there, after all! They were the people who had been following the children! Simon gazed at the lights in horror.

"Don't worry, they can't get here," said Milagros. "It's next to impossible to breach the village. The currents will keep them on the fringes of the lake and my birds will see to it that they're uncomfortable. You only got in because I sent the albatross for you."

Milagros was right. The boats never seemed able to get past a certain point. As the children watched, the lights would seem to make headway, but then without fail the extraordinarily powerful currents would spin them abruptly away and they would resume their restless circling.

"That means we've led them right here!" said Simon in dismay.

"We're so sorry," said Maya. "We didn't know . . ."

"You've given nothing away," said Milagros calmly, in a low voice that was more of a rumble. "Our village disappears each morning and is reborn each night. By morning, when the currents change and allow them in, the village will be gone. The rafts split up and we go our separate ways deep into the marsh, where intruders have little hope of finding us and where, should they venture, we can hear them coming from a mile away. Sometimes a raft will travel hundreds of miles in a single day before it rejoins the current that will return it here at nightfall."

Simon was still squinting at the Red Coral boats in the distance.

"At least for tonight, the Red Man isn't out there," said Milagros. "Just some of his Maroong who have been tracking you."

Simon relaxed slightly at this news, but glanced nervously at Milagros. He didn't want her to know that they knew Dr. Fitzsimmons.

"I know from the birds about what is happening across Tamarind," said Milagros. "I know from what they bring back in their beaks and talons. I've read the signs in the earth. The Red Man is causing what is only the beginning of unspeakable destruction across Tamarind. Already the plague in the seas has begun—that's how it starts. Never in my lifetime have I seen something happen so fast. What in times past took generations, has now happened in a matter of moons." The strange old woman sighed deeply and regarded the children. "I assume the señoras have sent you. They *would* choose this way for you to come," she said irritably. "And only they would send children."

"They said you could help us," said Simon, embarrassed

by how shaken he had been, and eager to appear confident once again.

"Not as much as they think, I'm sure," the old woman said. "They always expected miracles, those two," she muttered. The birds suddenly shifted along her arms, disgruntled cooing spreading up and down their ranks. They fought for space before they settled down again. "I only hear from anyone when they want something!"

"Isabella Obrado is looking for you, too," said Simon. "Everyone thinks you can help Tamarind."

"Oh," said Milagros. "I'm popular again, I see."

"But the señoras sent us," said Simon. "Their nephew is our friend. They're trying to find him. You sent a bird—a green parrot—to protect him, a long time ago, and they thought you could help to find him now."

Simon was startled to see Penny withdraw one of Seagrape's emerald feathers from her pocket and hold it out to the old woman.

Milagros was quiet. She seemed stirred for the first time since they had arrived. For a moment her face looked more human than it had.

"I remember, yes, I remember well," she said. "The child and his mother both." Outside the window the scales of the water tree gleamed in the moonlight. The children waited.

"I know the señoras," Milagros said finally. "They haven't sent you empty-handed. I know already what you've brought with you. Let me see it."

Simon opened his backpack and took out the ophallagraph. Light at once flooded the filthy, feathered corners of

145

the shack. The ophalla's glow was reflected in the eyes of the birds as they tilted forward on spindly legs to peer into the image of the boat, quivering with light. "They're starting this up again," Milagros said wearily, closing her eyes. Again, the children waited for her to speak. "You don't know what you're here to do, do you?" she asked finally. "You don't even know what you're looking for."

Simon and Maya looked at each other. "We're looking for the rest of the ophallagraphs," ventured Simon.

"The ophallagraphs are just clues," said Milagros impatiently.

Simon and Maya looked at each other helplessly. Everyone had counted on Milagros being the one who would know what to do: Isabella, the señoras, Dr. Bellagio. What were they going to do if she couldn't advise them?

Simon frowned, thinking, then a sudden stroke of intuition made him bold. What if there were a connection between the place hidden in the ophallagraphs that the señoras believed would save Tamarind and . . .

"Faustina's Gate," he said. "That's what we're looking for."

Milagros looked sharply at him. Suddenly the birds roosting on the rafters began dipping their heads and weaving their necks back and forth. A bird squawked loudly from its nest in the eaves. "Where did you hear that name?" she asked.

Simon swallowed. Faustina's Gate *was* important. "We know that the Red Coral are looking for it."

"This is very bad," said Milagros, settling back into herself. "I hadn't realized they knew so much. Things are worse than I thought."

"We asked the señoras about the gate and they didn't know what it was," said Maya.

Milagros took a deep, whistling breath and leaned forward. "Listen closely," she said. "You *are* looking for Faustina's Gate. That's the purpose of the ophallagraphs—that's what they're helping you do. The gate is a sacred place, hidden in caves deep in Tamarind. It isn't enough just to defeat the Red Man by force. Too much ophalla has been mined already. In order to save Tamarind you have to close Faustina's Gate and to close the gate you'll need certain tools—the clues inside the ophallagraphs will help you find them. The tools were scattered long ago—I have no idea where they are now, so don't ask me." She eased back then and again looked immovable.

"I don't understand," said Simon. "How will closing this—gate—stop the Red Coral Project?"

"I've already said all that I can," wheezed Milagros. "The señoras thought I could help, but I can only add to your puzzle. There are things you need for this journey—both tools and understanding—and until you have them, the gate, even if you could find it, would be meaningless to you.

"As for the Red Man . . . I don't know what his ideas about Faustina's Gate are," Milagros went on, "or what he wishes to use it for." She paused. "But it will be nothing good. You have to find it before he does."

"But . . . what do we do next?" Maya asked.

"As always, we must start with what we have already," said Milagros.

"All we have is this ophallagraph," said Simon.

"And now another," said Milagros.

She went then—slow, heavy-limbed, rustling as she moved—to a slim-barred golden birdcage in the corner. It was empty, its door open. A sweetgale bird watched silently from the window as she pushed to one side soiled papers from the floor of the cage. From beneath them she slid out a fresh sheet of paper. As she turned around the children saw it—another copy of the *Gazette Extraordinario*! And in the lower corner of the page, an ophallagraph, this one glowing, too, not brilliantly, but like embers still holding heat in a fire that had gone out. They stepped closer and peered into the image.

Two men stood side by side; the one on the right had his arm around the other, and with his free hand he held an umbrella over both their heads. They stood in the foreground of the image, and behind them were three stone cottages thatched with palm leaves and set at angles to one another. A tall palm swayed in the background and a lush kitchen garden flourished between the cottages. Flowers spilled from window boxes. A crop of low, eroded hills stood in the distance and set in one—Simon leaned in to get a better look at it—was a tiny blue square that glowed dimly. Clouds banked the background and across them were tiny black etchings of birds flying in formation. Simon thought that he saw something glinting, a thick thread, around the neck of the man on the left. The image was not in as good shape as the one of the *Pamela Jane*, as if things in it were unclear about whether they planned to reveal themselves fully or not. Suddenly Simon looked back at the umbrella.

"Wait!" he said. He took the umbrella that Dr. Bellagio had given him out of his backpack and held it up. "It's the same one as in the ophallagraph," he said joyfully. Maybe things were starting to come together after all!

"You're right," said Milagros, inspecting it. "It appears you have one of the tools already."

Simon looked up at her, his eyes shining. He wanted to hear more about the ophallagraphs.

"I wouldn't have this ophallagraph at all, except that the person who had it died," said Milagros. "It was passed from person to person all the way from the far north, crossing the island and eventually arriving here for safekeeping—I don't know what they thought I could do with it. Don't expect me to explain it," she said before Simon could ask. "I told you—I don't know where the tools are anymore, and without them anything else I could tell you would be useless. Now, what else have the señoras given you?"

"A map," said Simon, taking it out and smoothing it so that Milagros could see.

The old hag began to chuckle deeply. "One of General Alvaro's old battle maps," she said.

"You knew him?" asked Maya. "You knew the general?"

"I knew them all," said Milagros. "Long ago. So this is

what they gave you, is it? People always know more than they think they do—it never ceases to amaze me." She reached a long, filthy, curved fingernail to the map. She ran it from Maracairol up through the mountains, over blue knots of rivers and across the baked yellow desert of the Neglected Provinces. Then she stopped in the middle, on the border of the West and the Neglected Provinces, where there were arrows drawn to mark some military maneuver.

Her fingernail, curved like a talon, trembled as it roved over the symbols and drawings.

"This is the site of the Battle of Hetty's Pass," she said, tapping a spot on the map. "General Alvaro's greatest victory. Now, there's a person I'd like to have on my side in future battles."

Milagros paused, about to say something, then decided against it. Instead she stretched her arm out and pointed to the window, where sweetgale birds perched like blue tongues of fire on the boughs of the water-tree.

"In the morning I advise you to go to Hetty's Pass, in the Borderlands. I promise nothing, but I suspect that you may have some luck there. You're going to need all the help you can get to defeat the other Outsiders. You can borrow a gondola. Stay in the same current you're in until you see a single yellow harpy eagle circling in the sky. There will be a toro tree there with an almost spherical trunk and a large nest in it. As soon as you can, get onto dry land and let the gondola go—it will return here in a loop on the same current at nightfall. From the toro tree, walk northeast and keep the mountains in front of you." She traced a shaky line on the señora's map with her finger.

"You'll come to a plateau facing a mountain in the distance that casts a triangular shadow. You'll be in the Borderlands between the West and the Neglected Provinces. It's very important that you stick to the map. I warn you, the Neglected Provinces are a strange and inhospitable place. No child who enters there will leave with his youth."

"What will we find there?" Simon asked.

"That's for you to discover," said Milagros. "However, if you find all the tools—and your friend and the bird you call Seagrape—if you ever need my help again, put a piece of zala root in the parrot's talons and she'll find me.

"There's a room across the way where you can sleep," she went on. "It belongs to a man and his wife. Tell them I sent you. You'll find it more comfortable there than here."

The children shifted from foot to foot, reluctant to leave when they felt more confused than ever.

Milagros was silent for a minute. "I will caution you, that which appears alive is dead and what appears dead is alive," she said. "Things elude understanding until they are understood."

Simon's head swam, but Milagros brushed further questions away.

"But, please," insisted Maya, her eyes luminous in the dark, "what about Helix? How can we find him?"

Milagros regarded the girl and after a moment she smiled, a surprisingly gentle, knowing smile. "The green parrot is there to watch over and protect your friend," she said. "Right now he has his own things to discover, as you have yours. If he's to be found, it will be when the time is right, not before. Go now, I've told you all I can."

⚝ ⚝ ⚝

The room across the way belonged to a tiny, wrinkled old couple who swept the floor and laid down grass mats for the children to sleep on. The wife brought them a jug of water and a plate of steaming fried fish and boiled shoots of reed grasses and star fruit, which the children thanked them for profusely. The boat turned on its hinges and the village swung into view.

"It's amazing," said Maya. "I've never seen anything like it."

"I suppose not many people ever have," said Simon. He had studied the umbrella from handle to rod to the sturdy brown fabric between its spokes without figuring out what made it special, and now he put it carefully aside.

While they ate they listened to the lap of the water and watched neon life zigzagging beneath the water out across the lake. Strange currents distorted the surface. Cooking grease was splashed out to bait the fish and a fatty gleam ventured out across the water. In the darkness they heard the *sssssswack-swshhh, sssssswack-swshhh* of nets being cast. Penny was afraid of scaly wooden dragons carved into the bridges that grimaced down at the people passing beneath them. "They're just pretend," said Maya, but Penny had to sit so she wasn't facing them. Deeper inside the

152

village women came to bathe and wash their hair in a canal, and when they were finished the canal was opened to men. The murmur of human voices and activity reached the children as the invisible citizens of Tamarind went about doing all the things they could not do by day.

Whooo? Whooo?

Simon jumped, startled. It was an owl in the window, his face as round and yellow as the full moon behind him. He sat there only an instant before he took flight again, a single of his feathers drifting to the floor beside Simon.

He picked it up and examined it. Its quill glowed dully in the dim room. "It's got ophalla in it," he said. "The birds must absorb it somehow. Just like the glowing sea life. Sorella said there was ophalla in everything here." He paused, looking around at the faintly shimmering bark of the water-trees and at the glowing fish in the lake, glimmering like stars reflected on the surface.

He frowned, thinking.

Maya looked across the lake to where the Red Coral boats still spun in futile circles. "I wish they'd go away," she said. "They're too close for comfort. I wonder how long they were following us."

"I don't know," said Simon. "Anyway, we'll do what Milagros said and leave through the reeds tomorrow to reach Hetty's Pass. They won't be able to follow us."

"What do you think we'll find there?" asked Maya. "Why wouldn't Milagros just tell us?"

"She knew a lot more than she told us," said Simon thoughtfully. "But at least now we know what the ophallagraphs are for—we need to find those tools. And we know that Faustina's Gate *is* important. The Red Coral were on to something, unfortunately."

"What I'd like to know is how closing a gate is supposed to save Tamarind," said Maya. "It doesn't make any sense."

A cool breeze flowed over the lake.

Maya sighed. "I wonder if Helix is still with the *Pamela Jane*," she said. "I hope he's okay. Wherever he is."

"I'm sure he's fine," said Simon. "Helix can take care of himself." He looked out over the dark water. Their friend was somewhere in Tamarind, maybe quite far away from where they were right now.

"He doesn't even know we found his family yet," said Maya quietly.

"When are we going to see Helix again?" Penny asked.

"I don't know," said Simon. "Soon, I hope."

"I wish he was with us," said Penny.

"So do we, Pennymouse," said Maya.

Simon studied the two ophallagraphs, side by side, but he couldn't for the life of him see anything in them that might be the tools Milagros had spoken about. Finally his eyes grew heavy and he put away the ophallagraphs and lay back, hands under his head and his elbows sticking out. Usually if he didn't understand something, he would ask Papi. Now he had to figure things out on his own. It was harder than he thought.

What kind of gate was Faustina's Gate? How had Dr.

Fitzsimmons known about it, and why had he been so sure the children's parents could help him?

Simon's questions circled restlessly, like the Red Coral boats on the fringes of the village, never getting anywhere, until eventually sleep took over.

❧ Chapter Eleven ❧

"Wake up," said a voice in Simon's ear. He opened his eyes to see the old woman from the night before, whose room they had slept in. "Hurry now, you don't have much time!"

Simon woke Maya and Penny, and still half-asleep, they clambered into the wide gondola that Milagros had left for them. Milagros's raft was already gone. The woman untied the gondola and gave it a shove into a current. The lake was still dark but the village was disbanding. Whole streets floated off together for a moment before splitting up, each houseboat carried swiftly off on its own current back into the reeds. The breeze was cool and the air smelled marshy.

The children lay down flat so they couldn't be seen, but after a few minutes Simon peeked over the gunwale of the gondola and saw the lights of the Red Coral boats out on the far fringes, still spinning in futile circles. Soon the currents would release them and they would be able to penetrate the lake and the vast marshland that surrounded it. All around the children the town was melting away as dawn was breaking. Boathouses disappeared into the rushes, their inhabitants already settling down to sleep. Birdcages hung on poles at bows of gondolas; the children could hear the birds' sweet song from somewhere inside the rushes before that, too, was gone. The next time Simon looked back the lake was empty—with a mysterious whisper of grasses, the village had effaced itself. The birds had vanished, too, all but a black kestrel that wheeled silently high above the lake, now glowing pewter in the low-lying fog. Only the Red Coral boats remained, starting to make their way toward the middle of the lake. But the current the children were on had already brought them to the far side. Soft, tall reeds parted and then Simon, Maya, and Penny headed deep into a green and gold world.

When the current had borne them a great distance without any sign of the men following them, Simon took out General Alvaro's old map and the two ophallagraphs. On the map he found Hetty's Pass, the sandy plateau on the edge of the Neglected Provinces where they were headed. He examined the ophallagraphs once again but discouragingly they yielded nothing new. He wondered how many they would need before they made sense. To pass the time, Maya played games with Penny, counting the tiny silver fish that whizzed past the gondola and pointing out things they saw in the clouds.

A couple of hours later they saw the toro tree with the bulbous trunk and great snaggle of nest that Milagros had promised. The yellow harpy eagle wheeled in the air above it. Kneeling, Simon grabbed on to a root that grew out of the muddy bank and held the boat steady so his sisters could disembark. He followed them up, and when the current wrestled him for the gondola he released it and it continued on its track and within seconds it was gone among the reeds.

"I hope this is the right place," said Maya, looking around. "We're in the middle of nowhere."

They were indeed in the middle of nowhere—the Borderlands of the West and the Neglected Provinces, Milagros had told them. But it was a clear, bright day, the sky blue and hopeful, and although the earth was spongy, they were happy to be back on land. They soon found a dirt road that unrolled through the rice paddies and past a distant windbreak of trees whose tops were turning silver in the sunny breeze. Simon took out the compass and took a bearing northwest.

"I guess we go on this for a while," he said. He and Maya each held one of Penny's hands, swinging the little girl every few steps until their arms got tired. Putrid masses of waterweeds gave way to broad plashy rice fields, stretching green and luxurious on either side. It seemed that there wasn't another soul for miles. For the first time in a while, Simon began to relax. At least for the time being they were safe from the Red Coral. Penny ran ahead and dug in puddles for oily little tadpoles that wriggled in her palms. Every now and then a lone tree cast a cooling shadow on the road.

The sun was high when Maya stopped in her tracks. "What is that?" she said, turning her ear to where the red dirt road disappeared into the scalloped golden hills in the distance.

Simon listened. "I don't hear anything," he said.

"*Shh,*" said Maya, lifting her finger to her lips. "There it is again!"

Whump! Sssaaaa!

Simon heard it then, too.

Whump! Whump! Sssaaaa!

Simon grabbed on to the smooth-limbed branch of a tall tree growing beside the road. He wedged his foot in the fork, hoisted himself up, and climbed boldly, foot over hand, like a monkey to the top. He popped out at the top and looked around to get his bearings. Yes, there was the way they had come, and ahead of them the golden hills. The marshy earth spread all around, standing pools of water reflecting the swift-streaming clouds, and—

Whump! Whump! Sssssssssssssaaaa!

The wind picked up the final hiss of the *sssaaaa!* and carried it at speed up to him at the top of the tree. He squinted but couldn't see anything—where was the sound coming from? A breeze swished through, flattening the leaves, and suddenly Simon had a clear view out of the tree to a cloud of dust rising on the dirt road in the near distance. Wrapping his knees around the branch, he struggled for his binoculars, and when the next breeze swept the leaves back what he saw almost made him topple out of the tree. Dropping the binoculars to hang around his neck, he began to scramble recklessly back down.

"A whole lot of people are marching this way," he said, jumping down from the last branch and landing on the ground near his sisters. "There was a lot of dust—I couldn't really see them—but they're definitely marching. We need to hide!"

Maya grabbed Penny's hand and ran into the boggy earth off the road toward the tree. The rice was too short to hide in. Simon was about to follow them when he stopped suddenly.

"Footprints!" he cried, rushing back to the road and jogging alongside it to make sure that there were no telltale prints anywhere. Happily the road, raised out of the paddies, was hard and dry in most places. He was about to turn back when he saw Penny's heel marks in a mucky hollow—she had been playing some sort of hopscotch there, he remembered. He kneeled to pat them smooth. The steady thumping and answering rattling was growing louder and Simon could feel the vibrations through the earth.

"Simon—come on!" Maya called to him from the tree.

Simon clambered quickly up the tree and joined his sisters. Penny was sitting snugly in the fork of a branch and Maya was next to her. Simon climbed a little higher and crouched down to wait. The group was fast approaching, singing something, something without words and without a tune, just a series of guttural thumps and whumps. Even the breaths between the cries sounded fearsome. Who were they?

Whump! Through a break in the trees Simon saw a bare foot come into view. Then another, and a horde of them after that.

Whump! Whump! Sssaaaa!

They weren't singing, Simon realized. The thumping sound was from their feet, beating the ground in rhythm, and the *sssaaaa!* sound was from some jangling instrument they carried over their shoulders.

"The Maroong," he whispered.

Through the leaves he caught fragmented glimpses of enormously tall men and equally tall women. Their faces were pinkish in the sun and their shiny shaven heads were painted with jungle dyes. He saw a helmet with polished sea tusks that stuck out at awkward angles and reptile scales glittering like armor over torsos. Jewels flashed in lips and ears. He saw that they carried crude weaponry—spears tipped with giant tusks and heavy wooden clubs set with ragged sharks' teeth. *Whump, ump, whump, whump! Sssssaaaaaa. Whump, ump, whump, whump, sssssaaaaaa!* There had to be a few hundred of them. They raised their clubs, glistening with poisonous resin, up to the blue sky.

Then Simon realized this was not an ordinary work gang heading to the ophalla mines. They were warriors ready for battle.

What was the Red Coral planning that needed not just workers, but soldiers?

Where were they marching? Isabella had been kidnapped and the government was in shambles—was the Red Coral going to take over all of Tamarind? *Where are you, Helix?* Simon thought. If he were with them Simon was sure he and his sisters wouldn't be stumbling around so blindly.

The children kept quiet as mice. They waited until the

footfalls were far away and then Simon slid down from the tree and crept out to the road.

"All clear," he said. Maya and Penny climbed down after him.

"What do you think the Red Coral are up to?" Maya asked, dusting off her hands and looking down the road where the Maroong had vanished.

"Whatever it is, it's bad," said Simon grimly.

Penny was bending down to look at a tooth that had fallen off one of the Maroong's weapons. "Whoa," said Maya. "What has teeth that big?"

"Some animal in the East, where they come from, I guess," said Simon. He looked at his little sister then and wished that her legs were longer. "We've got to go a little quicker now, okay?" he said to her. "Piggyback?" He bent down and she jumped onto his back and latched her arms around his shoulders.

With greater urgency, they pressed on.

⚔ ⚔ ⚔

The land grew rapidly hotter and drier over the next few miles and soon the children left the lush rice paddies behind. The earth they trod on now yielded little life. A rare shady tree stood here or there, sucking up all available water for a mile around it, allowing nothing else to grow. The fuzz of a type of hardy dandelion drifted in the breeze from somewhere far away but found no place on the arid soil to make purchase. Simon had never seen anywhere in Tamarind like this before—where was the lush, humid jungle they knew? A mountain range loomed blue in the distance, like a chalky heap of rubble. He checked the map to be sure they were going the right way, then they kept walking until they saw the mountain that cast the triangular shadow Milagros had described to them.

"I think this is it," said Simon. "This is Hetty's Pass, where Milagros said that big battle was ages ago that the general won. And there's the triangle shadow she told us about."

"Now what?" asked Maya. "Milagros never really said what to do once we got here."

Simon took out his binoculars and scanned the valley.

"There's a hut on the plateau up ahead," he said. "Let's start there."

As they walked, Penny tilted her head sideways and looked at the mountain ahead of them. "I see a face," she said, but the others weren't paying attention. "In the mountains, see? There's the nose and there's the mouth and there's the chin."

"Mmm-hmm," murmured Maya, taking Penny's hand. "Now, come on, you have to keep up."

Penny trotted to catch up, but she kept her eye on the ridge in the distance, sure of what she saw.

✹ ✹ ✹

The sun beat down brutally and the dry breeze sapped the moisture from their skin. Simon had to veer to miss a parched tumbleweed that rolled past. Soon they drew close to the little adobe hut on the plateau. A few pieces of faded washing, dried stiffly by the sun, flapped in the breeze.

"There's laundry," said Simon. "Someone must live there."

Maya stopped to wipe the sweat off her face. "Question is *why* anyone would choose to live here," she said. "Can this really be where Milagros meant?"

As they drew near they saw a man sitting on a bench outside the hut, chewing olives and spitting the pits onto the earth as he watched the children approach. A pair of polished boots sat on the stone steps, their leather soft and worn with age.

"Wait," said Maya in a low voice. "We have no idea who he is—he could be dangerous . . ."

"I don't think Milagros would have sent us to someone dangerous," said Simon. But as they neared the hut he grew nervous. Maya was right; they didn't know who this man was. He was old, but he was far bigger than Simon and looked very strong. How would Simon protect his sisters if he had to?

The man didn't rise when they stopped awkwardly in front of him. The shadow he cast, even when sitting, was enormous. He had great hands, a broad face, a flat nose, a big mouth, ox-broad shoulders, and a torso like the barrel of a tree. His hair was white but his skin was bronzed dark and leathery from the sun and deep creases cleaved his thick neck. The sleeves of his shirt were rolled up. He moved only to kick the front door of the hut closed with his huge, filthy bare foot so they could not see inside.

Simon felt his knees trembling slightly. Penny huddled close to Maya. But then the man spoke and put them at ease.

"Water's there," he said, nodding to a pump beside a roofed well near the house. "Well's dry but the pump's good. Help yourselves."

Gratefully the children cranked the squeaky pump and rinsed the dust out of their mouths and took a long drink. A mule with soft floppy ears grazed on stubbly roots of grass in a tiny enclosure. It looked up at them and blew gently through its nostrils. Simon saw that around the side of the house was a pen with three ostrillos, like the one Señora Medrano had but bigger.

He stood up, refreshed, and regarded the man thoughtfully. Something about the straightness of his back and the focus of his expression, intense but unrevealing, gave Simon the impression that he might once have been a soldier. Simon wondered why he had kicked the door of the hut shut when he saw them coming. Now that they were there Simon wasn't entirely sure what to do. He was growing tired of explaining who they were and what they were doing there, and trying to gauge how much information to reveal and how much to withhold. Also, he was weary from walking all day and in the end his weariness made him bold: He opened his backpack and took out the two ophallagraphs from the *Gazette Extraordinario*.

"I'm Simon and these are my sisters, Maya and Penny," he said. "We've come to see if you know anything about these."

The man got to his feet abruptly, knocking over his chair, and looked in astonishment at the ophallagraphs. Suddenly finding themselves in his shadow, Maya and Penny took a step back but Simon stood his ground. The images glowed brighter in the shadow the man cast. He looked down at them, the white-blue light reflecting on his sun-worn face.

"Where did you get these from?" he asked harshly.

Simon felt sweat trickle down inside his shirt. Had he miscalculated in showing the ophallagraphs? "One is from Señora Rojo and Señora Medrano—" he began but got no further.

The man's face suddenly turned deep purple.

"Those devils!" he roared. "What do they want with me now! Where are they and what are they doing together? I thought they hadn't spoken since the day they tried to kill me!"

Enraged, the man clenched his bulging fists and turned and looked down the hill all around them as if he expected to see other people coming. What had he meant . . . since the señoras had tried to kill him? Simon took a big step back, Penny dived behind Maya, and the three of them stood there quaking.

"We're alone!" Simon said hurriedly. "We've come alone!"

A breath of cool air from the mountains blew open the door of the hut and before the man could close it again Simon caught a glimpse inside. Leaning in the corner was a cluster of rifles. Pistols hung on the wall in between maps depicting wavy lines of marching regiments; mounted armies fording rivers; fleets of boats slanted in the wind; and Xs and arrows had been drawn to mark supply lines, advances and retreats, defeats and victories . . . They were all battle maps. Simon felt a jolt of recognition.

They were right now standing on the site of the Great Battle of Hetty's Pass.

Who had won that battle? Who else would choose such an inhospitable place to eke out a life?

What had Milagros said? *What appears alive is dead and what appears dead is alive.*

Crafty Milagros—she had led them right there! Only how had she known that he was still—

"Alive!" Simon practically shouted. "You're General Alvaro and you're alive!"

Maya looked at Simon in confusion and the general's face immediately turned seven deeper shades of violet. With one hand he picked Simon up by the arm and hauled him three feet off the ground. "Who are you?" he bellowed, shaking him. Simon's teeth rattled and he couldn't speak.

Suddenly Penny roared and charged the general and began kicking his leg viciously. "Leave my brother alone!" she shouted. The general looked down at her in astonishment. "GET THIS CADET OFF ME!" he hollered at Maya. "CONTROL YOUR SUBORDINATE!"

Maya ran forward and scooped Penny off the ground and Penny immediately burst into tears. "He's hurting Simon," she wept.

The general dropped Simon, who stumbled backward. "Who are you?" General Alvaro growled.

"Simon Nelson," said Simon, rubbing his arm. "Sir," he added for good measure. "And these are my sisters, Maya and Penny."

The general glowered at Penny. "That cadet should be on probation," he said. "She's got wicked little feet. And that racket is maddening—make her stop, for the love of all that's holy."

"I won't stop, I won't stop," Penny sobbed, but Maya patted her back until she quietened down and her weeping subsided to hiccups.

"It's okay, Penny, I'm fine," said Simon. He was so pleased with his discovery that he didn't even care how roughly the general had gripped him. Milagros thought he could help them; that's why she had guided them here, Simon was sure of it. She had said the general was someone she'd want on her side in a battle! And they had just seen the army of Maroong marching west to join the Red Coral—surely a battle of some sort was what they ultimately faced against the Red Coral.

"We've come to ask for your help," Simon said urgently. "The Red Coral Project—"

"I know there are Outsiders here!" snarled General Alvaro. "And I've seen the changes beginning again. But the Extraordinary Days are over! They've been over for a long time. I'm retired! I came here so I would be left in peace!"

"But Milagros sent us here—she knew you could help," said Simon.

"Milagros!" said the General, aghast. "She's involved in all this, too? My, oh my, oh my . . . you can all turn around and march right back to those insufferable señoras and that witch Milagros and tell them I am *done* with all three of them!"

"But the Red Coral Project is destroying Tamarind!" said Simon passionately. "How can you just sit here?"

"If you had eighty-year-old bones, you'd just sit here, too, I assure you," said the general, scowling. "Those two crows—they almost killed me! I still have shrapnel from Medrano's Infernal Machine in my leg and if I had been just a few seconds slower that boleadaro from Rojo would have cut me in half instead of the twenty-foot palm that it felled! If Bellagio hadn't helped me escape I have no doubt whatsoever they would have finished the job!"

"Dr. Bellagio?" asked Maya, gazing enraptured at the general. "He knows you're alive?"

"Of course he does!" said General Alvaro dryly. "The man's my doctor—I hope he knows the difference between when I'm alive and when I'm dead. Those two señoras of yours, they got their knickers in a twist, but I was a free man—I'd made no promises! It wasn't my fault if they— Ah, to hell with them!"

Simon signaled Maya to be quiet. She obviously very badly wanted to keep asking questions, but with what Simon knew was sheer will she clapped her mouth shut and waited.

"Milagros—" began Simon, but the general cut him off.

"I'm an old man now!" he said testily. "My time has passed. We protected Tamarind for as long as we could. Many among us lost their lives for her. We were part of something then—we were needed. But that time is dead and gone. What you're talking about is a job for young people. You do it!" He paused before adding, "I'm already forgotten. I'd like to stay that way."

Just then a cold wind came down from the mountains where Penny had seen the face, making them shiver. Then it was gone and the sun was warm once again. The general glanced up at the hills. At last he sighed. "Let me see those ophallagraphs. Maybe I can help you with them at least. Come inside with me." He looked down at Penny. "White flag, cadet?"

Penny wrinkled her nose suspiciously but followed her siblings.

"How are the señoras?" grunted the General as he went into the hut.

"They're okay," said Maya.

"*Hmph*," muttered the General.

The adobe hut was a single room. There was a table and near to it some chairs made of brown jacaranda wood so dark it was nearly black. A single straw cot sat in the corner. Dented copper pots and pans hung on the wall next to a stove fueled by dry ostrillo dung, the odor of which filled the hut. A wooden trunk with an imposing A carved into it crouched beneath a fur of dust, and on it reposed a cigar case filled with musty old cigars, a bronze sextant, a silver inkpot, and the moth-eaten flag of an army that no longer existed. They sat at the table and Simon took out the ophallagraphs.

"I'll be damned," said the general, picking one up.

"They're supposed to have clues about how to help save Tamarind," said Simon.

"I know what they're for," grunted the general.

"We're meant to decipher them, but we don't know where to start," Simon continued. "We have the umbrella, and this boat, the *Pamela Jane*, is ours, but we don't know where she is right now . . ."

The general said nothing as he studied the ophallagraph of the two men standing beneath the umbrella. Then he tapped the image. "The man on the left," he said finally. "Maybe that's your clue."

"Why?" asked Simon, puzzled.

"He's dead," said General Alvaro.

"Dead?" exclaimed Simon.

"But he's standing up," said Maya.

"He's being *propped* up," said the general. "I think I've seen death enough to know, young lady. Look closely, you'll see."

Simon and Maya squinted at the ophallagraph again. The general was right. There was an unnatural stiffness in the face of the man in the green-striped jacket, and his eyes stared blankly ahead. Milagros's words came back to Simon . . . *what appears alive is dead.*

"Why would they take a picture of him then?" Maya asked, shivering. "It doesn't make sense."

"That I can't help you with," said the general. "I haven't the foggiest. That fellow Maroner designed them and he went and got his throat slit when he went into the jungle in search of some sort of plant he wanted for something or other."

"Wait," said Simon. "I thought Davies Maroner died in a fire."

"Well, maybe he did," said the general. "That's just what I heard, and who knows what's the truth or not around this place. Anyway, burned, drowned, murdered, the fool almost blew himself up hundreds of times with all his experiments. What got him in the end, who knows?"

Simon opened his mouth but the general cut him off. "Let a man think," he said. He pulled the ophallagraph of the two men under the umbrella closer to him and studied it. Then he pointed a thick finger at something set into the hills in the distance on the far right-hand side. "That there behind him . . . I wonder if—my eyes are old, tell me what that looks like to you."

"Um," said Simon, squinting. "A blue square—wait, it could be some kind of door—"

"That's what I thought," said the general. "The Little Blue Door."

"What's that?" Maya asked.

General Alvaro rubbed his chin. "People used to say that any question could be answered at the Blue Door. There's supposed to be something hidden behind it, something important, but I don't know what," he said. "It's supposed to be hidden in the middle of nowhere out in the Neglected Provinces. I don't know where, so don't ask me. It's just a story for all I know."

Penny had wandered to the window to look out at the three ostrillos in the pen. Suddenly her eyes grew wide. "Hey, look!" she shouted, pointing furiously. Simon, Maya, and the general looked up. A cloud of dust appeared in the distance, coming fast towards them.

The general lifted a spyglass and trained it on the far hills. "It's the Outsiders," he said. "They have six jeeps, all armed . . . I count at least fifteen men. We're outnumbered. We can't stay here—they'll surround us." He focused the spyglass again. "The Red Man's with them," he said darkly.

"Oh no!" cried Maya. "How did they find us?"

"They mean business," said the general, lowering his binoculars. "Can you shoot?" he asked Simon.

"No," he stammered.

"Hah!" spat the general. He swiped everything off the top of the tack box and flung it open. A breath of the past was exhaled as he took out two ivory pistols wrapped in felt. He tossed one to Simon. "It's a sparkle pistol," he said. "You'll figure it out."

Simon looked at it in horror. He'd never shot a gun before and he didn't want to—not really. What if he actually hit someone?

"The only chance we'll have is to split them up," the general said, glancing back through the window. He turned to Maya. "You and the cadet will take a path up through the hills where they'll lose you quickly. Halfway up is an entrance to a series of tunnels; you can see it from here. Once you enter the tunnels, it's very simple, you bear left at every third fork. It will take you out to the other side of the hills a few miles away. There are farms there. You'll be able to get a ride to Prince's Town, on the coast. It'll be the closest and safest place for the child." He turned to Simon.

"You and I will have to take the open plain to draw them out and give your sisters time to escape. I'll ride directly for the Outsiders, and you'll bear east. Go across the plateau until the Borderlands end and the Neglected Provinces begin—you'll know it when you see it. Stay on the edge of the Neglected Provinces, in the Borderlands, and head north—they won't want to follow you there for long. *Don't go into the Neglected Provinces.* You'll never find your way out again. When you reach the mountains in the north, follow the pass through them, and from there head west along the coast and you'll reach Prince's Town."

"No!" said Maya frantically. "There has to be another way. Simon, I don't want us to separate!"

The general's eyes narrowed as he looked back at the horizon, where the cloud of dust was now much closer, and from which the outlines of the hard metal of the jeeps, bristling with gun racks, were now emerging.

"I promise you that if you don't do what I say, in ten minutes from now you'll wind up prisoners," said General Alvaro.

"Go," said Simon to Maya, squeezing her arm and kissing the top of Penny's head. "I'll meet you in Prince's Town, don't worry."

Everything was happening so fast. The children ran out of the hut after the general, who seconds later had lassoed and bridled an ostrillo. He swung both girls on its back and Maya stopped clinging to its neck long enough to seize the reins that the general passed to her. Penny hung on to Maya for all she was worth. The ostrillo pranced around, jittery, and Maya looked down at Simon, her eyes wide with fear.

"Go!" said Simon, trying to be brave. "You'll be fine!"

Maya wrenched her gaze away from Simon. She looked at the approaching trucks and her eyes grew dark. Anger gave her courage.

"Be careful, Simon!" she called down as she leaned forward and spurred the creature on. The ostrillo sprang up on its powerful legs and then they were racing across the plains toward the tunnels.

Then, to Simon's surprise, instead of bridling another ostrillo, General Alvaro hurried to the well and lowered a long, hooked pole into it. He bent over so far that he half disappeared inside it but a moment later he emerged and withdrew a canvas bag, and from that a thin parcel wrapped in oilpaper. He threw the parcel to Simon. Simon started to look inside, but the general stopped him.

"Later, later!" he cried urgently.

He slipped a bridle on one of the remaining ostrillos and tossed the reins to Simon. Simon swung himself up onto the giant bird's back. The ground seemed very far away. The Red Coral jeeps, however, were already frighteningly close and growing nearer each second.

"Head east!" the general shouted as he vaulted onto his own ostrillo. He took off down the slopes like a wild man. Halfway across the plateau he raised his arm over his head and let out an unholy war cry that sent shivers down Simon's spine. Simon heard a bang and seconds later the air itself seemed rent by a crackling, yellow-white flash. It sounded as if a train of tremendous firecrackers were exploding. Even at that distance Simon was blinded for a moment and he raised an arm to shield his eyes. The general disappeared inside the white blaze and when he appeared again one of the jeeps had been struck and was fishtailing across the hot sand. The general was already fifty yards away, galloping toward the rest of the jeeps. Simon heard the sparkle pistol go off again and the explosion rang out across the packed earth of the plateau.

The jeeps were still coming.

Simon had to escape.

Taking a firm grip of the ostrillo's feathers, Simon turned the creature to face east and urged it on. In seconds it went from a standstill to a sprint, racing as if it was outrunning a storm. Simon held on for dear life.

❧ Chapter Twelve ❧

A Wild Ride ❋ A Third Ophallagraph ❋
The Neglected Provinces ❋ Miraculous Creatures ❋
Saber Teeth and a Sparkle Pistol ❋ Home to Roost ❋
Emerald Oasis ❋ Strange Fruit

When the Red Coral realized that Simon was escaping, a few of the jeeps peeled away from the others and came roaring after him, firing shots in the air. Simon ducked, pressing his cheek into the ostrillo's neck. He expected a jeep to pull alongside him any moment, or to lose his balance and end up facedown in the hot sand, but neither happened. To his surprise the shots grew more distant and when he looked behind him he saw that the jeeps were losing ground, no match for the sand that was growing deeper and softer. The ostrillo, on the other hand, was made for this terrain and covered the ground effortlessly. When Simon next looked over his shoulder the jeeps had shrunk to the size of toys and then they were gone altogether.

Simon had little time to celebrate. The general had been right—Simon knew the Neglected Provinces when he saw them. Up ahead dunes arose suddenly, undulating into the distance like a great yellow sea. A miasma of hazy light— much like the salt spray that mists the air out at sea—hung over them, and even the slight breeze emanating from the east had a different tang, like animal dung and hot sand and scorched leaves.

The general had been adamant that he not enter the Provinces, so Simon steered the ostrillo to remain along the border. When he was confident that the jeeps were long gone he pulled gently on the reins and the ostrillo eased to a walk. Simon flexed his cramped hands and reached down to pat the creature. He hoped that Maya and Penny made it to the entrance to the tunnels—it hadn't been far away and the jeeps had been diverted by him and General Alvaro, just as the general had promised. Still, Simon was nervous and didn't want to think of them alone in some dank, dark maze. Should he go back and try to find them now? He looked over his shoulder. Though he could no longer see them, the Red Coral were still back there. Going back right now would be foolish. He might even lead them straight to the tunnels where Maya and Penny were. No, better to do what General Alvaro had told him. As for the wily general, Simon was sure he had outwitted the Red Coral and escaped easily into the hills.

Suddenly Simon remembered that the general had given him something. Being careful not to lose his balance—even walking the ostrillo was a bumpy ride—he eagerly opened his backpack and unwound the parcel. As he peeled the layers back it began to glow and he looked at it in amazement.

It was another ophallagraph!

The new image proved to be just as much of a puzzle as the first two. It was a close-up of a deep-limbed deciduous tree, its branches laden with radiant globes of fruit that looked like oranges dipped in mercury. A single humming-bird hovered in the air, wings drumming a fast blur, its stemlike beak sipping from one of the round fruits on the right-hand side of the tree. The image was otherwise nondescript. There were no people—no distinguishing characteristics at all, in fact, except for the glowing silver fruit and the hummingbird.

Not much help, thought Simon. *Not yet, anyway.* He turned to the other ophallagraphs, studying them closely. If there was a connection between the three of them he couldn't see it. Disappointed that the new ophallagraph shed no light on the previous two and only deepened their mystery, Simon was about to pack them away and head to Prince's Town when his eye stopped on the image of the two men beneath the umbrella. He had a faint chill, knowing that one of the men had been dead when the picture was taken. Why would someone take a picture of a dead person? His gaze shifted to the blue square in the distance. Was it his imagination, or was it glowing more intensely than it had half an hour ago? It seemed to be changing before his very eyes, as if he were watching something rise from the depths to the surface. And then it was there clearly: built into the rock face, a blue door in the middle of nowhere, the only spot of real color in the whole image. The Little Blue Door, General Alvaro had called it.

Simon thought hard. He was certain that nothing in the ophallagraph was there accidentally. Each object was significant somehow. The door must be important. Were they supposed to find it? Would whatever lay behind it shed light on their mission?

The general had told Simon to stay on the edge of the

Borderlands and ride north until he reached the mountain pass that would take him to the north coast, from where he could head west for Prince's Town to meet his sisters. He had warned Simon *not* to enter the Neglected Provinces, as had Milagros.

But . . . the general had also said that the Little Blue Door was in the Neglected Provinces, and there it was, glowing up at Simon from the ophallagraph, practically begging him to pay attention to it. What if he just went a little way into the Neglected Provinces to look for it? He didn't have to be gone very long. It was possible he was very near it already. He wondered what Maya would say. She would probably tell him he should go straight to Prince's Town. But Maya wasn't there, and this might be the best chance he had to find the Blue Door.

He withdrew his compass and took a bearing east. He would head due east for an hour or two into the Neglected Provinces. Surely during that time he'd find a town, or at least a few huts, and someone who could tell him where the Blue Door was. If not, he could turn around and head back and wouldn't have lost much time at all. He contemplated the sparkle pistol—its ivory handle, the serrated wheel of its cylinder, its gleaming silver barrel—if there was danger, it would keep him safe.

Feeling confident and determined, with a final glance over his shoulder, Simon nudged the ostrillo with his heels and it set off eastward at a run. Soon the mountains, once so towering, were lost to sight. Then something extraordinary happened. The landscape began to change, swinging rapidly from one extreme to another. Simon and the ostrillo would reach the height of a steep sandy slope, the earth lifeless except for a stunted cactus or two, and then from its ridge they would look down into a lush valley where flowers waved, wild-armed trees swished in the warm breeze, and grazing animals teemed. Desert spiders, catching a breeze, spun bubble wings for themselves and drifted iridescent through the air. Brilliant scarlet birds carved arabesques in the salt-bright sky. Creamy-colored camel-like animals with lumpy backs and thick, velvety eyelashes over gentle, cowlike eyes ambled in single file. Fleets of water lizards floated down the current of a stream only inches deep, their heads poking above the surface, the rainbow-colored flags of their tongues flickering. Simon had never seen such creatures before, in life or in books, and he looked about him in wonder.

They would pass through one of these rich, miraculous worlds, then once again there would be nothing but earth baked almost to stone, without leaf or petal, or creature winged or hoofed. Simon wished he could tell his father what he was seeing—Papi would be fascinated by such bizarre microclimates. The ostrillo was far from a smooth ride but Simon got used to it, and the speed and the wind on his face were exhilarating. They came across a herd of fellow ostrillos at one point and ran among them. Simon looked out atop a sea of purple. The creatures' small heads twisted and rolled expressively on their long necks as they turned to stare at the newcomer and her strange passenger. Then, skittishly, threatened by something real or imagined, they sped up and swerved to the left and Simon's ostrillo, carrying his weight, was unable to keep up, and again they were alone.

The scientist in Simon wished there was time to study the animals he was seeing and catalogue all the quirks of nature and environment that had driven their strange evolution. A herd of spotted marsupials, almost impossible to see, moved in shifting camouflage as they chased the shadows of clouds. A small, horselike animal with gigantic ears that swiveled like saucers was the first to hear him coming, and when it took off across the plains its drumming hooves alerted dozens of lumbering, slow-moving tortoises who vanished into their shells, leaving a sudden rock bed. Micelike rodents leaped dozens of feet into a stand of cactus, fleeing from birds that veered away from the unforgiving spikes at the last second. Simon watched in fascination as these dramas unfolded around him.

The sky over the Neglected Provinces was low and vast. In some places it was scorching, and Simon opened the umbrella and rode beneath its shade. In others great cumulous clouds gathered in cool, fresh masses, building and tumbling when they grew too top heavy, marbled slate gray and charcoal and pristine white. It was a relief to ride beneath them and they almost seemed to lay a cooling hand on Simon's forehead. But they never seemed to result in rain, and it wasn't long before Simon regretted not stopping at the single stream he had seen earlier. He rode for another hour till eventually there were no more clouds, only leagues of dazzling sky. He was surprised not to have stumbled upon a town or even a single hut yet. He was growing thirstier and thirstier. He needed to find water soon.

The plants began to peter out and, with them, most of the animals. Simon and the ostrillo headed into an ever drier and more barren landscape where the wind whistled hollowly over shifting banks of yellow sand. What had turned the Neglected Provinces into a desert when the rest of Tamarind was lush jungle? There was evidence it had not always been this way: petrified trees thrust up from the dunes, a gnarled branch here, a twisted trunk there, and occasionally the sand turned up fossils that the ostrillo trod upon.

There were more recent signs of civilization, too: Every now and then Simon would come across the crumbling ruins of abandoned stone cottages. Whatever wood had been there had been digested by termites long ago. Creeper vines had nosed their way through cracks in the stone, driving larger wedges that over time had caused slabs to tumble down onto the earth. Some of the cottages smelled from the waste of animals that had sheltered there. Others were roofless and open to the sun and to winds that had scoured them clean. Why had they been abandoned? Mute and forlorn, they could tell him no stories. The elements were erasing them a little more with each passing day; at some point they would cease to be, and there would be no more record of their existence.

Simon began to question if it had been wise to come into the Neglected Provinces after all. He was sure he would have seen someone by now. The ostrillo was getting tired and had slowed to a lumbering walk. Finally Simon pulled gently on the reins and it halted. He was disappointed, but without knowing which direction to go in, it seemed foolhardy to continue. Reluctantly he decided to head back. The Red Coral men would be gone by now and he could catch up with his sisters. He took out his compass. He waited for the arrow to settle, but it kept circling. He tapped it lightly. He tried turning it over. He rapped it hard with his knuckles. But it was no use. The arrow just kept spinning in a slow, mindless drift. It didn't work out here. In spite of the heat, the sweat on Simon's skin suddenly felt cold.

Deep in thought about his predicament, he didn't notice the figure shadowing them, head dropped, muscular shoulders braced, paws treading silently in the sand. It was downwind so the ostrillo was oblivious, too. Then, from the corner of Simon's eye, he saw a sand-colored streak tearing out from behind a rocky outcrop—a huge yellow cat with great saber teeth! Instantly the ostrillo bolted. Simon hung on for dear life as the animal ran like the wind. Sheer will and terror kept Simon from falling. The landscape melted in a blur around him. After a few minutes the ostrillo suddenly slowed. Hopeful that this meant they had shaken off their pursuer, Simon looked over his shoulder and as he did, the ostrillo jerked to the right, throwing him. Simon sailed through the air and landed with a thud in the sand. He scrambled to his feet but he was too late. He watched in dismay as the creature ran off. He heard paws thundering on the earth behind him and turned in time to see the cat bearing down on him.

It screamed—an awful, tearing sound—its thick, yellow

tail whipping stiffly behind it as it sprang. In terror Simon reached for the sparkle pistol. The creature was only feet away and Simon could smell its foul breath. Hands shaking wildly, he pulled the trigger. White light exploded and he was lost in the blinding glare. It felt as if lightning had struck just feet away from him. He pulled the trigger again and again and the recoil threw him back.

As the glittering light faded around him he found himself lying on the hot sand, quaking but alive. He had not been mauled. His blood wasn't soaking the sand and his limbs were all still intact. He clambered to his feet and saw that the cat, terrified by the explosion, was running away in a fast lope across the plains. Simon watched him go, but it took a while before the shaking stopped. He had had a terrible fright. He looked down at the sparkle pistol. It had saved him. With no one to see him, Simon took a shivery breath and brushed a tear from his cheek. He realized the pistol was out of bullets. He looked at it a last time and put it in his backpack. Now he had nothing to protect him. Rubbing his bruised ribs, he gazed out at the desolate landscape. The ostrillo was gone from sight—losing it was the worst thing that could have happened. He was alone. Very alone.

He had no idea which direction he should go to get back to Hetty's Pass, or on to Prince's Town. Between the mad dash on the ostrillo and the ever-changing landscape, he was hopelessly lost. There was no turning back now.

Shading his eyes with a shaky hand, he tried to take his bearings from the sun. He decided to walk north—or where he thought north was, anyway—in the hope that eventually he would reach the coast. *You'll be fine*, he reassured himself. He wished it was easier to believe.

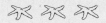

Simon had been walking for a long time without coming upon any signs of civilization and he was growing more and more worried. The day had moved on and before long the sun would set. He realized he would probably be spending the night in the desert.

Then he saw a single brilliant red bird, stiff as an arrow, flying purposefully overhead. His heart leaped. It was the first trace of life he had seen in hours. Wildly, he hoped it might be a sign from Milagros. At the very least he knew that birds headed home to roost in the evening—maybe it would lead him to shelter. Spirit buoyed, Simon followed the direction the bird was heading in. Before long a slender-necked pink bird flew overhead, and shortly after it a pair of plump, spotted birds that cooed as they passed him. Simon's mouth was dry and pasty and his stomach grumbled, but he marched doggedly on and eventually he saw a green blur floating on the horizon.

He squinted. Was it a mirage? But as he got closer he knew that his eyes weren't deceiving him. A tiny island of jungle—an oasis—stood in the middle of the hot, lifeless sand. It was no Blue Door, but all the greenery meant there must be water, and maybe food, too. This was where the birds had been heading.

A spring in his step, Simon hurried on, and soon he

entered the cool green fringes. Suddenly he was in another world altogether. The air was soft and moist. Vibrating clouds of hummingbirds floated through the crooked paths between trees. "Hello," said Simon softly but there was no one there to answer. Deep pools of fresh water stood here and there and he immediately dropped to his knees and drank deeply—the water was clean and cold. Finally he stood up, wiping his mouth. He felt refreshed and the grassy taste of the water tingled in his mouth. He looked all around him.

It seemed that the plants of the oasis were somehow immune to the searing heat and piercing glare of the sun that baked the earth just footsteps away. The trees looked primordial. Crimson pods dangled from branches. Plush mushrooms grew in moist cups of soil in hollows of branches. Sumptuous emerald moss flowed in luxurious waves from the branches. The air smelled like freshwater and ripe fruits. A fuzz of insects furred the air. Apricot-colored flowers bloomed in the lower branches. Famished, Simon tried to pick a fruit that looked like an orange from a big tree in the middle of the oasis but it was puzzlingly hard—like a stone on the end of the branch—so he left it and moved on to the next tree, where he found a sweet green fruit that he reached up and knocked free. Hungrily, he devoured several in a row. He found bananas and nuts, too. Finally sated, he wandered on.

The oasis looked almost aquatic, like something that would have appeared under the sea. The plants growing from the crannies of the trunks and the crooks of the branches looked like broad sea fans, pink coral, supple anemones. The

187

air itself seemed murky and green, as if algae were growing in the microscopic droplets of humidity suspended in the atmosphere. Creatures that looked like starfish were suctioned onto tree trunks. Orange-and-blue-striped slugs as big as sea cucumbers journeyed down the branches. Simon could hear them chomping through the moist green forest with their miniature jaws. Long-legged birds had snowy caps of hair that drifted over their eyes with the dreamy sway of anemones caught in a current, hiding their expressions.

For what environment had these strange creatures been made? His father would know, but Simon could discern no rhyme or reason in the long, triple-jointed legs of the fluffy-headed birds or the almost perfectly spherical shapes of the pair of spotted birds he had seen flying in, who were now perched together on a branch peering at him curiously. But the little world was peaceful and safe. When he had entered the light had been fading. Soon it would be dark.

"I'm going to sleep here tonight, birds, frogs, bugs, whoever else is here," he said softly. "Hope you don't mind." It was comforting to hear a human voice, even if it was his own. Simon thought about his sisters and was glad they at least were together. He hoped powerfully that they were already through the tunnels and safely in Prince's Town.

Simon was looking for a place to settle when he noticed that something had begun to happen. The striped slugs were all creeping down the branches and trunks to join a colorful carpet that crept across the oasis floor. They were heading on all sides toward the deep pools of water! As Simon watched, they paused for a moment at the water's edge before launching themselves in. Each was a tiny, vibrant raft that floated for a moment on the surface of the water before sinking toward the bottom of the pond. Other insects followed suit. Ants, beetles, brassy-winged dragonflies, apple green caterpillars—a whole diminutive army—hurled themselves into the pond. Simon tried to peer down into the water, but in the dimming light he could see only a few inches below the surface. Other animals crept into deep hollows inside the trees. Birds took flight, wings thumping as they headed out of the oasis. Only the woolly-headed birds remained. With their mechanical-looking legs, they levered themselves into the water, taking big steps down the rocky sides until they were submerged except for their beaks.

"That's so weird," muttered Simon. "What are you guys doing?"

The oasis, emptied of its inhabitants, was almost completely dark now and Simon was tired. He settled down in a hollow between two tree roots and laid his head on a pillow of moss. Weary to the bone, he drifted right to sleep.

He was awakened by a powerful strobe of light shooting through a gap in the treetops above him. He didn't feel that he had been sleeping for very long, but night had fallen and outside the strobe of light it was dark. He recognized the scent of burning. Something was being singed. The light seemed to be growing brighter and coming from more directions—Simon realized that where earlier there had been moss overhead, now there was none, and the moonlight was pouring down to the forest floor. It was like being inside a giant, brilliant diamond. The silhouettes of trees sharpened.

The burning smell grew stronger. Simon was wide awake now, crouching and looking all around him. The temperature had dropped and he found he was shivering. What was going on? Then he realized that the moonlight was scorching the moss. Huge, shorn flanks of it dropped to the forest floor, burned to a crisp, and crumbling to ash before his eyes. Leaves and fruit came tumbling down after it. The moonlight was devouring the forest! In a few moments it was over, and there was nothing left, just great, smooth-limbed trees, castle-shaped, the wood smooth and polished. Nothing alive remained. The cold, pocked face of the moon looked very close and a wind breathed through the oasis.

Then something caught Simon's eye. Round lights glowed up ahead, bobbing gently in the breeze. The wind subsided and the lights grew still. Simon got to his feet and approached cautiously. Clouds slid over the moon and the only light came from the lights in the forest ahead of him. Simon followed them through the trees, disappearing and reappearing every now and then. He pushed a final branch aside and, hardly daring to breathe, stopped before the great tree that stood in the center of the oasis, the one he had tried to pick the orange fruit from earlier.

Except that now the orange fruit had turned silver.

A tremor passed through Simon.

It was the tree from the third ophallagraph.

Globes of glowing fruit hung lanternlike from the boughs. Simon reached up to touch one of them. It was the size of a grapefruit. It was harder than any citrus and didn't yield beneath his touch. It was neither hot nor cold. These were what had been glowing so distinctly in the ophalla-graph. *What were they?* Simon wondered. *What were they for?* And what was he supposed to do with them? He reached up with both hands and plucked one of the mysterious spheres. It popped free and the branch bounced back and the other lights nodded and swayed. He lifted it to his nose but it was scentless. Whatever secret it contained was locked safely within. But it was important somehow, Simon was sure of it, so working quickly in the eerie half forest, he filled his back-pack with the strange fruit.

❧ CHAPTER THIRTEEN ❧

A Breakthrough ✸ Alone for the First Time ✸
Thirstier and Thirstier ✸ Pillars of
Unnatural Light ✸ The Little Blue Door

Simon woke to the sound of creeping over leaves and opened his eyes to a colorful parade of newborn slugs flowing out of the deep pools. The stilt-legged birds walked around the shallows, their long necks curved, feasting on the unlucky ones that did not make it out in time, but such a horde kept coming that hundreds still escaped. A lime green fuzz of moss was sprouting from the smooth bark of the trees. Bright-colored mushrooms grew before Simon's eyes and the plants that looked like sea fans sprang once again from the crannies. The previous night seemed almost like a dream. Simon opened his backpack and took out one of the weird fruits to see it in the light of day. Its silver sheen had dulled, but otherwise it had not changed from the night before. He returned it to his bag. He refilled his canteen from one of the pools, but all the fruit had been burned off the trees so his stomach went empty.

He figured out his bearings as best he could and set out. When he had been walking for half an hour he stopped and looked over his shoulder to see that the oasis had sprung back to life. A verdant green mist seemed to hover on the

192

plain and as he watched, it expanded like a cloud—a cool breath of life on the barren yellow sands. The next time he glanced over his shoulder it was gone from sight and the hot, sandy void spread all around him.

Simon had expected to come across people before now, but he hadn't seen a soul. Even the Red Coral Project had not infiltrated this deeply into the island. It seemed that no one at all was there. It struck him that this might be the first time he had ever been alone, completely, entirely alone, in his whole life. He realized that he had rarely ever been without Maya. Growing up on the boat together they had always been a team. When they had been to Tamarind the first time, Simon had been only nine years old. He had been frightened at times—many times, in fact. But Maya had been in charge, really. Even after they moved in with Granny Pearl and they had been separated in school, she was never farther away than a few classroom doors. As much as she infuriated him sometimes, underneath everything he knew that she was one of the few people who really loved and understood him— look at everything they had been through together. Now he was on his own and lost. Not only that, but he had the ophallagraphs and he was responsible for figuring them out and for getting them all home safely.

Simon thought about his friends at the boatyard at home and the boat they had spent months working on. It had taken up so much of his thoughts back then, but it seemed like such a simple problem now: put this there, move that there, connect these two things, add a third, and there you had it—a working engine. Simple, easy, satisfying.

A flash of anger seized him. If his parents had done something about the Red Coral they wouldn't be in this mess. It was their father's job to keep them safe—it was *his* fault they were here like this! Guilt swiftly quenched Simon's anger. Whatever the Red Coral had been doing to his parents, it had been bad. It wasn't fair to blame Papi.

Long ago, in that magical time when they had lived on the *Pamela Jane* and sailed the sea, Simon had trusted his father with all of his being. Whether they were caught in a thunderstorm or stranded in the doldrums, or the fog was so thick that they couldn't see beyond the deck of the *Pamela Jane,* Simon never felt afraid because his father was there, and he would keep them safe. He wished it were still like that now.

Just then a violent rainstorm began out of nowhere. The drops fell so hard they left welts on Simon's arms. He had been walking past a group of abandoned cottages, the type he had come across from time to time earlier in the Neglected Provinces, and he ran toward one for shelter. He dashed through an open doorway and crouched in a corner under a bit of roof that was still intact. He began to put the umbrella up to shelter him more, but quickly realized that it could be put to better use catching rainwater, so he turned it upside down and gleefully watched as a pool of water began to form in it. He kneeled down and guzzled it noisily then, thirst quenched, sat back with a sigh. But he'd had no food since the night before and he was hungry. His stomach grumbled.

He took out the ophallagraphs but they didn't make any sense. Suddenly he felt frustrated. They were too hard—he was never going to figure them out! They were just meaningless fragments. In the beginning it had been easy to be optimistic—the discovery of each new image brought the hope that the pieces would suddenly fall into place, but Simon was starting to wonder if that was ever going to happen.

He took a deep breath. *What do you do when you're stuck?* he asked himself. *You remain calm and approach the problem from a different angle,* he heard his father say, as he had heard him say so many times before.

But still nothing made sense.

The rain stopped as suddenly as it had begun. Simon poured the rainwater caught in the umbrella into his canteen, careful not to spill a drop. He was putting on his backpack when he looked up through the window and saw something startling. He ducked quickly and peered over the edge of the windowsill. The thick gray rain clouds were being sucked at high speed over the horizon. Simon had never seen anything like it before. In seconds the clouds were gone altogether and the sky was blisteringly blue once again, mirrored in the deep puddles that stretched across the landscape, each holding a single blinding reflection of the sun. It was going to be a sloppy walk now, through all that dazzling water. He was about to set out when suddenly he heard the sound that fat makes when it strikes a hot griddle. He looked up to see steam rising from the puddles!

The air quickly grew too thick with steam to see more than a few feet in front of him. A minute later it cleared and the landscape was revealed once again—dry and cracked, the earth baked. All that was different was that the scrawny cacti were now plump and green and brilliant red flowers bloomed from them.

Simon wished that Maya and Penny were there to witness the strange sight.

The abandoned cottages were unpleasantly forlorn and the sight he had just witnessed had unnerved him a little, so Simon was happy to be on his way. As he left the ruined cottage he suddenly had the sensation of déjà vu. He turned and looked behind him at the cottages. They looked familiar. Suddenly he was afraid that he had been there earlier and was walking in circles.

He looked again.

Three cottages. Sitting at angles to one another. Suddenly Simon's heart began to beat faster. There was no palm tree but he looked for a stump. He saw it.

He hadn't been past these cottages already, but he *had* seen them somewhere before!

He slung his backpack onto the ground and opened it quickly. He took out the ophallagraph that he was looking for, hands itching with excitement. It glowed brightly, even in the sunlight.

He held it up to the scene before him.

He broke into a big smile. *The two scenes matched up.*

The two men under the umbrella, standing roughly where he stood.

The three cottages, all in the same place, though in the ophallagraph the cottages had thatched roofs and freshly painted doors and windows. Flowers bloomed from the windowsills and vegetable gardens were planted high to stock the kitchens. A tall palm by the right-most hut shimmered in the sunlight. Now the buildings were just empty shells. Roofs, doors, and windows were gone. The only sign of life was a stand of cacti that encroached, hemming in the farthest cottage with vicious spikes. All that remained of the palm tree was a petrified stump.

Simon looked at the ruins triumphantly. He found the Blue Door in the ophallagraph, oriented himself, and looked up to see where it should be in real life. He looked out on to miles of flat, baked earth stretching to the horizon. There was no Blue Door in sight. Holding his breath, he narrowed his eyes and searched the horizon. He saw a low cluster of rocks resting very far away on the horizon. Could the Blue Door be there, in those rocks?

Simon's initial excitement gave way to frustration. The rocks were so far away! He flexed his ragged toes, wincing, and gently touched the sunburn on his forehead. But there was nothing to do but start walking, so he set off toward the outcrop of rocks in the distance. He was tired, blistered, and hungry, and each step was more of an effort than it had been the day before, but he pressed gamely on. He was right to have come into the Neglected Provinces.

The Blue Door was out there and he was going to find it.

As the day wore on, the sun beat down mercilessly and Simon walked beneath the umbrella to give himself some relief. All the big animals were gone but he had seen lizards and insects from time to time, then eventually even they petered out. He longed to see a single blade of green, but instead he walked across graveyards of giant bones, picked clean by carrion birds, hearing them snap beneath his feet. They rattled horribly as a wind picked up. The canteen was bone-dry now. And that was just water—he hadn't eaten anything in almost a full day. His mouth was parched and his lips cracked. His eyes felt like sandpaper. There was no moisture sufficient to form the tiniest puff of a cloud. His feet were swollen and grains of sand chafed the sores on his heels. Everything he knew seemed terribly far away. For a while he had been able to look back and see the tiny dot of the three ruined cottages behind him. When they finally slipped from view he felt even more alone.

He wondered how such a bare, empty place could exist in Tamarind. He half wished that the Red Coral would appear and find him. He would have felt relief to see one of their jeeps driving across the sands to pick him up, would have waved them down with all his might. He didn't care what they did with him afterward. But even the Red Coral Project hadn't penetrated this place.

Hunger and thirst made his mind fuzzy and he couldn't stop the drift of his thoughts. Sometimes he hallucinated. He saw his father, sitting at his desk, turning the radio dial restlessly, his face growing sallow, his brows sternly knitted.

A memory from long ago kept returning to him: sailing

on the *Pamela Jane*, on an evening watch with his father. His mother and sisters were in the cabin, and it was just Simon and his dad. Papi had been explaining how the sonar of dolphins and whales worked, allowing them to "see" with sound, even in complete darkness or through the sediment. Some species could even focus the sound into a blast to stun prey. Simon could hear the deliberate way his father spoke when he was explaining something, how he could make even the most difficult and complex ideas come alive. Simon had been fascinated that day, had sat there imagining great whales beneath the boat as his father spoke. The evening sun gilded the ridges of the waves, catching the metal on the *Pamela Jane*. A warm breeze flowed over them and below in the water ran the shadows of albacore tuna, and down far, far below these schools, the promise of a plenitude of miraculous and wondrous deep-sea animals so impossible looking that they seemed creatures only of invention. There were hundreds of days like these. Simon's memory was like a tide pool abundant with all sorts of life; he had only to dip his hand in it to draw up some rich remembrance.

Simon missed his dad.

He would have given anything to see Papi coming to find him.

There was something else that Simon's thoughts kept returning to. He knew in his heart that he had fled home rashly. Sure, he'd had a good reason—Tamarind needed help, and obviously their parents were in some sort of trouble because of the Red Coral Project. Only he had not left just to stop the

Red Coral Project, but to prove himself—to show his parents that he wasn't a kid who needed to be kept in the dark about everything, to prove to them that he *could* help. He was bored with life on land and angry that his father had changed so much, and he wanted to show him that. He, Simon, the most logical of thinkers, the scientist who weighed things impartially, who had been gifted with a rational problem-solving brain, had made an emotional decision. He had been able to argue it rationally to Maya and convince her—that was what he was good at. But deep down Simon knew why he had wanted to come back to Tamarind. And now he had put his sisters in danger, too. His heart was heavy.

All afternoon the hot, dry wind whipped up sandstorms that stung Simon's arms and legs. He had to huddle beneath the umbrella and breathe through his shirt held over his mouth. When one storm passed the dunes had moved, the landscape reshaped and reshuffled, so that everything looked alien to him all over again. And then the wind returned, tunneling over the earth and howling in his ears and blasting grains of sand into his eyes. The suspended sand made an orange haze to the horizon, so thick that Simon could no longer see if he was still heading toward the outcrop of rocks where he hoped to find the Little Blue Door.

He'd had nothing to drink since a mangy, shriveled cactus he had found that afternoon, whose juices had been sour, and he was desperately thirsty. He had tried to see if there was juice in the strange silver oranges from the oasis, but they were so hard they only bent his pocketknife when he tried to pierce them. They were heavy and he considered abandoning them but couldn't bring himself to—it would have meant there was no reason at all to have come here. Often he had to stop walking and rest beneath the umbrella, too exhausted to take another step. But then he would force himself back to his feet to shuffle forward, the hot sand pouring into his tattered shoes.

That night the wind died down and the sand settled. Simon took the ophallagraphs out and they lit a small circle of light. He did not fear the light attracting the notice of wild creatures because he knew he was utterly alone. The last living thing he had seen was a lizard with a prehistoric ruff and little jewel eye that morning, and even that seemed like a lifetime ago. He sat before the images as if they were a fire, but their warmth was false, and he shivered as the temperature plummeted. He fell asleep, and awoke once in the night to find that the ophallagraphs had grown brighter, shooting a beacon straight up into the sky for anyone who might be out there to see, though Simon had given up hope of any other humans finding him.

He saw other pillars of unnatural light, great white beams ascending the sky in the distance. Afraid he was hallucinating, he opened the umbrella and hid beneath it and tried to sleep. Lying there, he thought he could feel vibrations emanating from deep within the earth. He closed his eyes tightly and wished for morning.

✳ ✳ ✳

Morning. Still no water. Simon's head pounded. Every fiber of his body felt pain.

Daylight had swallowed the strange beams of light from across the desert and Simon wondered if they had just been a dream. Thoughts roved loose in his mind. He had stopped sweating altogether. It was a bad sign, he knew. In spite of the searing heat, his body felt cold. He coughed a rattling cough—the dust had scoured his throat and his voice was almost gone. His vision was blurred and sometimes things appeared double before him. But the sandstorms were over and he found himself not too far away from a long outcrop of rocks. He stumbled to his feet and trudged on, and some time later he walked into a strange new landscape of chimney-shaped formations sticking out of the earth. They had been created long, long ago by winds and water—back when there had been water in this forsaken place—and now they stood there, forlorn remnants of some long-ago age. Simon wandered delirious among them.

And then . . .

Something caught his eye.

A square of blue, there in the rocks.

Yes, it was—he was sure it was . . .

Or were his eyes deceiving him?

Simon began to stumble weakly down the steep rocks of a gulley and back up the other side to where a small blue door was built into the side of a great column of rock. He reached the door and fell against it—it wasn't a mirage. It was solid and real. The mysterious Little Blue Door in the middle of nowhere—he had found it! He could be close now—very close—to solving a big part of the mystery.

Strength he didn't know he had left flooded him. He tried to turn the handle eagerly but found it locked.

He knocked and waited hopefully, but when there was no response—not even the shuffle of footsteps or the murmur of a voice from within—he pounded it weakly with the heel of his hand. Nothing. He felt all the way around it carefully to see if there was a hidden catch, but his hands met nothing. With a growing sinking feeling, he threw his shoulder into it. If all else failed, perhaps brute strength would work. But the door failed to budge.

"Hello!" he shouted as loudly as he could. "Hello!" But his throat was so dry that he could do little more than bleat hoarsely. His voice echoed off the desert walls and gorges and came back to him, hollow and alone.

Simon grabbed on to the handle with both hands and braced his foot against the wall and, mustering all his remaining strength, yanked it. The door flew open and Simon tumbled back. Dazed, he leaned on one elbow and looked up. The door had opened not into a room, but on to solid rock. There was nothing behind it, only stone. Dizzy, he laid his head on the earth. He had come so far for this—for nothing—a false door that opened on to the rock in a forgotten place in the middle of nowhere. If his body hadn't been so parched he would have wept.

The adventure had gone too far. *I'm sorry, Mami, Papi*, he thought. *Maya, Penny, Granny Pearl*. He closed his eyes but the world still spun in the dark. He wanted nothing more in that moment but for it to stop.

At first he confused the echoing under the earth with the thunder of his pulse pounding in his ears. But then a deep rumbling began, coming from the rock behind the Blue Door. As he tried to sit up he heard the grinding crunch of heavy stone, and the last thing he remembered was being blasted by a blaze of dazzling, unnatural light.

❧ Chapter Fourteen ❧

The Mole Monks ❖ *An Ancient Library* ❖ *Triptych*

Simon opened his eyes to find that the brightness of the sun had been snuffed out and a strange new radiance was pouring over him. Dimly he remembered seeing a rock being rolled back from the Blue Door, and the sensation of being lifted and carried.

"Shh, he's waking up," said a voice floating somewhere above his head. The voice sounded as if it were trapped in a bubble bumping gently back and forth between the walls.

"It *was* the Little Blue Door!" Simon mumbled, struggling to sit up. "I went the right way." He leaned back on one elbow, feeling some satisfaction through the fog of hunger and weariness.

As his eyes adjusted, he saw three men looking down at him with nervous concern. They weren't ordinary people, he realized at once. Their eyes were very large, their ears small and nubby, and brown robes hid their pale skin. Fine, downy whiskers grew on their ageless faces, even on their cheeks and foreheads, giving them a faint silvery sheen. Simon realized that whatever he had said was the wrong thing. The men's concern had deepened to worry. One looked downright frightened.

"See—he *was* looking for us," hissed the nervous-looking one. He appeared unpredictable, like a cornered dog. "We should put him back out, before he wakes up more."

"He's here now," said another of the men calmly. He had a broad, kind face. "I won't send him back out to die. Let's wait a while. We may learn something from him."

"It's a bad idea, Eusebio," said the nervous one through clenched teeth. "I'm telling you . . . he's with them, I know he is—"

"That's enough," said the broad-faced man. "He's only young. And he's here now."

There was murmuring back and forth for a moment. Simon struggled to speak. He knew it was very important to tell them why he was there, but his mouth wouldn't obey him and he couldn't find the words. He was too exhausted. Then the broad-faced man said, "Oh, all right, Nicodemus, just for now . . ." Simon saw a rag being lowered to his face. He fought as he felt his nose and mouth being covered, but sweetish fumes burned his throat and suddenly he felt all his energy draining away and he was powerless to stop himself from sinking back into darkness.

When Simon woke again he realized he had been moved. He blinked, getting his bearings. First, he was alive. Second, he was lying on a rough blanket in some type of glowing sub-terranean chamber. Mud had been daubed on the round walls to dim the brightness of the rock. He became aware of throbbing in his feet. Moving only his eyes—if anyone was there he didn't want them to know he was awake yet—he looked down to see they had been salved and bandaged. Past his feet, a round doorway opened onto a long tunnel. A bluish glow came from his right, and Simon turned his head slightly to see the broad-faced man sitting at a table several feet away. The glowing was coming from something he was looking at on the table. The other two men weren't there. To Simon's dismay, he saw the man lift the ophallagraph of the *Pamela Jane* and hold it up to study. They had gone through his backpack while he slept! Simon tried to take a deep breath, but he wheezed and the man looked over and saw that he was awake.

"Here," he said, bringing him a clay mug of water.

Simon sat up. After the first sip, he began to guzzle it.

"Not too much at once," said the man, taking the mug away. "We don't know how long you've been dehydrated. You can have a little more in a minute."

The water had revived Simon and as he began to feel less groggy, fear set in. He had no idea where he was.

"You've been asleep for a whole surface day," said the man. "Not that we really know night and day down here."

"Where am I?" Simon croaked.

"On the other side of the Blue Door," said the man, handing the water back to Simon. "My name is Eusebio," he went on. "We wouldn't usually be so inhospitable, but you see, the Outsiders are nearby and we thought that you must have wandered off from their group. I apologize about the chormetten that put you to sleep. My brother Nicodemus doesn't believe in taking any chances."

"I'm not with the other Outsiders," said Simon, clearing his throat. He drank slowly.

"We've realized that," said Eusebio. "There are portholes—air vents, really—that open here and there in the desert floor. They're our eyes and ears down here. And yesterday we became aware that someone was lost in the Provinces. We were trying to figure out what to do about you when, to our surprise, you came straight to us."

Simon recalled the massive towers of light he had seen in the distance the previous night and realized he must have been seeing the glow of ophalla through the vents.

"I thought there was nothing out there," he said. "I thought I was alone."

"That's only how it looked," said Eusebio, smiling. "We planned to carry you through the tunnels and release you somewhere closer to civilization, but then we saw these—" He nodded at the glowing ophallagraphs. "Please pardon us for going through your things; you realize we had to."

Just then one of the other men Simon had seen earlier appeared in the doorway.

"Frascuelo, our visitor is awake," said Eusebio. "Would you get some food for him?" It was the second man, not the nervous one, but the one with the long face. He nodded to Simon and hurried off.

Simon realized he hadn't introduced himself. "I'm Simon," he said. "Simon Nelson." The fog in his head was clearing and he looked around. "What is this place?" he asked. "Why are you here?"

"We belong to an ancient Order, the Underground

Monks," said Eusebio. "Tamarinders call us Mole Monks. Any that still remember us, that is."

Underground Monks? Simon took another sip of water, wondering if he was still dreaming. Frascuelo returned with a bowl of soup, which he gave to Simon, then left. Simon devoured it hungrily. It was made of boiled cactus and herbs and he felt his strength returning.

"As for what this place is," Eusebio went on, "it's an underground library for the ancient books of Tamarind. Long ago, during a period of turmoil, our ancestors went deep into the earth to preserve a record of Tamarind's history, her myths and lore. An order of us has lived here ever since. We make sure the records are safe and the story of Tamarind survives. You can think of us as librarians."

Eusebio looked both plump and wizened, with exceptionally large eyes in a surprisingly shriveled face.

"How long have you been here?" Simon asked.

"I was born above and I came to study here in the archives when I was twenty," said Eusebio. "That was ninety years ago. Frascuelo is one hundred and five. Nicodemus is one hundred. Mole Monks live to be older than most because we live surrounded by ophalla." He tapped the ice white wall.

Simon finished his soup. He shifted, knocking his blistered heel on the ground, which reminded him of the harsh terrain he had come from.

Eusebio looked at Simon's feet. "Can you walk?" he asked.

"I think so," said Simon, standing up. Whatever the

monks had put on his feet was healing them quickly, but they still hurt.

"Good," said Eusebio, tucking the ophallagraph under his arm. "Because from what we've been able to tell, you don't have much time. Come with me. We'll join Nicodemus and Frascuelo in the library. It's a rather interesting triptych you have."

"A what?" asked Simon, starting to follow Eusebio.

"A triptych," Eusebio repeated over his shoulder. "This is quite a significant quest you're on."

"You mean the ophallagraphs?" Simon asked. "I don't really know what they mean, or what I'm supposed to do with them . . ." he said, hurrying to keep up with Eusebio.

"I didn't expect that you did," said Eusebio, going through the doorway into a long bright tunnel. "Otherwise you wouldn't have come here. Don't worry, they weren't meant to be decoded easily. We'll help you if we can. Come on."

Simon followed Eusebio through a labyrinth of tunnels cut out of the bedrock of ophalla. The cave had no need of gas lamps or sulfur lights—ophalla provided all the illumination they could need. At times it would begin to glow an aqueous blue-green and Simon felt as if he were underwater in a sea lit from the surface by the sun. As in the room where he'd awoken, the walls of some rooms they passed were painted with mud to allow respite from the perpetual glare. Every now and then they walked beneath vents to the surface and Simon smelled fresh air. Simon heard muffled mechanical banging sounds somewhere far ahead in the tunnels.

"The Red Coral are just beyond where we are," said Eusebio. "This is one of the few veins of ophalla remaining in the Neglected Provinces—they found it with their machines."

Simon felt instantly afraid. He was too weak to run from the Red Coral now.

"Can they get in here?" he asked.

"No," said Eusbio. "Not yet, anyway. There's a natural split in the vein that creates a barrier between where we are and where they are. They're getting to the end of that part of the vein now. We are much deeper underground—too deep for even their machines to detect. We know they're planning to move on to a new mine site very soon—a much bigger site, with far more frightening consequences for Tamarind."

Simon had no time to ask further questions because at that moment they turned a corner and entered the biggest and most marvelous library he had ever seen. Shelves carved out of gleaming ophalla stretched all the way across the cavernous room, where they disappeared in a luminous white blur. They were lined with thousands of books. The glow from the ophalla illuminated the titles on the spines: *Ophalla: Secrets of the Stone; Lore of the Lesser Islands; Book of Magic Vegetables; The Story of the Lost Islands of Tamarind: An Outsider's Account; Official Record of Dark Women; The Great Age of Ophalla;* they went on and on. Hope tingled all the way down to Simon's blistered toes: what better place was there to come to for answers than a library with three scholarly librarians on hand to help him.

He beamed at the other two Mole Monks, who were

sitting at a long table. Each had one of the remaining oph-allagraphs beside him and was poring over several huge open books. Simon also saw his backpack with the umbrella and mineral-fruits beside it.

"Nicodemus, Frascuelo, this is Simon Nelson," said Eusebio.

"Thank you for helping me," said Simon. "You saved my life."

"No time to waste thanking us," admonished Nicodemus, the nervous-looking one. "We've studied this triptych and we believe your quest is a critical one for Tamarind. We have to work quickly—what was hidden must be found before it's too late!"

"I'm afraid I don't know what a triptych is . . ." said Simon.

Nicodemus looked exasperated, his thin face twitching.

"Simon, please sit down," said Eusebio calmly. "Brothers, I think we should start by explaining to our young visitor what a triptych is."

Simon sat on a rough-hewn bench at the table. Eusebio settled across from him.

"Of course, of course," said Frascuelo. "You see, Simon, since ancient times, triptychs have been used as a device to hide important secrets in Tamarind. A triptych is comprised of three different images."

"Three!" cried Simon. "Does that mean I have them all?"

"Yes," said Frascuelo. "But don't get too excited yet—we have all the images, but now we have to interpret them."

"Oh," said Simon, feeling silly. Of course it wasn't going to be that easy.

"Usually triptychs are painted or drawn," Frascuelo continued. "But this one—it's clever, we've never seen anything like it before. The images seem to be doctored photographs enhanced with ophalla. We suspect it's the work of an inventor named Davies Maroner."

"That's right," said Simon. "He's the one who made them."

"Now," said Frascuelo. "The images are often made up of parts of many different pictures put together. Meaning is concealed in the details. Each detail has significance."

"Each and every detail!" interjected Nicodemus. "You can't miss a single one!"

"Nicodemus is right," said Frascuelo. "All the details are important. What you're looking for are tools—there are always three tools hidden somewhere in a triptych. Now, we think that you have two of them already—the mineral-fruits and the umbrella—which we found in your bag and identified in the ophallagraphs. We haven't yet found the third."

"What about our boat, the *Pamela Jane*?" asked Simon, pointing to it in the ophallagraph. A froth of light broke around her hull. "Could she be the third tool? We know that she has ophalla in her frame that enables her to cross the Blue Line. That's how we were able to sail here."

"We think the *Pamela Jane* is important," said Frascuelo. "And that she's the one that must be chosen for a journey. But a tool will be smaller, something that you can hold and use."

"But let's start at the beginning, shall we?" said Euse-bio. "You're searching for Faustina's Gate."

"Yes," said Simon curiously. "But how did you know?"

"Symbol interpretation," said Eusebio. He held out the ophallagraph of the tree. "You see this here," he said, "carved into the trunk, right near the bottom?"

Simon squinted, for the first time seeing the funny squiggle that he had mistaken for a knot in the trunk.

"It's an old symbol for Faustina's Gate, inscribed in a square," said Eusebio. "There are others marked in the other two ophallagraphs, which show that they're a set—see, here's one on the hull of one of the boats. And here's another—you can only see it with a magnifying glass—on the door of one of the cottages."

"Hey, cool," said Simon, "I never noticed them before. How did you know it was the symbol for Faustina's Gate?"

"I had to look it up in the *Encyclopedia of Symbols* to be sure," said Eusebio, nodding to the book on the table next to him. "Don't worry that you didn't see it yourself—unless you know the encyclopedia by heart, you wouldn't have much chance."

"What *is* Faustina's Gate?" asked Simon. "I still don't understand how it can be so important."

Eusebio thought for a moment and the ophalla light reflected off his gray whiskers. "To explain that we have to go back in time," he said. "The Neglected Provinces weren't always neglected, you see. There used to be more life here than in all of Tamarind. When the Dark Woman Faustina was alive the region was covered in a jungle more magnificent than any in Tamarind—it was a lush, bountiful place with the strangest and most wondrous plants and animals, great and small.

"Ophalla has always been precious in Tamarind," he went on. "Because of the mining frenzy before the last war, the ophalla in the Neglected Provinces was depleted from the earth in all but a few tiny oases, where the ophalla was too deep to mine. But what people soon found out was that nothing could live here without ophalla—once the earth was stripped of it, everything else perished. You see . . ." Eusebio leaned forward, lowering his voice, "*all the plants and animals unique to Tamarind need ophalla to live*. In their lust for ophalla, Tamarinders destroyed their greatest jungle and wiped out most of the life that lived there— many things that had thrived there were never seen again. People abandoned their homes and moved out. Almost overnight it became a wasteland and has remained that way until today.

"All of Tamarind might have been destroyed like the Neglected Provinces were, except for the fact that the rest of the ophalla in Tamarind was buried too deeply for people to find. Milagros knew that if people ever discovered how to reach that ophalla in the future, the destruction of Tamarind would begin again. But . . . she knew of a miraculous gate that existed deep within Tamarind. She knew that closing it would restore the balance of ophalla lost from the mining. To save Tamarind in the future, she dispersed the tools to close the gate to a handful of Tamarinders, and divided the secret among them."

It was as the señoras had said, but Simon was no clearer. "I don't understand," he said. "How does closing Faustina's Gate restore the balance? How does it work?"

The Mole Monks hesitated and looked at one another.

"Even we don't know," said Frascuelo ruefully. "It's one of Tamarind's greatest secrets. Only the person who finds the tools and figures out how to use them can learn how the gate works. It's extraordinarily powerful and closing it can't be undertaken lightly."

"Do you know where the gate is?" asked Simon.

"It's in a cave," said Eusebio. "That much at least is well-known."

"Where is the cave?" asked Simon excitedly. "I'm sure if I could get there I could find the gate!"

The expression on the monks' faces made Simon's hopes fade.

"Herein lies the problem," said Eusebio.

Frascuelo retrieved another book—this one huge—three feet high and two feet wide, its binding turning to dust. He turned the pages slowly and Simon saw thousands of different maps of Tamarind, depicting topography, patterns of settlement, detailed sketches of rivers, and precise renderings of ragged bits of coastline. When Frascuelo reached a page showing the entire island, he stopped.

"Aha," he said. "Here we are."

In a box on the lower right-hand side of the page, in florid script, was written, *Possible Locations of Faustina's*

Gate. Then, across the map, dozens of those sites were marked.

Simon frowned and rubbed his eyebrow. "How am I supposed to find it then?"

"The answer is in the triptych," said Frascuelo. "We just haven't seen it yet."

"Let's start with what we do have," said Eusebio. He picked up the umbrella and rolled a mineral-fruit across the table.

Over the next hour they pored over more dusty books. They discovered that the mineral-fruit was called "citrus fertil," from the ancient Citrus Fertilanza tree. It used to be grown in plantations across Tamarind, but was now very rare. Only a dozen of them were growing in oases in the Neglected Provinces over very deep ophalla deposits. The books confirmed what Simon already knew, that the fruit had a very hard rind that turned metallic silver during the full moon. No explanation was known for the mysterious phenomenon. The umbrella, however, left the Mole Monks stumped. To their chagrin, they could find no explanation at all for it in any of their books. They were excited to see the Little Blue Door in the image—"home," Frascuelo called it—and impressed by how Simon had found them.

When they had exhausted everything they could figure out about the tools, they lined the ophallagraphs up side by side and wracked their brains for anything else important about triptychs.

"Some things have a double use in an image," said

Frascuelo finally. "For instance, close your eyes a bit and look at the ophallagraph of the tree—see the fruit on the branches? It occurred to me that the fruit is clustered in patterns, perhaps like constellations of stars."

Simon frowned dubiously. It was no constellation he knew, and he had learned them all at a young age. "I don't think so," he said. "I know all the constellations in the northern and the southern hemispheres, from when we lived at sea." He remembered how when he was a small child his mother and father had held him close and traced patterns in the stars in the warm tropical nights. For a moment he could again hear his mother's voice: *Aquila, Capricorn, Aquarius, Cassiopeia, Scorpio, Perseus, Ursa Major, Ursa Minor, and look—one of my favorites, Simon—Andromeda . . .*

"Well, I'm sure you're right," said Frascuelo. "We don't see the stars much down here."

"Well," said Simon, scratching his head, "maybe it's not a constellation, but it's some kind of pattern." He half closed his eyes to look at the image. If there were a pattern there, what was its purpose?

"Usually triptychs have something in common," said Nicodemus at last. "The things they share are clues."

Simon had already spent ages studying the images and no connections had leaped out at him. But he'd never been looking for something they all had in common before. He decided to start in one corner of each and make his way across every tiny detail. Halfway through looking at each image for the second time, he suddenly saw what he had failed to notice before. Tiny, mostly in the background, often in the distance, but there unmistakably in all three ophallagraphs:

"BIRDS!" he said triumphantly. "All three of them have birds!" Did they have something to do with Milagros, he wondered. They must! But what were they trying to show him? Now that Simon had seen the connection he couldn't *unsee* it. There were birds everywhere! He studied each ophallagraph carefully.

In the ophallagraph of the boats in the harbor a flock of birds flew in a line alongside one of the waterfalls up to a tiny black triangle in the mountain.

In the one of the two men standing under the umbrella, a crooked line of birds flew across the big cloud in the background.

In the ophallagraph of the tree (which Simon now knew was a Citrus Fertilanza tree), a single hummingbird hovered in the air beside one of the fruits. Simon would have thought it was picking at it with its beak except that he knew the fruit would be too hard.

"They seem meant to draw your attention to where they're pointing," said Frascuelo. "Maybe they're supposed to lead you somewhere."

"But in the ophallagraph of the two men under the umbrella the birds are flying in the clouds," said Simon. "It can't mean that we're supposed to be there . . ."

"I suppose not," said Frascuelo.

They studied the images in silence.

"Some clues, of course, are just to lead you to other clues," said Eusebio. "The image of the Blue Door, for example, which led you here."

"Wait," said Nicodemus, peering through the magnifying glass at the ophallagraph of the fleet. "I've just noticed something else. The last boat, the one farthest away, see? Right here, almost off the edge of the ophallagraph." He let the others peer through his magnifying glass.

"It doesn't look like the others," said Simon. "It looks more like a raft. Yeah, it's a raft with a mast and a single, square-rig sail."

"I may be wrong," said Nicodemus, "but I believe it's the symbol for the Last Ferry."

As Nicodemus went to a shelf and returned with yet another book, Simon again heard the distant clanging and banging reverberating through the tunnels.

"There's a moraine—a mountain lake—where people in Tamarind used to take their dead," Nicodemus told Simon, flipping through the brittle pages until he found what he was looking for. He turned the book around so that Simon could see a small drawing—it was almost identical to the one in the ophallagraph.

"The Moraine of Lost Loved Ones is a sacred lake in the Grandfather Mountains," continued Nicodemus. "Long ago people in Tamarind used to carry their dead up the mountain to the moraine. They'd wait for a raft—the Last Ferry—and halfway across the lake they would release the dead into the water. Something special in the water preserved the bodies. Tamarinders believed that it was a place where they could go to remember and feel close to people they had lost, and to know that they were with them still."

The monks were solemn-faced. Nicodemus's description was haunting and Simon felt a chill.

"Where are the Grandfather Mountains?" he asked.

"The Grandfather Mountains are between Hetty's Pass and Prince's Town," said Frascuelo. "But I'm afraid we don't know precisely where in the mountains the moraine is."

"Prince's Town," said Simon. "That's where my sisters are. I was supposed to be there four days ago—I know they'll be worried. I need to find them before I do anything else. Can you tell me how to get there?"

"We can show you the way through the tunnels," said Eusebio. "You don't have to cross the desert again. You'll have to walk for the better part of a day, but you'll surface in the countryside in the North, and from there it won't take you long to walk to Prince's Town."

They had told Simon all they knew, but he still needed to collect the final tool and learn where Faustina's mysterious gate was hidden.

彡彡 彡彡 彡彡

Armed with his new knowledge about the ophallagraphs, Simon allowed the monks to blindfold him. They insisted on this as a precaution so that if he fell into the Red Coral's hands he would not be able to betray their location. They led him uphill through the vast system of tunnels that stretched like a rabbit warren through the earth deep below the Neglected Provinces.

Simon heard stone doorways being opened every now and then and shut quickly behind them, and twice he had to climb huge staircases that seemed to go on forever. He heard a dull roar rumbling through the earth from overhead and realized they must be passing beneath a river. The tunnel walls became slick and he found himself tramping through puddles and breathing damp air. They stopped. Simon heard a giant stone being rolled back. His blindfold was removed.

"This is as far as we can take you," said Eusebio. "A short distance farther is a fork. The tunnel to the left is the way you should go. The tunnel to the right is where the Red Coral are. The Red Man is with them and he's very dangerous. Stay away from them—go quickly until you're safely far away."

Clanking and muffled voices echoed somewhere up ahead. The enemy was very near. Simon's heart hammered. He shook the monks' hands firmly. "Thank you," he said. "I'm grateful for all your help—I would never have been able to learn all that stuff on my own."

The monks gave him an ophalla torch to light his way and wished him well, the torchlight gleaming softly on their gray whiskers. Simon hoisted his backpack higher on his back and, taking a deep breath, headed deeper into the tunnel. Behind him he heard the giant stone roll back into place. There was no turning back now.

✤ CHAPTER FIFTEEN ✤

Deep in the Lair ✹ *The Floriano Operation* ✹
Like Rats in a Maze ✹ *A Vast Crescent*

Simon proceeded cautiously, his body alert and tense. The clanging and hammering from the Red Coral mine echoed through the tunnel, and he could hear the river running faintly overhead. It sounded like being inside a very large shell.

He looked over his shoulder but the passage back to the monks was sealed—he could hardly tell where it had been. He kept walking, the ophalla torch lighting his way. The sounds from the mine grew louder. Soon he could see the fork the monks had told him about.

He slowed down.

Don't be foolish, he told himself.

But was it really foolish?

In one direction lay his sisters and safety.

In the other, tantalizingly close, lay the chance to learn more about the Red Coral Project. Even after all Simon had learned from the Mole Monks he still didn't know enough to find Faustina's Gate. Nor had he learned how Faustina's Gate was supposed to help them. He could keep going, slowly piecing together clues in the perplexing ophalla-graphs, or he could take this opportunity to get closer to the

Red Coral Project and perhaps learn something more immediately useful. No one suspected he was there; it would be easy to hide on the fringes.

Stepping as softly as he could, he turned right and began walking down the tunnel toward the Red Coral camp.

When he heard voices and saw lights up ahead, he stopped and stood very still. He wrapped the ophalla torch in a spare shirt and stowed it in his backpack so its light wouldn't give him away. Breathing lightly, he inched forward and pressed his face to a large crack in the tunnel wall.

He looked into a large chamber. It was an ophalla mine, but almost all its ophalla had already been chiseled out. Eastern tribespeople were loading the final blocks into a caravan of wheelbarrows that were constantly running in and out of the room. Maroong men were sweeping glittering powder into piles, then into bags. Giant machines were being dismantled and hauled out. The Mole Monks had been right: The mine was shutting down and the Red Coral were getting ready to move somewhere else.

Two Red Coral men passed near where Simon was. He crouched at once and hugged the wall. The men were talking about a guerrilla who had been tormenting the Red Coral camp recently.

"It's got to be more than one person!"

"No, I'm telling you—it's just one kid. I've seen him twice with my own eyes. Otherwise I'd think he was a phantom—appearing out of nowhere and disappearing without a trace. You always see that green parrot hanging around first, so keep your eye out . . ."

Simon's ears pricked up. Green parrot?

"We'll catch the little son of a gun sooner or later. He'll regret it when Fitzsimmons gets his hands on him . . ."

Simon couldn't suppress his smile. It was Helix, he was sure.

The men's voices faded, and Simon peeked cautiously through the crack again. He saw that a cart had appeared through a tunnel on the opposite side of the chamber and sat idling. He saw a flash of red beard. Dr. Fitzsimmons was driving it. Simon held his breath and watched. The two men Simon had overheard were striding over to the cart and as he watched, they climbed into the back and the three of them drove off down a side tunnel. Simon brushed a trickle of sweat off his temple. *That was close.*

He wished he could learn more, but it was impossible to go any farther without being seen. He'd got confirmation that the Red Coral were moving locations and heard the uplifting news that Helix was somewhere nearby—that was enough. He turned to go.

He froze. Inches from his neck was a serrated metal spearhead bound to the end of a thick, short baton. He looked up its length to see a giant Maroong woman standing above him. She must have been nearly seven feet tall, with shoulders broader than any man's Simon had ever seen. He had not heard her approach—even now as he watched her she barely seemed to breathe. Her lips were pulled back in a grimace, baring a full set of teeth shaved to sharp, menacing points. Her bald head was scabbed from the razor and painted bloodred.

She plucked the backpack from Simon's back.

"No!" he cried. The precious ophallagraphs, the mineral-fruits, and the umbrella were all in his backpack. He felt sick. What had he been thinking? He should have just kept going as the monks had told him to. He watched miserably as the woman began to rifle through the bag. She took out a mineral-fruit and tried to bite it, but even her sharply filed tooth could not pierce it. She opened and closed the umbrella. She shoved Simon's clothes and the map to one side, and withdrew the ophallagraphs and gazed at them rapaciously. She looked at him with a glimmer in her eye. She rooted through the bag once more, considering his compass and pocketknife and canteen, before she withdrew the sparkle pistol and tucked it surreptitiously in her leather skirt.

"Dr. Fitzsimmons will be back very soon," she said ominously. "He'll take care of you then."

With that, she shoved Simon ahead of her down the tunnel.

His knees felt like rubber. At any time Dr. Fitzsimmons was going to return and find him there. The roar of water overhead grew louder—they must be directly under the river here. In a few minutes Simon heard tuneless and relentless hammering and someone shouting.

He knew that voice.

It was hoarse, but he knew it.

He turned a corner with the guards, who unlocked a metal grate, shoved him unceremoniously into a cell, and left.

The cell's sole occupant—prepared for the unknown—looked fierce, but her expression quickly turned to surprise.

"Simon!" she cried. She looked behind him. "Where are your sisters?"

Simon glared at Isabella. She was among the last people he wanted to be locked in a cell with. He knew she must have told Dr. Fitzsimmons the children were in Tamarind after she had been captured and that's why the Red Coral had been chasing them.

"We had to separate," he said. "No thanks to you. If you'd listened to us in the beginning we might have been able to help you and we wouldn't be here right now!" He looked around the rough stone walls of the cell and rattled the door, but the lock was solid.

"I'm sorry," she said quietly. "I didn't mean to get you into trouble." Her hair was tangled and her clothes, the same ones she had been wearing the last time Simon saw her, were filthy. "It was only after Dr. Fitzsimmons caught me that I knew for sure you didn't have anything to do with the Red Coral."

"Too late," said Simon. He looked around the empty cell. "Where's *your* family?" he asked. "I thought they captured your mother and brother, as well."

"They're being held in Cabarro," said Isabella. "That's what one of the guards told me. If that's the truth . . ." She sniffed suddenly. Simon saw that her fingers were scabbed from a futile attempt to dig her way out of the cell.

"Listen," she whispered, her eyes suddenly bright, "I know you're angry, but I'm going to make it up to you. I've had a way out of here since this morning, but there's been too much activity in the tunnel. I've been waiting for it to quiet down so that once I'm out I'll have a good head start."

"What do you mean, you have a way out?" whispered Simon, instantly alert.

From within the folds of her clothes Isabella withdrew a long, thin tooth.

"The Maroong woman who brought me food this morning dropped it," she said. "You know they decorate themselves with bones and teeth—it must have fallen off her clothes. I'm sure I can pick the lock with it."

Making sure no one was coming, she kneeled and tried without success to unlock the door. It was clear to Simon that she didn't know what she was doing.

"You're going to break the tooth like that," he said. "Let me try."

Isabella kept an eye out for anyone coming while Simon set to work on the lock.

"They want your boat, you know," she said.

"Our boat?" Simon asked in surprise, pausing for a moment to look up at her.

"They're stuck in Tamarind," said Isabella. "They can't get out—whatever instrument they built that enabled them to cross the Blue Line was damaged so badly in the storms on their way here that they still haven't been able to fix it. They've been looking for somewhere called Faustina's Gate that they think will let them go back and forth, but they haven't been able to find that, either. Fitzsimmons thinks that the *Pamela Jane* is how you were able to get here. It wasn't anything you actually knew—it was the boat itself."

228

"She has ophalla in her hull," said Simon, putting his ear to the lock to hear the gears clicking. "It's attracted to the Line."

"You didn't tell me that when I asked you how you were able to cross the Blue Line," whispered Isabella. "You weren't exactly up front with me, either!"

"Can you blame us?" asked Simon. "You didn't trust us from the moment we got here. What else have you found out while you were here?"

"The Red Coral have just discovered a huge new ophalla deposit in a place called Floriano," said Isabella. "They're packing up and leaving for there now."

Floriano, thought Simon. That's where the señoras were.

"I've heard them say that the Floriano operation is at least as big as the total of everything they've mined already," said Isabella, dropping her voice. "If the mining is what's been causing the chaos in the environment, then what they're going to do at Floriano will be devastating. Excavations are set to start in three days."

Simon's heart plunged. Three days—what could they do in three days?

The lock opened with a click.

"Hey, you got it!" said Isabella.

Simon looked quickly both ways down the tunnel. "They took my backpack from me," he said. "I've got to find it."

"Forget your bag!" said Isabella. "We need to get out of here before anyone sees us!"

"It's important," said Simon. "It has the ophallagraphs in it."

"The what?"

"The ophallagraphs," whispered Simon. "I'll explain later—right now I have to get my bag. The Maroong woman kept it. Do you have any idea where she would have put it?"

"Dr. Fitzsimmons has a room," said Isabella.

"Good," said Simon. "It should be empty now—I saw him leaving just before the Maroong caught me."

"But he could come back any time," said Isabella, looking nervously down the tunnel. "Oh," she grumbled at last, "all right, I know where it is. Come on."

They hurried silently through the passage. They heard voices far ahead, but to Simon's relief they saw no one.

"This is it," said Isabella finally, stopping in a stone doorway. "Be quick! I'll keep watch."

The makeshift office was empty. Papers were strewn across the single desk, along with a microscope and several tools. A small laboratory was in the process of being packed up and crates were open, half-filled with equipment. Samples of ophalla had been tossed into a cardboard box. At once the haphazard disarray reminded Simon of his father's study at home. He saw his backpack on top of a stack of papers on the floor beside Dr. Fitzsimmons's desk. He grabbed it and quickly checked its contents. With relief, he saw that everything except the sparkle pistol was there.

He was about to leave when he noticed that a large map hung on the wall nearby, darkened by scores of mysterious black circles.

"Hurry up!" whispered Isabella.

"Hang on," said Simon. "This looks important."

He tiptoed closer. In a box at the bottom of the map was printed *Future Mine Sites*.

Shocked, Simon looked back up at the sinister circles. There were so many of them! They spread like a pestilence across Tamarind, from north to south and east to west, beneath towns, deep in jungles, in valleys, on hills. Nowhere was spared. Xs marked the sites that had already been mined, but the staggering majority remained to be excavated. Even Maracairol was marked for demolition. The Red Coral Project had only just begun their plan to upend Tamarind.

Isabella had crept into the room and together they looked at the map in horror.

"They aren't going to stop," whispered Simon.

He turned frantically to Dr. Fitzsimmons's desk, looking for anything that might help them. As he rifled through the papers his eyes fell on a folder. A chill crept up his neck as he recognized the handwriting on the cover. It was Papi's. He opened the folder and scanned the pages quickly. The research was all dated at the top. It was his father's early conjectures about ophalla, from soon after they returned from Tamarind. But his father would never have given his research to Dr. Fitzsimmons. Dimly Simon remembered that around that time two men had come to Granny Pearl's house. His father had pretended they were old colleagues. Simon had been reading on the porch when he had seen them leaving with boxes of documents. He was only nine or ten then and, thinking that the men were fellow scientists of his father's, he had chatted obliviously with them and even offered to help carry the boxes until his father had called him indoors sharply.

What a dumb kid he'd been! The men had been taking his father's work by force to give to Dr. Fitzsimmons! The research was stolen! Knowing what he knew now, Simon felt sure that the Red Coral would have made threats—maybe even threats about him and Maya and Penny—and Simon's parents had been powerless to stop them. They had done the best they could to keep the children safe and have their lives be normal. Simon flushed with shame when he remembered how impatient he'd been.

He hated Dr. Fitzsimmons.

He couldn't be any more different from his father.

Papi loved knowledge for its own sake and for the good it could do for other people. Dr. Fitzsimmons only wanted information so that he could be powerful and control people and possess things. He didn't care who he hurt or exploited in the process. Even Simon's family.

Isabella had returned to the door. "Someone's coming," she whispered anxiously.

Simon snapped back to where he was: in Dr. Fitzsimmons's room, where he could return to find them at any moment.

He hurried to the door and he and Isabella dashed down the tunnel.

"I think we should head toward the sound of the water," he whispered. "It must come up to the surface at some point. Can you run?" He thought that after days trapped in the small cell her legs might be weak, but she nodded gamely.

Simon took his ophalla torch out of his back to light their way, and they ran lightly on the edges of the tunnels out of the puddles. Dripping water echoed all around them. The air smelled like cold mud. The rumble of water overhead got steadily louder and Simon was sure they were getting closer to a way out. But suddenly they realized they had overshot the river and the roar was growing more distant.

"Let's double back and try another tunnel," he said.

They twisted and turned down winding passages. One moment the water boomed overhead; the next it faded to a whisper. Finding a way aboveground wasn't going to be as easy as Simon had hoped. Cold water dripped down their necks from the dank ceiling. Isabella slipped on the slick stones and skinned her knee. Simon helped her up and they kept running.

"At least we must be far away from them by now," said Simon at last. But the words were barely out of his mouth when a cry rang out in the tunnel ahead of them. He and Isabella stopped dead in their tracks.

"We're not far at all," she whispered breathlessly. "We've been going in circles!"

More voices filled the tunnels. The stamp of running feet echoed off the walls. Simon took Isabella's hand and they ran faster, sloshing through puddles, turning this way and that. Several times they reached a dead end and had to double back. Simon had a wild hope that the Mole Monks would hear and appear to save them, but no one did. The cacophony of footfalls reverberating through the passages made it impossible to tell how near or far their pursuers were. Simon caught a glimpse of a group of men rounding a corner up ahead. Seconds before they would have been seen, Simon and Isabella ducked down a new tunnel.

"We haven't been down this one before," whispered Simon, his breathing ragged. The tunnel was widening, the ceiling getting higher, and they were going uphill now. The thunder of water grew louder and louder, drowning out the sounds of the Red Coral behind them. Simon realized he was breathing fresh air. Just a little farther . . .

A moment later they emerged from the tunnel into the great dark night.

Freedom!

They stopped, out of breath. Simon closed his eyes, drawing in deep lungfuls of pure, cool night air. Being outside had never felt so good. The water roared beside them. Then he felt Isabella squeeze his arm. He opened his eyes.

They were standing on a mossy ledge that jutted out over the most enormous waterfall that Simon had ever seen. A vast crescent of tumbling ivory foam stretched on either side of them, receding into opaline mists in the distance. Just a few yards from their feet, water poured glassy over the edge and shattered into thunderous, muddy surf two hundred feet below. The sheer immensity and power rendered them dumb. Simon looked down into the colored bands of rainbows that spangled the mists. Hardy tufts of vegetation near the base of the falls were slicked down and gleaming in the spray. Nocturnal butterflies jittered through the air above them. Within seconds the heavy mists had doused the children.

There was no way to go but over the falls or back underground. Simon and Isabella turned to run back into the tunnel to find another way out. But before they could reach its mouth they saw lights flashing from inside, and seconds later Maroong men burst out.

They were trapped!

The men pulled up short just as Simon and Isabella had done. Their fearsome painted heads bobbed. The tips of their bayonets gleamed in the moonlight. Torches bobbed inside the tunnel and more guards appeared, sealing the entrance.

"There's nowhere to go!" gasped Isabella, squeezing Simon's hand.

Simon felt dizzy. For a moment it was as if the earth slowed and the noise of the water fell silent. A strange calm descended on him. He reached for the umbrella in his backpack and undid the catch that held it closed.

"We'll jump," he said.

Isabella looked at him as if he were crazy, but she grabbed hold of the umbrella with him and they locked arms. Simon heard the men shouting anxiously from the mouth of the tunnel as they realized what the captives were preparing to do. Simon took a deep breath and got ready to jump.

But he couldn't.

Suddenly the roaring thunder of the falls returned to him at full volume. What had he been thinking? An umbrella! It was too flimsy to hold them aloft or slow their descent. They would plummet to their deaths. Even if they survived the fall, the force of the water would tear them from limb to limb. It was lunacy. No, they would have to take their chances with the Red Coral men, who were shouting and edging closer along the ledge to them, their bayonets stabbing the night air. They wouldn't kill them here—they would take them back to Dr. Fitzsimmons, who wanted them alive, at least for the moment. If they were prisoners, at least they would still have a chance.

Simon turned back, steeling himself to face the men. As he did, Isabella lunged forward and hurled them both over the edge of the falls.

❧ CHAPTER SIXTEEN ❧

A Dark, Violent World ❈ *A Key* ❈
A Light up Ahead

Simon felt nothing but pure shock for the first few seconds after Isabella shoved them over the edge of the falls. The wind pushed his mouth open and he felt the cold and pressure on his teeth. He clawed the air but there was nothing to grab. They kept plunging and then—

Whoosh!

The wind snapped the umbrella open, wrenching Simon's arm upwards. Pain radiated through his whole body.

He looked up to see that the umbrella had bloomed above them and the tough fabric was acting as a parachute, slowing their free fall. Simon and Isabella hugged each other tightly as the winds swept them back and forth across the turbulent river. The furious white water and dark banks were coming up fast. In the final moment before they struck, they closed their eyes and held on to each other for dear life.

They landed in the water.

The river engulfed them instantly, immersing them in a dark, violent world. They were no match for the powerful current and Simon quickly lost all sense of where the surface was. The force of the water had driven their arms between the spokes of the shredded umbrella and they were caught together, struggling against each other. The burning in Simon's lungs grew unbearable. He needed air desperately, but no matter how much he struggled, the river kept him pinned beneath it. The pain in his lungs was agonizing. Isabella was weakening beside him. But the next time he felt his feet strike rocks he pushed himself up with all his might and at last broke through the surface.

AIR!

Sweet, pure air—thick with mist but *air*! He gasped it in as Isabella popped up beside him. Simon saw the black diagonal of the shore before the river plowed them back under. For the next few miles they fought for the surface whenever they could, swallowing water and choking as the mighty river sped them along.

At last the current slackened. Simon felt his knees grind into stones on the riverbed. He discovered he could stand. Or he could have if his legs hadn't felt like they were made out of rubber. He got to his feet as best he could and helped Isabella up—she was shaking, her long hair plastered wetly across her face—and they half crawled, half staggered the rest of the way.

They collapsed on the shore, breathing heavily, unable to move. The cuts on their arms from the spokes of the umbrella throbbed painfully. Isabella winced when Simon finally sat up and disentangled them. They were bleeding quite badly but the cuts were not as deep as he had feared. Isabella ripped the hem of her trousers and bandaged both their arms.

The bleeding staunched, they sat there for a moment as

their hearts slowed. The night air was cold on their skin after the icy water. They looked back where they had come from. The falls shone in the distance. Simon shivered—how had they survived such an enormous drop?

"Do you think they'll be after us?" Isabella asked when she could speak.

"I doubt they'll think we survived," said Simon.

"That gives us a little time," said Isabella through softly chattering teeth.

Simon looked over at her. "Are you okay?" he asked.

"I'm fine," she sniffed. "I'm just cold."

Simon turned away and looked back to the hill above them. They were back in the jungle, at least, which was a huge relief. Simon never wanted to see a desert again. In panic, he remembered the ophallagraphs. What if they had been destroyed?

Frantically he emptied the contents of his backpack. To his surprise the images were crisp edged and unharmed. The señoras had been right—they really were indestructible. In fact, their glow seemed stronger now.

"What are those?" Isabella asked curiously.

"I'll tell you later," said Simon. "But now I have to get to Prince's Town." He fanned the images dry and after squeezing out everything else in the backpack as best he could—the mineral-fruits were too hard to have even been bruised—he put everything away and got to his feet.

Cradling her arm, Isabella began walking up the hill to get a better view. "There's a light up there," she whispered, cringing as she flexed her arm.

Simon looked up the hillside. There was indeed a light, shining through the trees.

"What do you think?" asked Isabella.

Friend or enemy? It was impossible to know. Simon looked back at the falls in the distance. "We've come a long way from the Red Coral camp," he said. "I vote we take our chances."

"Agreed," said Isabella. She started up the hill.

Glancing behind him one last time, Simon caught sight of the battered remains of the umbrella. He had almost forgotten it! The pole had cracked and the umbrella lay in a crumpled heap. It was one of the precious tools and now it was ruined. The fabric had been torn away entirely by the force of the water, leaving only the skeleton of spokes. The ornate handle was lodged in the mud. He looked at it despondently. When he pulled it out, the handle came loose from the pole. He leaned over to rinse it off in the clear water and then he noticed something that he had not before. He raised it over his head and looked at it in the moonlight. It looked like . . .

"A key," he whispered.

The handle of the key had been the handle of the um-brella. The teeth of the key had been hidden inside the pole and only revealed when the umbrella had broken. It was made of pure white ophalla without any blue-green tinge. Creamy swirls spiraled into the palely glowing stone. While the handle was carved ornately, the key itself was crudely made and had only three teeth, each of slightly different lengths. Simon turned it over in his hand. He had already opened the Blue Door.

What else would need to be unlocked?

His heart quickened.

A gate. A gate might need to be unlocked.

Faustina's Gate, in fact.

The key was one of the tools they were supposed to find—he'd had it all along!

He glanced up to find Isabella already partway up the hill, making a path through the tall sugarcane grass. He nestled the key safely in the pocket of his backpack, and with new energy he hoisted the bag, soaking wet and heavy, onto his shoulders and hurried to catch up.

The roar of the falls changed pitch as they climbed. Simon's gashes stung, but he gritted his teeth and tried to ignore the pain in his arm and the bruises on his legs. Near the top of the hill they slowed and made their way forward cautiously.

The light held steady through the trees.

They were close to it now.

"I don't think anyone's here," whispered Isabella at last.

Carefully Simon pulled aside a branch and they saw the source of the light.

❧ CHAPTER SEVENTEEN ❧

Train to Nowhere

"It's a train!" said Isabella.

Simon's hopes sank when he saw the old relic, a locomotive, abandoned in the jungle, carbuncled in rust. They went closer to examine it. The light they had seen came from a headlight made out of a convex lens of ophalla. Vines threaded through the grates and in and out of the open windows. Simon reached out and pushed the side gently and it groaned. The whole thing looked as if it were about to crumble to dust before them. He noticed a simple plaque near the cab window that read DAVIES MARONER, INVENTOR.

Davies Maroner again! "Man, would I have liked to talk to *that* guy," said Simon. "What's a train doing out in the middle of nowhere, anyway?"

"Hey," said Isabella, "I think I know what this is . . . It was a provincial revival project—a train to connect the North to the South, but they never made it that far because of the war. Eventually they just stopped working on it and the tracks finished—well, in the middle of nowhere."

"I have to go north," said Simon. "I left my sisters at Hetty's Pass four days ago. We're supposed to meet in Prince's

Town." He took out his compass. Outside the Neglected Provinces it worked once again. They found that the tracks indeed ran north. He withdrew the map and smoothed it out on the ground. Made of oiled paper, it had survived the river remarkably well. "Where do you think we are now?" he asked.

"There are the Mumbagua Falls that we just went over," said Isabella, pointing with a stick to a curling blue sweep painted almost in the dead center of the map. "And we're somewhere around here right now, I'd guess. And here's Hetty's Pass." She brought the stick down on a place far to the northwest of where they were. Then she moved it all the way up to the north coast. "And here's Prince's Town."

"All the way up there," said Simon. "I'm still miles away!" He gazed in disappointment at the map.

His eyes traveled over the barren expanse on the map where he had wandered lost for three days, and he took a deep breath. At least he wasn't out there anymore. He was making progress. He had found the final ophallagraph, the mineral-fruits, and the key. He knew about the Floriano operation and about the Red Coral's deadly plan to take over all of Tamarind. Isabella was free and perhaps now they could work together to stop the Red Coral. Simon's journey hadn't been in vain. He squinted at the map—it looked as if Prince's Town was just on the other side of the same mountains they had seen at Hetty's Pass, when they met the general. It wouldn't have been a long journey for

Maya and Penny—they were probably safely in Prince's Town right now waiting for him. Simon could keep going for a little longer.

He looked up at the train tracks, gleaming between soft grasses and prehistoric ferns, unfolding across the plateau. He chewed his lip.

"These tracks head north," he mused.

"That's an idea," said Isabella. "We can walk along them at least and know we're going the right way. I believe they stop somewhere up"—she waved the stick over the map and brought it down to rest with a sharp knock in the middle of a vast, sandy stretch in the north—"here. From there we could walk to Prince's Town easily. I'll go with you that far. From Prince's Town I can get a boat to Cabarro, farther down the coast, where my mother and brother are being held—it will be faster than going over land."

"It would be a really long walk from here to Prince's Town," said Simon. "We'd lose a couple of days at least. And we don't have that much time—the new mine in Floriano will open in three days." He sized up the dilapidated old train.

"You're joking," said Isabella, skeptically following his gaze to the rusty old contraption.

"It would be faster than going on foot," said Simon.

"It *would* be," said Isabella. "If it worked."

"Well, then, it's worth a few minutes to try," said Simon. He hopped up into the engine room. A quick study revealed that the train had an old-fashioned steam engine. Beside it was a chute that led to what looked like a furnace. On the other side of that was a closed bin filled with crude charcoal. When Simon looked closer he saw that all the parts were made and fitted together slightly differently from those in a regular steam engine. He wondered if Davies Maroner had had to figure it out all on his own. Either way, it was impressive and unlike anything else he'd ever seen in Tamarind.

He jumped back down to the ground, dusting off his hands. "I think we can get this thing moving again," he said. "We need water—a lot of it—the boiler's only half full, and we need to get a fire going in the furnace."

Isabella went to see if she could find a bucket and Simon climbed back in the engine room and hunted around until he found an old flint and strike hanging on a wall. He took it down and gave it an experimental strike. A small shower of sparks flew out. "We've got fire!" he called.

"And there's a tub here," called Isabella. "It's a bit leaky and it's big—I'll need you to help me carry it. I can hear a stream just over there—we won't need to walk all the way back down to the river."

Simon and Isabella spent the next hour carrying water up from the stream to pour into the boiler, and gathering armloads of kindling from the underbrush for the furnace. They attacked the vines and weeds ensnaring the train carriage with gusto and Simon cleaned the grit out of the engine. Sweaty and dirty and feeling gallant, they climbed up into the train.

Simon sparked the igniter and after a few tries the tinder caught. He blew it into a larger flame, then added it to the firebox. He and Isabella waited, hardly daring to breathe. If this didn't work they had wasted time and energy and still faced a few days' walk to Prince's Town. Isabella wiped sweat off her face. Simon tossed in several more handfuls of coal and closed his eyes, wishing desperately for it to work. He was exhausted and the thought of walking farther tonight was almost too much to bear.

Then a puff of white smoke appeared from the funnel.

The engine coughed once, then again.

With an unholy shriek of protesting metal, the train lurched forward and pulled sluggishly away from the vines and roots and leaves that entrapped it. The breeze swept out the last of the dead leaves on the carriage floor.

"It's working!" Isabella cried joyfully as the carriage chugged forward, flattening the shrubs and ferns on the tracks. "It's actually working!"

Soon they were picking up speed. The magnificent waterfalls came into view once more, jets and fits of spray brilliant in the moonlight. Black palms stood silhouetted against the pure white mists. They stretched for miles— white curtains and combs of them, the most distant of them so far away that they appeared frozen in midair. Finally, Simon and Isabella left them behind as the train trundled steadily through the dark night.

Isabella stuck her head out of the window, breathing the fresh night air deeply. "I think we can climb onto the roof," she said, and disappeared through the window. Simon replenished the firewood and followed her up. The air was fresh and smelled of grass and earth. They sat and looked up at the great vault of sky and the big orange moon and the lush grasslands unfurling on either side of them. Butterflies came and settled on the roof, brown until they blinked their wings open for a second, revealing astonishing shades of purple, blue, and saffron. The train passed herds of elegant fleethorns, and Simon and Isabella saw stocky waterbeasts and tiger buzzards sitting shoulder to shoulder around watering holes. Lightning storms flashed in the distance and the fleethorns, disrupted by the threat of the storm, raced on under the moon.

"I'm going to return to Maracairol and get rid of that horrible Red Coral Project," said Isabella fiercely. "I won't let them hurt my home."

Looking out over the land, Simon felt his own deep love of Tamarind. This was why he and Maya and Penny had returned. Tamarind was part of them. He would find his sisters and they would close Faustina's Gate and stop the Red Coral.

Whatever it took, they would find a way.

※ ※ ※

Simon and Isabella took turns fueling the train throughout the long night, sleeping when they weren't on watch. At dawn, through the mist, they kept an eye out ahead on the tracks.

"This is it!" cried Isabella finally.

Simon stopped loading the engine with sticks—they

were down to the last few, anyway—and went to the front of the carriage to look out. Less than a hundred yards ahead of them the tracks came to an abrupt end in a great sand dune. Simon tried to pull the brake but it wouldn't move. Its handle was soldered with rust and though he pulled on it with all his might, it didn't budge. Isabella helped, too, but it was no use. The train bore down on the end of the tracks, unstoppable.

"Hang on!" Simon shouted.

Seconds later the tracks ended. The cow catcher drove into the sand. Simon and Isabella hung on for all they were worth. The back of the carriage swung around to the front and shimmied sideways across the sand, screeching and groaning and kicking up a blinding cloud of dirt. Simon and Isabella were thrown to their knees.

Then, with a deep rumble, the carriage tilted, teetering for several desperate seconds, before it thumped on its side and didn't move again.

The cloud settled and Simon and Isabella waited a few moments, catching their breath, before they climbed gingerly out of the window and hopped down onto the hot sand. A tumbleweed somersaulted past them and, caught for a moment, nudged the train carriage before the breeze loosened it and it rolled away. The wind blew the sand over the tracks behind them. Sand trickled down into the overturned carriage, filling it like an hourglass.

"Well, that's the end of that," said Isabella, rubbing her newly bruised knees.

Simon got the map and his compass out and took a

bearing. "Thirty-eight degrees northwest should get us straight to Prince's Town," he said. "I have to get to Maya and Penny."

Isabella had to hurry to keep up with Simon, who set out walking as fast as he could. Maya and Penny were so close now.

❧ CHAPTER EIGHTEEN ❧

Prince's Town

They soon found a road where they flagged down a farmer's cart that took them all the way into Prince's Town. The town, nestled between the sea and the same icy blue mountains Simon had seen from the general's hut, looked as if it were about to slide into the sea. Recent storms had torn off roofs and planted them in the surrounding fields. Homes lay collapsed in heaps. The roots of fallen trees had yanked up great stretches of the road and gusts of salt spray had silvered what trees still stood. Down by the shore, big sea-smoothed boulders had been rolled by the waves and lodged between buildings on narrow streets. Landsides had driven several feet of mud down some roads and the scrape of shovels on pavements rang throughout the town.

"It shouldn't be like this," Isabella muttered grimly as she surveyed the damage. "This area never gets storms . . ."

Simon didn't care about the state of Prince's Town right now; he only wanted to find his sisters. He covered his nose as they passed rotting fish flung into gardens by the wind and waves. Down at the foot of the town he caught a glimpse of a grotty little harbor jammed with boats. Of course—the docks!

"They'll be down there," he said to Isabella. "When the

Pamela Jane was our home we'd live on board the boat in different ports—that's where they'll go to wait for me." He broke into a jog.

"I'll come with you," said Isabella. "I need to find a boat to take me to Cabarro."

Now that they were so close, Simon began to feel ill. What if Maya and Penny weren't in Prince's Town at all? What if they had never made it out of the tunnels? He came out onto the street that ran along the waterfront and paused, letting his eye rove over the mossy old fishing boats and barges knocking together along the docks. He saw no women there at all, only crab-handed old fishermen and ancient dockhands.

He ran down the length of the waterfront, but afraid to reach the end without seeing his sisters, he slowed down. His eye ran over the people on each boat, skipping over the boats with no one aboard them.

And then he stopped.

He saw a boat that looked very familiar.

He held his breath. He peered hard. Despite the blue paint on the hull, the battered old burlap-colored sail, and the name *Blue Duck* painted crudely on her starboard stern, he would know her shape anywhere.

"That's our boat!" he said. "That's the *Pamela Jane*!"

Isabella followed his gaze. "The *Blue Duck*?" she asked, confused.

"Helix must have disguised her, after he took off," said Simon.

He began to sprint down the dock. If the boat was here,

Helix must be, too. And if Maya and Penny had reached Prince's Town they would certainly have found the boat and would be on it or nearby! Then a dreadful thought brought him up short. What if Helix hadn't disguised the *Pamela Jane*—what if someone else had? Helix might have abandoned her somewhere and perhaps someone else had stolen her. If that was true, Simon should approach cautiously.

Suddenly he felt frantic. More than anything, he wanted to see his sisters and know they were safe. He was blistered, sunburned, hungry, and his arm throbbed where the spokes of the umbrella had cut it. He stood still and whistled, a code whistle that they had used when they were hiding in the garden at Granny Pearl's as children. He waited. The sun came out from behind the haze of clouds, rolling out over the town and docks, and lighting the shifting points of wavelets and glinting off the fish scales that littered the wet dock. He whistled again.

At that moment he saw Maya emerge onto the deck of their boat, Penny behind her. Maya's hair was tucked under a mussel diver's cap. Penny was tanned and still wearing her pink pajamas. They were okay! His heart felt as if it would overflow.

Maya's head shot up and her eyes searched the dock. She saw him and a huge smile broke out over her face and she leaped from the deck onto the pier. Simon ran as fast as he could down the dock.

"Penny, Penny!" Maya cried. "He's here! Simon's here!" She grabbed Penny's hand and pulled her up onto the dock just as Simon barreled into them, wrapping them both up in a giant hug.

"You're okay," said Maya, wiping away tears. "I'm so glad! I was really worried! We didn't know what had happened to you . . ."

"I'm so glad *you're* okay," said Simon. "I'm sorry it took me such a long time to get here. I'll explain everything. But first, you found the boat! Is Helix here, too?"

Maya hesitated. "No," she said. "We just missed him."

Simon's heart sank a little at this news. He was eager to hear what Maya knew about Helix, but Penny had been jumping up and down and now she leaped into Simon's arms. He squeezed her tightly and swung her around. As he spun he caught sight of Isabella jogging down the dock. He had totally forgotten about her. She stopped awkwardly a few feet away, breathing hard.

Maya caught sight of her, too, and her eyes narrowed. "What's *she* doing here?" she asked, staring icily at the other girl. Then she glanced furtively down the dock. "Come onto the boat," she said. "We shouldn't stay out in the open all together like this. There were Red Coral boats here just yesterday—who knows who's lurking around. I guess *she'd* better come, too."

Still holding Penny, Simon followed Maya onto the *Pamela Jane*. It had never felt so good to set foot on her deck as it did then. He offered Isabella his hand and she jumped down after him.

"Are you hungry?" Maya asked. "I was just fixing lunch,

let's all eat." As they went into the cabin Maya caught sight of Simon's bandaged arm and feet.

"I'm fine, I'm fine," he said quickly, waving her off. And he really did feel fine now—like new. He was so relieved to know that she and Penny were okay, and so happy to be together again on the *Pamela Jane*. Their boat had been their home for such a long time and he loved her fiercely. His sisters, too—he couldn't believe that they had ever gotten on his nerves.

"We had to go in the dark," Penny told him.

"She means the tunnels," said Maya. "Our flashlight went out near the end and we had to feel the rest of our way out. Then we arrived here three days ago. We met the city children. Remember Jolo and Small Tee? They're mussel divers here! I guess islands are like that—you're always running into the same people. We went looking for you all through town. That's when we ran into them. We found the *Pamela Jane*, too, obviously. Helix had disguised her, but we recognized her straightaway. I couldn't believe it—we missed him by hours, we were so close. But he'll have to come back—I don't think he meant to leave the boat for good."

Maya returned with a plate of mussels, bread, and olives for them to share. She banged an empty bowl for the shells in front of Isabella, ignoring her.

"Mussels again," said Penny, wrinkling her nose.

"Don't complain," said Maya. "At least we have food—something's happening in the water here," she said to Simon. "So many fish and so much sea life is dying . . . Every day the fishermen and divers come back with less."

Simon moved the plate of mussels over to Isabella so she knew she was welcome to them. He wished Maya would be a little friendlier.

"Do you have any idea where Helix went?" Simon asked.

"Some fishermen nearby said he went up into the mountains," said Maya, sitting down and pushing her hair behind her ears. "To a place called the Moraine of Lost Loved Ones."

Hungry as Simon was, he was so surprised that he stopped with a hunk of bread halfway to his mouth.

"The Moraine of Lost Loved Ones?" he asked.

Maya frowned. "You've heard of it?"

"It's in one of the ophallagraphs!" said Simon excitedly. He rummaged in his backpack for the ophallagraphs. His sisters hadn't even seen the most recent one. He had so much to tell them. Isabella leaned forward, curious. Penny sat eating olives, swinging her legs under the table and listening carefully as Simon explained everything he had learned from the Mole Monks. He pointed out the Last Ferry in the ophallagraph of the boats in the harbor.

"It's the symbol for the moraine," he said. "It's called the Last Ferry—it's a raft that drifts around the moraine, taking people from one side to the other."

"That's where Helix went?" said Maya. "That's too weird to be a coincidence."

"I think so, too," said Simon. "Do you know how to get to it?"

"I've asked everyone, but nobody knows," said Maya. "I don't think anyone has been there for a very long time. Only the oldest people knew about it, and even they couldn't tell us how to get there. All they knew was that it's in the mountains somewhere—those there," she said, nodding at the mountains visible through the porthole. "But they're huge— where would you even start?"

Simon looked through the porthole at the glimmering peaks of the mountains towering over Prince's Town.

"Do you know where it is?" Simon asked Isabella, but she shook her head.

"I thought it was just a myth," she said. "I didn't think it was real."

"What else did you find out?" Maya asked.

Simon paused and then unhappily he told Maya about Dr. Fitzsimmons and the Floriano operation. She looked at him gravely. When a whiff of rotting fish came through the open porthole she got up to close it.

"So what now?" she asked.

Simon explained how the ophallagraphs formed a triptych, which was an old method of hiding secrets. He showed them the two tools that they had so far: the mineral-fruits from the oasis in the Neglected Provinces and the key that had been hidden in the umbrella Dr. Bellagio gave them. Maya and Penny gazed at the objects reverently. He told them that the Mole Monks thought the *Pamela Jane* was important, too.

"So we're just missing one tool," he said.

"And you think that the moraine has something to do with it?" Maya asked.

"I think it might," said Simon. "Anyway, it's our only

lead at this point. Not that it's much use to us if we don't know how to get there."

They stared at the ophallagraphs. Finally Isabella spoke. "I keep thinking I see something glinting around this man's neck," she said, pointing to the man on the left beneath the umbrella. "Like a chain or something. Could that be important?"

"I don't see how," said Maya dismissively. She frowned and Simon knew she was irritated that Isabella was involved. Maya wound a strand of hair around her finger. Then she gasped softly.

"Maybe . . ." she whispered. Eyes shining, she turned the ophallagraph of the two men beneath the umbrella around so that Simon could see it. She pointed to the man on the left. Isabella was right. There was some sort of chain gleaming around his neck, as if the sun was reflecting off it. Simon had noticed it before. "The general said he was dead," said Maya. "Remember? He said this other man was propping him up. Maybe there's a link between this man and the moraine— maybe he's in the water there and we're supposed to go there to find this chain that's glowing around his neck! Maybe it's one of the tools!

"And Helix is there now," Maya went on. "Milagros said we would cross paths when the time was right—maybe this is it!"

"I think you're right," said Simon, slightly enviously. "I wish I'd seen that!" But his excitement faded when he looked out of the porthole. The mountains were long and treacherous. "We know the moraine is up there somewhere," he said.

"But we can't just start climbing without knowing where we're going—the mountains are huge and the moraine could be anywhere. We don't even know if Helix found it."

They fell into silence, staring at the ophallagraphs, each hoping for some new pattern to spring forth, for some element within to suddenly make its purpose known.

"There's the face," said Penny suddenly.

"What?" asked Simon, not really listening.

"The face," said Penny. She pointed at the ophallagraph with the two men and the umbrella. "The one I told you I saw outside, on the mountain. It's here."

"What do you mean, Penny?" Maya asked.

"See, it's in the cloud there, where the birds are, it's the same face I saw in the mountain." Penny turned the ophallagraph ninety degrees and then the others saw it, too—a human profile in the puffy white banks of clouds. "See," she said. "There's the nose, there's the mouth, there's the chin, that's where the eyes are and that's the forehead." It had been there all along, but none of them had seen it before.

"Show me in the mountain outside," said Simon.

Penny tilted her head sideways and pointed through the porthole to the mountain, purple-blue with shadow. "Look," she said. "In that part of the mountains right there. It's the same face. Like someone's lying on his back looking up. I saw it when we were walking to the general's house, before we rode the ostrillo and went in the tunnels. Only it was the other way around then. I said I saw it then, but nobody listened."

And then Simon saw the profile for the first time: sloping forehead, shallow place for the eyes, blunt nose, jutting chin. Maya exclaimed when she saw it, too.

"You're right, Penny," said Simon. "There *is* a face."

He looked at the ophallagraph again more carefully, alert to any details that would appear afresh to him. Then he remembered: The tiny black etchings of birds were a clue. They carved a path across the cloud—or mountain, depending on how you looked at it—starting in a narrow pass between two distinctive formations before making their way up in loops and switchbacks, all the way to what looked like the chin of the profile.

"The birds mark the path from the bottom of the mountain to the top!" said Simon excitedly. "Right there, in the dip of the chin—it must be there!"

"Helix is up there," said Maya, looking through the porthole at the icy mountains. "We have to go!"

Isabella cleared her throat. "If I may," she said.

"What is it?" asked Simon.

"First, I would like to apologize for the reception you received when you arrived in Tamarind," she said, her tone lofty and presidential. "Please understand, my family had just been kidnapped by Outsiders, the same Outsiders who were wreaking havoc throughout the island. I thought you were involved with them somehow. But I was wrong—clearly you're friends of Tamarind—true patriots, even if you aren't from our shores—"

"Get to the point," said Maya sharply.

Isabella leaned forward across the table. "I need a boat," she said. "I can't help you until—'

"Every time you try to *help* us, we end up in trouble," Maya interrupted. She glared at Isabella. "We don't want your help anymore. We'll find Helix and get to Faustina's Gate ourselves."

Simon, too, was suspicious. He knew that when it came down to it Isabella would do what was best for Tamarind— even if that would harm the children. He remembered how the Peace March four years ago had almost resulted in them ending up at the bottom of the ocean. But beggars couldn't be choosers—they needed someone who could rally the people and raise an army to stop the mining, and except for Isabella there wasn't exactly anyone else around who had the resources to do that. And . . . he and Isabella had survived a plunge over a mighty waterfall into a roaring river together just yesterday and now he felt a bond to her.

"What's your plan, Isabella?" he asked.

Maya folded her arms and Simon listened closely as Isabella told them what she hoped to do.

"I'll get to Maracairol by boat," said Isabella quickly. "I'll rescue my mother and brother along the way and we'll organize a resistance army. The three of you—with Helix, if you find him in time—will find the missing tool from the ophallagraph in the moraine, then return to Floriano. The señoras and the colonels—they were the greats of the last war—they'll be able to help us, too. Tell them what's happening so they can mobilize the people of Floriano to join the army when it arrives."

She paused. "You said that Milagros and the Mole Monks told you that Faustina's Gate is the only way to restore the balance and save Tamarind," she said. "I think it's too late to simply defeat the Red Coral—too much ophalla has already been mined. You'll have to find the gate and close it, whatever it takes."

This time they all wanted the same thing: to save Tamarind. And Isabella couldn't do it on her own. She needed their help, which, Simon decided, was ultimately the only safe and logical reason to trust her. "All right," he said. "It's a plan." Reluctantly Maya nodded.

"But right now I need a boat," said Isabella.

"Well, you can't have ours," said Maya firmly.

The two girls glared at each other.

"Why don't you ask Jolo and Small Tee if you could use their cousin's boat?" Penny asked Isabella, swinging her legs under the table. "They're coming back now."

Simon glanced through the porthole and saw that the fishing boats were indeed returning. A few moments later a boat sailed in alongside the *Pamela Jane* and a couple of boys leaped nimbly onto the pier and tied it up. Jolo, followed by Small Tee, hopped across to the *Pamela Jane*.

"There's a fleet of Red Coral and Maroong coming!" called Jolo as he came down the companionway. "We just heard! They're sailing down the coast now—they'll be here by tonight—they're on their way to Floriano!"

He broke off as he saw Isabella and Simon. His face lit up.

"You made it!" he said to Simon. "And Isabella, I mean Madam President!" He bowed awkwardly as Small Tee came down the companionway, bumping into him. Overjoyed to see the beloved woman who used to come to the city to read him stories, the little boy ran and threw his arms around Isabella, who picked him up and kissed him. Maya looked on in surprise.

"We need your help," said Simon to Jolo, and quickly he explained their plan.

Jolo nodded at once. "My cousin will let us take his boat," he said. "It would be our honor to take you, Madam President!"

"We'll have to disguise you," Simon said to Isabella.

Fifteen minutes later Isabella's long dark hair was lopped off—courtesy of Maya, who wielded the scissors with relish—and what was left was shoved under a cap. Her face was smudged with grease and she wore a grubby old mussel diver's uniform belonging to Jolo's cousin.

"Excellent," said Simon. "No one will look twice at you."

"Twenty-four Rua Santa Flora, in Floriano," Isabella said. "I know where to get a message to you—we're going to need all the help we can get."

She left with the city boys and within minutes they had released the dock lines on their fishing boat and were making their way out toward the open sea.

Simon calculated quickly. Jolo had said that the Red

Coral fleet wouldn't pass by until nightfall. That meant the children had until then to get to the moraine and be back in time to leave well before the Red Coral arrived.

He turned his gaze to the gleaming peaks of the mountains. "Bring any spare clothes you have," he said to his sisters. "It's going to be cold up there."

≫ CHAPTER NINETEEN ≪

The Moraine of Lost Loved Ones ✸
The Children Come to the End of the World ✸
"Look, green feathers!"

Simon, Maya, and Penny left the boat and Prince's Town and hiked an hour to the base of the mountains where they began their climb, following the track the birds made in the ophallagraph as best they could. Excited by the prospect of finding Helix, they ascended energetically at first, but soon the steep inclines and wobbly footing slowed them down. Every now and then they found rotten old rope elevators or steps hewn into the mountainside—at one time there had been a real route, but now it had fallen into disrepair and they had to scramble, crawling or scooting along precarious ledges. The air began to smell cold long before they reached the first snow, tinged blue at the edges, which appeared on the sides of the path. They put on all their clothes—Penny wore a big sweater of Maya's—but they were still cold, and it grew even colder the higher they went.

Simon was tired and his feet were still sore from the Neglected Provinces but little Penny barely made a peep, and it was this that kept him going.

They turned a bend in the path near the top, near the "chin" of the mountain, and a frigid gust of wind nearly blasted them off the narrow ledge. Penny tottered and Simon had to haul her back from the brink of an icy chasm. Simon, in front, dug his shoulder into the wind, and arm in arm like a chain they hugged the mountainside and muscled their way around the corner, a few hard-won inches with each step, until they made it into the lee. They stood out of the wind for a moment, breathing hard, blinking snow off their lashes.

When they could see again they found they were on a plateau between the mountain peaks that had been impossible to see from the earth below. Simon took the ophallagraph out and found the path the birds made. They were going the right way, he was sure, and now they were supposed to head across the plateau. He would have liked to curl up for a nap, but before the drowsy, peaceful feeling could overtake him, he shook himself and scrambled to his feet.

"Come on," he urged his sisters. "We have to keep going."

They began walking again, and to their great surprise, when they rounded a jagged crop of ice they found a stone road lit by ophalla lanterns. They stopped and looked around them in wonder. The lanterns glowed in the false twilight of the fog that was swirling down toward them. Everything around them was white.

"It's like it isn't even Tamarind at all," said Maya in a hushed voice.

Snow crunching beneath their feet, they followed the lanterns. There was not a shiver of wind. Puffs of frost hung in the air from their breath. Simon kept an eye out for footprints, but if Helix had come this way, newly fallen snow had covered his tracks.

When the fog cleared they saw it—a vast lake stretching out before them like a flat blue pan at the top of the world.

"The Moraine of Lost Loved Ones," Maya whispered.

The three of them stopped where they were and looked out over it. Maya held tightly to Penny's hand.

There was such a feeling of stillness and eternity, of peace and sorrow. They had come, it seemed, to the end of everything. On the other side of the moraine was a steep wall of ice, blue light glowing from inside its crevasses. Ice birds must nest in them for they flew in and out. They looked like bits of snow blown against the sky, itself full of snow that had yet to fall.

Simon dropped onto one knee, overcome by melancholy, and gazed out across the blue limits. His heart ached; he didn't know what for exactly. Had Helix been here? What had their friend been seeking? He wished they could find him and tell him about his aunts. He needn't have come here—he had family in Tamarind who wanted desperately to see him.

And was the man in the green-striped jacket really here, lying beneath the milky turquoise water? Simon was afraid to go to the edge to look, but he told his sisters to wait and went alone. Now that they had stopped climbing, he felt the sweat on his skin begin to prickle icily. The air was sharp in his lungs. He stopped a foot from the edge of the lake. The water trembled and pulsed almost imperceptibly against the pebbled shore. Taking a deep breath, Simon looked down.

It took his eyes a moment to adjust to see through the watery lens.

Then he realized there was a body below in the water, perfectly preserved. And another next to it. And then others beside that, and then hundreds beyond it, all the way out into the middle of the lake. Bodies reposed at ten feet deep, twenty, forty, eighty. Loved ones had taken them here, lit by the lanterns through the high plateau, and offered them up to the blue abyss.

He looked for some time at the figures arranged in eternal slumber—old men and women; fathers and mothers; someone's brother, another's sister; and here and there a child; and around them too many young soldiers to ever count. Simon felt as if he were utterly alone in space and time. Then he felt Maya and Penny come closer. Penny leaned against him and Simon clasped her small fist, and Maya put her arm around both of them, and there on the banks of the high, lonely lake, the living huddled together.

A single, unmanned raft with dragonfly-light sails, barely big enough to hold the three of them, came around a curve in the lake.

"We have to go across," said Simon quietly, breaking their silence.

It was the Last Ferry, the raft the monks had described. It sailed alone, making its way toward them, then stopped at the shore beside them as if it sensed their presence there.

They stepped gingerly aboard. Simon felt the coldness of the deep water permeating the wooden boards. A subtle wind filled the sails and began to drive them toward the opposite shore. The children looked down and saw all the bodies that lay beneath. Currents animated their clothes and hair, which floated weightless in the water. A breeze stirred the lake into silvery ripples and beneath the molten surface the bodies below grew distorted, as if life had been breathed into them and they moved again. Each face looked as if it knew a secret unknown to any on the other side of the silvery divide.

"Look for something glowing in the water," Simon whispered.

Mist came down from the glaciers and for a moment the little raft sailed blindly through the water. Every now and then Simon caught a glimpse of an icy shore looming on the opposite side of the lake. Now that they were here, he wondered if they had been wrong about the man in the ophallagraph. What if the man with the glowing chain wasn't here at all?

But then Penny pointed.

The others saw the peculiar muffled glow, too, twenty feet ahead, off the starboard of the raft. As they all leaned to one side the raft turned and they began to head toward it. They held their breath as they drew alongside it, and looked down to see a figure lying two feet underwater, a glow emanating from a chain that hung around his neck, its end tucked into the breast pocket of his green-striped jacket.

"It's him," whispered Maya. "It's the man in the

ophallagraph." She paused. "I can see the chain there," she said softly.

"I'll get it," whispered Simon. "He's very shallow—I think I can reach him." He hesitated only a moment before he removed his jacket and rolled up his sleeves. He took a deep breath and plunged his hands into the water, disturbing it as little as he could. The water was cold as needles and his arms quickly went numb. His heart was racing. He had never touched a dead person before and his dread made him suddenly start to sweat. He could reach the figure, though, so bolstering his courage, he took hold of the lapels of the man's coat and drew him to the surface very slowly.

"Don't bring him out of the water," Maya said nervously. She and Penny held on to each other and watched. "Do you want me to help you?" she asked.

"It's okay," whispered Simon. "I've got it." The man, once he started rising, seemed weightless in the water, and it was easy for Simon to let go of him with one hand and pull the thin chain over his neck with the other. Simon felt a quick horror that the man would suddenly open his eyes, or that the frigid grip of death itself would seize Simon and tear him off the raft and drag him underwater.

But the man was dead and not to be feared. He had been somebody's father or brother or uncle, Simon thought, not so different from Simon himself or the people he loved, and he felt ashamed for feeling afraid. Aside from the pallor of his skin, the man looked as if he was simply asleep.

Simon had pulled the chain over the man's head, but it was attached to something in his jacket pocket that wouldn't budge. Simon reached down and felt something round and cold and metal nestled in the pocket. He worked it gently free and drew it out on the end of the chain. It was a stopwatch. He lifted it out of the water and Maya leaned forward and took it from him. Then he lowered the man gently down. "I'm sorry to disturb you," he whispered, barely moving his lips. This time the body came to rest all the way down on the lake floor, his face perhaps even more peaceful now than it had been when they first saw it. Simon withdrew his freezing arms from the water. He dried them roughly on his jacket and put it back on, shivering.

"I think it's broken," said Maya, handing the watch back to him.

There was an ornate winder, but the watch hands must have fallen off, and any internal workings must be totally waterlogged. There seemed no catch, no way to open its face. It looked soldered together by the cold water. Simon's disappointment was tempered by the cold in his hands and arms—he would look at the watch more closely when they had left the snow. Right now, all he wanted was to get back to somewhere warmer.

The ferry had begun moving again and in a few moments it had stopped at the far shore. They waited but it didn't move again, as if it were waiting for them to disembark. "I think we get out here," said Simon. "We can walk around the edge of the moraine and go back the way we came."

His legs felt like frozen blocks and his teeth were chattering. It was going to be a long, painful walk back down the mountain.

They stepped out onto a snowy verge at the foot of a giant mineral blue wall that rose high above them until it got lost in the fog. Deep inside the ice they could see chunks of pure ophalla hanging suspended like asteroids in space, each emitting a violent glow. The children heard the faint trickle of water down icy gorges. Ice birds carved the air high above them but made no sound. The blue light made Simon want to sleep forever. He yawned. They had to get away from there—the cold, the sadness. If Helix had been there he wasn't anymore. "Come on," he said. "It's time to go."

Then Penny saw something.

A little way down from where they stood a crisp green feather lay on the snow. There was no wind there to have stirred it. Penny ran to it and held it up triumphantly. They all looked at it, thinking the same thing.

"Seagrape!" Maya called. She spun around. "Helix! Seagrape! Helix!"

They had been here!

The others joined her but their voices echoed unanswered off the glacier. Albino ice spiders scurried across the ice ahead of the vibrations of their voices, and moments later at the other end of the lake the glacier calved and a mammoth block of ice crackled as it sloughed off the glacier's face and splashed—*boom!*—into the water. The sound died away and within moments the water was locked still again. But there was no answer from Helix, and no green bird flew into view.

"Look," said Penny, pointing to the ground. "Parrot poop."

"It's not even frozen yet!" said Simon, poking it with his shoe. "They couldn't have been here that long ago."

They tried calling again but their calls echoed forlornly from the desolate mountaintops. Snow began to fall. The ice birds grew nearly invisible, pale arabesques in the dimming sky. Suddenly, and with overwhelming intensity, Simon wanted to be away from that cold and lonely place. He wanted to see their friend; he wanted to go home.

As the others scanned the sky one last time, Penny wandered off and peered over an icy ledge into a great blue hole that descended into the wall of ice. By the time the others saw her she already had one leg over the edge.

"Penelope!" shouted Maya. "No!"

But Penny quickly hoisted herself onto the ledge. She disappeared.

"Penny!" shouted Simon.

He and Maya ran to the edge and looked aghast over it. Penny was all right, but she had scooted down a smooth-sided ice tunnel and was just out of reach.

"I'm getting the feathers," she called, her voice echoing against the narrow walls of blue ice. "There's more down here."

"Forget the feathers," said Maya in frustration. "Penny, this is *dangerous*. Come back up, okay? Come on, crawl back out to us!"

Penny's voice sounded farther away as she looked back down the tunnel. "But the *feathers*," she said. "Helix and Seagrape went this way. Maybe it's a shortcut."

"It isn't a shortcut," said Simon sternly. "Turn around right now and come back to us."

The tunnel went at an angle down into the ice before it turned a bend and Simon could no longer see where it went. Reluctantly, Penny turned and tried to crawl back up the slope, but a thin layer of surface ice had melted slightly under the heat of her body and had become too slippery for her to grip. Each time she moved she slid another couple of inches farther into the hole.

"Stop!" cried Maya. "Don't move." She took off her jacket and tossed an arm of it down to the little girl. "Penny, grab on to the end of this and we'll pull you out."

But the jacket wasn't long enough. Maya leaned in as far as she could and Penny stretched her hand up as far as *she* could, but it still wasn't enough. Penny looked distressed for the first time and she started scrabbling against the ice, but that only made it melt faster.

"Keep very still," said Simon, trying to stay calm. "We're going to get you."

They should have brought rope with them, he rebuked himself. He took off his jacket and one of the shirts he was wearing. His hands were numb and the fabric was stiff with cold and it was hard to tie a knot. But eventually he managed to tie his shirt and jacket and Maya's jacket together. He lay down at the mouth of the tunnel and tossed one end of the makeshift rope down to Penny. "Grab hold!" he said.

But Penny had slid farther, and stretch as she might, the

makeshift rope didn't reach. Suddenly she slipped a few more feet. She was inches from the bend in the tunnel.

Quick as lightning, Maya tied the jacket rope to her ankle, hopped onto the edge of the ledge, and began to lower herself down. "I'm tallest," she said. "Penny, grab on to the jackets—Simon, you're strongest, try to pull us up!"

Penny let go with one hand and grabbed the jacket just in time. She pulled herself up until she was sitting between Maya's legs. Simon, braced on the outside of the tunnel, had a firm grip on Maya's wrists.

"All right," called Maya, relieved. "I think we're okay!"

Inch by inch, Simon succeeded in hauling them back up the tunnel—in another few moments they would all be on solid ground again. But the ice was melting beneath him, too, and he was beginning to slide. Sweat poured down his face.

"Don't let me go!" Maya cried, feeling Simon's grip loosening.

"If Penny can crawl over you up to me, then she'll be out and it will be less weight," said Simon.

He hung on to Maya with all his might but it was no use—suddenly the ice broke beneath him. Maya screamed, the sound changing pitch as the three of them slid into the tunnel. They swung around the corner and the slope steepened and they found themselves zooming through the polished blue ice, deep into the mountain.

Simon tried to grab the sides of the tunnel to slow their descent but the walls were too slick and they kept going faster. The tunnel narrowed and they had to lie back flat.

And then, abruptly, the tunnel widened and grew brighter and brighter and then—*whoosh*! The ice walls and roof broke open and they were whizzing along in the open air and for a few surreal moments they could see out across Tamarind! Ice was all around them yet the steamy hot jungle was within sight. They were halfway down the mountain and going fast. In the next instant the tunnel closed over them again and they were hurtling, numb with cold, through the wintry passage, going faster than ever. At this rate they would reach the bottom soon, Simon thought. All he could do was hope fervently that they weren't heading into a frozen pit at the foot of the ice where they would be trapped and never heard from again.

Without warning, they shot out into the world again, into the bright, hot day. The ice slide had brought them to the foot of the mountains and when they stopped skidding they found themselves sitting in a puddle of water. The air was immediately hotter and the chill at once began to leave their skin. Not yet able to speak, they sat there catching their breath.

"Everyone okay?" Simon asked finally.

Maya nodded. Penny looked back up at the towering wall of ice they had come through, her eyes shining. "I want to go again!"

"Penny," said Simon. "That was really bad."

"*Really* bad," said Maya.

"You knew you shouldn't have climbed in there," said Simon.

"But the *feathers* were there," said Penny. "And look!"

Simon got slowly to his feet and squinted in the direction Penny was pointing. Then he saw a person walking, a distance away but still big enough to make out. Above the figure flew a green parrot. As they watched, it turned and squawked and began to fly toward them.

Maya stood on tiptoe and shaded her eyes. "It's Helix!" she cried. "Helix! Helix!"

Simon could hardly believe it. He and Penny set off after Maya, who had begun running toward the figure.

"Helix!" the three of them shouted.

Helix stopped and turned around and moments later they reached him. Maya threw her arms around him and hugged him, then stood back to look at him.

Helix looked thin and strong, his hair uncombed, his skin darker, the blade of the knife on his belt recently sharpened and shining brightly in the sun. Camouflage mottled his face and his clothes from the Outside were worn to shreds and he looked once more like the boy they had first met in the jungle. As much as he had wanted to see Helix now that he was there in front of them, Simon felt a little unsure. Helix could have betrayed them back at Isabella's, or earlier, even, before they had left home. Maybe he hadn't been entirely honest with them about the other reasons he had wished to return to Tamarind. Perhaps he had put Simon, Maya, and Penny in danger in order to return.

But before Simon could say anything, Maya blurted out, "Why did you just leave like that, back in Maracairol? You left us locked up in Isabella's tower!"

"I'm sorry," said Helix. "I didn't think I'd be gone so

long. I saw a chance to escape and I took it. It didn't make sense for the *Pamela Jane* to be captured and all of us locked up. It seemed like the right thing to do. I thought you'd be safe in Maracairol until I could figure out what the Red Coral were doing." He looked at them, his face open, and Simon thought he really did look sorry.

At the moraine, Simon had felt a glimmer of Helix's sad secret burden, a burden that was his alone and could never really be shared with others. Helix had lost people who were never coming back. If he had reasons for returning to Tamarind that had nothing to do with the Red Coral Project, Simon forgave his secrecy. The decision to come back had ultimately been made out of necessity—the Red Coral Project had to be dealt with. If there were other reasons that Helix hadn't shared, well, that was okay. Simon, too, knew he'd had his own reasons for wanting to go back to Tamarind so urgently. They all had.

Simon cleared his throat. "It's all right," he said. "You had to make a decision. We figured that's what happened." He wanted to tell Helix about his aunts there and then, but he hesitated. How was he supposed to break such momentous news out of the blue? It was enough of a shock right now that Helix and the children had found one another again.

Maya burst into a flood of tears and she threw her arms around Helix. Simon looked at her, feeling something between annoyance and amazement—one second she was furious at Helix, the next she was sobbing in his arms. Maya really made no sense sometimes. Penny jumped up and down until Helix scooped her up and squeezed her tight and kissed her. "Hello, starfish," he said. Maya straightened up, the squall over, and stood there sniffling and looking red-eyed and slightly chagrined.

Simon and Helix shook hands and clapped each other on the shoulder, which meant that everything was all right between them. Maya wiped her eyes and the four friends stood there in the golden light smiling at one another, a brisk breeze rolling across the earth, the sea twinkling in the distance and the icy blue point of the top of the highest mountain casting a shadow behind them. Seagrape flew high above them. Penny sat down then—her short legs needing a rest—and the others followed.

"I found Seagrape's feathers in the slide," she said.

"Wretched bird," said Helix. "I had to fight with her to get her to go in there with me. But I'd been told that was the fastest way down. I think it used to be a gradual slope all the way, but over time it's melted and become steeper. I was wandering around in the mountains for days before I finally found the moraine today. We must have just missed one another."

"Tell us everything," said Maya. "Where did you go when you left Maracairol?"

"We found the boat," said Simon. "The *Blue Duck*? Seriously?"

"It was all I could think of," said Helix sheepishly. "I was in a rush. The first thing I did after I escaped was to stop somewhere so that I could disguise the boat. I ducked into a cove and hid and watched Isabella's fleet sail right past—then I sailed to a little town where I painted the hull and changed her name.

"I tried to find out what I could about Faustina's Gate," he went on. "I asked people all across Tamarind, but no one I talked to had ever heard of it. I think that the Red Coral must have gotten it wrong. Or whatever it is has another name."

Maya was about to say something but Simon motioned for her to wait.

"I caused some trouble around the Red Coral camp and found out more about what they're planning," Helix said. He paused. "You know that Fitzsimmons is here. I saw him, from a distance. The red hair gave him away."

Simon nodded grimly. "We know," he said.

"He started out planning to just gather a cargo of ophalla and return home to study it," said Helix. "Now it's turned into something else. He wants to take over all of Tamarind. He's out of control. Right now there are thousands of new Maroong heading west—"

"To Floriano," finished Simon.

"You already know," said Helix. "There's no resistance to speak of. Everything's a mess and it's getting worse. Floriano is going to be their biggest operation yet. The huge steel ship they came in is sitting off the north coast, ready to be filled with even more ophalla. And even more Maroong are marching to Floriano from the East."

Simon listed gravely. "We were actually on our way back to Floriano now," he said. As quickly as he could, leaving out the señoras, he told Helix about their plan with Isabella. He

279

took out the ophallagraphs to show Helix, as well as the mineral-fruits, the key, and the newest tool, the stopwatch. Simon held it flat in his hand and they looked at it, glinting when the sun caught it. The metal was still cold.

"I'm afraid it's broken," said Simon. "Here, look, you can wind this knob and it makes a buzzing noise, but that's it. I think the water sealed it shut."

"I wonder what it was supposed to be for," said Maya.

But none of them knew. Simon had thought that the final clue would help all the others make sense, but now he began to think that the frustrating, mystifying secret hidden in the ophallagraphs would elude them forever. Perhaps they had done everything they could already and the problem lay in the riddle itself. Perhaps it was incomplete or unsolvable. Either way, it seemed less and less likely that the secret—whatever it was—would be able to save Tamarind before the Red Coral opened the mines at Floriano.

"So you went to the moraine because it was in the ophallagraph, and because you heard I was there," said Helix.

Maya nodded. "Why did you go?" she asked.

Helix dropped his gaze as if he were ashamed. "Going there had nothing to do with the Red Coral," he said. "I thought that if I came back to Tamarind now that I was older I might be able to find out who my family was. I know now it's impossible. I went to the moraine to . . . to say good-bye, I guess."

Simon and Maya looked at each other.

"We have something to tell you," said Simon.

The yellow sunlight was growing weaker. A breeze came

down from the mountain and ran across the tall grass. The glazed peaks of the mountain shone behind them. Simon took a deep breath, then he and Maya told Helix about his aunts.

"They've been looking for you all these years," said Maya softly.

Helix looked as if the wind had been knocked out of him.

After a few minutes, without a word, his face sealed, he got to his feet. "Let's get started," he said.

The others let him be. Who knew what it would feel like to find out after all this time that you had a family after all, and you were about to meet them again? Though their legs were weary they walked as though they were not tired. Seagrape flew high overhead, her shadow dipping and bobbing urgently on the ground before them. A few hours later the *Pamela Jane*—still disguised as the *Blue Duck*—was setting sail out of Prince's Town as the sun set, and heading swiftly toward Floriano.

❧ CHAPTER TWENTY ❧

Reunion ✸ "It's a ghost!" ✸
Beneath the Aliandis Tree ✸
A New Edition

Late the following afternoon, the children and Helix left the *Pamela Jane* in a secret, sheltered inlet near the bay in Floriano, as close to the town as they could get. They furled her sails and hid her deck beneath palm leaves. Maya made Helix wash his face in the salt water to scrub off the camouflage. He combed his hair with a wet comb. His ears were bright red. They walked into Floriano on foot late in the afternoon. Finding no one at home at Señora Rojo's, they slipped through the bars of Señora Medrano's tall iron gate and climbed the hill to the pink stone mansion that Simon had previously glimpsed through the trees.

"I don't know if this is such a good idea, after all," Helix whispered nervously. "Maybe one of you should go first." He looked so uncharacteristically pale and edgy that Simon was half-afraid that if they let him out of their sight he would run away and not be seen again.

"It'll be fine," Simon said reassuringly. "They really want to see you."

No one answered their knock—maybe whoever was home was too deep in the house to hear—so the children and Helix walked in through the open door.

Expecting that he would have to call again, Simon was surprised when Señora Medrano appeared suddenly through the parlor door, Señora Rojo behind her.

They stopped in their tracks.

No one spoke.

Everyone was watching Helix. Simon and Maya held their breath.

Simon had never seen Seagrape alight on a shoulder other than Helix's, but now she flew first to Señora Rojo and then Señora Medrano. Then she coasted once around the room, stirring up the thick dust that had rested there for so long, before she returned to Helix's shoulder. The señoras turned very pale and took each other's hands. Finally, through her tears, Señora Rojo spoke.

"This is the happiest moment of our lives," she said. Her sister nodded.

✺ ✺ ✺

In the past few days, Simon had wandered lost in the Neglected Provinces, been taken prisoner and escaped, plunged over a waterfall, scaled a frozen mountain, and sailed at speed all night and day so that the Red Coral wouldn't catch up with them—he couldn't stop yawning as the children sat in the great room, telling the señoras about their adventures.

When they had first arrived, the señoras had ushered them into the great room, where for a while they sat together, stunned. Later Helix went out on his own to the purple aliandis tree, beneath which they told him his mother was buried. The señoras prepared dinner and when Helix returned they all ate together. It was decided that nothing could be done until morning. They hoped to have word from Isabella by then and could assemble the colonels and decide what to do next. The señoras told the children that an advance guard of Maroong had arrived in Floriano a few days ago to begin clearing land for the new mine.

Now night had fallen and candles glowed softly in the black windows. A slight dampness seeped in and the scent of animals was carried on a light breeze. Every now and then they heard rumbling deep within the earth, and the herd of ostrillos came galloping out of the trees and moved across the open grass like a cloud pushed by a swift wind.

None of them noticed that someone had come and sat beneath the window and was listening to their story, every now and then nodding. He sighed once, deeply, but if any of them heard it, they thought it was the wind or a bullfrog or the sigh of a bird's wings. Only Penny saw him looking in, but she had seen him before and was not afraid. He winked at her and put his finger in front of his lips, and she knew that he didn't yet wish to be noticed.

Soon Maya motioned to Simon, and saying good night, they took Penny upstairs to the rooms the señoras had prepared for them, leaving Helix and his aunts alone to talk. Maya carried Penny. At the top of the stairs the little girl took her thumb out of her mouth.

"I want to go home," she said for the first time.

"Me, too," said Simon.

"Me, too," said Maya. She hugged her little sister close to her. "Soon," she said.

Maya and Penny went to sleep in one room and Simon in another. He lay awake in the dark for a while. Every now and then from downstairs he could hear the señoras' voices.

"We could tell you stories about your mother for days and never get to the end of them . . . It's good to remember . . ."

"On the coldest nights, we would sleep together in a big bed, all three of us—me, Estella, and your mother—huddled together under a mountain of blankets. Your mother was a kicker when she slept, but because she was littlest, we always put her in the middle . . ."

Their voices drifted away and Simon concentrated on the ticking of the grandfather clock coming from the landing.

He couldn't imagine losing anyone in his family, and though he was tired, he tossed and turned, anxious about what lay ahead. The Red Coral Project were set to open the mine in Floriano the next day, and Simon still had no idea if Isabella would be able to stop them, or how he and his sisters were going to reach Faustina's Gate. The clock chimed, echoing through the rooms. Time was running out.

Simon was woken the next morning by hammering. Dazed, he rolled out of bed. Helix, who had not come to bed until late the night before, rolled over and pulled the pillow over his head. Simon realized that the hammering was loud, persistent knocking coming from the front door. He dressed

285

quickly and came downstairs to see the señoras walking briskly toward the door, Maya and Penny following behind them.

"Who the devil can that be?" said Señora Medrano. "Nobody comes here."

When she flung the door open and saw the figure standing there, she and Señora Rojo nearly jumped out of their skins.

"It's a ghost!" gasped Señora Rojo.

It was General Alvaro! Simon's initial excitement at seeing the general—he must have come to help, after all!—was swiftly replaced by apprehension when he looked back at the señoras. In the emotion of the night before, it hadn't even occurred to them to tell the señoras that the general was alive and well.

Señora Medrano took a deep breath and a big step forward and pinched the figure on the arm—harder than was really necessary, Simon thought. She stood upright. "He's no ghost," she said darkly.

"But we killed him!" said Señora Rojo.

"Apparently not successfully," said Señora Medrano.

The general stood there, clothes rumpled, hip stiff from a night on the damp earth, expression aggrieved.

"Oh, but he's grown old," sighed Señora Rojo, putting her hands to her own wrinkled face. "Has it really been this long?"

"Enough of this infernal babble!" General Alvaro shouted, though whether he was insulted or exasperated Simon couldn't tell. "Ladies, I've just traveled all the way from the Borderlands and I spent an uncomfortable night in your garden because I didn't want to intrude on what I realized was a reunion," he said. "Now, please let me in—we don't have time to waste!" He nodded at the children. "Good morning, children. Cadet," he said, nodding last at Penny. She smiled at him, the only one not surprised to see him, pleased to have shared a secret.

"You know who this is?" Señora Medrano asked the children sharply.

"Um, we . . ." Maya floundered.

"Yes," said Simon decisively. "We can explain—"

But he was saved from having to give an explanation because at that moment Dr. Bellagio appeared at the top of the hill. He was in a hurry and carried something tucked beneath his arm. When he reached the doorstep he stopped in surprise, first to see the children and then to see the man standing among them.

"General Alvaro!"

"Dr. Bellagio," said the general.

The men shook hands warmly.

Señora Rojo gasped. "Wait—you *knew*!" she said to Dr. Bellagio. "All this time you knew he was alive!"

"Spare us your dramatics, you antique!" growled General Alvaro. "Bellagio's the very reason I *am* alive—no thanks to you and your equally iniquitous sister!"

"I'm sorry, Conchita," said Dr. Bellagio, pained. "I felt it was for the best . . ."

"But we buried him," said Señora Rojo. "All three of us were there, that day . . ."

"To be entirely accurate, we buried an unidentified soldier," said Dr. Bellagio.

Señora Rojo's face turned from white to red to white again. Simon, Maya, and Penny inched away nervously. Señora Medrano, not taking her eyes off the general, raised her hand to her mouth to stifle a snort, but her eyes shone with glee.

"You old possum," she said delightedly.

"But, Dr. Bellagio," said Señora Rojo reproachfully. "In my home every week all these years and all this time, you let me believe I had killed this man . . . How could you?"

"How you could have even tried it at all is what baffles me!" retorted the general.

A parrot squawked, bringing the conversation to a stop as everyone turned to look at Helix, who had come quietly down the stairs and had been listening to everything unfold. The señoras' eyes lit up when they saw him.

"Well, I'll be damned," said General Alvaro, taking off his hat. "There's no mistaking *your* face."

Dr. Bellagio was speechless for a moment. "I'm very glad to see you alive and well, young man," he said finally. "Your aunts searched for you faithfully since the day you went missing. It—it's been a very long time."

Helix could not have looked any more uncomfortable. The señoras dabbed their eyes.

Seeing his opportunity, Dr. Bellagio cleared his throat. "I hate to interrupt such momentous reunions, but I have important news. Word just reached Floriano that Isabella Obrado escaped from the Red Man—she's raising an army and planning a revolt against the Outsiders! People say the army will be here today!"

Simon breathed a deep sigh of relief and smiled. Isabella was safe! Suddenly everything seemed more possible. Isabella was free and she was determined to stop the Red Coral. And a determined Isabella was a formidable ally. He remembered the look in her eye as she had pushed them over the waterfall.

"But that's not all . . ." Dr. Bellagio went on. "I found this just inside the gate on my way up the hill," he said, smartly handing Señora Rojo the newspaper that had been tucked under his arm. When she refused to take it from him, he opened it himself and everyone stepped forward for a closer look.

"It's the *Gazette Extraordinario*," said Maya wonderingly. "And it's a brand-new copy!"

At first Simon thought Maya must be wrong. It couldn't be a new copy—the señoras said no one had printed a newspaper in Tamarind for years. But it was. It was the same size, it had the same name and the same typeface, and it bore the unmistakable scent of fresh ink. There was nothing sensible printed in it, just a jumble of letters.

Señora Rojo examined it closely. "It's from the old Printing House in Rivas, I'm sure of it," she said excitedly. "The pattern on the edge of the paper is identical—it's from the old machines!"

Milagros's words returned to Simon again: *What appears dead is alive.* Someone was sending them a message, and he knew who it was.

"How far away is Rivas?" Simon asked.

"About ten miles, just northeast of here," said Señora Rojo.

"Well, if no one else has any announcements or surprises we may as well go inside and figure out what to do," said Señora Medrano.

They all trooped inside and settled around the long wooden table in the kitchen. Helix reported everything he had seen in the North of the island. The general listened intently to his accounts of the numbers and movements of the troops of Maroong. Simon updated the general and Dr. Bellagio about the ophallagraphs. "We know that it's essential that we close Faustina's Gate," he said. "And we have all the tools now. But we still don't know how to get to it or how it works."

There was a sober pause. General Alvaro pressed his lips together and his jowls quivered; Dr. Bellagio stroked his silver moustache; and the señoras' wrinkled walnut faces grew very serious.

"The Red Coral are supposed to open the new mine later today," said Simon. "There's hardly any time left. And we still don't know where Faustina's Gate is. General Alvaro, would you contact the colonels and mobilize the town? I'm sure that Isabella will make contact with us very soon. When she does we need to be able to tell her that Floriano is ready to join her in the fight. We know Dr. Fitzsimmons is looking for the *Pamela Jane*—we've got to get her somewhere safe as soon as possible. Helix, Milagros told us that if we really needed her again we could put a zala root in Seagrape's talons and she would fly to her. I think we need her help now.

"Finally, this newspaper . . ." He slid the new copy of the *Gazette* to the middle of the table. "I'm pretty sure I know who printed it, and I'm sure he can help us figure out what we're supposed to do at Faustina's Gate and how we can get there. I propose that I leave right away for the Printing House in Rivas. This paper"—he tapped it—"is an invitation."

General Alvaro looked at Simon with something akin to admiration. "That's the soundest plan I've heard since Hetty's Pass," he said. "And I came up with *that* myself."

CHAPTER TWENTY-ONE

The Mad Inventor ❀
An Explanation, at Last ❀
A Very Old Radio

There was a peculiar sallow cast to the air when Simon reached Rivas later that morning on the back of one of Señora Medrano's ostrillos. The village was in a state of damp, lichen-chewed decay. Washerwomen beat laundry on stones down by the river and children sailed homemade toy boats in the lazy eddies. Lanky cranes waded on the shores of the river, and the sweet reek of low tide hung in the air. The cobblestone streets, smoothed by time and the traffic of cart wheels, were buckled here and there from tree roots, and the town, mossy in its shadowed bits, was slowly turning to rubble. Simon asked for directions and finally a bent old crone pointed him down a series of streets to a dilapidated brick warehouse on the far side of the town.

The building's windows were boarded up and its doors locked and chained. The yard around it was deserted. The place looked abandoned. Simon tied the ostrillo to a fence post in the shade and left it eating weedflowers. He had to walk twice around the perimeter before he discovered that a door at the rear of the building was askance on its hinges.

He pushed it to one side and, with a last deep breath of fresh air, turned his shoulders and slid inside.

It took a few moments for his eyes to adjust to the gloom. The breeze that had entered with him was swallowed by the great vault of stale air, and Simon heard before he saw the warbling pigeons crowding the eaves. Their droppings frosted the tops of printing equipment, and the floor was littered with the broken shells of eggs that had hatched or fallen from nests in the rafters. A light snow of termite dust sifted down from the ceilings and spiders big as octopuses shifted in the corners.

Simon began to feel sure he had made a mistake. How could anything still be running here? It didn't look as if anyone had even set foot in the place for years. He made his way past stacks of rotting paper and rusting hulks of machinery with unoiled wheels and turbines that hadn't turned in decades. A thick cushion of dust covered everything. It looked as if the señoras had been wrong—the new copy of the *Gazette* must have come from elsewhere. When time was so precious, Simon had wasted hours getting here, and would now go back empty-handed. His disappointment was keen.

But then, to his surprise, he heard a soft scraping sound. He kept going, treading carefully on the rotting floorboards.

As he went farther into the building, he sensed that something was stirring. Some tremor of life traveled through the air. A turning of wheels and gears; the simmer of a Bunsen burner; the sound of paper rubbing against paper; of feet shuffling on a creaky floor.

Someone was deep in the Printing House.

Simon proceeded gingerly. When he reached a lighted doorway he stopped.

"Davies Maroner?" he asked.

The man standing in the room at the end of the Printing House was exactly what Simon would have expected a mad inventor to look like. His white hair was wild and frazzled, as if he had been playing with electricity. More hair spouted from his ears. He reminded Simon of a very old lemur. His clothes were streaked with grime and grit, and thick rims of dirt were buried deep beneath his finger-nails. Long-ago chemical burns had healed patchily on his hands and arms. But deep in his wrinkled face his eyes were bright and lively. Though he moved with a limp, he was still spry, and he stepped quickly to Simon and shook his hand energetically.

"Pleased to see you, young Outsider," Davies Maroner said warmly. "You've come from a world far away! It is my privilege to meet you!"

Simon had first suspected that Davies was alive when he kept hearing conflicting accounts of how the scientist-inventor had died, but it wasn't until they received the new copy of the *Gazette* that he felt certain. Davies was the person the Dark Women of the Extraordinary Generation had turned to for help to find a way of hiding the secret they had kept hidden for hundreds of years. He had invented ophal-lagraphs and created the triptych, and Simon had high hopes that he would be able to shed light on Faustina's Gate. Simon felt sure that only a scientist could answer the big questions he still had, and he was nearly trembling with excitement at the chance to talk to the clever and unusual man.

"When I learned you were pursuing clues in the ophallagraphs I hoped that we would have real time to speak with each other," said Davies. "But we both know how little time is left, so I'll share with you what I know as quickly as I can. Please, please, have a seat! You wish, I'm sure, to hear what I know about Faustina's Gate." Davies did not stand still as he spoke, but hopped nimbly here and there, fiddling with knobs and opening and shutting things.

Simon sat obediently on an overturned box. He wasn't surprised that Davies somehow knew who he was, or that he had summoned him here—Davies seemed to be everywhere and know everything. Simon felt as if he already knew him. Even his voice sounded oddly familiar.

"Yes," he said excitedly. "Faustina's Gate. Do you know where it is?"

But Davies shook his head ruefully.

Simon's heart sank. If Davies didn't know, who did?

"I've gone in search of it many times, but never found it," said Davies. "No one alive today—even Milagros—has ever been inside it. But never fear, never fear! I have found many smaller ophalla gates and I base my theories about Faustina's Gate on those. Don't worry, young Outsider. I wouldn't have called you here today if I couldn't help you."

"I still don't know how Faustina's Gate can help Tamarind," said Simon. "I still don't even really know *what* it is."

"Yes, yes," said Davies cheerfully. "It took me many years to figure out. Let me try to explain my theory. Faustina's Gate, you see, is one of many 'gates' in Tamarind that help control the amount of ophalla sediment that reaches the Blue Line. The Blue Line requires a high concentration of ophalla in order to remain stable and support the life of all the marine organisms specially adapted to Tamarind's waters."

Simon listened carefully.

"Faustina's Gate isn't a real gate," continued Davies. "It's actually just a deep hole. Like a very, very deep well made naturally out of ophalla. At the foot of the well are underground, water-filled tunnels that run for miles until they open into deep-sea vents. These vents release pure ophalla into the sea around Tamarind. When this free-floating ophalla reaches the open sea, a type of natural barrier is formed—the Blue Line—separating Tamarind's waters from the Outside ocean."

"So Faustina's Gate acts as a direct conduit to the Blue Line," said Simon.

"Exactly," said Davies. "Now, the Blue Line isn't really a line, it's the outer edge of a gyre—a circular body of water that surrounds Tamarind. There is very little mixing of the water inside the gyre with the water outside it."

In the corner something in a crude iron pot bubbled softly and Simon heard the low whine of a radio coming from behind a curtain.

"Usually this replenishment happens through a natural—if often slow—process of percolation," explained Davies. "The ophalla in the earth in Tamarind breaks down naturally and percolates into a deep system of aquatic caves that run beneath the island, then it's released offshore."

In a flash Simon understood. "But all the mining means there's not enough ophalla reaching the Blue Line!" he exclaimed.

Davies nodded.

"And the Blue Line is breaking down," said Simon in amazement.

"Yes," said Davies soberly.

Simon remembered the news reports back at home about the mysterious glowing sea creatures found dead. The Blue Line was weak: That's how the creatures were getting through! Suddenly it was starting to make sense.

Davies leaned forward and spoke slowly to emphasize what he was about to say next. "The Blue Line is the key to the whole ecosystem of Tamarind," he said. "Everything alive in Tamarind today relies on the health of the Blue Line. Even the relatively small amount of ophalla that the Red Coral have removed from the earth has severe repercussions on the concentration of ophalla in the Blue Line. And once the line is compromised, lifeforms on the Outside can breach Tamarind's waters, causing destruction of species not equipped to withstand them. That's why you're seeing sea life dying. Life on land is beginning to follow. A domino effect gets set off through the whole ecosystem, including shifts in weather patterns—we're only seeing the beginnings of this now. Because Tamarind is such a small system, really, the changes can happen very fast. The danger is that if the Blue Line finally collapses, it will be sudden, not gradual."

Thunder grumbled ominously in the distance and just then the heavens opened and heavy rain pelted the tin roof of the Printing House.

"So destroying the Blue Line would destroy Tamarind," said Simon gravely.

Davies nodded. "The best I can figure, the island would become a denuded rock. The intense variety and richness of life—all the native species, plant and animal, that have evolved here and exist nowhere else—everything would perish. Oh, over many hundreds of years, plants and animals from the Outside would colonize Tamarind, but then it would just be an ordinary island, like any other. Tamarind as we know it would cease to exist."

"And at first it would all be like the Neglected Provinces," said Simon.

"Yes," said Davies. "Like the heart of the Neglected Provinces, where not even a sandbug can survive."

They were silent for a moment.

"So," asked Simon. "How can Faustina's Gate help? You said that it's only one of many gates?"

"That's true," said Davies. "It is, however, perhaps the oldest and biggest, made up of the most concentrated ophalla. The ancients knew about it long ago. Percolation, as you would imagine, is a very slow process, but the gate may offer us a way to speed up the release of ophalla from Tamarind to the Blue Line. Somehow—and I still haven't figured out how—closing the gate triggers ophalla to be released into the sea.

"You see," he said urgently, "it's too late to just stop the Red Coral from mining—too much damage has already been done. The process must be reversed! Faustina's Gate must be closed in order to release more ophalla into the sea to bolster the Blue Line!"

Simon listened intently. In the background he was dimly aware of the sound of static every now and then. "And somehow the tools we found that were hidden in the ophallagraphs will help us close the gate," he said.

"Exactly," said Davies. "Now, did you bring the triptych with you?"

Simon took the ophallagraphs out and their glow spilled into the dusty room, illuminating bracket fungi growing out of the floorboards and cobwebs thick as smoke in the corners.

"They did work!" said Davies, beaming. He regarded the ophallagraphs with the pride of an artist admiring his work. "I wasn't convinced they would. It was quite a tricky process to refine the ophalla crystals enough to be able to use them. Then of course there was the problem of pigmentation. Not to mention the biggest thing—knowing if such small crystals would respond the way I wanted them to when the time came."

"We have the tools now," Simon said. "The mineral-fruits, the ophalla key, the stopwatch. But how do they work? What do we do with them?"

Davies Maroner shook his head. "Regrettably, I can't help you with that," he said. "I just don't know. The secret of Faustina's Gate was shared and passed down by the Dark Women over the centuries. Dark Women never tell ordinary Tamarinders their secrets. Milagros only told me parts of it, never the whole. People from the Extraordinary Generation who she had entrusted with parts of the secret came to me with pictures of the mineral-fruits, the umbrella, the *Pamela Jane*, and so on—all the things you've already discovered in the images. I assembled these fragments without knowing their full significance. I never saw the actual tools that you've now found."

He looked at the images. "I added the Blue Door myself because I knew whoever would eventually try to solve it would need help," he said. "And the birds—yes, they were hints in honor of Milagros, who had risked her life to help me at a time that was very dangerous for Dark Women! The people who gave me parts of the secret told me that certain elements of the images were especially important, so I pointed the birds toward those things, but they never told me *why* they were important. After I had created the ophallagraphs, I had to go into hiding, which was my agreement with Milagros. That's why I spread so many stories about my death."

Simon sat quietly, processing everything Davies had told him.

Now he knew that Faustina's Gate was linked to the Blue Line, and the Blue Line was responsible for the health and survival of everything in Tamarind. He knew that if the Blue Line was destroyed, Tamarind as they knew it would disappear.

What Davies hadn't been able to tell him was where Faustina's Gate was, or how to use the tools.

Simon heard the squeak of a pigeon's wings overhead. He looked all around the room at tables set up with Bunsen burners and microscopes, scattered piles of notes, twisted bits of wire, chipped ophalla stones, and all sorts of other oddities.

"It *is* beautiful, isn't it?" said Davies, picking up a piece of ophalla and looking at it reverently as he slid it under a microscope. "I find it utterly mesmerizing."

He motioned for Simon to look. In the grainy, suffused light that the stone emitted, Simon could make out an irregular honeycomb pattern. For a second he thought he saw an almost imperceptible movement, then it was gone. It must be his tiredness. He rubbed his eyes.

Just then Simon heard the crackling again, followed by a hissing, whining noise. Davies must have some sort of radio back there. Suddenly Simon realized where he had heard Davies's voice before: in his father's study when he had gone to collect the compass right before they had left for Tamarind! Simon pulled the curtain aside and saw a very old radio purring on top of a table. He looked sharply at Davies.

"It's you," he said in amazement. "It's you Papi was trying to communicate with!"

"It is, it is," said Davies cheerfully.

Simon gazed at him dumbstruck. "Can we talk to my dad?" he asked.

"Unfortunately, we've only actually been able to hear

each other a handful of times," said Davies. "I spoke to him; they know you four made it here safely. That's another reason I knew you were here. I'd try to get him now but the reception has only ever worked very early in the morning or late at night. But I'll do my best to reach him later, and if I can, I'll tell him you're safe."

Simon looked at the radio. He wished more than anything he could hear his father's voice, just for a moment.

"Which brings me to another reason I wanted to see you today," said Davies. "So much of what I've invented in Tamarind was inspired by stories I'd heard about the Outside or by objects the rare Outsiders who came here brought with them. I would like to return the favor. I'd like something I've worked on to inspire scientists on the Outside—worthy scientists like your father and mother. This is my research. I want you to take it to your parents. In the right hands ophalla—just a few tiny pebbles of it— can be used for marvelous things to help many people." He handed Simon a big sheaf of papers covered in very tiny print.

Simon looked at the papers in surprise. "Thank you," he said solemnly. He put them carefully in his backpack. Around him things ticked and burbled in the makeshift laboratory and the static of the radio whirred and popped.

"Now hurry," said Davies. "Time is running out! You should get back to Floriano before the Red Coral get there. As for where Faustina's Gate is—I would study the birds if I were you. I suspect they hold the secret."

Simon shoved the papers into his backpack. "Thank you!" he called as he left. Back outside, he untied the ostrillo and vaulted onto its back and urged it on. He had learned the secret of how Faustina's Gate could save Tamarind, but he still had no idea where it was.

✧ Chapter Twenty-Two ✧

The sky was dark and overcast and the hour felt later
than it was as Simon and the ostrillo loped back to Floriano.
Clunk! At first he thought someone had thrown a stone at
him. But then another landed and another on the path before him, and then—ouch!—one struck him in the face.
Quickly, he and the tall bird took cover in an empty lean-to
on the edge of a farmer's field and looked out in amazement.

It was hailing.

In the tropics.

The mining was turning the weather upside down.

Soon the air had faded to white and hailstones the size of
marbles rattled across the landscape. The sound on the tin
roof was deafening. When it showed no signs of abating,
Simon retreated to the back of the shelter and settled down to
wait it out. He took out the ophallagraphs and prepared to
study them. Now that he was sitting down, Simon felt tired.
It seemed to have been a long day already—every day since
they had arrived in Tamarind had been strenuous. He was
looking at the ophallagraph of the boats in the harbor for

several seconds during an especially extended yawn before he realized it was upside down.

Sometimes a tired mind will recognize patterns more easily than a mind that is alert and concentrating and sure of what it's looking for. In the strange half light, the three waterfalls on the mountains in the background were glowing, gliding down the mountainside like liquid mercury. Suddenly the pattern they made looked familiar—very familiar. But why? From where? Simon turned the picture the right way up. He turned it back around. Now he was certain he had seen it somewhere before, but where was just out of reach, like an itch he couldn't scratch.

In a flash it came to him. Eagerly, he rummaged in his backpack for Señora Rojo's old battle map. He lined it up beside the upside-down ophallagraph.

The three "waterfalls" in the ophallagraph were mirror images of three of the rivers that branched and forked their way across Tamarind on the señora's map.

"They aren't waterfalls at all," he said. "They're rivers!"

The rivers were labeled on the map: the Jal, the Ror, and the Sassalla.

But what was the significance?

Simon kneeled, his head in his hands, and stared at the image. Freezing drops of water fell on his back but he barely felt it.

Look for the birds. They were the clues.

He searched the image and found the line of birds. They followed what Simon now knew was the Jal River, up to where it disappeared into a dark triangle at the base of the mountains. The Jal was the smallest river, and the one closest to Floriano. It started in the East and looped around near Floriano's bay before it flowed north.

The birds were pointing the way.

In this light, the dark triangle could be the entrance to a cave.

Not just to any cave, Simon was sure, but to the cave that held Faustina's Gate.

"I found it!" he shouted joyfully, but the roar of the hail drowned out his voice. If the lean-to had been taller he would have jumped up and danced around. Faustina's Gate was in their reach. It had been staring them in the face since the day they had met the señoras. Now, after all this time, he knew where to go. Not even the immensely clever Davies had figured it out.

Simon calculated that Faustina's Gate was only a few hours away from Floriano. Nothing was stopping them now. They could leave as soon as he got back. They would have to figure out how to use the tools once they got to the caves.

With a satisfied sigh, Simon gazed at the rest of the oph-allagraph. It was beautiful, the boats shuddering gently in a molten silver sea, the birds twinkling, the light reflecting off the water. It was like something out of a dream. His eye fell on the *Pamela Jane*. Then Simon noticed that she was point-ing directly to the black triangle in the distance. He remem-bered what Frascuelo had said, that perhaps she was the one that should be chosen for a journey.

Two revelations struck him at once and his heart began to pound.

One, the *Pamela Jane* was heading for Faustina's Gate.

Two, she wasn't just meant to sail *up* to the entrance to the caves—she was supposed to sail *inside* them.

Davies had said there was a huge underground system of rivers and caves. A big enough cave system and the boat *could* conceivably sail into it. And for some still secret reason the *Pamela Jane* was the boat that was supposed to do this.

Hardly able to contain his excitement, Simon waited impatiently for the hail squall to end, which it did, abruptly. He hurried from the shelter, leading the ostrillo by its bridle, but got only a few steps, noisy from the crunching ice, before he stopped and gazed, stunned at the devastation.

The hail had stripped trees of their leaves and the jungle was stark and skeletal. Pulverized crops lay beneath a crust of white ice. Birds' nests had been knocked to the ground, their eggs smashed, and yolk ran yellow on the ice. Lizards limped to the ends of branches. Frozen corpses of beetles and scarabs and spiders and wishing bugs gleamed wetly between ice pellets. Everywhere was silent except for the creak of ice melting and the drip of water from bald tree branches. Then, all of a sudden, from trees all around, birds began to shrill mournfully. The ostrillo ducked its head on its long neck and made a deep sound like a horn.

Simon leaped aboard the ostrillo and urged the creature on, desperate to get away, but the slippery ice forced them to slow down. On the fringes of the battered jungle he passed a motionless heap of brown fur. It was an infant slothe-slotha, too slow-moving to escape and too fragile to withstand the sharp pummeling. Its disconsolate mother crouched keening over it. Then the ostrillo began to run. The ice was melting fast and soon its talons were pounding down on dry earth and, finally, they left the swathe of destruction behind.

Simon's backpack with all the papers from Davies jounced heavy on his back.

He had to get to Faustina's Gate before it was too late.

$$\times \quad \times \quad \times$$

The closer he drew to Floriano, the more sure Simon became that something was very wrong. One moment it was pouring cold rain, the ferocious wind flailing the branches of trees, the next the atmosphere was eerily still and dark, the heat suffocating and the sky split by steely flashes of lightning. The changes in pressure made his ears pop. The ostrillo's feathers were wet and bedraggled.

As they neared Floriano fog was rolling in and the early afternoon was dark as dusk. Simon noticed a strange brightness in the sky above the town, but it wasn't until he reached the crest of a hill that he saw its source.

Moored in the bay, looming over the waterfront, was the biggest ship he had ever seen in Tamarind. She was huge and modern, her steel hull somehow heartless. Electric lights glowed from her portholes like dozens of eyes of a predator spying hungrily on the town, braced to attack.

Her smokestack belched sooty black ghosts that hovered over the town, darkening its roofs.

Simon looked at it in dread.

The Red Coral had arrived.

An explosion rocked a nearby hillside. They were already breaking ground for the mines. The ostrillo danced nervously. Dusk moths fluttered like miniature bats and the odd jungle firefly had begun blinking on and off, but otherwise they were alone. Thunder rumbled in the distance. Simon could feel the air cool—they were going to be rained on. Lightning flashed and thunder growled. He clicked his feet against the ostrillo's sides and it began half skidding down the hillside to the outskirts of the town, Simon keeping a watchful eye out for any prowling Maroong or Red Coral. The steady whirr and pulse of insects buzzed in the dark trees. To Simon's relief, he made it to Rua Santa Flora and opened the gate to Señora Medrano's. There was a crack of thunder overhead. He reached the porch just as the dark sky opened and the rain came pouring down.

Inside, Simon found everyone—his sisters, Helix, the señoras, Dr. Bellagio, and the general—gathered in the kitchen, where there was an atmosphere of nervous excitement. Maya was sitting at the table scrubbing gray paint off Penny's arms with a wet cloth. Helix was crouching in the corner, sharpening his knife, which rasped against a whetstone. Simon smelled mud, and in the muffled light he saw the camouflage daubed on

Helix's face. Up since dawn, the señoras were wearing their best dresses and had spent most of the time pacing anxiously, their cheeks flushed and their eyes bright. Simon collapsed gratefully into a chair and Señora Medrano hurried to get food for him.

An explosion echoed from the mine site.

"They arrived almost as soon as you left," said Maya, looking apprehensively out of the window. "They must have started mining right away. The weather has been going crazy since they got here." Outside the wind picked up and threw drops of rain at the windows as if they were stones. The kitchen grew darker.

"Well," barked the general, "did you find Maroner?"

"Yes," said Simon, and as quickly as he could, he told them about the link between ophalla and the Blue Line and about the strange and terrible loss of life he had witnessed on his way back. Señora Medrano put a plate of food in front of him, but Simon was too excited to eat.

"We have to leave for Faustina's Gate straightaway," he said. "Davies said that the Blue Line is on the verge of collapse—if more ophalla doesn't reach it soon the line will break down completely. If that happens Tamarind is done for."

In the distance another explosion rang out. Everyone but Helix and the general jumped.

"Did Davies tell you how to get to Faustina's Gate?" Maya asked.

"No, but I figured it out," said Simon, his eyes shining. "It was in the ophallagraphs all along. And," he said, turning to Maya, "Davies was able to communicate with Mami and Papi—they know we're okay."

"Good work, soldier!" said the general, hammering the table with his fists and getting to his feet. He looked strong and vigorous. He was in his element. Mud was caked on his boots and he stamped them vigorously on the kitchen floor.

"Isabella's scouts were in touch with us a few hours ago—the army is coming!" he said. "All hell is about to break loose! Everyone in Floriano has been alerted and is prepared to join the fight."

"As soon as people heard they'd be fighting with the general they rallied," said Dr. Bellagio. "They're marching in from all around!"

"And," the general said, pausing gleefully, "a surprise: Our boy Helix here is a real revolutionary like his father—he sneaked out to the Red Coral ship in the fog earlier this morning and opened the seacocks and bolted the doors to the bilges. The vessel has been slowly taking on water for hours. By the time the problem is spotted it will be too late!"

Simon grinned and looked at Helix, who shrugged self-consciously.

"Now," said the general, "if the Red Coral start fleeing, they'll be looking for any nearby boat to make their escape in—the *Pamela Jane* isn't safe where she is anymore. You have to leave now while you still can."

Outside the rain had stopped suddenly and the fog had rolled in, so heavy it seeped through the windows and drifted through the rooms of the old mansion. The kitchen was dim. Maya looked worriedly out of the window.

"We won't be able to see five feet in front of us!" she said.

"We don't have a choice," said Simon. "The mining is causing this weather—it's only going to get worse. Anyway, it will help us stay hidden."

More explosions rocked the hillsides in the distance.

"Time to go!" boomed the general.

The señoras hurried to pack warm bread and fruit, which Maya tucked in her backpack for later.

"Wait—what about Seagrape?" asked Penny.

"Seagrape will find us," said Helix, standing up and tucking his knife into his belt. His hair was wild, face mottled with dyes from the jungle, but he looked calm and cool.

Simon was the opposite. His heart was pounding, he was breaking out in a sweat, and his whole body felt as if it were buzzing. After all this time they were finally going to Faustina's Gate. But first they had to make it out of the harbor in the *Pamela Jane*, past the Red Coral. The thought of going anywhere near Dr. Fitzsimmons made his knees weak. What if the *Pamela Jane* was spotted?

"You'll have to be careful," General Alvaro said briskly. "Floriano is crawling with Red Coral and Maroong. But the colonels are posted throughout the town as lookouts."

Another explosion cracked, echoing off the hills, and the bitter smell of explosives drifted in.

"Good-bye," Maya said, flinging her arms around the

señoras' necks in turn. "We'll come back and tell you all about it, after we close the gate."

"We'll see you soon," said Simon as Señora Rojo embraced him. Her head wobbled slightly, and she held him tightly for an extra second. Suddenly Simon was reminded of Granny Pearl.

He hoisted his backpack onto his back, Maya took a firm grip of Penny's hand, and with Helix and the general they hurried across the wet grass toward the path down the hill. The shrill whistle of a single frog pierced the air. Fog hugged the earth and the drip of dew ticked like clocks. Ostrillo eyes blinked on and off through the gloom. When they reached the border of trees, Maya and Penny went ahead down the path, but General Alvaro stopped, taking Helix's shoulder.

"In case things don't go well here, there's something it's time to tell you," he said, his voice low. "Years ago I knew your father. He's a good man—I never met anyone braver. Your aunts don't know this, so don't blame them for not telling you, but the last I knew, he was living in a small town called Barella, on the far northeast shore, where the jungle meets the coast. He may still be there."

Helix froze. "Barella," he whispered.

"Yes," said the general briskly. "You get to it by the Cassandor Road."

Maya stopped and looked back up at them. "Come on," she whispered urgently.

"I wish I could go with you all the way," General Alvaro said, a youthful light in his eyes. "Good luck to you!"

Then he raised his hand and—to Simon's surprise—the old hero saluted them.

The *Pamela Jane* was hidden in a cove on the other side of Floriano's harbor, and to get to her Helix and the children had to cross the town, skirting dangerously close to the Red Coral base camp.

"There's so much fog I think we're safe to go along the waterfront for most of the way," said Helix as they hurried down the hill. "That'll be quickest. We'll duck back into the town when we have to."

They set off through the back roads, sticking close to Helix. Simon held tightly to Penny's hand so she kept up. They followed the beach for a while, jogging silently on the sand and shingles, every now and then leaping over a heap of fishing net or dodging an overturned rowboat that had been dragged up onto shore. To their left, Floriano was silent, the damp streets empty. To their right, past the swishy gurgle of the water, the giant Red Coral ship, already beginning to list ever so slightly to starboard, was a dark shadow looming through the mist.

His jitters had passed and Simon felt strangely calm. A short time ago he had been a boy, complaining about his parents and tinkering with boat engines, going nowhere farther than school and the boatyard. Now here he was, in a strange and dangerous place, on the brink of the most important thing he had ever had to do in his life.

The fog distorted sound, but when they heard the noise

of the Red Coral camp growing louder, Helix put his finger to his lips and hurried them deftly along. Soon they could see clusters of tents. Equipment unloaded from the Red Coral ship was being transported up into the hills to the mine by a convoy of Maroong. Every now and then the fearsome glinting of the bones and teeth of their armor flashed through the fog. Simon kept his eyes peeled for Dr. Fitzsimmons, but the fog grew thicker and soon Simon could barely see the others next to him. The world stopped in white just inches from their faces. He held tightly on to Penny so they didn't lose her.

They had to duck into the town to get around the Red Coral camp. They ran silently down the cloudy streets, past the deserted market and the closed doors of the bakeries. The town was eerily desolate, but Simon knew that it was only because everyone was waiting inside until the call went up that the army was here.

They left the town and scurried back around the edge of the harbor to where they had left the *Pamela Jane* hidden in the mangroves. Simon could smell the cold water before he could see it. They battled their way across the swampy earth through the mangroves and soon were walking waist deep in water. Helix swung Penny up onto his back and they tried not to splash too much.

Green water flowed over their legs and lizards watched them from the upturned roots, their orange dewlaps flaring now and then through the mist. Simon still didn't see their boat. Maddeningly, the fog was rolling in thickly again. It was like being in the middle of a cloud. He stared blindly into it.

Maya tramped ahead in the water. "There!" she whis-pered loudly at last.

Simon heaved a sigh of relief as the fog parted, revealing the boat.

The *Pamela Jane* had undergone her second transforma-tion. When Simon had gone to Davies Maroner, Maya, Penny, the señoras, and General Alvaro had painted her hull gray-blue to disguise her once again. Her name had been covered over and in its place, in Maya's finest script, were the words "Silver Witch."

Brushing cobwebs and spiders off their shoulders, the children scrambled through the murky water and climbed aboard. They rigged the sails quickly and soon the *Silver Witch* was creeping furtively through the swamp, veils of moss trailing across her deck, silk spiders rustling as they rushed down her sails and leaped onto overhanging branches. Maya steered at the cockpit and Helix and Simon stood at the bow, slashing vines and holding back branches to let the boat pass. The fog had engulfed the sun and the air was humid. Mist clung to the roots of the mangroves. In the back-ground explosions rang out from the mines.

Simon heard flapping and gasped as a green flame swept past inches from his face. Seagrape landed on the deck. She shuffled sideways over to them, murmuring and muttering cantankerously. Her wings were wet and lustrous from the mist, gleaming deep emerald. They greeted her quietly but enthusiastically. They knew now that Milagros had gotten their message. Simon looked all around, half expecting to see her appear. He hoped she would do what she could to help.

As they neared the end of the cove of mangroves, the children saw a strange light up ahead. At the moment they entered the harbor the wind rose, pushing the fog away. Now the boat was exposed, but the children had a clear view to the astonishing sight in the middle of the harbor.

The Red Coral's great steel ship was already down at the stern. She listed slowly and water poured into her hull, then in front of the children's eyes she began to sink. Her vast ophalla cargo spilled out, illuminating the sky and water. The mangroves all around the harbor were lit silver, and slippery eels and schools of ballyhoo appeared clear as day through the bright water. Blue vapor rose from the surface. Everything seemed to hover ghostly in the ophalla's phosphorescent glow.

The children watched in delight. If there were any Red Coral left after the army moved in they would be stranded in Tamarind! But if anyone on shore had noticed the event they had no time to react, for at that moment a cacophony erupted just beyond the hills.

Boom! Boom! Boom!

Simon jumped, then looked gleefully at the shore. "That isn't the mining!" he said. "The army is here!"

A chilling war cry went up, echoing off the hills and out over the water. As the children watched, a dark seething line appeared on the ridges, and a moment later the army came pouring down the steep slopes. There were so many people that the hillside was soon dark. At the same instant, all the doors of all the homes in Floriano were flung open and people flooded the streets, running to join the army and encircle the Red Coral. In seconds the town went from peace to pandemonium. Penny shouted, catching sight of the advance guard galloping down the hills on ostrillos. She didn't look frightened at all, Simon realized. She was thoroughly enjoying herself! Good—better she thought it was all a game. He glanced at Helix and could tell that he wanted to be out there fighting, but he remained steadfastly with the children.

There were a few more explosions at the mines as the Red Coral kept on heedlessly, but then the explosions stopped and the din of battle began. The acrid scent of smoke hung heavy in the air. The sky was dark with storm clouds. As they crossed the open harbor, the children had a majestic view as the action unfolded. They saw a few Maroong already deserting, running along the shore with armfuls of ophalla.

As the *Silver Witch* approached the other side of the harbor the children saw the sinuous Jal River. The tang of salt air washed over them, and gusts of wind filled the mainsail, and then they were sailing at a fast clip up the river. The sounds of the battle in Floriano grew fainter and the glow in the sky from the sinking Red Coral ship faded from sight.

The riverbanks were mostly deserted and it was only occasionally that the children saw the twinkle of lights of a tiny village through the heavy fog and rainstorms. There was no way to tell the hour of the day. Insects confused by the darkness into night song chirruped unseen on the riverbanks and nocturnal hunters prowled the shores. They passed towns waterlogged and abandoned, half-buried under the mudslides of recent storms, and saw more and more signs of the havoc the weather had wrought. Every now and then they felt tremors and heard the earth rumble, and the river swirled muddy around them. Simon had to steer around the swollen carcasses of animals drowned in floods, debris, and trees felled.

After they had been sailing for an hour the children saw a lightweight craft skimming up the river. It caught up to the *Silver Witch* and a man leaned out.

"The Red Man has escaped!" he shouted. "No one has seen him anywhere—keep a sharp watch!" Then his boat glided off quickly to keep searching up the river.

Simon felt a chill. "Where can he have gone?" he asked.

"It doesn't matter," said Helix. "He can't hide for long. He sticks out like a sore thumb here."

Dr. Fitzsimmons was still a threat. He could have spotted them sailing across the harbor and could still come after them, perhaps with a contingent. Now that his ship had been sunk, he would be desperate to secure a way home. He would want the *Pamela Jane*. It was more important than ever that the children make it to Faustina's Gate. Even if Isabella was victorious in battle, they would achieve nothing unless the gate was closed.

Simon took out the map, now dog-eared and grubby. They were making good time and would soon be at the entrance to the caves. He checked his backpack several times but the ophalla key, the stopwatch, and the mineral-fruits were all still there.

It had all come down to them.

Only they could save Tamarind now.

❖ CHAPTER TWENTY-THREE ❖

A Warning ❋ *Penny Objects*

Finally the sun burned off the storm clouds and emerged. Afternoon light shone exhausted on the river. The children began to notice more and more birds. Sloop wingers cavorted around a lemon tree, a white whalla carved the sky high above, and a flock of bluebandas passed low overhead. Seagrape squawked up to them and they down to her.

The *Pamela Jane*, disguised as the *Silver Witch,* turned the bend and up ahead the children saw a few large golden birds strutting regally on the shore. Then, as they got closer, standing on a hill above the river they saw a figure wearing a great cloak of iridescent feathers, peacock blue with navy eyes, shimmering in the hazy daylight.

"Milagros!" said Simon.

They drew alongside the riverbank and Simon and Maya quickly leaped ashore and tied off the boat. Helix helped Penny onto the bank and the four of them climbed the soggy hillside to meet the Dark Woman. Up close, though she had worn her finest cape, the sunlight laid her filthiness bare. Bird droppings encrusted her clothes and a feather caught in her hair shivered in the breeze. Her skin was tanned from grime.

The hilltop looked out to sea on one side and out across

the jungles of Tamarind on the other. The S of the river curved below them, twinkling in the light, heading toward the low humps of ancient, time-eroded mountains that stood on the coast. The faint sparkle of the river disappeared into a dark triangle at their base, just like in the ophallagraph.

Milagros stretched out her arm and Seagrape landed on it. "Hello, my friend," she murmured. "You have more to do." Bird and woman regarded each other, then Seagrape returned to Helix.

"You knew where the cave was all along," said Simon. "Why didn't you tell us when we first came to you?"

"It would have been no use to you without the tools," said Milagros. "You would have tried to come here straight-away, but without the tools you would have perished in the caves, to say nothing of the fact that without them, even if you found the gate you would not be able to close it.

"I couldn't tell you where the tools were because I no longer knew," she went on. "Once I gave them to others I had no idea where they went. I knew, though, that if you were clever enough to find them by using the ophallagraphs, you'd be clever enough to find your way to Faustina's Gate through the cave. You have to be very sharp to survive—its chambers are home to deadly creatures and its passages are tortuous. If you choose the wrong way you'll never see the light of day again. You must remain alert the whole time and never let your guard down."

"We have the tools," said Simon, taking them out to show her. "Can you tell us how to use them?"

"Unfortunately, I cannot," said Milagros. "Part of their

secret lies in figuring out how to use them when the time comes. I've never seen the gate myself. I've come here now only to warn you about something very important you must know before you close it."

The children waited, listening.

"If you succeed in closing the gate, you'll emerge on the other side of the mountain, in a cove in the Green Vale," said Milagros, speaking deliberately. "It's said to be the most beautiful place on the whole island. When you sail out of the cove, there's a current that will carry you out to the Blue Line. You have only a short time—minutes—to reach it."

"But we're not going home yet," said Maya. "We told the señoras we'd be back. We didn't even say good-bye properly."

Milagros shook her head. Her eyes were dark beneath her drooping eyelids. "Once you close Faustina's Gate, you have to leave Tamarind at once or you'll have lost your chance," she said. "In closing the gate you'll be saving the Blue Line—it will be restored. Very quickly, the line will become so strong that you won't be able to make it across— you'll be trapped in Tamarind. And once the gate is closed, it can't be opened for a very long time."

"Even the *Pamela Jane*—can't she still make it back across?" Simon asked.

"No," said Milagros. "Not even this boat can. Not once the line has been strengthened again."

Simon was stunned. Never come back again? Simon and Maya looked quickly at Helix. He had just met his family! How could he leave them so soon?

"If we close the gate, how long will it stay closed for?" Helix asked, gazing steadily at Milagros.

"No one can answer that," said Milagros. "Perhaps forever. Or for such a long time that it may as well be forever."

Helix cast his eyes down and stared quietly at the ground. Maya watched him worriedly.

Simon gazed somberly out over Tamarind. From there he could see the whole lie of the land: the green jungle; the band of Jal River, shining in the sun; the red dust rising over the old mines. Somewhere, too far away to see, clouds were shifting across the shining peaks of the snow-clad mountains between whose cool depths lay the Moraine of Lost Loved Ones. Forever.

The first time Simon's family had been to Tamarind, his mother had been imprisoned on a pirate ship and his father had been trapped in the Ravaged Straits. They had seen only a small stretch of the southwest shore and the tiny tin towns there. But even though they were in Tamarind so briefly and saw so little of it, in the years afterward they stood up to the Red Coral Project valiantly in order to do what they believed was right. Now they would never have the chance to see the place that had haunted their imagination for so long.

Simon was filled with fierce love for his parents then. He felt a new respect and a tenderness. Standing there, as all this flooded through him, he felt another strange sadness.

He was not a child any longer.

He felt it; he knew it. In the end, in the moment it happened, it was the simplest of transformations.

Simon loved Tamarind, but more than Tamarind he loved his family. It was time to go home.

The children looked at the great old woman solemnly.

"Thank you," said Simon. "Good-bye."

"Good luck—to all of you," said the Dark Woman, bowing her head. She turned and left, disappearing into the jungle, and for the first time the great mass of her seemed strangely ephemeral, as if any breeze coming through it would leave only feathers where she had been. The great gilded birds went, too.

"Come on," said Helix. "We have to get to the gate."

They went quickly down the hill. When Simon looked back a few buzzards circled high overhead. The boat rocked uneasily in the water and Penny began to dig her heels in the ground as they approached.

"Come on," Simon said, tugging her hand.

But Penny was gazing intently at the boat. She reminded Simon of a cat staring—almost in a trance—at something invisible. When Simon went to pull her along again she balked.

"No!" she said, her face growing stormy. "No—I'm not going!"

"Penny," said Maya impatiently. "Let's go—we don't have time for this!"

"Nooooooo!" shouted Penny, and when Simon tried to pick her up she burst into angry tears.

"What's got into her?" Maya asked.

"She's had enough," said Simon. Poor little Penny. She was always so brave and she made such an effort to be grown-up like the others. Finally it was all too much for her. The strange old woman had probably frightened her.

Helix looked slowly all around them, his expression dark.

"Penny!" said Maya. "Sweetheart, don't cry! Here . . ." But Penny just kicked Maya away.

"Listen, mouse," said Helix, bending down and scooping her up. "We're going to get you home, okay? But we don't have much choice—right now we have to get back on the boat."

Penny kicked and screamed. "I don't like it," she cried. "Something's bad! Something's *bad*!" Her howls echoed off the riverbank.

"She's just scaring herself more," said Maya.

Helix carried her onto the boat and on the deck she curled up in a ball, arms wrapped around her knees. Her outburst subsided to sniffles, but every now and then a sob broke through. Maya stroked her hair. "It's okay, Penny-mouse," she whispered. "We'll be home soon."

It went unspoken between the older children that perhaps they wouldn't be home soon—they might not, in fact, make it through the caves.

"Here, you be in charge of this," said Simon, giving Penny the stopwatch from the ophallagraph to hold. He slipped its chain around her neck. Distracted, she fiddled with the knobs and listened to the soft whirring of the gears.

Soon they were sailing back up the river. Helix whistled for Seagrape and she coasted down the hill and landed on the main mast, but she wouldn't come down on the deck with them.

Though no one said anything, Penny's reaction had spooked them all.

CHAPTER TWENTY-FOUR

Cave of the Musical Winds ❀
Ancient Masks ❀ *Tools and Treachery*

They sailed in silence and the dark entrance at the base of the mountain grew enormous as they drew closer. Before they reached it, Helix lit several torches and lashed them to the railings. Simon reached into his backpack and touched the mineral-fruits and the key. He had to be ready to use them. Penny kept twisting the winder on the stopwatch and watching it spin down, entranced by the gentle buzz it made. Seagrape seemed very interested. Finally she dived down from the mast and sidled up to Penny and leaned over, peering at it with one eye.

Sailing into a cave in a fifty-two-foot schooner was a profoundly strange sensation. The children gazed around them in awe as the *Silver Witch* glided soundlessly through the towering entrance. At once the world outside was left behind, and they found themselves in a vast, yawning cavern whose far reaches dissolved into darkness. As they drifted deeper into the cave the triangle of light from the entrance shrank and finally disappeared. Even with the torches, it took a while for their eyes to adjust to the dimness. The wind died and the sails collapsed. The boat sat becalmed. The children didn't know what to do—without wind or current they were powerless. Simon peered with all his might into the darkness. What was out there? Then, above them, a mournful moaning started up. Penny took Maya's hand.

"Is it ghosts?" she whispered, her eyes wide.

"Of course not," said Maya at once, but she looked up nervously.

The boat rocked in place. Helix lit a new torch and held it high above his head and a ceiling of carved masks suddenly appeared.

"The Ancients must have put them there," he whispered.

The masks, big as shields, were suspended a hundred feet overhead and painted with dyes from the jungle. Untouched by the sun and elements, their paint was preserved, their faces bright. They rippled like the surface of water under a skidding breeze, and looked down on the children as they passed beneath them. Penny whimpered.

"Don't be afraid," said Simon, squinting. "The noise is from the wind blowing across their mouths. Like the sound that the wind makes over the mouth of a bottle."

A light breeze, barely a whisper, came down from the roof of the cave and filled the sails and the boat began to drift forward. Simon trimmed the sails, eager not to head too quickly into the unknown. The wind sighed and groaned through the tunnels. The *Pamela Jane* left the chamber with the masks and headed down a long, wide passageway. Simon and Maya stayed at the wheel and Helix went to the bow with a torch to look out. Penny fiddled fretfully with the stopwatch. Seagrape perched on the bulwark.

Simon heard a splash off the lee, but when he whipped

his head around there was nothing there. Helix hurried back from the bow.

"Don't freak out," he said in a low voice, "but there's something up ahead."

He held the torch over starboard and light was flung on the opposite side of the passageway, where a shelf of rock rose a few feet out of the water. At first Simon thought he was looking at odd rock formations, but then they moved and he realized that they weren't rocks at all. Heaped on the ledge, like seals basking, were giant salamanders, the biggest Simon had ever seen. The greatest among them was easily seven feet long. They were white as drowned corpses and a thick ooze of mucus covered their skin. Phlegm wattled their jaws. They lifted their heavy heads and with their lazy, opaque eyes they watched the boat pass.

One of them opened its impossibly wide mouth and hissed, swiveling its head slowly back and forth. The others followed suit and hissing reverberated through the passageway. Suddenly the first creature lumbered to its feet and wriggled down the ledge and dived into the water. Its head surfaced a moment later, swimming toward the boat. Other lumps in the shallows lurched to life. Simon shuddered. They didn't try to attack, just followed the boat, swimming lazily, keeping their eyes trained on the children.

The *Pamela Jane* continued down the passage, her ghoulish escort patrolling languidly alongside. More salamanders slunk along the ledges. The water pillowed silkily around the hull. Here and there Simon saw bluish tinted foam where the water lapped the oystery sheen of the cave walls. Curtains of rock poured down around them, looking to Simon like ice cream that had melted and refrozen.

The children heard rustling and as the boat turned a gentle bend in the river, they came upon a colony of albino cave crickets. The size of rats, they were gathered in a crevasse, munching on something, their backs to the boat. As they heard it coming they looked around. One slipped and fell into the water and began swimming with long, easy kicks like a frog back to the shore. Before it could make it, a pale salamander burst up through the water. The cricket disappeared down its gullet in a single gulp. A shrieking noise erupted from the rest of the crickets, who began hopping wildly and noisily down the tunnel. The salamanders surged up onto the rocks with surprising speed. Swiftly and ruthlessly, the crickets were devoured and the passageway fell creepily silent again. Frothing at the mouth, many of the salamanders returned to the water and stared up at the children in the boat.

"I don't like those things," said Penny, a quiver in her voice. She stopped winding the stopwatch and it began to unwind, buzzing on the chain around her neck.

The ceiling of the long, watery corridor grew jagged. Stalactites hung everywhere, like an upside-down forest. As they glided under them, the children began to notice the rustling of small hairy bodies in the dark nooks and crannies. Countless little eyes reflected the orange torchlight. *Bats*, thought Simon with relief. *Nothing to be afraid of*. Granny Pearl loved bats and would sit on the porch in the evenings watching them in the dimming sky.

"Hey, Pennymouse, look up there!" said Simon softly. "Mice like you, but with wings!"

"Simon," whispered Maya, squinting up at the ceiling, "they're not bats—they're spiders."

As Penny's stopwatch wound down, the buzzing ceased and the cave was quiet.

Suddenly a heavy black spider dropped on a sticky thread and landed on the back of a salamander that had been slithering along the ledge. The creature hissed in pain and terror, and in a flash the others dived underwater to escape. Almost instantly the poisoned salamander stopped fighting and went rigid. The thick-legged spider ran up and down its back and within seconds the salamander was trussed in sticky threads. A Penny-size lump lay cocooned like a mummy on the ledge. Other spiders poured down the wall to feed. Simon shivered in revulsion.

He became aware that the huddle of spiders on the ceiling had begun to move, as if someone was stirring under a fuzzy brown blanket. Suddenly one swung down, its deadly string landing like a tentacle across Helix's shoulder. He cried out in pain and dropped his torch. Seagrape exploded in a blur of feathers, beak, and claws. She snatched the creature up and dropped it in the water before it had a chance to bite her.

More spiders had begun slowly levering themselves down on strings, all hanging at different lengths and swaying in the thin wind.

"Why are they all coming now?" wailed Maya, recoiling in horror.

Simon pulled Penny to him. As he did so he noticed the stopwatch on its chain around her neck.

"That's it!" he cried. "Penny, keep winding the stopwatch!" Penny grabbed the watch and immediately began winding it. As soon as she stopped, the watch began buzzing again.

The effect was instantaneous. A giant spider that had just landed on the deck stopped in its tracks, stretching up onto the tips of its legs and trembling horribly for several long seconds before it crumpled into a furry pod. Its legs twitched and then it lay motionless. The spiders that had been rappeling down from the ceiling turned and began climbing back up in a panic. Some shuddered and fell into the water, where they floated stiff and brittle for a moment before slowly sinking. Others leaped back onto the stalactites and scuttled away, shrinking into the dark recesses of the ceiling, only the orange dots of their eyes still visible.

"Keep winding the watch, Penny," Simon told her, taking a shaky breath. "It must send out some sort of vibration that the spiders can't tolerate."

"Good job you figured that out," said Helix.

Simon looked at Helix, who was rubbing his arm. "Are you okay?" he asked.

"I'm fine," said Helix, but his face was pale and his right arm hung useless at his side. "It's like a bad jellyfish sting; it'll wear off."

Penny insisted on being the watch winder for the duration. Simon and Helix kicked the husks of the dead spiders into the water and kept a watchful eye on the ceiling of the cave. The boat drifted on, the soft hum of the stopwatch keeping the spiders at bay. Somewhere far up ahead was the sound of rushing water.

The wind drew the *Pamela Jane* on through the cave system. To the children's relief they left the corridor of spiders behind and entered a majestic, cathedral-like cavern with a vast, soaring ceiling. They sailed out into a huge dark lake and gazed around in wonder. They were deep inside the mountain now. The walls and ceiling glittered with ophalla stones, naturally inset like gems into the rock.

"They look like stars," said Penny.

"It's as if we're in the middle of the ocean at night," whispered Maya.

The breeze carried them into the middle of the immense black lake. Seagrape flew up and coasted around the cave, a dark silhouette crossing the firmament.

The faint purr of water grew louder as they approached the other side. As Simon's eyes adjusted he saw five colossal entrances to different tunnels, opening like great black maws in the cave wall. Each tunnel entrance was a hundred feet high, but barely wider than the boat. And that rushing sound—he realized with alarm—was coming from the tunnels, some of which must drop steeply from the lake.

"Which do we take?" Maya asked, worry creeping into her voice.

Just as she was asking, the wind began to rise and the boat started sailing purposefully toward the opposite side of the lake. Within seconds she had picked up speed and was slicing swiftly through the water. Seagrape returned and perched on Penny's shoulder and Maya sent them both to stand in the companionway. Maya and Helix reefed the sails to slow the boat down, and Simon tried to tack away from the tunnels to give them more time to figure out what to do.

But the water was converging into powerful swells heading toward the tunnels, and despite their best efforts the boat skimmed across the water like a skater sliding across ice. The water echoed loudly in the tunnels. Simon didn't know which one they were supposed to take. The boat pitched wildly in a gust of wind and waves cuffed her hull. The wind was rising steadily. A storm was starting, deep in the cave! The false stars glittered dizzyingly around them. They were almost at the tunnels—they had to make a decision!

Then Simon realized that something felt familiar.

It looks like stars, Penny had said.

Stars. Why was that reminding him of something? Who had he been talking to about stars recently? Then he remembered. The monk, Frascuelo, behind the Blue Door! *"Some things have a double use in an image,"* he had said. *"For instance, close your eyes a bit and look at the ophallagraph of the tree. . . . it occurred to me that the fruit is clustered in patterns, perhaps like constellations of stars."*

"Get me the ophallagraphs from my backpack!" Simon shouted, struggling to hold the wheel steady as the water grew wilder. "The one of the tree in the Emerald Oasis!"

Maya found it and quickly brought it to him. She held the wheel while, hands shaking, he lifted up the ophallagraph. Frascuelo had been right. The pattern of fruit on the tree mirrored the patterns of the stars in the cave!

But how does that help? Simon thought, starting to feel frantic. The boat was hurtling closer and closer to the tunnels and they had to decide quickly. "The birds," he muttered. "The birds point to clues."

He found the bird, the only one in the image, a long-beaked creature that hovered over a large mineral-fruit—or star—at the tip of a Z-shaped constellation. It took Simon only a moment to locate the same constellation and the bird star in the ceiling of the cave. It shone brightly over the right-most door.

"That one," he cried, pointing. "That's the one we want!" He shoved the ophallagraph back in his bag just as a gust of wind blasted them from the other direction, blowing out the torches and causing the boat to roll violently to port and the wheel to spin out of control.

The *Pamela Jane* was caught in a current heading for the wrong door. Seeing that Simon was in trouble, Helix ran back to help. With his one good arm he leaned into the wheel with all his strength. Simon tacked and the boat rolled to starboard. Simon braced himself against the wheel to stop it from spinning the opposite way. For a moment he was afraid the boat would breach. But she steadied and they were on the right path, speeding toward the tunnel under the bird star.

In an instant they passed through the entrance and were racing into darkness. Simon's stomach flipped.

"We need a torch!" he shouted. "We have to be able to see!"

A moment later there was a *whoosh* as Helix lit a wooden torch. When he saw where they were, Simon was horrified. They were hurtling through an underground gorge whose sides closed claustrophobically around them. The mast was barely clearing the top of the tunnel.

One wrong shift of the boom, one inch too far a turn of the wheel, and the boat would smash into the wall of the gorge. The boat was solid and the first hit might be all right, Simon thought, but if the rudder or mast was damaged he would no longer be able to steer. She would crash into the rocks and her hull would splinter and soon she would shatter into scattered bits of driftwood. The children would be at the mercy of the river.

The water flowed fast and dark all around them, its roar deafening in the claustrophobic space. Simon had to keep them steady in the middle. Maya and Helix clung to the railing and Penny braced herself in the companionway, only her head sticking out of the hatch.

All of a sudden the gorge walls and roof widened and lifted, the current slackened and soon the boat was sailing in a slow drift through a dark cave.

"Everyone okay?" Simon asked, trying to keep his voice steady. He wiped sweat off his forehead with his arm.

Everyone was. Helix held the torch up. The current carried them along slowly, but spiky stalagmites poked through the water and they had to pay attention. In some places stalactites from the ceiling met stalagmites from the floor in

337

great and ancient columns. Simon steered deftly around them.

The children were so busy making sure they didn't hit anything that they didn't immediately notice the cave was growing steadily brighter. But then a faint sizzling sound came from the water and the *Pamela Jane* shivered.

Simon looked over the side. In shock, he saw that the outside of the boat's hull was half-eaten away. Hundreds upon hundreds of oily black leeches, big as fists, crept along it, ravenously devouring the wood. Beams of bright light emanated from the holes. Suddenly the boat shook mightily and a fizz of bubbles shimmied away from her hull. Seconds later, the last of the wood was gone, and one by one the bloated leeches popped off and drifted away. The boat rocked gently. The children gazed down at her in astonishment.

Before their very eyes she had undergone a staggering transformation.

The wood of her hull had been stripped to reveal not merely the solid crossbeams and ribs of ophalla that Simon had expected back when he had first investigated the glowing from the boat's porthole, but an underlying hull built wholly out of ophalla that had long been hidden beneath a thin wooden veneer. The children no longer needed the torches—the light from the boat itself lit the cavern and illuminated their shocked faces. The *Pamela Jane* looked like a vessel carved out of shining ivory. No new leeches could climb her gleaming sides and they retreated to the gloomy shadows to wait, a dark ring outside the hull's glow.

"Milagros never said anything about this," said Maya, gazing down over the brilliant side of the boat in wonder.

"Maybe she didn't know," said Simon. "I guess this is why the *Pamela Jane* was the only boat that could make it through the caves—an ordinary wooden boat would have been chewed right through."

Just then a hushed sound came from the cabin. Simon's heart sank.

"I hope she hasn't sprung a leak . . ." said Maya.

"I'll check the cabin to make sure no water's coming in," said Helix. He disappeared down the hatch.

Simon leaned nervously out from the boat to look at the hull, but saw no sign that the *Pamela Jane* was taking on water. He felt anxious, though—if the ophalla wasn't completely watertight, even a tiny crack somewhere would be the end of them out in the open sea. Penny crouched down and reached over to touch the bright ophalla.

As she did so, the children heard a shout and a thud from the cabin.

"Helix," Maya said.

Simon dashed toward the hatch.

But before he reached it he stopped short.

It wasn't Helix coming up the companionway. It was a tall man with red hair. He wore a sweat-soaked shirt. He was all elbows and cheekbones and jutting forehead. His face was streaked with mud. His pale hands clutched a trembling gun.

Dr. Fitzsimmons.

With cold, spreading dread, Simon realized he must have been on the boat the whole time.

His gun was pointing right at Simon.

"Maya, get Penny!" Simon shouted.

But like a flash Dr. Fitzsimmons leaped out of the hatch and seized the little girl. Penny immediately burst into tears. He waved the gun in Simon's face. "Stand back!" he shouted.

Maya was near the bow. Hands raised, Simon took a few steps backward toward the wheel. "It's okay, Penny," he said. "Don't be scared." He locked eyes with his little sister, who was now sobbing uncontrollably. The blood drained from Simon's head and he felt dizzy. How was this happening? There was no sound from the cabin below. Helix must have been knocked out. Or worse.

Simon felt his knees begin to shake but he fought to keep still and hold his ground. He mustn't show fear.

Slowly his fear was replaced by outrage. Dr. Fitzsimmons had sneaked onto their boat. He had taken their little sister and he was hurting her and she was terrified.

It was *their* boat.

This was *their* family. This had gone on long enough.

Simon's heart was racing, but a calm descended on him. Anger focused him.

"Let Penny go," he said.

"I'll let her go when we're on our way," said Dr Fitzsimmons. "I'm coming with you." In the ophalla light cast by the hull, his brow was white as marble.

Simon concentrated on keeping his face expressionless as he tried to figure out what to do. Penny's tears had subsided to hiccups and she was shaking. Dr. Fitzsimmons held her arm roughly. A breeze picked up and the boat began to sail slowly forward.

Fitzsimmons was desperate, Simon realized. He had probably been terrified to see all the Maroong deserting him in droves and the army moving in. But he had fled, deserting his crew and his workers, and now he was using a small child to get what he wanted. Simon couldn't believe that he had ever known this person. *He's a coward*, Simon told himself. *You don't have to be afraid of him.*

"You shouldn't be here," said Simon quietly. He had to get Dr. Fitzsimmons talking to buy himself some more time. Maybe Helix would wake up—then they might have a chance. Penny looked very small.

"When did you board the boat?" he asked.

"When I realized the army was coming I escaped," said Dr. Fitzsimmons. "I was going through the mangroves when I found your boat—I didn't realize at first it was the *Pamela Jane*, but then I heard you coming. I hid in the cabin. I knew that I'd be able to get rid of a bunch of kids when I had to."

It was strange to hear his voice again after so long.

The breeze freshened and the boat began to pick up speed. Simon kept a hand on the wheel. He saw that Maya, still up at the bow, was trying to tell him something. Without making it obvious he was looking at her, he watched from the corner of his eye as she mouthed something. What was she saying?

Then he realized.

Jibe! Of course! Dr. Fitzsimmons was standing in the arc of the boom.

It was taking a big chance. But he may not get another one. Sweat poured down Simon's face. He tried to steady his breathing. He met Penny's eye so he was sure she was paying attention to him. He took a deep breath.

"COME ABOUT!" he shouted, and immediately he spun the wheel to port.

The heavy boom came cracking around. Startled, Dr. Fitzsimmons instinctively raised his arms to shield himself. Penny shrugged out of his grasp and ran toward Simon, who dived nimbly across the deck, grabbed her, and rolled over to shield her at the same instant that the boom hit Dr. Fitzsimmons square across the jaw. The gun went off. There was a splash followed by a howl.

The children ran to the stern to look over.

Dazed, Dr. Fitzsimmons was swimming back to the boat. Simon lunged for the lifebelt and tossed it over the railing. They could tie him up until they got home. But shadows were moving in fast from the fringes of the lake. The leeches started attaching themselves to Dr. Fitzsimmons one after another as he frantically tried to claw them off. Simon reeled the lifebelt in and cast it out again, trying to get it to land closer to him. But the creatures were a swarm now, and Dr. Fitzsimmons was panicking. He didn't even appear to see it. His hand, tarred with leeches, splashed blindly.

"We've got to help him," cried Simon, desperately reeling in the lifebelt again.

Maya covered Penny's eyes and held her close as she

and Simon saw the leeches crest Dr. Fitzsimmons's shoulders, then his neck, then his face. The last they saw was his hand reaching out of the water, still trying to claw them off. Then the current bore him away and he disappeared down a narrow side tunnel into the darkness.

"Simon, stop!" cried Maya as Simon prepared to throw the lifebelt out again. "It's too late—he's gone!"

Just then Helix staggered up from the cabin, a cut on his head bleeding. He put his hand on Simon's shoulder and took the lifebelt and dropped it onto the deck.

In a moment Penny broke free of Maya and peered over the railing, but there was nothing to see.

None of them spoke.

Simon sunk down and cradled his forehead in his hands and closed his eyes. For all that he loathed what Dr. Fitzsimmons had become, he would have saved him if he could. Seagrape crept over to sit with them, warbling softly. Maya crouched beside him for a moment.

"You did the best you could," she said quietly. "It was too late to help him."

After a few minutes, Maya let out the mainsail until the breeze caught it. There was only one passage open to the boat and she floated down it. Penny wound the watch dutifully. Helix, furious to have been caught off guard, paced angrily.

The *Pamela Jane* rounded a corner and the breeze petered out.

"Simon, look," Maya whispered.

Finally Simon opened his eyes. The foul odor of the

343

leeches had left the air and the boat hung suspended in the luminous waters of a large, calm grotto whose sides rose up to a domed roof a hundred feet above. Great rays of light shot down through the crystal water from the luminous hull.

On the steep wall before them glowed paintings of sea creatures, a breathtaking fresco of the sea creatures of Tamarind. As the children looked, mouths agape, it shone brighter and brighter.

Simon scrambled to his feet and leaned over the bulwark to try to get a better look. "The Ancients must have created it out of some sort of paint made of ophalla powder," he said in awe.

Familiar sea creatures mingled with oddities unique to Tamarind, all lit with a strange silvery spume of ophalla. Moon jellies pulsed on the surface of the water, swept along in an invisible current. Spotted dolphins raced. Gently scrolled tentacles of octopuses unfurled toward caravans of lobsters marching in single file. Turtles with great hawked beaks nosed along, speckled eels with gaunt faces shimmied across the open, and a strange fish with dozens of decorative fins flowing like garments swam alone. From the humblest limpets and fluted sea sponges to the grandeur of a magnificent whale and her calf, it was an artful panoply of life in the ocean.

"My ancestors did this," said Helix softly.

The creatures, rendered larger as they rose up from the underwater wall, ascended in a long train of luminous, ethereal bodies, swimming and floating and drifting, hoisting

344

shells on their backs, bearing themselves from the dark depths of the cave up toward the highest point. Simon's eye followed them up and, high above the others, he saw a porcine fish with big bright eyes and a single, twisted horn that pointed up near the top of the cave. Breathing shallowly, Simon squinted up and could just see a thin, bright outline of a door behind the strange fish.

A thrill went through him.

"It's up there," he said. He couldn't stop smiling. They had found it. He pointed to show the others the outline of the door.

"I see it!" said Maya. "You think that's it? That's Faustina's Gate?"

"I don't think so," said Simon. "Faustina's Gate is supposed to be like a well. But I bet that it's behind the door."

But the door was a hundred feet up a steep cliff face. How would they ever reach it?

Simon looked closer at the wall.

"It's almost as if there're handholds as well as footholds," he said. "One of us will have to climb."

The others looked at him. They were all tired and dirty. Maya's hair was tangled and mud from the mangroves back in Floriano streaked her face. There was blood on Helix's head from where Dr. Fitzsimmons had struck him. Penny's pink pajamas were now a shade of grubby gray, torn and tattered and frayed. She looked very small and serious as she held Seagrape on her shoulder, stroking her.

Helix glared at his injured arm. The sensation was returning and he was able to wriggle his fingers now but it wasn't enough. Reluctantly, he nodded. "You can do it, Simon," he said. "You've figured out everything this far." He looked paler than usual, but smiled reassuringly.

"What about me?" asked Penny. "I'm not scared of heights."

"*You're* not scared of anything," said Simon.

"We need you to stay down here and keep winding that watch," Helix told her.

"I know that's not a real job," Penny grumbled. "They're not even in here." She looked around and quickly gave the stopwatch a couple of turns, just in case.

Simon waited until the boat was as close to the cliff as she could get. Maya looped mooring ropes around rock formations to hold it in place. Simon started to waver. Who knew what he would find at the top?

"All right," he said at last, securing his backpack with the key and the mineral-fruits in it. "Here goes."

He balanced on the railing of the deck until he got a good hold of a crevice in the wall above him, then he boosted himself up and found a foothold. He climbed carefully but quickly, and as he got higher he could see the door. It was carved and inlaid with faintly gleaming white ophalla, and in the middle of it was the dark eye of a keyhole.

"Be careful!" Maya called.

"I'm fine," Simon called. "There's a ledge by the door, I'm almost there."

He pulled himself up to the top of the cliff until he was sitting on the ledge, his legs hanging over the edge. He looked down for the first time. From up there the *Pamela*

346

Jane looked like a miniature. The water was shallow and the sharp points of stalagmites thrust up from the cave floor. If Simon fell on one of them he'd be in big trouble. Queasiness washed over him and he closed his eyes until it passed.

He took off his backpack and withdrew the glowing key.

"Here goes," he muttered under his breath. He hardly dared to breathe and his hand shook slightly—what if this didn't work?

But the key slid like butter into the lock. Seconds later both began to shine brightly. Something in the door rumbled faintly, like stones grinding, then the sound died away. Simon felt his heart hammering as the door swung smoothly inward.

He crawled through and found himself in a small, domed room chiseled out of ophalla. It was like being inside a giant, hollowed-out hive. Into the ophalla walls had been carved breathtakingly intricate pictures and patterns, whose meanings had been lost to time.

And there in the middle was Faustina's Gate.

Simon knew it when he saw it. It was a round hole, like a natural well, just as Davies had told him, and it descended deep into the earth below. Its sides and the floor all around it were made naturally of dully glowing ophalla—the whole room, in fact, was made from the stone.

After all their trials, here it was at last.

He ducked his head out of the door. "It's here!" he called triumphantly. "We found it!"

He crawled as close to the edge of the hole as he dared

and peered down into seemingly endless darkness. He knew that the bottom of the well opened into a tunnel that branched out in a network that led all the way out to the Blue Line. He felt around for a pebble and dropped it down the hole and waited, but there was no answering ping. He shivered—it was a long way down. What was he supposed to do now? He was stumped. For all his excitement, Faustina's Gate was only a hole in the ground—how was it supposed to save Tamarind?

But there was one last tool that he hadn't used yet.

Simon opened his backpack and took out the mineral-fruits.

What were they for?

He arranged them in a line and waited.

Nothing happened. Simon began to feel panicky. What if their journey had been for nothing? Perhaps the gate didn't work anymore. Or, almost worse, what if it did and he couldn't figure it out?

There was a rustling in the doorway and Simon looked up, startled. Seagrape was hovering in the air outside. She flew through the door and landed with a thump on the ground near him and began to sidle over.

"Hey, Seagrape," said Simon. "Come to help?"

As Simon kneeled there, thinking, Seagrape pecked slyly at the fruit.

"No!" said Simon sharply. "Don't do that!"

But Seagrape had rolled one of the fruits away, near Faustina's Gate. Before Simon could reach it, she put the sharp, curved tip of her beak to the depression at the bottom of the fruit and pulled. A single long ribbon of peel came loose. She kept pulling and the whole thing came off in one piece!

She squawked as Simon tried to take it, and as she lunged to peck him, she pushed the fruit, which wobbled towards the hole and disappeared over the edge.

"Now look what you've done!" said Simon in dismay. "Bad bird! Go back down to the boat!"

Seagrape flapped her wings and hopped over to the rest of the fruit.

"No!" Simon told her, but she squawked fiercely when he tried to shoo her away. She flew around the room once, screeching terribly, and as she flew past him she reached down and wrenched out some of his hair with her talons.

"What's got into you?" asked Simon in surprise. He had never seen her behave this way.

And then Simon noticed something that made him stop and stare, astounded.

The mineral-fruit that Seagrape had peeled and pushed into the well had left behind a trail of juice. And everywhere that liquid touched had begun to glow and bubble. As Simon watched, the ophalla on the edge of the well began to grow thick and lumpy, like dough rising. Deep inside Faustina's Gate a rumbling sound began, and the blackness of the pit lightened.

Then Simon remembered the ophallagraph of the tree— the bird in the image had its beak to the fruit!

"Sorry, Seagrape," he whispered. "You knew what you were doing, didn't you?"

Fascinated, Simon bent closer to inspect the stone. Something in the mineral-fruit was causing a reaction in the ophalla. As he watched, the stone began to bubble up and expand and tiny holes appeared in it. Suddenly the holes sneezed tiny puffs of dust. More dust drifted up like smoke through the well. Simon's nose started to tingle.

Simon had been out on coral reefs with his parents to see the coral reefs spawn. Triggered by the moon and the tide, the whole coral reef would suddenly release a cloud of trillions of gametes. This reminded him of that.

It wasn't dust coming from Faustina's Gate, Simon realized—these were *spores*.

At last he understood the true meaning of Milagros's words: *What appears alive is dead and what appears dead is alive.*

The ophalla was alive! Or if not the stone itself, something inside it. He remembered the wriggle of movement across the slide at Davies Maroner's. Simon had thought his eyes were tired, but perhaps something under the microscope *had* moved.

Did his parents know? Had they guessed?

The well was like a cauldron of life. Tiny specks vibrated in the stone, orbiting furiously, dozens of them within each marble-size chip of the rock. The ophalla was growing before Simon's very eyes and the well was getting smaller as the new stone was filling it in and sealing it. Faustina's Gate was closing.

Seagrape hopped over to the mineral-fruits again and this time Simon didn't stop her. As soon as she had peeled each fruit he broke it in his hands, squeezing out the juice, and tossed the pulp deep into the well.

The spores in the air were getting so thick that Simon was starting to have trouble breathing. He coughed. The air had a sharp tang, like ammonia. His nose was running heavily. Light was streaming out of the well now. He tossed the last mineral-fruit in and scrambled to get his backpack on. Seagrape squawked and flew out of the tiny chamber into the cave.

The ophalla was getting brighter and brighter, too bright to bear. Simon's eyes stung. He rubbed them but it only made them worse. It wasn't until then that he heard the others calling him frantically.

"I'm coming down!" he called through a sneeze. His eyes were watering fiercely.

He looked once more at Faustina's Gate, rapidly sealing shut, and he left through the door and began to climb back down. He didn't get very far before he froze on the face of the cliff.

"Something's in my eyes—it's getting worse—I can't see!" he shouted. "I can't tell where to go!"

"We'll keep talking so you can hear where we are," Helix called, his voice strong and calm. "Move your right foot down about two feet, there's a foothold there—good! Now if you move your left hand down about a foot and just a little more to the left . . ."

Simon made it a third of the way down before his foot slid and he lost his grip on the rock. Maya shrieked. He grabbed a small ledge but his fingers were slipping. His eyes burned unbearably. "I can't hang on!" he shouted. He heard pebbles loosened by his hands rattling down the cliff.

"Simon!" Helix shouted. "Jump away from the cliff, as far out as you can! Trust me!"

Steeling himself, Simon bent his legs up and kicked out strongly. He swanned out into the light streaming down from the doorway and felt himself tumbling backward.

He had a moment of terror as he fell through nothingness, but seconds later he landed in the curve of the *Pamela Jane*'s sail, bouncing once on it as if it were a trampoline. He slid down and landed in a heap on the deck. Helix had pushed the boom across toward the cliff, underneath Simon.

"Simon, Simon, are you okay?" Maya cried, running to him.

The fall had knocked the wind out of him and it was a few seconds before Simon could gasp for air. The spores had blinded him and he could see only shadows. The boat had pitched to starboard when he landed in the sail and now it was rocking back and forth as it righted itself. Rumbling began deep in the stone around them.

"It's alive!" he coughed, struggling to sit up. "Ophalla isn't the stone—it's what lives inside the stone! I saw it— something in the rock is alive—it's spawning! That's what Faustina's Gate will do—take the new ophalla organisms out to the Blue Line!"

"The Blue Line!" said Maya urgently. "It's going to close. We have to hurry. Simon, you rest here. I'll untie us and get us going."

The rumbling grew louder. The wind rose and a surge of water lifted the *Pamela Jane* and began propelling her through a narrow passage out of the chamber. Maya and Helix shouted to each other as they kept the boat steady. Simon could still feel the spores in the air, prickling his skin. Penny crouched beside him, Seagrape on her shoulder.

Simon was afraid that another violent cave storm was beginning like the one in the chamber with the stars, but instead in a few minutes the current slackened, a gentle breeze arose, and it was as if they were being expelled on a breath. He began to see light again—no longer the searing white of the ophalla, but the light that went with warmth—the sun.

❧ Chapter Twenty-Five ❧

A Choice ❋ *The Last Crossing* ❋ *Home*

They emerged out of the cave into the Green Vale. At first Simon saw everything through a milky blue haze. He blinked at shapes and shadows, but slowly outlines grew crisp and gradually color returned and the world grew bright and rich and saturated. He looked all around in awe. Milagros had told the truth. This was surely one of the most beautiful places in Tamarind. Steep green hills, thickly carpeted in vegetation, towered over them on three sides. Giant spotted flowers sprang from vines. Hundreds of multicolored birds hovered over the canopy. The air thrummed with insects. Striped-tailed monkeys capered up palms, chattering in surprise as they stared at the strangers on the boat. Sleepy-eyed slothe-slothas hung upside down on branches, munching lazily on juicy leaves. An amber cat prowled the opposite shore. There were no signs of civilization, just hundreds of miraculous plants and animals untouched by the Red Coral Project. A school of flying fish burst out from the trees, flitted across the vale, and disappeared into the underbrush on the other side.

"Look at all the animals!" said Penny in delight.

"We're here," cried Maya. "We made it! And Faustina's Gate is closed! Tamarind is going to be okay!"

Simon's eyes no longer burned. He felt fine again and he got to his feet. "Thanks," he said to Helix. "That was quick thinking with the sail."

"Of course, Simon," said Helix. "You're like a brother to me."

Simon looked at him and smiled. "You, too," he said.

Simon realized that this was it—they were about to leave Tamarind. Here the waters were tranquil, but outside the mouth of the Green Vale the glittering sea beckoned. The Blue Line was close to shore here and visible even from the deck of the boat. Deep beneath the surface of the earth ophalla was flowing from Faustina's Gate out to the line, strengthening it. Already water was massing blue on one side of the gyre and green on the other. Clouds were tumbling from the horizon. The *Pamela Jane* glided across the glassy green cove, her tall, elegant masts straight and true, her ophalla hull shining, ready to take them back home. Sadness filled Simon—he would never see this place again.

"Remember what Milagros told us," said Maya. "We don't have long—we have to hurry!"

Simon let out the mainsail and Maya raised the jib and the boat began clipping along. Simon breathed the air deeply, as he took his last look at Tamarind.

But then, just as they reached the mouth of the cove and were about to enter the open ocean, Helix turned and jumped overboard and began swimming toward land.

"Helix!" shouted Maya. "Helix!"

But Helix didn't look back. He swam steadily toward shore.

"What's he doing?" cried Maya. She turned frantically to Simon. "Stop! Let's turn around!"

But though it was still a shock to see him go, deep down Simon had known since he heard the general tell Helix that his father was alive that Helix wouldn't be coming back with them this time. A lump rose in his throat.

"It's the right thing," he said hoarsely. "He needs to find his father."

"We could have waited," said Maya. "We could have closed the gate later!"

"There wasn't time," said Simon. "You heard Milagros—it had to be done right away."

"But," said Maya, tears streaming down her face, "he isn't even going to say good-bye!"

"There was no easy way," said Simon, putting his hand on her shoulder. "This is best. This is where he belongs. He couldn't come back with us."

Simon knew that even if they had found Helix's father, Helix would not have returned with them. He was from Tamarind and Tamarind was where he needed to be right now—he had a family here, a whole past to discover, a life sundered long ago by unhappy events and misfortune that now had to be repaired and begun anew.

Helix reached the shore and turned and looked back toward the boat. He raised his arm and waved. Simon and Penny waved back at him, and then Maya did, too. Helix turned and began running along the beach toward the jungle. For a moment they watched him and then, just as suddenly as he had come into their lives, he was gone. Maya hunted for him with her eyes, but he could no longer be seen. There was no flicker of the undergrowth, no trembling branch or snap of a twig to give him away.

Good-bye, my friend, said Simon in his heart.

He wrenched his gaze away and looked back at the sea, at the long, great swells running up and down the coast. They were blazing at full speed out to sea now. Outside the Green Vale, the gyre was building force and the water was darkening. Simon narrowed his eyes and looked again at the sea. "We have to go," he said.

Tears spilling silently down her cheeks, Maya nodded. The water was already turning darker. The Blue Line was changing. Faustina's Gate was closing. They could see, in the lift of each swell, racing schools of wahoo and tuna and the shower of color of smaller reef fish. Clouds massed ahead of them. The storms of the line were brewing. But behind them, all over Tamarind, trees were beginning to bud, enveloping the island in emerald, the seas were receding from the streets of the shore towns, life was stirring again in the ground, and in the Neglected Provinces, a gentle steady rain began to fall on the parched earth.

Seagrape had followed them and was flying around overhead.

"Go back," Simon shouted to her. He waved his arms. "Go home!"

"Helix gave her to us," said Penny. "After we saw Milagros, he told me it was my job to take care of her now."

The parrot coasted along beside them and then flew across the sail, high up past the mast and coasted back down again. The sight of her comforted Simon. He turned and waved at the shore in case Helix was watching them.

He took out the ophallagraphs. They made a sound like burned paper and the touch of his fingers blackened their edges. They were changing. Brief images seemed to come to light for a moment, as if Simon were looking into oil on the top of water, rainbowed in the sunshine. Then they dissolved. The paper crumbled. Simon was looking down at palmfuls of ash, soft as talc, as they blew away in the wind.

Maya didn't look back as they drew farther away from shore. When at last she spun around and looked frantically behind her, it was too late. The island was getting smaller and they were heading into the storm.

This was the fourth time in his life that Simon had crossed the Blue Line.

Gusts of salty wind battered the *Pamela Jane*. Her sails flapped wildly as Simon and Maya furled them, and she surged forward into the rising waves. The first drops of rain landed like warm stones on the deck and soon the children could barely see one another through the blur of rain and salt spray. White mist and gray-churned sea closed in all around them. All color was gone from the world. It was as if they were sailing into a great void. Maya took Penny into the cabin and Simon secured the wheel. He tied himself into a harness and stayed on deck, happy for the rain to lash him. He waited until the last minute to join his sisters in the cabin.

And then, in an hour or two, they were out of it. It was as if the storm spat them out onto the other side of the world, and a current bore them away from it until it appeared to be merely a dark blot on the distant horizon, as insignificant as a cloud of insects drifting away on a summer wind. Somewhere hidden deep within was Tamarind, but it was lost to them.

They set a course for Bermuda and in two days they had reached it.

This time as they sailed back down the channel through the reefs to the cove, it was daylight and the sea was calm. Penny was bouncing up and down at the bow, waving furiously, as the front door of Granny Pearl's house opened and Mami and Granny Pearl came out onto the porch. Simon looked for his father but didn't see him. The children moored the boat and waded to shore.

Simon could feel the difference as he came across the lawn. The Red Coral Project men were gone. There was a lightness in the air, an absence.

And a presence: Papi. The door was opening and he appeared now on the porch.

Simon broke into a run after his sisters.

Mami picked up Penny and squeezed her tightly, Maya hugged Granny Pearl, and Simon stopped and stood in front of his father. Papi was standing straight and tall. His beard was shaved off and he looked at once years younger, like he had when Simon was a child. Simon was embarrassed, but could do little to stop the tears that sprang hotly to his eyes as his father pulled him close and kissed his head. Simon had never been so happy to see his family in all his life.

The Red Coral Project was so small and secretive that once Dr. Fitzsimmons and his men were gone, there was no one left on the Outside who knew about it. The men who had watched Granny Pearl's house were hired hands only, and when the money to pay them ran out they had disappeared. The Red Coral Project melted away. Their hold had been broken, and the children and their parents were free.

For a long time after they returned, Tamarind was all the children thought of or talked about. It took time to get used to Helix being gone.

Penny would often wander into Simon's room and look at Helix's half, as if she expected that he would come back at some point. Whenever they heard the latch on the gate, or saw a shadow in the moonlight across the garden, or heard the wind rustling in the trees, each of them would look up, hoping and half expecting that Helix would come through the door.

But, of course, he never did.

After they sailed away from Tamarind, Maya had discovered that, in addition to a letter he had left for their parents, written while he was alone in Tamarind, Helix had left his shark's tooth necklace on her bunk in the cabin. She never took it off, even when she slept. She would sit on the porch with the old conch shell pressed to her ear, listening to the sound of the sea inside it, until after it grew dark and Mami finally made her go to bed. She moped for longer than anyone, until one night they were eating dinner—a real dinner, everyone together, like it used to be, Papi, too— when Maya burst into tears.

"I can't believe we'll never see him again," she said.

"He gave us Seagrape, didn't he!" Penny finally said, exasperated. "That means we'll see him again."

After that Maya didn't cry at the dinner table anymore.

Seagrape had become Penny's constant companion. She strutted around the house after her, muttered grumpily when Penny dressed her in doll's clothes, and slept on a perch in the corner of Penny's room, tucking her head beneath her wing. Sometimes she would go off to fly around for a while by herself, but she always returned. Penny sneaked scraps to her under the dinner table and Seagrape would squawk indignantly if someone's foot accidentally jostled her.

Occasionally she would come to visit Simon, wherever he was.

Simon wondered about the señoras, the general, Dr. Bellagio, the colonels, Jolo and Small Tee, and Isabella. He often caught himself remembering the night she had thrown them both over the edge of the waterfall—how cold they had been when they finally crawled out of the river and how she had talked about Tamarind so beautifully and with such love on the train that night.

He hoped that Tamarind was at peace again, and the terrible storms and droughts and floods had ended, and the land and sea were healing.

Most of all, he wondered where Helix was, and how he was doing. Did he miss them? Did he ever wish to be back in his old room with Simon, or talking to Papi in his study, or sitting down with all of them at dinner? Had he found his father? Simon hoped so.

Simon's father received one last transmission from Tamarind: *Red Coral defeated . . . Tamarind saved.* Then the radio connection went out suddenly and never came back. Dr. Nelson left it on for a while, and checked it periodically, but it was only static. Eventually he turned it off for good.

✳ ✳ ✳

Simon gave his parents the documents from Davies and the bag of ophalla stones that they discovered Dr. Fitzsimmons had secreted onto the *Pamela Jane* when he had tried to escape. Dr. Nelson pored over Davies's research in wonder. "Davies Maroner has a very exceptional mind," he said. "I would have loved to sit down and talk to him for hours."

Simon couldn't yet understand all the complicated scientific formulations his father was working on but he was determined that one day he would.

A piece of ophalla sat on the desk between them, emitting a dull luster.

"Did you know it was alive?" Simon asked. "Or that something in it was alive?"

"I suspected," said his father. "But there was no way to know for sure. It doesn't grow outside Tamarind, that much was certain, though Fitz would never believe that. But whether it's actually dead here"—he picked up the ophalla stone and turned it over in his hand—"or whether it's in a state of dormancy, of suspended animation . . . well, I can't say."

"The compass was next to the book about stromatolites," said Simon. "I guess that should have been a hint."

"Yes," said Papi. "Stromatolites—living rocks. They're what first gave me the idea that ophalla could be alive."

Then his expression changed. He looked at Simon sternly. "You know, it was very dangerous of you to run off like that, especially with Penny. Things didn't have to turn out as well as they did."

Simon ducked his head.

"But I'm sorry, too," said Papi. "We shouldn't have tried to hide so much from you. We were only trying to protect you. Anyway, I'm proud of you. Not many people your age— not many people *any* age—could have done what you did."

Simon felt his ears getting hot. This was exactly what he had wished for when things were at their blackest in the Neglected Provinces—to be able to sit talking with his dad about science and, well, just anything.

"Thank you," he mumbled. "So," he said, "you think ophalla could be used to make medicine?"

"Yes," said Papi. "Well . . . ophalla *itself* won't be used to make medicine, but what we can learn from it will enable us to understand more about different cures. Ophalla is completely different from anything else we've ever seen. It shifts the whole paradigm. The important thing is not having great quantities of ophalla itself, but in studying the bits we *do* have."

His face became sad as his thoughts turned to his old friend and he sighed.

"I wish that Fitz had believed that," he said. "The worst thing is that he had such a rare mind. If only he would have used it for something better than he did."

☆ ☆ ☆

The *Pamela Jane* could not be left as she was—gleaming, moon white, magnificent—and so Simon and his father built an external hull around her once again. Simon's father left out a single patch, four inches square, near her starboard bow in which the alabaster-like carvings remained.

One day, some time after they had been home, many weeks after they had finished working on the *Pamela Jane*, Simon was sitting in his father's study at the desk opposite him, doing his homework. The *Pamela Jane* once again looked like an ordinary wooden boat and she sat peacefully on her mooring. Late-afternoon light poured in on the books and shells on the shelves and lit everything a mellow orange. The office smelled salty and musty. The curtains lifted for a moment, revealing the view to the green cove, where the *Pamela Jane* stirred gently on her moorings and Penny played down in the purple shadow on the sand. Maya was at a friend's house. Laundry hung dripping into grass and Granny

Pearl walked back across the lawn with her empty laundry basket. Then Penny came running and caught Granny Pearl on the porch.

"Tell me another one," she said.

"Another one?" asked Granny Pearl. "I'm running out of stories—anyway, you're the one who's been to Tamarind, not me!"

"Please," Penny begged.

"Oh, all right," said Granny Pearl, and Simon heard her sit down in the creaky porch swing and pat the cushion next to her. "Just for a little while."

Through the window, Simon and his father heard as Granny Pearl began to tell Penny stories about Tamarind, the same ones she had told to Simon's father many years ago. Though even Simon was too old for stories, they both stopped work and sat and listened.

When his homework was done, Simon left for the boatyard. It was late spring and the evenings were long now. Granny Pearl had gone inside, but Penny and Seagrape were still on the porch. Penny was lying on the floor drawing a map of Tamarind, murmuring to Seagrape, who was perched beside her, peering curiously over her shoulder. Simon paused on the stairs to look at them for a moment.

Then, smiling to himself, he ran out to his bike, leaning against the tree, and pedaled down to the boatyard. The bees drifted drowsily over the flowers, and far away, once more a dream, a wondrous green island lay under the sun.

❧ ACKNOWLEDGMENTS ❧

I would like to gratefully acknowledge the generous efforts of others on behalf of this book, including my agents, Sarah Burnes and Caspian Dennis; my editor, Amanda Punter, and the team at Puffin; Jean Feiwel and the team at Feiwel and Friends; Lexy Bloom; Julia Holmes, Lisa Madden, Lana Zinck; my parents; and Tim Hasselbring, who read countless drafts of this story with enthusiasm and a sharp eye that Simon himself would surely admire.

Don't miss Maya, Simon, and Penny's first adventure in

THE LOST ISLAND OF TAMARIND

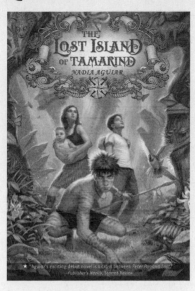

Now available in paperback from SQUARE FISH.

REVIEWS FOR *THE LOST ISLAND OF TAMARIND*

★"Aguiar's exciting debut novel is a cross between Peter Pan and *Lost*. . . . Developed with seeming ease, each new character advances the plot logically and fluidly. The storytelling, intricate as it is, builds to a whole that is greater than the sum of its parts."

—*Publishers Weekly*, STARRED REVIEW

"The book's magic . . . lies in Aguiar's precise, often lyrical, descriptions. A native and resident of Bermuda, she writes with authority about daily life in the tropics. . . . Aguiar uses her knack for realistic details equally well in the magical parts. . . . *The Lost Island of Tamarind* has a gentle spirit, tempering its dangers with warmth."

—*The New York Times Book Review*

"Stranded on a lost island, a teen faces nail-biting adventures searching for her missing parents in this fantasy cliffhanger. . . . As she bounces from one adventure to the next, Maya forgets all about having a normal life and longs just to have her family reunited. Spunky kids, perilous pursuits, and marine mystery make for a smashing good read."

—*Kirkus Reviews*

Excerpt from

The Lost Island of Tamarind

BY NADIA AGUIAR

Maya struggled after the boys, going as quickly as she could with Penny. Helix and Simon kept up a lively conversation, but Maya didn't join in. Instead, she fretted. She didn't like Helix or their situation one bit. Who knew where he was really taking them? They had no idea where they were going, not really. But Maya didn't know what else they could do. She kept her eyes peeled for the jaguars Helix had talked about, but she saw no sign of one.

Finally, Helix stopped and put his finger to his lips.

"From here on, we're going to have to be totally quiet," he said. "I mean it. Don't say anything and watch where you walk. Don't step on a twig even."

"Why?" whispered Simon.

"Because in a minute, we're going to come out into a grove of banyan trees and that's where the jaguars will be. They'll all be napping at this hour."

"Then why are we going this way?" asked Maya. "Shouldn't we be avoiding the jaguars?"

"We can't," said Helix. "They're on the shore all around here and my raft happens to be on the other side of those trees. Because of the way the currents run, this is the only point at which you can get to Greater Tamarind from the Lesser Islands. All the other currents drag you toward the Lesser Islands—that's probably why you ended up landing here. You have to know the waters really well not to get sucked into a current. The winds are bad, too. We don't have any choice but to go past the jaguars."

"Come on, Maya. We have to do what he says," said Simon.

Maya pressed her lips together. She didn't say anything, but she began following Helix, keeping one eye on the path in front of her so that she didn't step on anything that might make a noise. She hoped that Penny wouldn't wake up. When they got to the banyan trees, Maya and Simon stopped in their tracks and stared.

They were looking into a vast, magnificent, and spooky grove of gigantic trunks, covered in a shaggy hide of mottled green lichen. Their roots stood above the ground, forming dark, cathedral-like hollows large enough for the children to have hidden inside. Ropy vines with hairy tassels of roots stretched down from the branches to burrow into the earth and form new trunks, until over time the whole grove had become interconnected, and the canopy of leaves was so dense that little sunshine could get through, and the light beneath the canopy was just a murky green gloom. But it was not the banyans themselves that Maya and Simon could not take their eyes off of, it was what lay beneath them.

Lying beneath the majestic trees napping were forty or so jaguars.

The jaguars had thick, soft, honey-colored fur with black spots. Beneath the green glow of the trees, each animal looked like a pool of light with tiny blots of black shadow. Vines swept soothingly back and forth over their backs in a fine breeze, and a rumbling purring rose from the creatures.

"Don't worry," said Helix in a very soft whisper. "These vines aren't like the others. They're just sweeper vines— they put the cats to sleep. They'll only nab you if you move too quickly. Just don't make a sound and we'll be fine."

He put his finger to his lips and motioned them to follow him as he began tiptoeing lightly through the grove. Simon went after him, and a moment later, Maya took a deep breath and followed them. She watched where she put her feet, stepping gingerly so that not a single leaf would rustle, nor twig would snap, and disturb the cats' slumber. Though it would have been difficult for the creatures to hear them over the roar of feline snoring. By the time the children got to the middle of the grove, the sound was almost deafening. A tiny branch broke against Maya's arm when she brushed past it, and she froze in her tracks and waited, not daring to breathe, but the cats lay perfectly still, the vines sweeping in long, even strokes over their backs. The children crossed the halfway mark. Up ahead, Maya could see water shimmering through the trees. They would get to the raft and then they'd be safe. Cats hated water, after all. The water got brighter and brighter with each step toward it. Maya tried to clear her mind of anything but where to put her feet. The right foot on a patch of soft ferns, the left foot balancing on a root sticking out of the earth, right foot in the quiet, muddy place right there, left foot down just between those two rotting sticks . . .

Then the worst thing happened.

Penny woke.

And began to wail.

It was unlike Penny to wake from a nap crying, but perhaps she had sensed the danger around them in her sleep. Horrified, Maya stiffened. Helix and Simon stopped, too, and looked over their shoulders at her. She looked back at them helplessly. Around them, the cats began to wake. Whatever spell the vines had put them under couldn't withstand the cries of an eight-month-old infant.

A fat yellow paw slapped down on the ground in front of Maya's feet. Her breath caught in her throat and she looked into the furry, spotted face of a sleepy jaguar. The cat was stretching and yawning, its muscular jaw stretching out nearly in a straight line, its eyes rolling back in their sockets. When it opened its eyes again, it leaped up, startled. Its lips and whiskers drew back in a snarl, and it lifted one of its great yellow paws to strike. Maya looked at the enormous, dirty claws and imagined what they were about to do to her, but could not seem to make herself move. Her feet felt rooted to the earth. And even though she was petrified, she was able to think quite calmly that even if she did begin to run, the giant cat would catch up with her in a heartbeat.

She took a deep breath, preparing for the strike, but just as the jaguar's paw descended in a deathblow, from the corner of her eye, she saw Helix swing his bow down from over his shoulder and withdraw an arrow from his belt.

But Helix's arrow sailed through the air without striking its target, because suddenly a long dark vine came swinging across and flew right under the jaguar's ribs and lifted it up in the air. It hung, swinging slightly to and fro, twenty feet off the ground. The creature let out a surprised and outraged yowl that woke any cats that had still been sleeping. Suddenly, all the jaguars were on their feet, snarling, ears flattened, tails dancing like flames. Several cats leaped for the children at the same time, and as they did, other vines dropped down and looped around their middles and hauled them into the air, where they swung back and forth, howling in fury.

"Don't move suddenly!" Helix shouted to Maya and Simon. "Or the vines will grab you, too!"

Maya had been about to make a mad dash for the water, but she stopped and stood absolutely still.

"Very slowly," Helix said. "Very slowly, we're going to keep walking until we get to the raft, okay?"

"Okay," said Simon. He and Maya began following Helix again, and they walked through the rest of the grove, looking up in amazement at the jaguars swinging slowly back and forth overhead.

They only started running when they left the grove and

neared the shore. Maya breathed a sigh of relief to be back out in the sunshine again. But they stopped short when they realized that Helix's raft couldn't fit all of them. Growling noises still coming menacingly from inside the jungle, Maya hurried to collect driftwood, and Helix sliced a few thin, rubbery vines from the edge of the forest and began tying the driftwood to the raft to make it bigger.

"I can do that better," said Simon.

"It's true," said Maya. "He's the knot expert."

Working quickly, Simon tied a series of knots that bound the driftwood to the raft.

"Impressive," said Helix.

As Helix pushed the raft into the water and they clambered onto it, Maya looked nervously over the water. The channel separating the tiny island they were on from the bigger island was narrow, but the current flowed treacherously.

"Are you sure this is safe?" she asked.

"You can stay here if you like," Helix said. "The vines will let the jaguars back down in a few minutes, and I'm sure there'll be a big fight over who gets to have you for lunch."

That was it; Maya did not like Helix. She gritted her teeth and crawled onto the raft.

"Fine," she said. "I'd rather drown than be eaten."